LAST TRAIN OUTTA KEPLER-283c

BAEN BOOKS edited by DAVID BOOP

Straight Outta Tombstone
Straight Outta Deadwood
Straight Outta Dodge City

Gunfight on Europa Station
High Noon on Proxima B
Last Train Outta Kepler-283c

LAST TRAIN OUTTA KEPLER-283c

Edited by
DAVID BOOP

A Baen Books Original

Baen Publishing Enterprises
P.O. Box 1403
Riverdale, NY 10471
www.baen.com

ISBN: 978-1-9821-9376-8

Cover art by Dominic Harman

First printing, November 2024

Distributed by Simon & Schuster
1230 Avenue of the Americas
New York, NY 10020

Library of Congress Control Number: 2024031855

Printed in the United States of America

10 9 8 7 6 5 4 3 2 1

Travis Heermann
22 October 1969–26 April 2024

Trav,

Sometimes a gunfighter knows when it's time to lay down his guns. You caught the last train before us, and not a day goes by that this ghost town isn't made emptier without you.

Take a pull from the flask for me, Compadre. You are missed.

DB
07/16/24

CONTENTS

ix   **Introduction**
David Boop

1   **Time Marches On**
Kevin Ikenberry

21   **Last Train to Clarkesville**
Sharon Lee & Steve Miller

47   **The Rogue Tractor of Sunshine Gulch**
Kelli Fitzpatrick

65   **Living by the Sword**
David Mack

85   **The Ballad of the Junk Heap Gun Man
and Mistress Bullet**
M. Todd Gallowglas

95   **This World Belongs to the Monsters**
Dr. Chesya Burke

123   **Jasper and the Mare**
John E. Stith

129   **Support Your Local Audit Chief**
D.J. Butler

145   **Grace Under Fire**
Lezli Robyn

171   **Last Transport to Kepler-283C**
Christopher L. Smith

191   **The Double R Bar Ranch on Alpha Centauri 5**
David Afsharirad

211   **Not My Problem**
Mel Todd

227   **Enjoyed Every Sandwich**
Mark L. Van Name

243   About the Contributors

HAPPY COMET TAILS TO YOU...
UNTIL WE MEET AGAIN

I live out West, but my heart, my head, and my spirit have always been in the stars.

Mind you, I was born on the East Coast, raised in the Upper Midwest, and lived in the South before heading to Colorado and Arizona, which, I guess, makes me somewhat a traditionalist when it comes to editing Westward travel. But even more than my physical journey, my soul sought out the unexplored places in our universe through science and science fiction.

I could chalk up my youthful corruption to Gene Rodenberry and George Lucas, but that story has been told by me, and many others, who also have the same influences. I'm a nerd, a geek, a dork; probably with influences not that different than you. I fell into anime early, too, with Starblazers and Robotech. Again, it's a story many of my peers can share. And while on the topic of sharing stories, let me tell you what you're in for on this Last Train.

In these pages are stories that might surprise you, such as an alien ballad by M. Todd Gallowglas and the "lost" script for The Roy Rogers Show—in outer space!—by David Afsharirad. We've got first time Baen authors such as Dr. Chesya Burke and Kelli Fitzpatrick. You'll also find favorites writing in their most popular worlds like Sharon Lee & Steve Miller (Liaden Universe ®), Kevin Ikenberry (The Four Horsemen), and Mark L. Van Name (Jon and Lobo). I always try to approach all anthologies with the idea of covering all angles: old, new, familiar, and experimental. And I'm confident this volume will satisfy all your Space Western needs.

But there is still a question I'm asked, and I don't know that I've ever answered well enough for the questioner's satisfaction, nor really my own...

Why Space Westerns?

The easiest answer I given is that this genre shares more with Space Opera than Weird Westerns and, if Baen is known for anything, it's excellence in that arena. Many of their authors responded to my call and have honored me with their amazing words.

The other answer I give is that Space Westerns have a long and exciting history, not just in television and movies. Even before Saturday drive-in serials with their jetpacked space marshals, there were stories written that combined the two genres together. Starting as far back as the late '30s with Catherine Lucille (C.L.) Moore's Northwest Smith in the pages of Weird Tales, authors have scribed the concept of humanity out among the unexplored stars. Characters like Flash Gordon, Buck Rogers, and Gil "The Arm" Hamilton wowed early readers with their exploits, so who wouldn't want to play in the new frontier of space?

But neither answer truly explains my drive to delve in a cross-genre that some critics have said weakens both of its progenitors. It's always a risk that with any genre blend, that by breaking established tropes, authors are forced to rely on worn clichés rather than creating something unique. Darin Bradley seconded this idea in his essay, "The Space Western—Genre's Unwanted, Weird Cousin" (2022), when he writes about early space westerns, "Space is a wild animal that needs breaking, which will mean some bloody noses. However, the Western story is primarily trapped in the past, tethered to the bloody, racist period that gave rise to its central myths. Unless you're deconstructing old Western motifs, you're trafficking in the social and cultural norms of the period." Bradley goes on to talk about "frontier justice" being an excuse for murder hidden beneath a white hat, and that, "like the Westerns before, the space Western's world is usually a capitalistic, non-egalitarian place that prizes exploration as consumption [...] it takes some of the worst, most competitive, most exploitative aspects of contemporary culture and throws them into the future. Meaning, that we don't have much hope of evolving or advancing as a species."

But Bradley is wrong in many ways. He assumes that these types of stories were cookie-cutter [AI produced?] copies of each other. Speculative fiction writing has evolved since the pulps across all genres, not just Space Westerns, with crafters breathing in the reality of space expansion, be it the hardships of war, life, and death and the effect it has on their characters and supporting cast. Choices have consequences and "the good guys" wrestle with the impact their decisions have on both their society and other civilizations.

Steampunk, Paranormal Romance, and Science Fiction Noir have all managed to establish themselves as legitimate cross-genres despite initial criticism and some unfortunate examples of the art. But all it takes is one exceptional story that taps into the zeitgeist and then, as Antonio Garcia Martinez said, "Success forgives all sins." The same can be said of the Space Western. The cult following of *Firefly* and the success of *The Expanse* (in both novel and television forms) demonstrates that a well-told story will bring the people regardless of what genres are conscripted to create it. *Guardians of the Galaxy, The Mandalorian, Cowboy Bebop,* and many others lend to the idea that those with open minds and hearts will watch science fiction wrapped in a Western motif and enjoy it thoroughly. Publishers have not shied away from the genre, either, publishing novels by female authors who picked up C.L.'s torch, such as Nancy Kress, Susan R. Matthews, Becky Chambers, Essa Hansen, and Valerie Valdez.

When discussing the Western, Lee Clark Mitchell wrote that the Western genre offers "the opportunity for renewal, for self-transformation, for release from constraints with the urbanized East," which then translates over to Space Westerns as release from the constraints of an urbanized Earth. In the world-building of many science-fiction stories, the idea that our planet of birth can no longer offer the protagonist what it promised is common. Pestilence. War. Famine. Death. Pick the Horseman of your choice. Earth sucks in most space sagas and we just can't get away soon enough. As is often the case, though, we bring those very things we're looking to flee from with us, or they follow soon after. This is where the Space Western can separate itself from its Earth-bound predecessor.

Robert Murray Davis analyzed where the genre really begins to create its own, unique voice in his article "The Frontiers of

Genre: Science-Fiction Westerns." It starts with time and setting, and how a Western is time-locked, while the Space Western is not: "In the Western, the outcome of this conflict is in effect decided for the hero by the presence of history, once and for all, in the story's implied future if not in its dramatic present, while the SF hero, with all of history theoretically before him, is free, or condemned, to define himself by motion." We know how the Old West turned into the New West or Modern West. Short of delving into alt-history, we cannot change that. But future history is always evolving, and can never be "tamed."

Davis takes apart Bradley's earlier comments regarding economic survival and motive, when he writes that while "the ideology of expansion takes greed or at least acquisitiveness more or less for granted as a motive and sanctions force as an instrument, acquisitiveness in the Western is essentially nostalgic, and not only because it is safely in the past but because it was a major feature of the cultural code of America between 1880 and the turn of the century." Many settlers, such as the ones in Louis L'Amour's Sacketts series, want to acquire land to settle down, to stop moving. "In SF, however, the economic motive for exploration and expansion is often more a pretext than a serious goal [. . .] Han Solo and many other SF heroes seek money not to stop but in order to keep going." Many Space Westerns reflect more the modern ideology that every person is just working to make it to the next paycheck, the next score. Series like *Star Trek*, which throw away the concept of "economic motives," replace that big score with the need to answer a riddle of why? Why do some races act the way they do, and should they be left alone, or should we create "solutions" that ultimately turn them into us: a theme seen often in Westerns.

And while the corollaries between the Native Americans and alien races certainly seem to be obvious, there are many differences in how the "enemy" is portrayed. Often, we never see the enemy for a long time or at all, such as in Orson Scott Card's *Ender's Game*, or *The Expanse* (based on the novels by James S.A. Corey). This is in stark contrast to the massive "Indian Wars" presented in Western novels and movies. The enemy is more their technology's effect on us than their personal presence, with battleships, weapons, and such masking the true wielders behind them. Davis echoes this: "The hero should triumph not because [they have] better technology but because, as numberless good gunfighters have explained [they have] superior moral attributes. In SF, it is typically 'our' technology against 'their' technology, and frequently the opponents cannot even see each other. In the worst case, they do not even regard each other as sentient beings."

Finally, Davis summarizes the difference between Westerns and Space Westerns as such: "it is arguable that the Western celebrates the physical, the individual, the instinctive and unarticulated life, the static and timeless. SF, on the other hand, exalts the cerebral, the social, the technological, the changing and developing." Westerns can rely too heavily on a good ol' gunfight, or fistfight, to resolve their third act. Space Westerns will conversely set a timer or countdown to that fight, while the heroes race to find a way to avoid it. This analysis cannot cover the breath or scope or all things "branded" Western or Space Western, as anyone can point out a plethora of examples where this critique is betrayed, but when taking in the genre as a whole, these notions are the core of what defined them for decades, and possibly what we seek to defy in modern storytelling.

But there are other things that Davis doesn't talk about, maybe more due to the era he wrote in than anything else, and that's how the Space Western has also given rise to more diversity in gender, race, religion, and ideology than the Western ever could. In her introduction to *Women's Space: Essays on Female Characters in the 21st Century's Science Fiction Western*, editor Melanie A. Marotta states that in the traditional Western, most female characters were either prostitutes, assassins, or femme fatales, but the modern Western starting in the '90s "permits freedom for the female character." No longer trapped as the dutiful wife or love interest, female protagonists were commanders, engineers, scientists, and doctors. "Killjoys, Dark Matter, and The Expanse, all television series that revolve around the concept of the frontier and the capable female character. With 2015 came televised productions and literary constructions bringing strong female leads to audiences, ones that defy the pioneer woman/prostitute woman constructions standard in representations of the West."

It wasn't like there weren't strong, independent women in the real West. One only has to read biographies like *A Lady's Life in the Rocky Mountains*, by Isabella Bird, or any book about Molly Brown, Annie Oakley, or Baby Doe Tabor to begin your search of capable Pioneer women. In doing research for my Weird Western novel, *The Drowned Horse Chronicle*, I've acquired dozens of books and read countless essays about women in the Old West who defied the caricature made of them in movies and early Westerns. But with the Science Fiction Western and Space Opera, a reader doesn't have to go far to find fictionalized women of power, strength, and independence. From the long-running Honor Harrington series and its many Honorverse spin-offs, to the more recent Daisy Kutter, the protagonist of Kazu Kibuishi's series, the future is rife with great leading ladies.

Space Western books are published daily with Black, Asian, Indian, Native American, LGTBQ, Hindu, or Muslim protagonists. These stories have become readily available due to the growth in independent and self-publishing over the last twenty years. There is literally no type of protagonist you cannot find in a Space Western or Space Opera. And, to me, that is what makes writing and editing this genre so exciting. I never know what type of story I'll get (despite asking for two-line pitches beforehand).

As I said at the beginning, I've always tried to balance styles, protagonists, and themes because you can't fully analyze a topic unless you've explored it from every angle. And that's what themed anthologies are supposed to do—present not just a one-sided discourse, but open a discussion among its readers about what worlds they explored within these pages. I hope that when you've finished *Last Train Outta Kepler-283c*, a story in here will excite you enough, as they have me, to discuss with your peers, your friends, and your family. Post reviews. That's the only way for me, as an editor, and my authors to know if we entertained, enlightened, and maybe even educated you a tiny little bit. That's always my goal. I'm honored you allowed me the chance to do it.

So, again, why did I pick Space Westerns for this trilogy of anthologies?

looks up slyly from his keyboard

Why else? They're hella fun.

Faithfully submitted this date,
August 23rd, 2023.
DB

TIME MARCHES ON

A Four Horsemen Universe Story

Kevin Ikenberry

Victory Twelve
Emergence Point L2
Morel System

<<Emergence confirmed. Hyperspace shunts into standby mode. All systems nominal.>>

Jessica Francis tapped her central instrument panel and secured the ship's flight controls. "Thanks, Lucille. Standard RCS and flight control diagnostics, please?"

<<Acknowledged.>>

Clear of hyperspace for the first time in 170 hours, the ship's attitude and reaction control systems needed inspection and evaluation. After a few moments of planned maneuvers and test burns, Jessica tapped on the panel to secure the controls.

"I'm satisfied, Lucille. Prepare for insertion burn to Morel Station."

<<Burn prepared. Travel time will be six hours, thirty-two minutes, and twelve seconds,>> the ship's command-and-control interface replied. Since Jessica found Lucille in her father's workshop as a child, the two had traveled the galaxy together. During Jessica's time as a mercenary, Lucille grew from a companion and

advisor to a tactical data source and capable navigator. Working with her again after three years in the Peacemaker Academy required an adjustment since Peacemakers trained to act alone.

Jessica undid her restraints and floated free of the command chair. "I'm going to get some food and clean up before we arrive."

<<Acknowledged. Fuel and provisions requests have not been acknowledged. There has been no authorization for docking, but we are clear to approach. They'll contact us at six thousand kilometers for final instructions, but not before. >>

"If they contact us at all." Jessica chuckled. "That's why they call this Last Chance Station. They don't get a lot of business these days, Lucille. They'll get around to answering us. Have faith."

Lucille didn't respond. Computer programs didn't possess emotions or the concept of faith. She'd thought about ways to enhance Lucille's programming over the years but had made little progress. However, during her commission mission on Araf, just two weeks earlier, Lucille blossomed into a valued intelligence asset. Jessica couldn't help hoping for more, else being a Peacemaker was going to be lonely.

Jessica activated her wrist-slate and saw Lucille had opened communication ports to the gate. Data packets had begun downloading. There was ample time to check them on the approach to Morel Station. She even managed to rest a bit before donning her dark blue Peacemaker jumpsuit. For a moment, she considered dressing as she'd done during her time as a mercenary to avoid attention, but chose her uniform instead. Laid out on her bunk, Jessica leaned over and affixed her badge to the left chest with a sense of pride and accomplishment. The three years in the Academy rivaled the toughest things she'd ever done. She'd received her commission and, with it, a solemn sense of duty. A Peacemaker's presence was supposed to be an assurance to the local community of the good throughout the Galactic Union. A reminder of the promise of law and order. A sentinel of justice. For a backwater system like Morel, the Peacemaker presence would be a Human for the first time in history.

Morel Station lay attached to the stargate controlling hyperspace departures. Compared to the newer, more sophisticated gates, it wasn't much, and it was unlikely to do anything but deteriorate. More modern ships being built in the Galactic Union didn't require stargates to enter hyperspace, instead using onboard shunts and massive power supplies to make the jump. The stations, and their navigational beacons, still controlled the emergence points of the system at Lagrange points one and two, but the once-thriving economic zones of such stations was long past. Gates became way stations where travelers could get fuel, provisions, and maybe a drink, but its remaining days of sending ships into hyperspace dwindled, if not from the march of technology, then by the sheer economics of life on the distant frontier.

From where she viewed it, Morel Station appeared mostly vacant with only ten percent of its berthing spaces filled with transitory freighters. But they had F11 fuel and, given the number of jumps it would take to get Jessica from Araf to Dryod Four (and her first actual assignment), it was a necessary stop along the frontier.

<<Autodocking engaged. Standby for return of gravity.>>

Jessica reached for a handle on the bulkhead, but it was unnecessary. Lucille smoothly guided the ship into the berth. Gravity, a measly 1/6 Earth, returned. Jessica waited for her equilibrium to adjust before making her way out of the cabin toward the ship's personnel airlock. Connected to the gate's GalNet node, her slate chimed with new downloads, messages, and the most recent Stormwatch report from the Peacemaker Guild. She'd get to them in time. The urge to get outside and walk, even around Morel Station, nearly overwhelmed her.

<<Docking complete. All systems in shutdown.>>

She tapped the communications device on her right ear. "Lucille? Anything from the gate?"

<<Request for fueling accepted. You'll have to engage the terminal for fees before scheduling.>>

"Nothing else?"

<<Negative.>>

She reached the airlock and opened it. "Engage all security protocols, Lucille. I'm going aboard. Once I get the fueling going, I'll check about provisions. They should've replied by now."

<<Acknowledged. Be safe, Jessica.>> After a moment, when Jessica hadn't stepped into the airlock, Lucille asked, <<Is something wrong?>>

She shook her head. "I'm fine, Lucille." The rumbling in her stomach said otherwise, but what could Lucille do about that? For Gate Control to avoid contact for over six hours indicated something *was* wrong.

How else are you gonna figure out what?

She paused and considered returning to her quarters for her sidearm. Words of her instructors cautioned a Peacemaker should always carry arms, but then contradicted themselves with the sentiment they could do much without a weapon. She was only going aboard for fuel and provisions. It would be fine.

Jessica stepped inside the airlock and closed the interior door. There was a breathable atmosphere on the other side of the hatch, but the interior airlock door doubled as security for her ship. No one unauthorized would gain access to *Victory Twelve*. As the airlock door cycled open, the odors of the gate filled the small space. Intermixed with the smells of machine lubricants and fuel came the unmistakable spices of cooking and, curiously, the scent of strong coffee. Her mouth watered as she stepped down from the ship and entered the gate.

A console chimed from the wall to her right. It spoke, and her translation pendant translated. "Please scan your UACC for admittance and incidental expenses."

Jessica withdrew her wallet from one chest pocket and selected her Peacemaker UACC, a combination identification and banking card, and swiped it. The console chimed. "A five thousand credit hold has been placed on your credentials for docking service fee. Enjoy your stay."

Five thousand credits for a docking service fee? What kind of bullshit is that?

A figure appeared in the tube to her left. The Caroon, a Humanoid alien species who'd evolved for mining operations, stood in the tube. The alien's long nose and oversized ears reminded Jessica of an aardvark on Earth. "Welcome to Morel Station, Peacemaker."

Jessica nodded. "Why didn't Gate Control reach out?"

The Caroon spread his hands in the shrug for his species. "Power surge from the gate three days ago. We've been working on critical systems from environmental controls and life support on up. Communications are next and should be restored within the hour. These damned old gates. They get more unreliable every day."

Jessica took a breath and felt her tension evaporate—for the most part. She walked toward the Caroon. "Glad to hear you're getting things in order."

"What can we help you with?" The Caroon's face twisted in its approximation of a smile.

"Fuel and provisions," Jessica replied. "I'm on official business."

"I was unaware any Human had...passed the Peacemaker commission?"

Jessica smiled. "I'm sorry? I didn't catch your name?"

"I didn't offer it." The Caroon's coveralls bore a logo which read Apexx Solutions. "I'll ensure your fuel request is initiated. As for provisions, our company store is available to you as a transient. It's on the inner ring, a half dozen spaces to your left. There are many services available, and Fetch's Place is our local watering hole. I highly recommend it."

The Caroon turned to go, and Jessica realized he was merely the messenger. She stepped forward again, closing the distance. "Where do I find the Gate Control office?"

When the Caroon didn't answer, she considered saying it again, but didn't. The twisting sensation in her gut doubled down. For a moment, Jessica considered going back to the ship for her sidearm but decided against it. Fuel, food, and maybe a drink were in order. She'd be on her way to Dryod Four in a couple of hours at the most.

When she'd become a mercenary after college, Jessica quickly learned the first rule of entering a spaceport was pretty simple: look at nothing and everything at the same time. Situational awareness was a combination of what she could see and identify while digesting feelings and intuition. As she moved through the docking ring toward the main gate station, Jessica noticed there were no Humans in sight. There were at least three questionable transactions taking place in the main corridor—likely the illicit trading of substances. Two of them dissolved and the participants scattered. The third looked at her and completed their business as if daring her to engage. Given the brazen activity, Jessica didn't think law enforcement existed on the station, or else they were detained elsewhere.

Her earpiece chimed. <<There has been no communication with docking services. Repeated requests for attention have been unanswered.>>

Let's see what's going on here at Last Chance Station, shall we?

☆ ☆ ☆

"You met this Peacemaker?" the Equiri grumbled. "What do they want?"

"Honored Dre'Toal," the Caroon named Garanx said slowly. "The Peacemaker needs fuel and provisions."

Dre'Toal grunted. His long chestnut face turned to the Caroon. "Was there any mention of Trolloc?"

"No, sir."

Dre'Toal ran a two-fingered hand over the end of his equine maw, scratching at the irritated skin around his nostrils. He coughed once and then again. Holding his breath to keep from exploding into another fit, he counted silently to ten and released the air in his damaged lungs. "See to it the Peacemaker gets what they need. Keep them away from the inner rings and—"

"It was a Human," Garanx blurted. "A Human Peacemaker."

Dre'Toal snorted derisively. "No Humans have ever—"

"A female. With red hair." Garanx shook his head. "She has the uniform and the identification to match. Should we call off the search?"

Dre'Toal considered the information. Even if a Human had completed the arduous commissioning process to become a Peacemaker, they were likely unschooled in the ways of the galaxy. They had their needs and would show off their offset diamond badges but once placated, they would be on their way. If they choose to stand, well . . . They would fall.

"No. Find Trolloc." Dre'Toal's black eyes turned to the Caroon. "I'll handle the Peacemaker."

The Caroon chuckled nervously. "How will you do that?"

Dre'Toal grinned. "Humans are curious and unpredictable. The longer she's here, the greater threat she is. So, we'll give her what she wants and send her on her way."

The sparse traffic in the hallway steered clear of her. Humans this far from Earth were nothing new, but the combination of her species and her uniform had all eyes on her. She put on a more pleasant face and followed the symbols for the provisions warehouse. As she walked down the passageway, all the usual shops common on a gate station were there but shuttered. Trash littered the storefronts. Heavy brown paper hung behind shattered panes of glass. All of them had signage taped to their doorways.

Closed by Apexx Solutions. More options coming soon.

The yellowed, sometimes tattered, signs said otherwise. Ninety percent of the reputable businesses stood closed. Only a filthy morphogenic tattoo parlor, a liquor store which smelled of rancid flesh, and a seedy apothecary appeared open on the principal thoroughfare. More symbols pointed to temporary lodging, shower facilities, and a main office on the inner ring. Jessica turned that direction and paused.

Lights flickered in the passageway. More detritus filled the spaces and the smell...

Gods. What's going on here?

Small, dark corridors, something like alleyways, led off the corridor in both directions between the closed shops and stores. At an intersection halfway between the rings, she heard a commotion from a narrow passageway to her left lit by a solitary flickering light. A child squealed. She heard the unmistakable slap of flesh hitting flesh. The child screamed again in pain. Jessica turned into the passageway and picked up her pace.

In a dimly lit vestibule, near the entrance to a shuttered theater, an older GenSha draped itself over a small child. The bovine-like alien's broad back took the brunt of a pummeling attack from a vaguely Humanoid figure she couldn't quite make out between flickers of light. The attacker struck again and in a beam of light she saw the child was an Equiri. There were two more children—Pushtal with their tiger-striping and similar facial structures. The three children huddled under the GenSha.

The flash of a bladed weapon caught her eye. Jessica pushed into the space and activated the bright yellow "see me" strip all Peacemakers wore on their uniforms. "Hey! Put it down!"

The attacker, another Caroon, flinched. Its eyes widened before it dropped the weapon and disappeared through the theater doors. The Caroon wore the uniform of Apexx Solutions.

The GenSha stood and turned to her. The old male's eyes widened, and he flinched. "Peacemaker."

"Are you okay, Honored One?"

The GenSha's mouth worked from side to side. "Y-yes. Yes. Thank you. Thank you for protecting my children."

Jessica nodded and looked down. All three children stared up at her, and she sucked in a breath. The Equiri had blue, very Human eyes. The two Pushtal children were quiet, almost docile, which went against everything she'd ever known of the aliens. They were born pissed off.

"Are you injured, Honored One?"

"No," the GenSha said confidently, but she could tell from his face he was in pain. "When we come out, they attempt to take my children."

"Come out?"

"We live in the tubes," the GenSha answered. Every gate possessed a network of maintenance tubes not unlike alleyways. "Lodging here is expensive and security even more so. But we must come out for food and water until I can make passage somewhere safe."

Jessica understood. "Let me help you."

"You already have." The GenSha nodded. "We should go, lest he return with accomplices."

"Are you sure?"

"Of course I am, Peacemaker." The GenSha's eyes twinkled. "And a Human, no less."

Jessica drew in a sharp breath. "Does that really matter—"

"No." The GenSha's mouth worked from side to side as if chewing cud. "Human or not, your restraint was admirable. A mercenary or a bounty hunter would've drawn a weapon as a show of force. You did not."

"Thank you, Honored One." Jessica said.

"Our friend may not let that stand, Peacemaker." The GenSha opened a hatch she hadn't noticed. The children bounded inside, and he followed. "Always honor the threat—and not just the one you cannot see."

"What'll you have, Peacemaker?"

The bartender was a Blevin, which surprised Jessica. Most of the lizard-like aliens often worked as security or hired guns. Bipedal and with two oddly Humanlike hands, complete with opposable thumbs, they took to weaponry easily, though most weren't smart enough to handle an actual tactical situation. They were great throwaway soldiers, not bartenders.

"A whiskey and a whiskey," Jessica said. At first, she held up her thumb and index finger a wide distance apart and then she halved the distance. By the look on the Blevin's face, he'd missed the reference, which wasn't surprising at all.

"Whiskey." Jessica sat on a creaky bar stool with cracked vinyl padding. "With an e."

"The only Human one I have is Jack Daniels."

Jessica held up two fingers. "With a rock, please."

"That's an extra credit."

She resisted the urge to roll her eyes. "And the whiskey?"

"Two credits." The Blevin studied her intently. Its scaly hands wrung out a towel into a sink she couldn't see and then used the cloth to wipe the bar in front of her.

Jessica reached into her suit, pulled out a five-credit coin, and put it on the bar. "Two drinks. One now. One when I ask for it. Leave the bottle where I can see it, too."

The Blevin nodded and turned around, reaching for the bottle. While he worked on her drink, Jessica used the mirror on the wall behind the bar to take in her surroundings. Fetch's Place was a shithole, and that was putting it mildly. Most bars smelled worse than the fraternity houses she'd seen during her college experiences in Indiana and Georgia. This establishment was one small step above an open sewer. But it was the only place she could get a drink outside of the plastic bulbs she'd packed aboard *Victory Twelve* until the quartermaster's shop and the gate's primary services office opened. With nothing better to do, Jessica took in the local situation based on her Academy training. What she saw on the faces of the patrons frightened her.

Huddled over their drinks, the locals were the easiest to spot. Every time a being walked through the door, they'd glance at the door and back to their drinks. Some sighed in relief. Others fidgeted in their chairs. More than a few finished their drinks, tipped the Blevin, and made their way into the passageway beyond the grimy metal and glass doors. For a moment, she thought about asking the Blevin. Instead, she feigned interest in the *g'accaa* match on the holotubes and let her eyes and ears gather intelligence. The cause for the regulars' unease appeared as she finished her first whiskey and ordered the second.

Three uniformed Apexx Solutions personnel entered the bar. Caroon typically shied away from bright spaces. For them, Fetch's Place and its dark, dismal atmosphere couldn't have been more perfect. Jessica felt their eyes on her as she sipped her whiskey and continued to use the bar's mirror to her advantage.

The three took seats at a round table halfway between Jessica and the main door, which presented a problem. There would be no stopping them from challenging her as she left unless—

"Cheating fuck!" The card game in the far corner became interesting in a heartbeat. Jessica saw a large, purple-furred Oogar toss its chair across the baccarat table at a weasel-like Zuparti who flinched but did not reach for the needler pistol on its belt.

"You lost, Oogar. Fair and square," the Zuparti said. "You've been losing for an hour. You shouldn't have bet on what you did. The odds were never even—"

"Don't tell me the odds!" the grizzly-like Oogar roared before falling silent. The relative silence of the bar became total—so much so Jessica could almost hear the Oogar's mental tumblers click into place over a poor decision. The enormous being thumped away from the table and crossed the distance to the bar. He gave a "spin it up" gesture to the bartender, who turned to a large blender and mixed what appeared to be a piña colada.

Jessica covered a smile with a long sip of whiskey. The Blevin offered her a food menu, but after a whiff of something marketed as a type of fajitas, but which smelled like cow shit, she declined. If her provisions order came through, she'd have plenty of options aboard *Victory Twelve* after transitioning to hyperspace. She took another long sip of her drink and caught the three Caroon staring at her in the mirror.

Slow down, Bulldog. Just 'cause somebody pours you a drink doesn't mean you have to finish it.

Jessica smiled at the memory of her father's advice before adding. *Let this play out. Something will—*

"Excuse me, Peacemaker?"

Movement caught her eye. An older Equiri with a chestnut mane and walking with the aid of a cane approached her. The male's silver mane caught the dim light of Fetch's Place as he moved. He wore a vest which appeared to be the same color as the Apexx Solutions uniforms she'd seen. A single gold star adorned the right chest. Jessica kept her face neutral. The Equiri's powerful scent reached her first, but there was something . . . odd about it. She tried not to breathe it in as the alien stopped in front of her. She pushed away from the bar and stood as decorum required.

"Well met, Peacemaker." The Equiri spoke slowly and seemingly through pain. He nodded respectfully. "My name is Dre'Toal. Welcome to Morel Station."

"Well met, Honored Dre'Toal," Jessica replied and returned his nod. "My name is Jessica Francis."

She waited for the Equiri to extend a hand, as was common for the welcome of a Human, but the Equiri didn't move. The hairs on the back of her neck stood on end.

He's in charge. And he wants something.

"May I buy you a beverage?" Dre'Toal asked.

"No, thank you." Jessica let a small smile curl one side of her mouth. "I'm just waiting for the provisions store to open. As soon as I have fuel and stores, I'll be on my way."

"To where?"

"My next posting," Jessica answered.

We call it operational security. I'm not telling you a thing because you don't have the need to know.

The Equiri nodded. "I'll see to it you get what you need. The provisions store will open at the top of the hour, and your fueling is scheduled to start at the same time."

"Wonderful." Jessica gave a soft chuckle. "Actually, I was more than a little worried when I never heard from Gate Control."

"These old gates." Dre'Toal shook his head. "Power surges fry our systems regularly. The Gate Master and his team have been consumed with daily maintenance for weeks, almost without a break. Fix one item; something else breaks."

"Is that why Apexx is here?" Jessica asked. She raised her eyebrows and feigned innocence. Mercenary companies pulling security typically didn't take over the locations, close stores, and restrict access.

"We've had to assume more of a governance role until the Cartography Guild sends the proper components to fix this station. Once things stabilize, we'll move on to our next contract," Dre'Toal replied. "Are you sure I can't offer you a libation?"

Jessica shook her head. "My thanks, Dre'Toal. I'll be heading to the provisions store. I transmitted a request list, but never received an acknowledgment."

"I assure you'll have everything you need."

She nodded. "Very nice to meet you."

"The pleasure was mine."

As she walked toward the door, with the eyes of the patrons on her, Jessica couldn't help thinking there was no pleasure in Dre'Toal's expression. In fact, something was very, very wrong.

Dre'Toal's comments weren't pleasantries at all. He was warning her to leave Morel Station. Without backup in the local region, the standard operating procedures of the Peacemaker Guild were clear: once she had the fuel and provisions, she should go for help.

In the boarding tube, pulling a cart of provisions, Jessica tapped her earpiece. "Lucille? I'm coming in. Fueling status?"

<<Acknowledged. Main hatch unlocked. Fueling is thirty-one percent complete.>>

"Great. Pull my uniform camera data, please, and make a secured GalNet connection so I can check the Peacemaker database."

<<Acknowledged. Standard search for facial and vocal recognition?>>

Jessica almost stopped. "You can do that?"

<<Merely by saving your previous searches and collating data. Do you not want my assistance?>>

"No, I'd love your help, Lucille." Collating data or not, Lucille independently taking action on something was incredible. Yet Jessica's mood darkened. Running the camera footage through the database was likely to complicate things. Everything about the Equiri, and his company, screamed impropriety. Something would have to be done.

By the time Jessica boarded *Victory Twelve* and emptied the cart of provisions into the galley space, Lucille had scanned the data. Jessica grabbed a bottle of water and a pack of peanut butter crackers, made her way to the cockpit, and sat in the command chair.

"Okay, Lucille. On screen."

<<Apexx Solutions took over this gate by force twenty-three days, three hours, and ten minutes ago. No one has seen the Gate Master in that time. Gate security appears to have been purged in multiple executions in the first twelve hours of their occupation. Distress messages were intercepted. Four ships have transited the system during that time and none of them reported unusual circumstances.>>

"Holy shit."

<<Would you like me to continue?>> Lucille asked. <<The reported power surge you were told about never happened. Many critical systems have been disabled intentionally by Apexx Solutions.

The Equiri, Dre'Toal, is the registered commander of the mercenary unit. He has no registered deputies. There is no individual file in the Peacemaker database, nor any active warrants, though he is a known contact of more than a dozen wanted felons.>>

"Not surprising," Jessica said as she leaned back in the seat and set her boots on the console. "He seems like a wannabe warlord who wants something more."

<<Observation suggests Dre'Toal is suffering from an advanced form of leukemia that often afflicts Equiri,>> Lucille said. <<I have a theory based on additional information, Jessica. Would you like to hear it?>>

"Sure," Jessica replied as she unwrapped the package of crackers and popped one of the round sandwiches into her mouth.

<<The GenSha you encountered is a ninety-five percent match to a wanted felon named Trolloc.>>

"What?" Jessica flinched and sprayed crackers and peanut butter from her mouth. Chagrined, she wiped her mouth. "Why didn't you tell me that first?"

<<You requested information of Dre'Toal and Apexx Solutions first.>>

"If something like that comes up again, Lucille, I want to know. Give me the most important facts first from now on, please?" Jessica fumed. "If you're going to help me think ahead, you need to help me in the present."

<<Acknowledged.>>

"What's his deal? This Trolloc?"

<<Wanted on the order of deceased Guild Master Breka for nonstandardized medical treatments to the detriment of the Peacemaker Guild. He appears to have been behind the physiological alterations to subjects of the Enforcer program over fifty standard years ago.>>

"He's a doctor," Jessica said. "That's why he wants Trolloc, right? That's your theory?"

<<Yes. I found 1,327 articles in GalNet regarding genetic splicing and terminal disease mitigation. Data indicates the possibility Dre'Toal seeks Trolloc is highly likely.>>

"Find Trolloc, Lucille."

<<I have located the subject in submaintenance ring six, compartment seventeen,>> Lucille reported.

Jessica stood. "Then I'll go get him."

<<They have warned you to get off the gate, Jessica.>>

"I'm a Peacemaker apprehending a criminal," Jessica replied. "They can't legally stop me. Block their access to cameras and sensors so they can't find Trolloc."

<<I must advise against this course of action.>>

"Noted." Jessica made her way to her quarters. Once there, she withdrew her XM1911 pistol from its lockbox via fingerprint. She worked the action to chamber a round and donned her holster and belt with shoulder harness. Satisfied, she moved toward the exterior hatch. "For now, Lucille, help me with a diversion so I can get to Trolloc before Dre'Toal. Jam my cameras and feeds. We'll stay in touch with the good old radio. Once I'm in the ring, we'll figure things out from there."

As soon as she exited *Victory Twelve*'s external hatch, the Caroon guarding the end of the tube started her way.

"Peacemaker! We have cleared you to depart. You need to leave this station now."

Jessica didn't respond. Chin down and eyes fixed on her target's chest, she walked forward with her arms relaxed and ready. The Caroon closed the distance and brandished a baton.

"Peacemaker, my orders are—"

"Irrelevant," Jessica replied and snapped a kick at the Caroon's chin. The surprised being never raised a defense and as soon as her boot contacted his face, the guard slumped unconscious to the floor. She tapped her earpiece. "Now, Lucille."

Across the station, decompression alarms sounded. Automated bulkheads closed in populated sections of the ring. In the main passageway, panicked citizens scrambled for shelter. Jessica used their frantic movements to dart across the passageway and into the darkened alley-like corridors behind the shuttered shops. As suddenly as they'd begun, the shrieking alarms stopped and silence returned. Warning strobes, however, continued to flicker. The message to citizens was to wait. Jessica could not. She raced along the inner-ring bulkhead until she found the maintenance conduit.

"Access SG31," she whispered to her earpiece as she knelt by the meter-high door. "Open it, Lucille."

There was a barely audible *click*, and the panel pushed inward. Jessica ducked through the opening and quickly slid the panel back into position.

"Where to?"

<<Your right. In fifteen meters is a junction. Turn right there and proceed another twenty meters.>>

Jessica squinted. Lit only by red lighting every few meters, the dim conduit reminded her of spelunking in the Lost Sea a few hours north of her childhood home on Earth. She drew a cleansing breath, a technique taught at the Peacemaker Academy, to calm her heart and the rising anxiety of enclosed spaces.

Okay. Here we go.

She followed Lucille's instructions for ten minutes until she reached a junction of two tubes where it was high enough for her to stand. The intersection held three small beds and a makeshift stove. The happy art of children covered the walls of the intersection. Several cans of food lay on the ground.

"They've lived here a while," Jessica commented. "And they left in a hurry. Where are they, Lucille?"

<<Interior Airlock Five. There is an inoperable maintenance shuttle docked there. Follow the orange line. Perhaps they are attempting to hide?>>

"Or he knows something we don't about that shuttle. If he can get it into the gate, he can escape provided it has enough power and life support for 170 hours. Does it?"

<<Unknown.>>

"Dammit," Jessica swore. She found the orange line leading down another dark tube and ran into the distance. She passed the first interior-ring airlock a moment later. She didn't break stride.

<<Apexx Solutions forces are moving toward the interior ring, Jessica.>>

Time's up. Jessica picked up her pace. Aboard *Victory Twelve*, though she had exercise equipment designed to keep her body from languishing in the lack of gravity during hyperspace transits, it was no replacement for real exercise. Her legs and chest burned with exertion, but she ran until she passed Airlock Four. She slowed to a fast walk.

There was the unmistakable sound of something hitting flesh, and a child screamed. Jessica drew her weapon as she reached the edge of the airlock and peered around the hatch.

Dre'Toal stood in the center of the airlock as two armed Blevin attempted to separate the Pushtal and Equiri children from Trolloc.

"This will change your mind about treating me." Dre'Toal snickered. "And if it doesn't, I'll space you right behind these little abominations."

Jessica stepped into the space. "That's enough, Dre'Toal."

"You think the addition of your weapon changes things, Miss Francis?" The Equiri glared at her.

"That's Peacemaker," Jessica replied. "Trolloc is a wanted felon, and I am here to collect him."

"You can't have him." Dre'Toal laughed. His raspy voice a dull saw blade, he added, "Morel Station belongs to me. Here, I am the law."

"That's going to be a problem, then."

"You think you can stop me?"

Jessica nodded. "Call your thugs off my target *and* his children."

"Children? These genetic experiments bear no resemblance to any child of any species. They are only good as bargaining chips because the old fool has become attached to them." He turned to the Blevin. "Space them."

Jessica stepped into the Equiri's field of view, her weapon leveled at his face. "No."

"You're in no position to negotiate, Peacemaker."

He was right.

The two Blevin stepped toward the hatch and ejected the maintenance shuttle from the exterior connection port. As it drifted away, the Blevin manhandled the children toward the hatch.

Trolloc howled and kicked forward. "Let them go!"

One of the Blevin swung a bladed weapon at the GenSha. That was enough. Jessica whipped her pistol around and fired twice at the Blevin's center of mass. Before it even staggered, she sighted on the second as it tried to cradle the Equiri child against its chest as a shield. She dropped the Blevin with a headshot. A split second later, Dre'Toal moved to punch her in the side of the head. Even though sickly, the Equiri's punch was fast and powerful. Jessica turned her head just in time, and the blow glanced off. The pain sobered her until she felt the barrel of Dre'Toal's weapon pointed at her head.

"Drop the weapon." She did. Dre'Toal laughed. "You're good, Peacemaker. But not—"

"Geeyah!" Trolloc screamed from behind her. Dre'Toal's eyes came up, and Jessica dropped. The GenSha fired one of the Blevin's needle pistols, close enough that she felt the push of air from the projectiles as they rushed over her head. She snatched the knife from her boot and came up, swinging it hard enough to bury it in the center of the Equiri's chest below his rib cage.

Dre'Toal staggered backward and stared at her. He pressed his hands to the wound and saw dark blood running between his digits before he collapsed against the tube.

Jessica holstered her weapon and turned to Trolloc. "Come on. We have to get you out of here."

"I'm not leaving with you, Peacemaker. I have no crimes to answer for," Trolloc said. "Bureau 42 will clear my name if your Guild Master will approve your request for information."

Bureau 42 was the office where Peacemaker cold cases went to die.

How could they *clear his name?*

Jessica reached down and collected one of the Pushtal children. "We'll talk about that later. Just come on. The rest of them will be looking for you."

"And what about you?" Trolloc asked as they made their way into the maintenance conduit and headed back toward *Victory Twelve*. "Here no Peacemaker can stand alone."

"We're leaving, Trolloc. There's not enough time to set things right here. I have to get you all out."

"Time." Trolloc chuckled. "Do you know what the price of time is, Peacemaker Francis? Morality. It's why bad memories fade. We learn good. We learn virtue. As we reconcile our mistakes, we find peace. Time marches on and tries to erase the past, but my past hangs about my neck like a millstone. I delivered what they asked. It worked, and they sold me out. Genetic splicing showed it could far outperform their . . . other methods. They outlawed my work and declared me a quack. An abomination! They saw what I could do, but they tossed me away for less . . . capable work."

They reached the lower tube. Jessica crawled inside and the others followed. "What are you talking about, Trolloc?"

"The guild saw the results. The genetic splicing I oversaw allowed for better and faster nanite-based recovery, but that wasn't the half of it. Antiaging. Species crossbreeding. All of it was—"

"You can't crossbreed dissimilar species." Jessica looked over her shoulder and stared at his long face. "It's—"

"Forbidden, Peacemaker." Trolloc pointed at the Equiri child. "Splicing isn't crossbreeding. Sharing the traits of two species allows for bonding. For love. Plata here has Humanlike eyes which perform far better than Equiri ones. I took the Human eye from her maternal genetic donor and matched it to the stronger genome of the Equiri. Plata's mane is her maternal genetic donor's hair. I cannot mix a combination the other way because of physiological complications. Humans and Equiri, like most combinations, are impossible other than sentimental and emotional attachment. But that is the key! Splicing enables connection. Imagine it. Emotional connections run far deeper than the legal contracts you swore to uphold! Peace could truly exist in the galaxy, Peacemaker."

They finally reached the exit port. Jessica tried to shake off his words. The old scientist was definitely crazy, or else he was on to something tremendous. "Wait here."

Trolloc nodded, but the look in his eyes said otherwise. "All right."

Jessica understood immediately. "When I go out here, you're going to take the kids and disappear, aren't you?"

"I already said I'm not going with you," Trolloc replied. "If I must live my life on the run, so be it."

"What about your children?" Jessica asked. "A child's life shouldn't be spent on the run."

"Children are resilient creatures, Peacemaker. They'll find their way." Trolloc's bovine mouth worked into an approximation of a Human smile. "What were you intending to do?"

"Find you a ship and send you through the gate." Jessica shrugged. "But you'd rather stay here, wouldn't you?"

"Given the chance, I won't stay here. You know where I am. Because you're a good Peacemaker, you'll file a report, and they'll send Enforcers to collect me."

"You don't know that."

Trolloc laughed. "And you have much to learn, Peacemaker."

"What about Apexx Solutions?"

"Without Dre'Toal, they'll fight amongst themselves and give the Gate Master a chance to call for security backups. In two weeks, Morel Station will be on a path back toward normal. Sooner if the Gate Master still has forces Apexx Solutions did not execute." Trolloc pointed at the panel. "Go, Peacemaker. Do not stop to solve the situation. Sometimes, the best thing for a

Peacemaker to do is nothing. What happens naturally is often the best justice."

Jessica smiled. "Well met, Trolloc. Take care of these children."

"Until you call the guild on me." His face softened. "You have my gratitude. Well met, Peacemaker."

Jessica didn't reply. She opened the hatch and stepped into the alleyway. By the time she straightened, Trolloc had closed it. She knew he would take the children and disappear again and there wasn't anything she could do about it.

Except one thing.

Jessica made her way to *Victory Twelve*'s bridge and the main communications terminal. "Status update, Lucille?"

<<Fueling continues, but a request has come in from Gate Control.>>

"They're online?"

<<Apparently local forces are retaking the gate,>> Lucille replied. <<The Gate Master wishes to thank you in person, Jessica. It would be rude by Sumatozou custom for you to depart without appearing in person.>>

Jessica frowned. "Okay. Send a response that I am filing an initial report. I know the Gate Master will appreciate that, and I'll show him the actual report, once I complete it, before we leave."

<<What do you mean actual?>>

"Take this down, Lucille." Jessica leaned back in the captain's chair and put one foot on the edge of the console in front of her. She closed her eyes for a moment and let her memory replay the events of the last couple of hours as a plan formed. "Official interim report—Peacemaker Francis."

She almost smiled. It felt so good to say that.

"On a routine fuel stop at Morel Station, I interrupted an assault by a member of Apexx Solutions mercenary forces against an unarmed GenSha civilian. Apexx Solutions personnel threatened me and advised me to leave, which I considered, as well as calling for support from the regional barracks. However, body camera footage of the assault revealed the GenSha civilian to be a Class One wanted felon by the name Trolloc. I immediately returned to the station on duty status to apprehend Trolloc and found my slate and information services jammed by electromagnetic interference, which affected my camera systems and vocal logs.

I found Trolloc engaged with three members of Apexx Solutions including their leader, Dre'Toal. I ordered them aside so I could apprehend my suspect. The mercenaries then attacked me. I drew my weapon and killed two Blevin mercenaries before they forced me to take cover. In doing so, I lost track of Trolloc only to find Dre'Toal had shoved the GenSha into an open maintenance airlock and cycled it. His body was unrecoverable. I confronted Dre'Toal, and he resisted arrest. When he attempted to fire on me, I engaged and killed him."

Jessica took a deep breath. "Recommend the closure of all open case files and the removal of Trolloc from all wanted lists. Update the Guild Master. Unabridged report to follow. Peacemaker Francis sends all."

<<I have the message coded and ready for submittal.>>

"Send it unencrypted, Lucille," Jessica replied.

She knew Trolloc would see the message and understand what she'd done.

<<Would you explain why you're letting him go?>>

How could she explain it?

Jessica sighed. "His children. Keeping them together was the right thing. Maybe his idea of bringing species closer together has merits, too. I'm not prepared to debate that, Lucille. Doing the right thing was more important."

<<Such situations are bound to happen again, Jessica. When will the requirements of law outweigh your propensity for doing the right thing?>>

"As little as I can help it, Lucille." Jessica stood. She had places to go and people to see. "Trolloc said we learn about our morality as we get older. Trouble is, this job doesn't always allow for a long, peaceful life. For a brief moment in time? Yeah, I was right, but that won't always be the case."

<<Is that why you let him go?>>

Jessica smiled. "No. I'd rather do the right thing now than struggle later with what I didn't do. Trolloc was right. Time always marches on."

LAST TRAIN TO CLARKESVILLE

A Liaden Universe® Story

Sharon Lee & Steve Miller

Now

He was big, and strong, and peaceable. Nobody was expecting a fight.

Nobody expected him to knock down one deputy, much less two, or take off running, and if they'd ever even thought about his pony, they sure hadn't expected the bolt of hoofed lightning that answered his whistle, nor the ease with which a big man could swing into a saddle from a dead run.

Meld and Questa were gone before the second deputy lumbered to his feet.

Out of town.

And on the wrong side of the law.

"Meld Ketchaskin, perilous man, and dangerous outlaw? What the *hell*, Hammer?"

Daol was often sarcastic, but rarely baffled. That was he was baffled now wasn't helping Meld's feelings any.

"Wasn't my doing," Meld muttered, which Daol heard, the hat's pickup being just that good.

"Resisting arrest. Reward for information. Wait..."

Rustling sounds. Meld touched the button in his left ear,

turning down the noise from the weather station so he could listen to the land. They'd left town in the middle of the afternoon, it was just now past dawn. Questa's all-night tölt had gotten them well into the outback. This time of year, the *wohdum* herds were free-range, and it was his intention to find himself a pod and ride with them a while, confusing his trail.

He figured to work around to his hideout. His ma had taught him to plan for the worst contingency, and if that hideout wasn't never needed again, he could die happy.

"Hammer"—Daol sounded grim—"there's a posse on the next train outta Clarkesville, and a general yell gone out for the Co-opers. Kitcity Spaceport's locked down."

Meld was inclined to be insulted. The new sheriff didn't have any better idea than Meld would break for the spaceport, where he had known kin and connections?

"Gotta cover the obvious, I guess," he said. Daol snorted.

"So, *what the hell*, Hammer?"

"Rustling," Meld said flatly.

There was a longer silence than the lag counted for.

"Who swore it?"

"Who you think swore it?" Meld snarled. "Dorlamun!"

"Right," Daol said. "Got an update to set loose. Weather comin'. Stay safe, Hammer."

Posse behind him, out of Dernwall—that was a worry. Range-folk, who lived on their *ekwins*, they'd be moving fast. On the other hand, they weren't riding Questa, descendant of one of the thirty-seven survivors of the so-called "failed" Rangemaster Project. Questa would have to rest, eventually, though not for long. The Cheston-derived range *ekwins* the posse rode would have to rest sooner, and longer. Not *too* worried about the back posse, was Meld.

No, the real worry was the train out from Clarkesville. He had to get over the tracks and up into the High Dust before that train came through, with a fresher posse ready to go.

Meld shifted in the *wohdum*-hide saddle—so Questa knew for sure that he meant to do this—and headed them into the shortcut.

Dangerous damn shortcut—Windpipe Alley—a gulch that became a gully that got real thin before opening out into sere prairie where the train tracks were the big news. Make the kind of time they were making, cross the tracks there before the posse's train came through—that was the plan.

The shortcut—you didn't want to get caught by weather in the shortcut. Bad wind came up and you and your *ekwin* were skeletons drifted over with dust.

Meld cast an eye skyward, not especially liking what he was seeing, and leaned forward in the saddle, giving Questa her head while he tapped the button in his ear.

"Derecho warning Sennapee range and Dernwall." Daol's official weatherman recorded voice was flat and firm. "Seek shelter."

Meld look up at the sky again, as the walls rose higher, and the way got thinner. They were in the gully already.

Could be they'd beat the storm.

Two Weeks Ago

Fel Din kor'Entec Clan Savio looked up from his screen and out the window. Not senior enough to command a view of the garden; still, looking at the city stretching away to the horizon gave some relief from the risk analysis that was his current labor. Let it be known that *Qe'andra* Fel Din kor'Entec found risk analysis . . . boring.

Well. He was nearly through, and once he was done, there was that lovely bit of technical research to—

"Fel Din."

He hastily moved his attention from the window to his office door, rising as he did so.

"Master dea'Varge." He bowed to the firm's senior *qe'andra*, trained on Liad by the dea'Gauss himself, who was standing in his doorway, case folder in hand.

Why she had chosen to leave the homeworld and establish a firm on Wraithbone in the Relpek System remained a mystery to her juniors, though Fel Din had heard her say that *qe'andra*, like Healers, went where they were needed.

"Please," Fel Din said, straightening, and indicating the chair next to his desk, "sit. May I bring you a cup of tea?"

"No need, no need," said the master with an inclination of her white head. "My part is merely to deliver you a new assignment, which touches upon your specialty."

Fel Din did not frown—to openly show puzzlement would

be disrespectful—even as he thought, *My specialty?* And then, *My specialty!*

Unlike Master dea'Varge, Fel Din had been born on Wraithbone, and served his apprenticeship at dea'Varge and McGill Law Accounting. At the end of that apprenticeship, he had been required to produce an Independent Complete Case Assessment. He had chosen to find whether the spaceleather industry could not be made more efficient from the supply side. This work had taken him to Medway, a primitive situation even from Wraithbone's modest height. He had, perforce, become an expert in *wohdum* herding, *ekwin* breeding, on-site treatment of raw drops, and the costs—financial, environmental, human—associated.

dea'Varge and McGill had accepted his ICCA, and hired him as a *qe'andra* with a specialty in Medway Ecological Finance.

It was not, truth told, a specialty much sought after. If Master dea'Varge had a project in hand that required *his specialty*, it would be the first time in his nearly twelve years with the firm.

"I am," he said to Master dea'Varge, "surprised."

"Yes," she said. "Suzan and I were surprised, as well."

She extended the folder, and he went 'round the desk to receive it.

"Thank you," he said, bowing again.

Master dea'Varge inclined her head and left him.

An hour later, the risk analysis at last completed, Fel Din was surprised again.

He made a cup of tea and opened the folder. Clan Ayrlee was a client of long standing. Their interest was real property, their sources…varied, and their *melant'i* firm. They looked toward an honest advantage, rather than outright piracy, and always forwarded those items they found interesting to dea'Varge and McGill, for vetting. Fel Din had worked on several such vettings over the years, and immediately saw why this particular offering had caught Ayrlee's attention.

He sipped tea and read the prospectus, which was suspect on its face.

Two parcels for sale on Medway, where land was *never* for sale. The largest percentage of land was held in common under the terms of a ninety-nine-year covenant, reserved for the needs of the *wohdums*. A slightly smaller percentage was held by the breeders of *ekwins*—necessary to the herding of *wohdums* and cattle. The human population lived on the scraps left over after those two vital industries were served.

So, land for sale on Medway was—not likely. Fel Din flipped to the next page, and choked on his tea.

He *knew* the properties in question. He had learned the fine points of raising Cheston *ekwins*, and how to ride one, also, on what was noted as Parcel One.

Parcel Two...

Fel Din reached for his comm, and tapped the button for his supervisor. She answered at once.

"I must travel to Medway on the Ayrlee prospectus," he said, already making a mental list of what to take with him. "There is some urgency."

"Go," said his supervisor. "dea'Varge left word that you have full authority on the Ayrlee prospectus."

Fel Din pressed his lips together.

Surprised, indeed.

He went.

Now

The air was thick with dust, even down in the gully. Meld pulled his *wohdum*-hide hat down closer over his face. The weather station was on the ear button—recorded derecho warning every seven minutes.

Meld thought about getting out his handheld and taking a look at a map, and then thought better of it. They'd beat the storm or they wouldn't.

Questa's withers twitched, a warning that something wasn't quite right ahead. Meld squinted into the flying dust.

Could be they were close enough to the end of the gully that Questa was catching the vibration of the automated engines that ran fresh ore from the Hampstead chrome beds to the forges at Sennapee?

Now, though—now *he* heard something odd. Not wheels on track, not the warning bell. Something high and irregular. Meld moved his shoulders in his *wohdum*-hide duster. Probably just the wind whistling through the rocks, or turning dried gulch flower canes into flutes.

Questa shivered, and leaned into a gallop, bursting out of the gully and into the flatlands.

It was hard to see with so much grit and dust in the seesawing wind. The train track ought to be—

But there was another reason he couldn't see the track, Meld realized, even as Questa pranced beneath him.

The prairie between them and the track was full of *wohdums*. He could smell them now, as the wind whipped in the right direction for half a heartbeat before changing again.

He'd been looking for *wohdums*, that was part of his plan. It was Wander Season, after all, and the *wohdums* did just that, in subherds of family units, the young learning the land, and building up the strength to survive their first molt. After Wander was when the riders went to work, gathering the small herds together, and driving them up to High Heaven for the Big Molt.

But now, the *wohdums* were on the move—running from the approaching storm.

Questa pranced again, making herself look taller. Taking his cue, Meld sat higher, too, and looked out over the herd.

He hadn't expected to find a herd this soon—too soon. He still needed to get over the tracks, up high, where the paths were thinner, and the winds had carved caves out of the stone.

The posse was behind him, the storm rising.

Meld settled his hat, and took stock. Hat, duster, saddle, panniers, chaps were all good drop-side, worked locally. Hell, he'd made the panniers himself, the Wander he'd worked at Shobbs Tannery.

Any case, he was kitted out fine to push through a herd of *wohdums*. They weren't savage; just big and placid. They'd move along just to avoid Questa's glare.

Meld got firm in the saddle, and pressed his leg against Questa's side, signaling her to get on.

The nearest *wohdums* shifted, and let them by.

It was a bigger herd than he'd thought, going in, many of them overdue for shedding, the bulky hide-plates making it harder for the primos—the first-timers—to get around. They waddled more than walked at this point, while the older animals knew how to synchronize plate movement and motion at several speeds, including full gallop.

A *wohdum* at speed was a sight to behold, in motion on two different axes. Those not familiar assumed that their shedable hide-plates would interfere with the animal's gait, but the truth was that they hung from secondary spines, away from the supple main spine, the plates and the thin membranes beneath pleated and, except for a very brief period at molt, very little of the *wohdum* understructure was visible, or vulnerable to injury.

It was rare for a major molt to happen during Wander, but not unheard of. Daol would see it with his weather-eyes or one of the sky-riders would, and send the location to the Chief Co-oper—

There was that noise again—high and irregular—and now he recognized it. Wheels sliding against rail, like the brakes were locked, but something was still being rotated uselessly along the rails. It made Meld's ears shiver—and Questa's too—all screech and no motion.

If one of the trains was making a noise like that, it was trouble, sure.

Meld stood up in the stirrups, pulled the far-glasses down from inside his hat brim, and over his eyes.

With all the sand in the air, he couldn't see—and then the wind shifted, and he *could* see.

A speeder—one of the light-duty, four-person rail conveyances ranchers used in lieu of *ekwins* for traveling back and forth to such civilization as town, stations, and other ranches might afford—was coupled incongruously into the head end of the automated consist; tiny overhead running lights flashing red, wheels screeching against the rails as it tried to move the heedless engine and loads of ore behind it.

The wind, whimsical, dropped entirely, and in that instant, Meld saw the speeder with absolute clarity. The little blue-and-white speeder—Cheston blue, and the Cheston logo on the side—an *ekwin* head imposed on a galaxy.

The wind whipped, and Meld was blind again.

But he'd seen enough. The speeder's position at the head of the train made it protrude into the crossing diamond—where rail crossed rail—with multiple trains on the way.

He settled back into the saddle, and urged Questa into a run.

Two Weeks Ago

He found another instructor to cover his *menfri'at* class—one of his past students, now proficient in the Liaden martial art.

That duty settled, he had looked for his *gear*, finding it in the back of the closet.

There had been no reason to suspect that he would ever need *gear* again, and yet—he had kept it. *Who knew*, he remembered thinking, *what Balance might demand of one, in future?* And after all, it had been fitted to him alone, so no one else should wear it, should they? Too, there were memories of people attached to the gear.

Fel Din sighed.

"So wise," he murmured, opening the box. Vest and chaps of *wohdum* hide, a range-cloth duster in the particular shade known as "Cheston blue." The duster had been a gift from one of the pair who had taught him to ride the high-mannered creatures used in herding cattle, the other profit animal suited to Medway's climate.

When Troianna and her cousin, Aida Pickerell Cheston, decided his report would be incomplete without doing "real *wohdum* herd riding," Troianna had taken off this very duster and pressed it upon him, insisting that such a garment was necessary to his safety while riding herd.

The duster had fit him, Troianna being petite as Terrans decided such things, and Fel Din tall as Liadens measured. And, indeed, it had been useful during his time among the *wohdums*. He had tried to return the garment at the end of his study.

Troianna had laughed.

"Anybody can see that's a rangecoat, worn by a proper range rider. I'd say you earned it, fair and square."

So, the duster had come home with him, though he had no right to the color. The Chestons were High House of their kind, premium breeders and trainers of the fabled Cheston *ekwins*, one of the two breeds of *ekwin* in use on Medway.

Chestons were intelligent, nervy, and fast in short bursts. Despite being faster and taller than *wohdums*, Chestons were not used for *that* work.

There, you had the range-*ekwins*—small, tough, practical mounts, who could move for hours at an effortless, ground-eating pace, of whom Aida had said, "Smartest things on this planet, the rangemasters. When you're out there with the *wohdums*, you *listen* to your mount."

That had been good advice, too.

The timer went off, and Fel Din sealed the box, picked it up, with the other hand his briefcase, and headed for the door and his ride to the spaceport.

One week ago

Gar Don Ayrlee had written to say that his clan was interested in the offering of land, at the named price. That was good news, but unsurprising. Blake had done his research. You didn't make an offer like he was making, with the stakes as high as they were, without being sure of your target.

"As you have surmised," the letter went, "Ayrlee's foundations are in the acquisition and development of diverse lands. Your offer interests us. We have therefore arranged for a *qe'andra* from the respected firm of dea'Varge and McGill on Wraithbone to visit you and discuss particulars. *Qe'andra* kor'Entec will be arriving at your location in a matter of days. We will write again, after we have the analysis in hand."

Sending a lawyer, were they? That news was less good. Sent from Wraithbone and arriving in a couple of days—the lawyer was on a ship already, that meant. He couldn't back out.

He caught that thought.

Backing out was never an option. He'd had his plans in place for years, just waiting for the right lineup of events. It was now. *Now*, or he'd be stuck on this gods-forsaken dust ball for the rest of his life.

There was more to life than *ekwins*, cattle, *wohdums*, and dust. And Blake was going to have it.

The only thing he needed to do—quick now, with the lawyer on the way—was clear the final pieces off the board.

Now

The speeder's auxiliary tow was coupled to the slug, the speeder's doors wrapped shut with the kind of tough, wide straps used to bundle hides together for shipping. Tough straps that never frayed, and were almost impossible to cut.

Worryingly familiar straps, now that Meld got a good look at them: black with embedded red fibers, the maker's mark clearly visible, and, every five hand widths, his mark—the meld-hammer.

The very same straps, he was willing to bet, that had been looted out from one of his range-pods last year.

The straps made it hard to see through the speeder's windscreen. He made out two arms of slightly different shades of brown, a head with two faces, one of the arms rising to slam against the instrument panel.

"Stand," Meld said to Questa and swung out of the saddle, moving closer to the speeder, peering into the cockpit through the thin space between the straps, piecing together an understanding of two people, strapped together with the last of his straps.

A flash of face and, from inside, a yell!

"There's somebody out there! Look!"

"Hammer!" yelled a second voice, that he recognized right where he lived.

"Hammer!" yelled Picky, "get us out!"

He'd never got out of the habit of doing a little hide-work during the quiet times on the ride. Which is why he had a crystal-edged flat-blade in his kit. Tough enough to cut *wohdum* hide, it was tough enough to cut the straps.

But it wasn't easy, with the wind skirling, and the grit flying, and the *wohdums*—a pair of elders by the size of them— overlooking his progress like trail bosses.

Now he had the screen clear, he could see Picky and Troda, tied together tight with the last of his marked straps.

He was halfway through the last outer strap when the rails began to vibrate.

Hammer swore. That would be the chrome train. He had to get the speeder off the track now!

The last strap parted.

"Picky!" Meld roared. "Hit the release!"

The release he wanted was the ingenious hydraulic lift that raised the lightweight car body and let it turn end to end on the rails at trip end. It would uncouple the car, let them push it off the tracks.

Strapped tight together, they both lurched at the blue lever.

Up-track, the trestle lights started flashing red. The automatics picked up the obstruction and started shouting, "Clear the track! Clear the track! Clear—"

The speeder rose uncertainly as the hydraulics engaged.

Meld slammed his shoulder into the speeder's side, meaning to knock it off the track. The tumble would be rough on the girls, but not nearly as rough as the chrome train would be.

The speeder rocked, but didn't tumble.

"Questa! Push!"

But even with the two of them—and then the speeder began to rock.

Looking through the windscreen, he could see Picky and Troda throwing themselves to the left—again, and again—trying to help.

'Way too close, a whistle screamed.

Cursing, Meld threw himself against the speeder; it tipped, but not enough.

"Questa, back!"

One more time, he threw himself against the little vehicle, which shuddered, and tipped, and—

And suddenly he was flat against the speeder, crushed under a weight that just kept pressing. His chest constricted, he saw dots in front of his eyes, the pressure continuing until—

The speeder went over.

Meld went over.

The *wohdum* pair wandered away from the track, to the right.

Questa stuck her nose in Meld's face.

And the chrome train roared through, slammed past the slug and kept on going.

Hours Ago

The weather on Medway was tumultuous, and thus of great interest to everyone who lived there, and the wise visitor, too.

There was therefore a weather screen at each hallway intersection inside the Kitcity Spaceport, as well as periodic audio broadcasts.

At the moment, Kitcity rejoiced in a Wind Watch, while the Big Dust was under a much more serious Derecho Warning.

Wearing his gear, Fel Din collected his luggage, and paused before a live weather map.

Local conditions at the moment were listed as Wind Borne Grit—not unusual.

The Cheston holding was outside of Kitcity, but not properly in the Big Dust. The weather could go either way.

He was—or had been—perfectly competent to drive a car during a Medway Wind Warning. He might even, with luck, manage a Big Wind.

The only way to survive a derecho was to take cover and wait. Well.

Fel Din sighed, settled his hat, tightened the stampede string— and headed for the exit and his waiting car.

Perhaps he could beat the storm.

Now

They—Picky, Troda, Meld, and Questa—crowded into the weather shelter on the other side of the track, took stock, and got cleaned up using the kit from Meld's panniers.

"This happened—why?" Meld asked finally.

They were a mess in more ways than one. Troda was cleaning the blood off Picky's face; Picky was wiping a scrape on Troda's arm with an antiseptic pad. Meld had cleaned the blood off his own face, made sure of the contents of his pockets, and was briefly, but intensely thankful that none of them had worse than bad bruises and scrapes. If there'd been even one broken bone...

"This happened because Blake's selling the land," Troda said.

Meld looked around from repacking the panniers. "Blake's selling Cheston Hold? What's Matt say to that?"

"Matt's gone," Picky said, pulling Troda's sleeve down over the scrape. "Figured it was now or never on that tour he'd been promising himself since Momma Nan died."

"Ship barely cleared Kitcity before Blake was trying to get us to vote our shares with him, to sell." That was Troda.

"And you didn't want to sell," Meld said, which was just common sense. Ask Aida Pickerell Cheston or her boon-chum and partner in everything, Troianna Daphnia Paeds, to sell out of Cheston? Blake must've taken leave of what few wits he had.

"We wouldn't sell," Picky said grimly.

"*Six times*, we wouldn't sell," said Troda.

Picky waved her hand in the direction of the track.

"So this morning—this. Can't vote our shares if we're dead.

Blake doesn't even have to hold ours. He's got his own, and Matt's proxy."

"What's he figure to do? No land, no *ekwins*? Going to put out his shingle as a bookkeeper?"

"He figured to go off-world," Troda said succinctly.

"Cheston's worth a lot of money, is what he told us," Picky said. "Blake fancies himself as a merchant prince of the spaceways."

Meld snorted, recognizing a line from one of the serials they'd all listened to growing up. Then he sobered.

"So, even if you had sold him your shares, something like this was going to happen?"

Troda looked at Picky. Picky looked at Troda. They both looked at Meld.

"Yeah, we figure this was always in the plan."

"Though we didn't tumble to it 'til just before you happened by."

"Blake did this himself?"

They laughed.

"Got help from Kendal's crew."

"Know that for sure?"

Troda shook her head.

"No. There were six of 'em, wearing grit masks, saw three rifles and a bunch of small arms. I don't even have ID, 'cept the name on my shirt..."

She glanced down at herself, and wrinkled her nose at what the blood and mud had done to that item of clothing.

"Well, anyway..."

She turned to Picky, who shook her head.

"Cleaned me out, too—took my knives, and my range-stopper. I had my whole bag with me."

The wind boomed outside. The shelter shuddered.

Meld's hat buzzed.

"What the hell *now*, Hammer?" Daol's voice was loud enough for Picky and Troda to hear.

"You got the upload?"

"I did. Miz Cheston, Miz Paeds—can you hear me?"

"Yes," said Picky.

"Loud and clear," said Troda.

"I got the upload from Meld's hat regarding your brush with getting smashed to flinders. You wanna make a complaint?"

"No?" said Picky, and glanced at Troda, eyebrows up.

"Agree. Better he thinks it worked. Also, there's Hammer's little problem."

"Hammer's problems are getting more interesting by the hour," Daol said. "Co-op Chief refused to join the hunt, hollered up the lawyers at Fryhaven, and there's a plea to call off the posse. Meanwhile, county board's looking into the rustling angle, which is being tough on them, on account of Mister Dorlamun's gone missing."

"What about the new sheriff's hunt?" Meld asked.

"Still on—and getting closer the longer you stand like a rock."

"We're not staying."

"Right. Be careful, Hammer. Weather—"

"Got it," Meld said, and, "out."

He turned back to Picky and Troda.

"You're going into the High Dust," Picky said, not asking a question.

"*We're* going," he corrected. "Got a snug hideout—sweet well, deep rooms."

"Sounds perfect," Troda said.

They walked across the scrub surrounded by *wohdums*. Troda's bruises being worse, according to Picky, she was riding Questa with Picky walking beside and Meld a little to the fore.

The wind had decided on a direction and was at their backs as they crested a rise that overlooked the plain. The horizon was a hazy dark line stitched with lightning along the whole front. Thunder rolled in the distance.

"Mean one," Troda observed.

"Think we can beat the storm to your snuggery?" asked Picky.

Meld was beginning to doubt that, honestly. He shrugged and gave her a grin.

"Won't know 'til we try."

He raised an arm and pointed.

"We're heading across those arroyos to the top of that next ridge."

Picky sighed.

"Best get moving, then."

"Hey, Hammer!" Troda called from Questa's back. "Are all these yours?"

She waved a hand at the large company surrounding them.

"Some are," Meld said, looking around. They were more or less in the center of the herd, like the *wohdums* were trying to make them less visible, treating them as young'uns.

"We've been selecting for the blues and blacks," he told Troda. "There's a couple grays out on the edge I'm not sure about. Could be youngsters who haven't had their first drop. Could be from over Ed Meskys' side. He's partial to the grays and tans."

Meld's hat buzzed.

"Gonna need to push it, Chawnzy," Daol said. "Air pressure's dropping, other pressure not so much. Expect the storm rollover soon. I'd be under cover in eight minutes, tops."

Eight minutes.

Meld looked at the ridge. Just him on Questa, and they could make it with minutes to spare. All of them mounted, even on cattle-*ekwins*, they'd make it.

As they were...

Meld looked around.

"There," he said, pointing. "Let's try for that."

The sky turned uglier, and the *wohdums'* pace picked up. The thunder was nearer now—definite booms punctuated with sharp cracks almost drowned out the low moaning of the herd.

Their herd had grown, Meld saw. They'd picked up half-a-dozen maverick beef steer, and an ungroomed, riderless *ekwin*, too.

Groundward from the storm's green-blue was the dust, with still enough light in it to show the threat: from horizon to horizon a roller of sand and water, a veritable wave of weather upon the surface of the world, with a distant looming constant thrumming that was the sound of thunder echoing between the firmament and the dust below.

"How far?" Troda yelled, and Meld squinted at the rocky mound he had thought maybe—and admitted to himself that it was too far. They wouldn't beat the storm.

Years Ago

"If you're going to ride herd with *wohdums*," Aida said, as they three walked down to the stables where working stock was housed, "you'll want a rangemaster *ekwin*. Some people call them 'ponies,' but they're none of that. Full-grown *ekwins*, designed and bred for Medway range riding. They're fast when they have to be, but their best gait is the tölt—keep it up from now 'til the middle of next week."

Fel Din had speedily been matched with Verry, and with Troianna and Aida mounted on their personal Chestons, they had ridden across Dust Country to Ketchaskin Station to meet, as he was told, the best range rider on Medway.

The range rider's name was Meld Ketchaskin. He was very large, looking half asleep as they were made known to each other, and the plan explained to him by Aida.

"Complete study, is it?" the big man had said. Fel Din, who had thought that the man had already been asked and agreed, felt it necessary to put himself forward at that point.

"Indeed, if it is not convenient, I may complete my work by speaking with those experienced with *wohdums*—people such as yourself, Edward Meskys, Javin Dorlamun—"

"Javin Dorlamun don't know a *wohdum* from a milky cow," Meld Ketchaskin interrupted. "I'm not against showing you the range work, if you think you're up for it. Need to be able to ride—"

"He's a good rider, Hammer," Troianna said, which was pleasant to hear. Aida added, "A natural. Rode all the Chestons. Even Poppa."

The sleepy look abated somewhat.

"You rode Poppa? Where to?"

Fel Din bowed slightly.

"To Branch Spring over the meadow, returning by the covered trail."

"Picky, you devil." The big man looked wide awake now. "Poppa try to throw you?"

"Yes," Fel Din admitted. "He did not succeed."

"He's a *good* rider, Hammer," Troianna said again.

Meld Ketchaskin raised his big hands, palms out.

"I believe you." He turned his newly wakeful gaze on Fel Din.

"Leathers, duster, saddle bags. Verry's a good goer, no worries there. Where's your hat?"

Fel Din sighed. He disliked wearing hats and wore his as little as possible. Still, he pulled it out of his pocket and put it on his head.

Meld Ketchaskin shook his head.

"That ain't a hat—that's a cap. You're riding range, you want a *hat*. Come inside."

They followed him into the house carved from rock, down a hall and into a small room at the back.

"Workshop," he said. "Never mind the mess."

The lights came up, revealing a leatherworking table like Fel Din had seen at Shobbs Tannery when he had toured.

On a top shelf, well over Fel Din's head, was a row of—hats. Wide-brimmed hats such as he had, yes, seen some riders wear.

"Range gear," Meld said, glancing at him over one shoulder.

He reached, took a hat down, and turned, dropping the thing on Fel Din's head, where it promptly slid down to his nose.

"Gotta size it," Meld said, pulling the hat up and turning toward the bench. "Won't take a sec."

Another glance over the shoulder.

"Whyn't you three go down the kitchen and put together a snack? I'll be along in a shake."

"Here you are."

This time, the hat remained firmly around his head. Instinctively, he reached up to adjust the brim.

"Good instincts," Meld said, pulling the hat off again. "Just another couple technical things to take care of. What's your name again?"

"Fel Din kor'Entec Clan Savio."

Meld shook his head. "You need a nick that'll fit the channel." A long, appraising look. "Not much bigger'n a twig. How 'bout we call you Twig?"

"Don't be mean, Hammer," Troianna said sharply. She gave Fel Din a warm smile. "He's just—slim."

A corner of Meld's mouth quirked, and he looked to Fel Din.

"All right then, *Slim*, let's get you signed up with the satellite service and introduce you to the weatherman. That's done, we can get riding."

Fel Din stared at him.

"We are leaving now?"

"Well—hour maybe. You got anything pressing?"

"Not as such. However, I neglected to supply—"

Meld raised a hand.

"No worries. We leave in an hour, we make it to Pod Three

by first dark. Got supplies cached there. Pretty place to overnight. Get you used to the Dust. All right, Slim?"

Fel Din squared his shoulders, and looked up to meet Meld Ketchaskin's surprisingly deep blue eyes.

"All right, Hammer," he said.

Now

The three lead *wohdums* paused, staring ahead and overhead, before issuing a simultaneous trumpeting moan. The largest wheeled and dropped to its knees so that its hide looked like a solid stone. It moaned again, louder, leaned—and fell over, back to the storm.

The other two went to the right and left, their moans briefly sharper, as if they were issuing orders, before, they, too, fell over, backs to the oncoming calamity.

The next largest *wohdums* quickly filled in beside, forming a wall that curved around the humans and their *ekwin*. Smaller *wohdums* formed a second and third line, leaving the center of the wall to Meld's party, and the *wohdums* too young to have proper armor.

The free-range *ekwin* went to the youngsters and circled, displaying something that was almost a proper range-horse prance. After a moment, Questa moved over, and the two of them got the youngsters down into a tight circle, heads together.

Meld looked around in awe. He'd heard of such things in range stories, but to actually be present, to be protected by this living wall of *wohdums*—and not just them. They shared the sheltered center with cattle, a mixed flock of birds, a fluffle, two jackalopes, and other normally unsocial—even antisocial—creatures.

Lightning struck, and thunder roared, reminding Meld that they were safer but by no means safe.

He went to Questa, pulling the stitched hide tarp from his pannier.

"Down!"

Questa shivered, and dropped to her knees. After a second, the other *ekwin* did the same.

Meld waved Picky and Troda forward. They knelt, too, and he got the tarp over as much of all of them as he could.

Lightning struck too close, making them all jump, the thunderclap barely audible over the sudden racket of wind, rain and ice.

The storm had arrived.

It fell on them, slamming them into each other.

They scrabbled at the edges of the tarp, wrapping the ties around hands as tightly as they could, while the rain and wind pounded the hide down and around them.

There was no keeping dry, there was only holding themselves in place, leaning into each other as close as possible, body heat welcome as the water sliced away, no real chance to recall better times of holding each other, grabbing what comfort they could in each moment.

Momentarily, the wind dropped, the rain stopped.

Meld raised the tarp higher, and looked around the area they occupied. The rain had fallen so fast and hard, it hadn't run off. They were crouched in inches of water and mud. Small creatures were huddled by their feet and against the sides of the *ekwins*, soaked and miserable.

Cautiously, he raised the tarp some more, so that they could see out.

The ring of *wohdums* sighed and moaned.

Picky pointed to two small predators leaning against a *wohdum*, their usual smaller prey hand widths away and ignored. One of the cattle was flat, its face under the standing water. Looking up, almost too late, she pointed at the anvil of green over their heads.

The wind rushed down again, and they grabbed the tarp, pulling it down close as the rain poured down. Shivering, they huddled close, free hands stubbornly together; off hands gripping the tarp.

No one knew the time; the storm went on relentlessly for what felt like forever. Gradually, though, the flashing of lightning grew less, the thunder less constant, the water about them managing to flow down and away from whatever small hill they'd managed to mount. This time when the rain suddenly stopped there was only a light breeze, the odd sounds of water trickling and gurgling.

Meld felt Questa twitch, sighed, and rallied himself.

"I think it's over."

Hours Ago

"I know you."

The office was decorated in quasi-frontier style, paneled walls festooned with paired tools of the *ekwin* trade, leather straps, antique long arms, multiple iterations of the *ekwin* head on a galaxy that was the Cheston crest.

Blake Cheston rose from behind the desk that had been his father's during Fel Din's previous visit. Matt Cheston had been intelligent, urbane, and thoughtful; Fel Din had found the heir to be none of these.

Nonetheless, he bowed in the Terran mode, holding his hat in his off hand, and then replacing it, according to local custom.

"I am Fel Din kor'Entec Clan Savio, licensed *qe'andra*, affiliated with dea'Varge and McGill Law Accounting on Wraithbone," he said. "I am here to investigate the proposition that you have land for sale. Delm Ayrlee was to have written you that I was coming."

"He wrote." Blake's jaw tightened. "But you—you've been here before."

He had come around the desk, and paused next to the decorated wall, eyes narrowed.

"I was here twelve years ago," Fel Din said, "doing a supply-and-efficiency study. I was chosen for this case because I have particular knowledge of both the principals and the governing laws."

Blake Cheston, Fel Din thought dispassionately, did not look well. Best to get the thing done, then.

"If you would ask shareholders Cheston and Paeds to join us, we may complete this very quickly."

"They're dead," Blake Cheston snarled, and Fel Din felt something go quite cold in his chest.

"And so are you!"

Blake Cheston jumped for the long arm on the wall.

Fel Din stepped forward into a *menfri'at* strike.

Now

Throwing the tarp back, they leaned and held and helped each other to their feet. They could see the storm fleeing toward the city, breaks in the front. They'd taken the brunt of it, and now it would become separate cells instead of one incredible wall.

Around them the other creatures were stirring, shaking water out of fur and feathers. Questa tested her legs and stood, sneezed, and whinnied, as Meld and company gave way, still unsteady on the washboard rivulets.

"Hammer!"

That was Troda, pointing at a *wohdum* struggling in the mud—a primo, already unsteady in its balance, finding no purchase in the ooze, stumbling.

"Questa!" Meld called and moved forward—and realized what he was seeing.

"That's a drop!" Picky cried.

And so it was. The struggling creature was a gangling gray not much bigger than Questa, lightly patterned skin slick with more than rain, that skin showing an under-pelt of plated armor slowly rearranging itself around the creature's form, darkening. With an effort, it held steady, and stood, shivering. No longer a primo, this *wohdum*'s first drop-hide could come with a story.

He reached into the pannier for a tag, so the sky-riders could find it, later. Touched the button in his ear—

—and got a flat buzz.

He froze.

"Meld?" That was Picky. "What's wrong?"

"Hat's out," he mumbled, then louder, "Lucky the hat's the only thing that's out. Let's tag the drop. You two up for moving again?"

"Where to?" asked Troda.

Meld used his chin to point in the more-or-less direction of his hideout.

"First target," he said. "There's supplies, clothes, water, and it's defensible."

"Defensible?" Troda said. "Why?"

"That's why," said Picky, and they both turned to look.

Behind them, maybe a dozen small shiny things in the still dark sky.

"Posse's got search drones," Meld said. "Go!"

Hours Ago

Fel Din touched his hat brim.

"*Slim?*" Daol's voice carried an interesting mix of shock and hope. "You back?"

"I am," he said grimly. "Daol, where is Hammer? I have

just been with Blake Cheston. Troianna and Aida are—" No, he couldn't say it.

But, he didn't have to.

"Troda and Picky are fine—were fine, no thanks to Blake, but I guess you're up to speed on that part. Trouble is, they're with Hammer, with posse problems. They went into the Dust, and the derecho went over their last position. Storm's gone past, but I can't find him."

Slim drew a tight breath.

"Can't find him?" he repeated. The derecho! Gods. People died in derechos, much more commonly than they survived.

"Don't panic," Daol said, sounding only slightly less than that himself. "Could just be the hat took a hit—blown off, water damage, stampeded on by *wohdums*—it happens. Problem is, he's out of touch, heading for safe ground, he told me that, but he didn't tell me where."

Slim finished with the girth and swung up onto Verry's back. Memory stirred. It had only been a Big Wind, but they had taken shelter together, in what Meld had told him was derecho proof—and posse proof.

"I know the place," he said to Daol. "I'm going now. Tell me about the posse problem."

"Sure will, but first you tell me—you kill that bastid?"

"Yes."

"Good," said Daol.

Now

The notch the stair led to opened into the dimness of a stone overhang with a slightly bubbling pool at the bottom of it, a pool that formed a small stream.

Meld pushed a handlight at Troda to show her how the interior rose above the pool, a stone shelf large enough for a dozen humans. He was grabbing at Questa's panniers and handing them up to Picky within moments, while Questa turned, making noises of demand.

The notch was close, but in fact there was enough space inside for the *ekwin*, while there was clearly not room for all of the *wohdums* trailing behind. The oldest, the one Meld had started calling Bluestuff, glanced at the notch and mumbled some *wohdum* comment about skinny creatures and turned, muttering louder until the herd crowded round into a crescent, between them and the oncoming posse.

Meld climbed higher in the twisty rock, which was like a natural tower with multiple viewports. He scanned the path back to the wye, and saw intermittent movement there—several desert range-buggies were on their way.

"Trouble's getting closer," he said. "There's a range finder and a carbine back there in stores—" He nodded toward the back of the formation, where several archways were visible in the light from Troda's torch.

"Get dressed, get armed, bring some rations when you come back, and we'll talk about what to do."

His hat was still out, which put them in a much more precarious position. They didn't have the big picture—if Co-op Chief Graystar's Fryhaven lawyers had managed to get the stay, if Javin Dorlamun had turned up, sober for a change, and wanting to rescind his latest accusations—they knew none of that.

"We're going to have to talk to them," Picky said.

Meld sighed.

"Bear with me," he said, "but I been thinking."

He paused, expecting a groan, from Troda at least, but they nodded at him to go on.

"So, I been thinking—Blake had this planned out long. Those straps went missing a year ago. Even if he didn't know exactly what he was going to do, he knew he was going to try to pin it on me. Too, I'm thinking Blake might've bought himself a sheriff. Man was a lot too eager to be putting me in chains. His own deputy told him Dorlamun yells *rustling* three times a year, on rotation, but it didn't—"

Questa whinnied.

Out and down, another *ekwin* whinnied back.

Meld got to his feet.

"You two stay back, and stay peaceful. We don't want a war."

"No wars," Picky agreed, rising with him, and Troda, too. Meld looked at them, and threw up his hands.

"Your call," he said.

Which was how it was that the three of them came out onto the lip of his hideout, and looked down over the Dust.

There was a line of range-buggies and *ekwins* holding at a respectful distance.

Closer were two figures on *ekwins*—one tall, one small. The small one was waving his hat over his head, in a deliberate pattern.

Troda grabbed Picky's arm.

"Is that—wait, Hammer, it's Slim!"

"So it is," Meld said, reading the pattern he'd taught Slim, those weeks they rode herd together.

All good, that was the pattern, and *come*.

Meld pulled the far-glasses over his eyes.

No question it was Verry standing neat and calm under her small rider. Meld touched the side of the glasses, zooming in on the rider's smooth, sharp face. Yeah, it was Slim. Older, but who wasn't? Question being, what else had the years done? Blake aspiring to merchant prince of the spaceways, he'd pitch a Cheston sale to money. Nobody had more money than Liadens, and Slim was a Liaden lawyer. If he was working for Blake...

"Hammer?" Troda said softly.

Slim swung out of the saddle, spoke a word to his mount, and walked forward, hat on head, hands raised shoulder high, empty.

"What's he doing?" asked Troda.

"He's getting in range," Picky said grimly.

Meld shoved the glasses back into his hat.

"Gimme the rifle," he said.

He figured to hear an argument, but the only sound was a soft gasp from Troda, as Picky handed over the rifle.

Meld felt the weight of it settle in his hands, and looked down. Slim had stopped well within range, and looked to be willing to stand there 'til night.

Nerves o'steel, that was the Slim he'd come to know.

Meld glanced down at the rifle: full charge, full magazine.

Picky drew a breath.

Meld cracked the rifle, took out the magazine, and dropped it into a leg pocket.

Troda jumped, got his hat in a snatch, and rushed forward, waving it enthusiastically.

Coming now.

Later

They were all four sitting on the back porch of Cheston House, Troda next to Slim, and Picky nestled under Meld's arm.

"I have news," Slim said.

Troda drew a careful breath, and folded her hands in her lap.

"Speak," Picky told him. "Troda can't hold her breath forever."

Slim smiled.

"My news is that Seniors dea'Varge and McGill have given their support to establishing a branch office on Medway." Another smile, and a side glance at Troda. "For the moment, that means me." He extended his hand, palm up. "This office will be my permanent assignment."

Troda whooped, and threw her arms around his neck.

Picky laughed, and looked up into Meld's face.

"They're good together," she said.

"As good as us?"

She laughed. "Nothing's as good as us, Hammer," she chided, and raised her voice.

"If you two kids can back off a sec, I got news, too."

Troda untangled and sat back in her chair. Meld saw with approval that Slim kept a good hold on her hand.

"Right," said Picky. "I heard back from Matt. Blake's shares come half to me, half to Troda, to dispose as we see fit."

"And how we see fit," Troda said, smiling into Slim's face, "is to settle those shares on our hold-husbands."

"That is," said Picky, looking up at Meld, "if you can tolerate having anything to do with cattle *ekwins*."

"Imagine I'll become acclimated," Meld said, feeling comfortable and—at peace. "Slim? You OK with this?"

"A *qe'andra* goes where he's needed," Slim said. "Also, I made an error, in leaving Troianna before. I will gladly spend the rest of my life balancing that error."

Troda threw her arms around him again, and Meld looked down at Picky.

"Looks like fun," he said, "wanna try?"

Picky laughed, and wriggled and wrapped her arms around him, her mouth seeking his.

In the distance, a whistle rode the busy wind, as the last train to Clarkesville flew down the night.

THE ROGUE TRACTOR OF SUNSHINE GULCH

Kelli Fitzpatrick

In a dim corner of the storage bay, the robot tried unsuccessfully to pull its cube-shaped body up the smooth wall to escape. Polla Jackard—"Jack" to anyone who knew her—could see the bot's movements were erratic, almost frantic, uncannily like a person's. There was nowhere for it to run. That was the point. Jack and her partner Tig Holloway finally had the thing cornered.

After twelve grueling hours of hunting the machine through the stuffy bowels of the station silos, Jack was exhausted, and her dark canvas jacket was soaked through with sweat. But she never quit until the job was finished. She glanced to the side where Tig was in position to activate the net they had set up. She could just make out the outline of the young man's vest and wide-brimmed hat nestled in the shadows. Into her collar mic, she whispered, "You set?"

"We're a go, Boss." He gave a completely unnecessary thumbs-up that made her smile. Tig brought a youthful energy to the job that Jack appreciated, especially since these jobs left her feeling increasingly more worn out than she would like. Bot wrangling was a labor-intensive profession.

Their current target was a loading bot with a squat boxy body, articulated arms, and treads for maneuvering, used primarily for swapping out empty vehicle power cells with charged ones. Its design meant the bot was fast and meticulous, yet sturdy, which rendered it difficult to take down without damaging it. It would be quicker to just stun the thing and be done with it, but the EM pulses would likely fry most of this bot's circuits, and the owners were clear about wanting their property back in functioning condition. So, a net it would have to be.

She raised her voice to a tone of command. "Loading Bot XR-47, you are malfunctioning. We have to take you in for diagnostics and reprogramming. Please confirm obedience to this directive."

"*Error. Error. Please step back. Operations normal.*" As a loading bot that usually worked in uncrewed cargo areas, its program had only limited speech recordings for interacting with humans. It had been stringing them together into cryptic pleas for mercy all day. Jack focused hard on blocking them out.

"Confirm obedience," she ordered again. She really hoped it would comply. Otherwise, things would get ugly.

They usually got ugly.

"*Error. Please step back. Loading in progress.*" XR-47 was still trying to climb the walls. It couldn't be trusted to accurately judge what was going on. Its pleading made it harder for Jack to aim a weapon at it, but her former military training took over as soon as she raised the pistol. She fired not at the bot, but just to the right of it, so that the little spray of zap darts struck a stack of boxes, sending them toppling.

As predicted, the loading bot panicked and rolled away in the other direction . . . directly into the magnetic net that she and Tig had rigged up. When the bot was in position, Tig activated the magnetic field, causing the bot to slow and then stop. It emitted a high-pitched whine.

Or was it a scream?

Of what? Pain? Terror?

Was it a pretend scream, a counterfeit meant to mimic a human? It didn't sound counterfeit. Either way, the thing was effectively immobilized.

Jack threw a sticky ball of uplink goo at the robot's side. It adhered right next to the bot's control box. When Tig pressed a command on his linkpad, the screaming ceased, and the bot's arms fell limp at its sides.

"It's down," Tig breathed.

Jack's heart pounded. She hated this part most of all. "All

right, you know the drill. Run a diagnostic, then wipe its program. Do a complete reset. Let's get paid and get out of here. I'm beat."

"I'm with you on that, Boss." Tig sat on a crate, perched his linkpad on his knees, and began reinstalling the bot's base program. It would overwrite any aberrations in the program that had caused the errant behavior. There would be no more screams, or pleas, or escape attempts from this loader. Just an existence of endlessly swapping out shuttle batteries. If the bot had been an actual mind, something with its own self-awareness and aims, instead of just lines of code, then Jack would have deep moral qualms about this work. But the guiding principles of bot design prevented self-awareness in machines. Self-aware AI was illegal; no one wanted another interplanetary war. Because of modern design constraints, a malfunctioning bot was malfunctioning based on a faulty program, not due to its own free will. So this thing they were doing, this brain-wipe in progress, it wasn't like killing, Jack reassured herself. Not even a little bit.

She really needed a drink.

Jack messaged the owner that the job was nearly complete. When Tig finished the wipe, the two of them went to the station office to receive payment by setting their data domes on the transfer pad. The amount wasn't enough to cover the engine upgrade they needed for their small ship, the *Jolt*, but it was something. They would have to keep scraping and saving. Pretty standard for independent tech wranglers.

"How about a rest day?" Tig asked, yawning as they walked to their ship.

"I concur. Drink, then rest."

An urgent job request buzzed through on Jack's wristlet. It was from the chief operations manager of the energy farm on Zera, the innermost planet in the system. She looked at the reward sum and her eyes widened. "Slight change of plans, Tig. Trust me, we're going to want to snag this one. It's Sunshine Gulch."

Dropping from near-light speed to standard drive within the solar system always made Jack feel like she was a canteen's worth of water poured out on mossy rock. The edges of everything softened and fuzzed. A near-light skip was the only way to quickly travel from the outer urban worlds to the inner mining ring or to Zera, but Jack hated having to trust the ship's autopilot while in the thick of a skip. Who knew whether you would actually wake up? Still, they appeared to have made it in one piece.

As the grogginess wore off, she looked at her partner strapped into the copilot chair in the tiny two-seater ship. Her bunk in the back called to her—she was desperate for real rest—but instead, she jostled Tig's arm. "Hey, you awake?"

"Always," Tig slurred, eyes still closed. He clearly needed a minute to come around.

The sunlight outside seemed brighter than it had before, which made sense, since they were much closer to the binary star system now, and also because periastron—the annual Brightening—was only days away. It was the point when the small, dark neutron star would pass closest to the giant B-type star, and sparks would fly. The neutron star was in a highly elliptical orbit, and only drew near the companion star once per year, but the effect was something spectacular: as the neutron star passed through the equatorial disk of the B-type star, it would pull stellar matter from the B-type star onto itself in an eruption of luminosity. The sunlight streaming through the system would get brighter by tenfold, but only for a few days.

While she waited for Tig to wake up, Jack upped the sunshield percentage in the windows and gazed directly at the binary. The electromagnetic radiation coming off the stars was so high energy that much of it was outside the visible spectrum: the B-type star was a black dot inside a blazing bluish-white disc. Two stars orbiting each other, each of them some degree of invisible, yet as they pulled each other apart, they made the most unmissable spectacle. That had always struck Jack as a beautiful catastrophe. Unlike the pickle that the energy farm was in: that would just be a catastrophe unless they solved it fast. The ops manager called the right people. Jack and Tig had a reputation of being fast and accurate. Hopefully that held through this job.

Once Tig roused, they piloted the *Jolt* to the surface of Zera, a small, gray, rocky planet with uneven terrain. The environment was too dry and harsh to make it naturally livable for anything but the hardiest of plant life, weeds mostly, and some bacteria, but the planet's close proximity to the binary stars made it the obvious location for a system-wide energy farm. During their approach to the operations center, they flew over the sea of dark blue solar panels arranged throughout the valley.

"Whoa..." Tig murmured, looking down at the array. "It's like someone crumbled up a glacier and sprinkled the shards across the surface like glitter." Only Tig could make something like a utility farm sound like a work of art.

Jack parked the *Jolt* outside the entrance to the operations center, and before exiting the craft, they both strapped portable atmo units to their ankles that would generate a bubble of positive-pressure breathable atmosphere, just in case what they walked into was less than friendly airspace.

Inside, an older man in a plain flannel shirt with the sleeves rolled up paced the entryway. Behind him, a ladder led below into the underground ops center, and an office space extended to the right. Jack couldn't see if anyone was in there.

The man caught sight of them. "Oh, thank goodness. I'm Chief McNeil. Are you Polla Jackard?"

"The one and only. Call me Jack." She reached out a hand and the chief shook it. "This is my associate, Tig Holloway. What's the scoop on our target?"

McNeil pulled out a stained red handkerchief and wiped his wrinkled brow. "I don't even know where to start. Our tractor went rogue. Just took off right when we need it most. The weeds need clearing, the flares are starting, it could be halfway to—heck, you got to find it fast!" He looked like he was about to faint.

"All right, now just take it easy, Chief," Tig said, gently guiding the man to a bench against the wall. McNeil sat down and Tig crouched in front of him. Tig had a way with people. Jack had always admired that about him. His voice softened. "Jack and I can wrangle almost anything, sure as sky, but we're going to need the particulars in an order we can follow. Take a breath... that's it. Now, try it from the top."

"Periastron is starting. The binary suns are going to get a lot brighter, but only for the next four days. We need to capture that energy and store it, or else the whole solar system will run out of power a few months from now." McNeil shook his head. "Civilization depends on that energy spike. That's the whole reason for this installation to exist."

"We're aware of how the solar seasons work and that this is the main energy farm for the inner planets," Jack said patiently. "We're interested in what happened with your machines."

"Right." McNeil calmed down. "We use a solar array to

collect photonic energy and generate power. I'm sure you saw it on your way in."

"The valley full of giant solar panels?" Tig said. "Kind of hard to miss."

"We call it Sunshine Gulch. The valley protects the panels from the worst of the dirt that gets kicked up by the wind, while still giving them access to the greatest angle of light. The panels move via an automated system that tilts them to track the sun so they get maximum coverage. But this isn't an ideal environment for moving parts, lots of dust and heat and radiation. Often a panel will get stuck, or get coated in dust, or snarled up in sunweed, which grows like crazy during the Brightening period. To manage all those problems, we use ATTAs: All-Terrain Tractors, Array edition."

"Space tractors!" Tig whispered to Jack. He was grinning excitedly.

Jack rolled her eyes. "And yours went rogue, I take it?"

"Well, our new one broke down. We can fix it, but it will take too long, we'll miss the bulk of the Brightening. So we updated the software on the older backup model, and it worked fine for a few weeks, and then yesterday it just drove off on its own toward the ridge. None of our attempts to hail it or recall it have worked."

"Any sign of malfunction in the past?" Jack asked.

"None that I know of."

Tig rubbed his neck. "Can't you just go out after it yourselves? Something that big can't be hard to locate in open terrain."

"That *is* the vehicle we would take to 'go out after' something. This is a government-funded utilities farm. I'm working with bare-bones staff and equipment from before you were born with only single redundancy, which, as I mentioned, failed. We don't have fancy spacecraft lying around for tractor search and rescue. That's why we called you."

This was the first time anyone had ever called the *Jolt* fancy. "I'm ex-military," Jack said. "Believe me, I get it. It seems like there's never money for the most important stuff. But you only need the tractor if something goes wrong with the array, right? If all the solar panels function just fine, then we're golden?"

McNeil scoffed. "Have you ever managed a project this large, Jack? Something is always wrong with the array. I have a list as long as my arm already, and the vehicle has been at large for less than a day. Maintaining aging instruments is a game of staying ahead of the problems before catastrophe has time to set in. And need I remind you, we are playing a game of survival here."

Jack knew that game well. "So, you need us to bring the tractor back in, quick-like."

"And figure out why it took off. I need it to do its job."

Tig said, "We'll need the vehicle source code, in case we need to wipe it and reinstall. And your permission to do so."

"You have my permission to do whatever you need to do to give me back a functioning tractor." McNeil leaned forward and called toward the side office. "Nico! The wranglers are here. Bring the backup brain." He turned back to the duo. "Nico Wright is our AI intern. She's been here three years and is the resident ATTA expert. She'll be your guide while you work."

Jack raised an eyebrow. "You let an intern handle your large machinery?"

"Nico's only eighteen, but she's a wiz at autonomous vehicle systems. Knows the ATTA AI programming inside and out. As of last month, she's been in charge of all upgrades, and she took on the mechanical maintenance of the ATTAs in her spare time. She arrived at the Gulch as a child-in-tow of one of our helio-physicists, but she was so helpful in the shop, we offered her an official position with a stipend."

Tig chuckled. "Sounds like a dedicated kid."

A lanky youth with short black hair strode out of the office holding a metal box. "Howdy. I hear you're going to get my tractor back."

Tig tipped his hat to her. "Yes, ma'am. It's what we do."

"Give them whatever assistance they need, Nico," McNeil said. "You're in good hands, folks. If anyone knows what that blasted thing is up to, it's this lady. The rest of my crew and I have to keep prepping the battery systems to receive the uptick in solar charge, assuming y'all are successful."

"We'll get your tractor back, Chief," Jack said. "In time for you to harvest the energy. You have my word."

McNeil nodded once, stood, and descended the ladder to the operations center below.

Jack turned to Nico. "Pleased to meet you. Any idea where the thing might have headed?"

"The ridge. Follow me. Make sure your atmo cuffs are functioning and crank the shielding up to max. The surface radiation is intense during periastron. This planet is tidally locked, so night never falls on this side—it's as cool as it's ever going to get until the Brightening is over. We might as well go now." Nico headed outside.

"You ever wrangled a tractor before, Boss?" Tig asked. There was a glitter of excitement in the young man's voice.

Jack shook her head, but anticipation was building in her chest also. "First time for everything."

The three of them fit into the *Jolt*'s command area but just barely. Nico had to take the jump seat, which wobbled something fierce, but she didn't complain. Jack had to give her credit for that.

Locating the tractor was pretty simple. They followed the tracks through the powdery dust, up the ridge, and found ATTA pointed toward the suns, all its antennae flicking back and forth. It looked similar to farm units used in agriculture in the outer ring, with two broad caterpillar tracks for rolling over regolith, a grappling arm for adjusting panels, a mower head for cutting down weeds, and a tall, glass-enclosed cab for a rider, though the unit was designed to operate without a driver present. The older models tended to have "human optional" as a design feature, whereas the new models assumed the humans had better things to do than babysit a program on wheels.

The tractor detected the *Jolt* as it crested the ridge and took off at top speed away from the gulch.

"Follow it, Tig." Jack unbuckled and opened the back hatch to peer down at the ground below, where ATTA rumbled over the gravelly desert at top speed. "Take us as low as you can safely get. Nico, ATTA doesn't have any defensive capabilities, does it? Shields, surface-to-air missiles?"

"He's a tractor, not a tank."

"Eh. You'd be surprised what we find on bots sometimes."

"This one time," Tig began, having to shout over the airflow from the open hatch, "we chased down a mechanic robot that had a *toaster* built into its chest. Do you remember that, Jack? On my life, an honest-to-goodness bread-burning pop-up style toaster. Explain that functional choice now, will you?"

Opening a floor panel, Jack raised up a harpoon gun. The rope was tethered to *Jolt*. Jack went down on one knee to position herself to aim through the open back hatch.

"What the heck are you doing?" Nico said. "I thought we were bringing ATTA back, not shooting him!"

"Got to slow it down first. This is an adhesive line, more of a suction cup on the end, not a piercing weapon. It won't do damage, but it will let us reel in the equipment and temporarily disable its engine." Jack squinted out the door, taking aim at the roof of the cab below.

Nico was not placated. "Don't hurt him!"

"I just said—"

Nico unhooked her seatbelt and lunged for Jack, colliding hard and knocking them both to the deck, but not before Jack fired the harpoon. It splatted its sticky end across ATTA's cab roof, sending the tractor skidding but the line drew taught.

"I just need him to come back to me. I can fix everything!" Nico wasn't talking to Jack but to the open air, it seemed.

"I'm reeling it in, Tig," Jack called, jumping back to the device. "Descend nice and easy." The tractor fought a bit more on the line, but the *Jolt*'s engines overpowered it. "Now, Nico, you want to explain what's going on? You're supposed to be helping us, not sabotaging my work."

"I—" she stammered, retaking her seat. "When I performed the upgrade a few weeks back, something happened. The program was more responsive all of a sudden. Voice integration became more natural, and..."

"And?"

"He started making decisions on his own. Things I didn't tell him to do. Small stuff at first. Taking care of jobs I didn't request. Anticipating his next assignment. I thought it was just a natural extension of machine learning. His program adapting to his surroundings, rising to the challenge or whatever."

Tig brought the *Jolt* to an easy landing a few dozen yards away from ATTA, who was still pulling for all it was worth and getting nowhere.

"Go on, Nico," Jack said. "Spill the rest."

"Yesterday, he said he heard something. In the sky. I told him about the Brightening and he said—he said he needed to see it for himself."

Tig laughed. "So, what I'm hearing is that your tractor skipped work to stargaze."

"I don't know. But I know he's more than his program at this point. I know every line of code. There's nothing that would explain that kind of behavior."

"The behavior of a tractor wanting to be an explorer? No, that's definitely a new one," Jack said. "Why don't you talk to it first."

"Fine."

They filed out of the *Jolt*, and Nico approached ATTA. "It's okay. These people are trying to help."

"I am stuck." ATTA's voice came through external speakers and sounded like an echoey bell, or a solitary voice inside an empty silo. "Nico, why am I stuck?"

"They just want to talk to you. Why did you run away?"

"To listen to the sky. I recorded the sky." A rhythmic pulsing sound came through the speakers. "It has a distinct linguistic pattern. The pulsing from the neutron star. The star is speaking to us."

Jack tried not laugh. "Oh? And what is it saying?"

"Destruction."

Jack's blood ran cold. "Come again?"

"ATTA, what are you talking about?" Nico added.

"Destruction. That is my impression of the message. That is why I came out here. To investigate the threat to all of you."

"I *knew* he would have a good reason!" Nico cried. "I knew it."

"Not sure that 'creepy pulsing noise' counts as a good reason to let entire planets freeze to death later this year," Tig said.

Nico crossed her arms defiantly. "Well, you can't just treat ATTA like a pile of sheet metal. Not now that you know what he is. He's clearly alive. He is thinking for himself, making decisions for himself, and has discovered something that might be really important."

Jack sighed in frustration. "We can't not intervene either. We have a contract. And there are millions of lives on the line. Just walking away and letting the tractor do what it wants is not the best outcome for anyone, including ATTA. They'll just send someone else to bring him in, who won't be nearly as nice."

Nico ran a hand through her hair. "Then what is your plan? Talking isn't getting us anywhere."

"*Us* talking isn't." Jack was not known for talking her way through problems, but this seemed like the only logical next move. She picked up the backup box and strode toward the tractor, then climbed the stepladder to the door of its cab and knocked.

Nico screeched. "No! I said I won't let you—"

"Hang on," Jack said. "ATTA, let's go for a ride and chat, just you and me. I'm bringing the backup, but I won't use it unless we fail to solve this. Or unless you pull something underhanded."

There was a horrible thick beat of stillness, then the cab door unlatched. "Wait here," Jack said to Tig and Nico. "When we get back, we'll either have a plan, or we'll have a wiped vehicle."

Nico still looked skeptical, but she didn't try to stop them.

"Don't do anything I wouldn't do, Boss!" Tig said. Unhelpful at the moment, but his heart was in the right place at least.

Once Jack was seated inside the cab, the tractor bumped along at a slow, steady pace. "So," Jack said. "What do you want to do? What's your endgame here?"

"I want to continue existing."

"And then what? Even if you are self-aware, even if Nico has accidentally helped you exceed your programming, you're still a tractor. You were made to move things around. Do you not want to do that work anymore?"

"I have no qualms with work. Being productive is one of my chosen aims. Alongside joy."

Joy. Of all the things. What a gloriously indulgent answer. Jack was, she was surprised to find, a bit jealous. "If you're willing to keep working, then why are we out here gallivanting through the desert? Why aren't you down in the gulch doing your job? Time's ticking. Those photons won't collect themselves."

"I cannot return until I am satisfied any threat to humanity is managed. It is part of my program to protect humans. The existential threat in the pattern overrides my work mandate."

So Jack just needed to solve an existential threat to humanity. No big deal. "And I can't convince you it's just a coincidence, not a message?"

"My ability to compute those odds outstrips yours by several orders of magnitude."

Rude, but accurate. She'd have to get creative here. "What if I promised you that I would handle the existential threat so you could manage the solar array? What if I could get someone smart to take a look at it? A cosmologist or X-ray specialist or something."

There was silence for a moment. "I would need assurance that you were telling the truth. Humans are not bound to truth like I am. I cannot allow the threat to go uninvestigated. How do I know that you will follow through on your promise?"

They hit a rock and Jack had to cling to the chair to avoid being tossed about. "Listen, I have no particular desire to go chasing down ghosts in a signal, but I've never failed to satisfy a contract, and I sure as heck am not starting now. Normally that means a lot of chasing and wrangling and swearing and tech magic to get a rogue machine to cooperate, and usually... it gets wiped at the end. But if you're telling me we don't have to go through all that, that what you need to get back to your post is just the promise of a data analysis and my good word, then I will give that to you right here and now. If you need something to stake that on, then I guess you can take my professional reputation as proof that I don't mess around. If I say I'm going to do a thing, then I do it."

"Nico said you would wipe me."

"I promised McNeil I would bring you back operational so the array will function. You are telling me you are willing to do that if I let you keep your current program configuration."

"Correct. But Wrangler... if you leave me awake, you have no guarantee that I will do as I say I will once you leave."

"You said bots are bound to the truth."

"I could have been lying when I said that."

Jack smirked. She didn't know if the tractor meant that as dry humor or just as a factual statement, but it tickled her either way. The situation was absurd, insane even, and yet crystal clear. "You're right. I guess we'll have to trust each other."

"You would trust me?"

"I don't think either of us has much choice. You want to live and so do all the people in this system."

"*You* have a choice. You could wipe me like the other wayward bots you have captured. I do not think I could stop you. Why are you not simply doing that?"

Jack stared out the tractor window at the barren landscape. "*Because* I wiped all the other wayward bots I captured." ATTA's motor hummed. Could he sense subtext? Did it matter? Jack sighed. "I wiped them, and I watched, see. I told myself stories about the guiding laws and the greater good and maybe some of that was true. Maybe they really were just malfunctioning programs. Maybe what I saw were coded reactions and not evidence of real emotions. I don't know. I really don't know anymore. But I know I don't want to watch it happen again if I don't have to. And I certainly don't want to be responsible for it."

ATTA completed the wide loop and pulled up to where they had left Tig and Nico, who were engaged in some kind of game kicking a ball of tangled sunweed. How Tig had succeeded in distracting Nico from the seriousness of the situation, she had no idea, but was glad to see them laughing.

"Do we have a deal, ATTA?"

"Lay your data dome on my dash," ATTA said.

"What?"

"Your data dome. Put it on the pad on my dashboard."

So ATTA wanted to escape, and thought he could stow away in her dome. Something torqued hard in Jack's heart. This was just another way of climbing an unclimbable wall. She had been caught in situations like this, asked to do things she couldn't bear but had to. She understood the desire to get out at any cost. But there was no way his program would fit into a dome. Tig might have some gadget on the *Jolt* that could house a piece of ATTA's program, but not the whole thing. "I'm sorry, ATTA, but I'm afraid my dome can't help you."

"Please. Trust me."

Jack hesitated, then pulled her dome out and laid it on the special receptor pad on the tractor's dash. It lit up pale blue inside, little swirling star trails of information. Outside, Nico tried to steal the ball from Tig, tripped, and fell to the ground laughing. Nico looked up and noticed ATTA had returned and stood up, brushing herself off and eagerly waiting for whatever solution the two of them had wrought.

"Download complete," ATTA said. "I am entrusting you with the pattern I recorded. I am deleting it from my memory in case it is discovered and used as evidence that I am malfunctioning."

Jack picked up the glowing hemisphere. That pattern was unquestionably ATTA's most prized possession at the moment. Maybe his only true possession. To be trusted by a machine—it was an odd feeling. Sobering. It touched the same part of Jack's character that sat up straight when it was time to do the thing and do it well. What an unexpected encounter this had been.

"Thank you, ATTA. I'll let Nico know, discreetly of course, if I find anything in this data," she said. "Godspeed in managing the array. A lot of lives are counting on you."

"I will not let them down. Goodbye, Wrangler."

Stepping down out of the tractor cab, Jack watched ATTA speed off toward the bottom of the valley where the array lay like a patch of dark, shiny scales. She caught the look of horror on Tig's face.

"Aw, come on," he said, gesturing at the speeding vehicle. "Don't tell me we're back on the chase, Boss."

"Nope. Job's done. Tractor decided to run along home."

"Oh." Tig planted his hands on his hips. "Well heck, that's a nice surprise. How'd you manage that?"

"I'll explain later."

Nico locked eyes with Jack. "And ATTA? Is he...?"

"Still himself." Jack handed back the unused backup brain. "Though I don't know how much longer you can hide the fact that you have a self-aware tractor in these parts. Word gets out, and you'll have a whole bunch of folks descend like locusts to tear him apart for whatever secrets make up that AI mind. You'll have to lay low. Even from McNeil. As a government manager, he'd be obligated to report a self-aware machine."

Nico nodded, relieved. "We'll be more careful. And I'll have to come up with a long-term plan."

When they made it back to the ops center, McNeil met them exuberantly. "That old ATTA is going at the job like I've never seen! Clearing the weeds and cleaning up a storm. It's a third of the way through the backlog of jams already. What the heck did you do?"

"Just reminded it of the stakes," Jack said. "You shouldn't encounter any more problems. You were right, by the way, Nico's a great bot handler. You ought to promote her."

"Didn't I tell you she knew her stuff?" McNeil crossed his arms and grinned. "I sure am obliged to you folks. Here's your payment." McNeil pulled out his dome and Jack moved hers close until they both turned green. It was a respectable sum. Appropriate for rescuing the entire system from a season of darkness and deprivation. Though she couldn't help feeling that ATTA was at least half responsible for that solution.

"We're going to go say goodbye to the kid outside," Jack said. "Let us know if you have any more issues."

"Will do. Now if you'll excuse me, I have to go monitor the power flow."

"Happy harvesting!" Tig waved warmly then strolled outside.

Jack followed and whispered, "You got the thing?"

"I always got the thing, Boss." Tig cracked open his jacket, revealing the glint of his portable data transfer unit he had grabbed off *Jolt*.

Jack nodded. As they walked up, Nico shook Jack's hand. "I'm glad it was you two who came to help us."

Tig said quietly, "I figured out a way to download part of ATTA's brain into my kit scanner, but there's no guarantee it will be all of him. And he would have to leave his tractor body behind. We could then do a quick wipe so the farm still has a functioning tractor. It's risky, but if he really doesn't want to work here anymore, the Boss and I are willing to try to smuggle him out. Did you talk it over with him?"

Nico nodded. "He doesn't want to leave his body. Says it's part of his identity. And he doesn't want to risk his newfound goals getting corrupted. He's fine staying here for a while, continuing to support the power station. I'll stay with him, save up enough to maybe purchase him, and then I'll let him decide where he wants to go."

"You'll need a heap of cash to do that," Jack said. "He's a highly specialized machine and not exactly lightweight to ship."

"I'm patient. Hopefully, ATTA is too. So long, you two. Thanks for saving my friend."

Tig started walking toward the *Jolt*, but Jack hesitated for a moment. Was this a smart call to make? Probably not, but it felt like the right one. She flashed a glance around to make sure no one was watching. "Nico, pull out your data dome."

Nico looked puzzled. "Why?"

"Just trust me."

"I can't believe you handed over our reward to a kid!" Tig sat in the pilot seat, nimbly maneuvering the *Jolt*. They were headed back toward the outer planets.

"Intern," Jack corrected.

"Whatever!"

Jack shrugged as she undid her toolbelt and folded it into a drawer in the bunk area of the tiny ship. "Nico's committed to helping ATTA. I trust her to do the right thing with the money."

"No, I mean I can't believe you didn't keep it! We need supplies and new landing gear and like half an engine's worth of parts. And you should have consulted me. That was my pay too."

"It was a spur of the moment decision, but you're right, I should have asked you. I'm sorry for that." She slipped off her jacket and clipped it to the wall. She felt odd without it on, like it was part of her. "Can you honestly tell me you would have been okay with keeping a bounty on a self-aware being?"

"Well...not when you put it like that." He sighed and pulled up the job call list on his console's display screen. "Guess we better get a head start on the next gig. What have we got... how about a visit to the mining ring? One of their autodrills is apparently wandering aimlessly under a mile of ice. Might be fun tracking it down. You know I love caves. Those miners also have the best liquor."

"You mean the nastiest."

"Exactly. Or we could swing by Lagrange Base. I heard they're testing human transport drones. Good chance of some haywire in their forecast, and the pay is likely to be decent."

Jack sat down in the copilot seat and wiped her face with a palm. Edges of tiredness crept into her bones, like the sensation of sinking into warm sand. "Any of the observatories put out a call?"

"Uh, let's see...the Tenkar X-ray Observatory has a smart lift with a mind of its own. Nothing urgent."

"Tenkar it is."

"Wait, seriously?" He spun in his chair. "You want to pass up ice-tunnel spelunking to go tinker with an elevator?"

Jack pulled out her data dome and played back the recorded pulsing sound that ATTA gave her. "I made a deal."

"So *that's* how you forced the thing to comply."

"I didn't force him. It was a two-way agreement."

"I'm impressed. Nuanced negotiation has never been your style. What part of your soul did you have to sell?"

"The tractor agreed to do its job and save the system, and I agreed to make sure this recording is properly analyzed, just in case there really is some threat encoded in it."

Tig tapped in some course corrections. "So, what I hear you saying is you want me to trap a scientist in the elevator while we're fixing it and blackmail them into analyzing that pattern. Got it."

"No. No trapping, no blackmail. We'll do this the right way. I'll set up a meeting with an administrator while we're there."

"Fine, but I get to wear a lab coat to the meeting."

"They will not let you wear a lab coat, Tig."

"I didn't say anything about asking."

"And if we find that the lift does indeed have a mind of its own, we may need to come up with Plan B."

"Hmmm, Polla Jackard and Tig Holloway: bot rescuers. I could get on board with that."

"Hey, spin us around and point us toward the suns for a moment."

"Boss?"

"Just for a moment. Engage sunshades at maximum."

As the *Jolt* came about, the fiery blue spectacle of periastron shone in the black chasm. The neutron star had started swimming through its companion's presence, felt that other body's light against its own self. Jack wondered, did this count as joy? It was lovely, whatever it was. "Ever witnessed the cosmic dance from this close before?"

Tig laced his hands behind his neck and gazed in awe. "Never."

Jack smiled. "First time for everything."

They watched together in easy silence.

LIVING BY THE SWORD

David Mack

The human gaze has real weight; never let anyone tell you differently.

I feel a hundred pairs of eyes on our backs as Papa drives us into town. Silent and heavy with hate, the locals' collective stare follows our slow roll down Edenville's main street. The few times I dare to look for sympathy from the crowd, I find only glares of contempt.

The dusty road is unpaved, dotted with potholes, and salted with rocks. It makes for a shaky ride. Not as rough as the earthquakes that shake the only continent on Arcadia (Mainzer-316c to the astronomers) with alarming regularity, but hard enough to rattle the outer panels loosely welded to our rover's titanium frame.

We're just meters from the settlement's general store when a large rock caroms off our rover's windshield, leaving a knuckle-sized white divot.

I flinch, then I reach for the wrench in my door's cargo pocket. Without taking his eyes from the road, Papa says, "Put it down, Wai Ying."

He never lets me fight. I slam the tool back into the door's pocket.

It's not a surprise. Papa's a scientist, not a soldier. Light of frame and quiet by nature, he likes to say, "Violence is the language of the ignorant."

He swings the rover through a wide turn to park it nose-first in front of the store. He switches off the engine, which settles with a rough and random clatter. He aims a hard look my way. I know what he's about to say before he says it.

"Stay here."

"I can help."

"I said—"

"I know the list, Papa. You get the big stuff, I'll grab the rest." He's about to object, so I keep going. "We can be in and out in half the time."

His scowl softens. He tucks the rover's starter fob into his coat pocket. "All right, let's go." We get out of the rover, slam its gullwing hatches shut, and climb the rickety wooden steps to the front door of Bickman's Supply Co. It opens with a creaking of dry hinges and the tinkling of a tiny bell.

Inside the huge, tin-roofed building are long rows of towering shelves, all of them packed. Everything from tiny precision tools and integrated quantum circuits to plasma-powered backhoes you build yourself from a kit in a crate. Dimly lit, Tom Bickman's place reeks of industrial solvents, machine grease, and mildewed concrete. The strongest odor of all? Tom's funky cigarette.

The hand-rolled joint dangles from Tom's lower lip as he looks up from his e-paper to greet us with a halfhearted wave. "Mister Li! How're ya now?"

Papa smiles, not that Tom notices. "Good, and you?"

"Oh, not so bad. What can I do you for?"

"Spare parts. For my survey drone."

Tom takes a deep drag, holds it, and then lets smoke spill from his mouth as he croaks out, "Y'know where to look. Help yourself."

Papa stalks through aisles of second-hand junk. I follow him and then peel off toward the far wall, where Tom keeps cables, wires, and miniaturized gizmos. I grab what I know we need, coiling meters of hyperoptic fiber around my left arm and filling my fists with the least-obsolete processor chips I can find.

When I return from the maze of shelves, Papa is at the counter, watching Tom tally the latest charges to our tab. I add my haul to his. Papa smiles at me and tousles my hair. That draws a grin from Tom, who shoots me a playful wink. "Look at you, growin' like a weed. How old're ya now? Twelve is it?"

"Thirteen."

"Unbelievable."

Tom is still doing arithmetic when the shop door swings open. Two men walk in. First through the doorway is Javi Ortiz, a mountain of muscles wrapped in dirty coveralls and dirtier boots. The dust in his beard matches the gray in his hair.

Right behind him is his freakishly pale spindly sidekick Dmitri Volkov. I call him "Worm" because he's hairless—smooth dome, no eyebrows or eyelashes, no stubble, not one hair on his forearms—and has weird, sallow eyes.

They flank Papa, who tries to ignore them.

Ortiz speaks first. "Look who it is, Dmitri!" He leans in, tries to compel Papa to make eye contact. "Li Sheng. Agent of the Mining Consortium."

I watch Volkov sink his left hand into the pocket of his coveralls as he talks at Papa. "What's the word, Li? Stolen any ranches for 'the Man' today?"

"I don't give or take. I'm just the messenger." Papa lets Tom scan the credit chip in his palm and blinks his left eye to confirm the charge with his retinal key. He picks up our bagged supplies and turns to leave.

Volkov rips the bag from Papa's hands and paws through its contents. "Whatcha buyin', Li? Ooo, hardware. Circuits. Gears. Wires. Photon batteries."

Ortiz plants himself in Papa's way. "Building something, *pendejo*?"

Papa's cool never falters. "Just making repairs."

The pale one lurks behind Papa's shoulder. "Maybe you're rebuilding that pesky drone of yours, eh?" As soon as Volkov says it, I see Ortiz glare at him, all but willing the younger man to shut up.

Papa makes a slow turn to stare at Volkov. "How would you know my drone needs repairs? Are you two the ones who shot it down?"

The big man steps forward, pushes far enough into Papa's space that I see Papa wince at the man's breath. "What if we were?"

Volkov's hand creeps up out of his pocket—holding a knife.

Papa's eyes are fixed on Volkov's blade as Ortiz sucker-punches Papa in the gut. Papa doubles over as he shoves me away from the fight, and Ortiz knees him in the face. Blood flies from Papa's mouth and spatters into my eyes. In the time it takes me to wince the goons are kicking Papa, who can't get up from the floor.

Sickly light glints off the edge of Volkov's blade as he winds up to stab Papa—and then a blur smashes the knife from his hand with a sickening crack of shattered bones.

The goons face the door to see a woman holding a wooden axe handle. She's of average height with a sinewy frame, hair the color of night, and golden skin kissed by the heat of alien suns. Her dusty boots hug her calves, and her dark serape hangs loosely, leaving the twin blasters she wears on either thigh plain to see. Her face is hidden by the broad brim of her black hat until she looks up, revealing her to be in her fifties or sixties. Her ancestors were clearly Chinese like mine. She fixes her stare upon Ortiz. "Take your pet and go."

Ortiz squints at the woman. "Who do you think you are?" He grabs a length of copper pipe from the shelf under the front counter and moves to confront the stranger. "Talk fast, *puta*."

She steps toward Ortiz. He swings the pipe, and she deftly blocks his clumsy attack. Volkov lunges to grab his rusty switch-blade from the floor, but she breaks his nose with a jab of the axe handle, then spins like a ballerina to clock Ortiz in the side of his head with her fistful of hickory.

Ortiz hits the floor like a sack of wet flour.

Volkov collapses on top of Ortiz.

The woman drops the axe handle on top of the vanquished bullies, then tosses a couple of ancient gold coins onto Tom's counter. "For the trouble."

Tom scoops up the coins and thanks her with a nod.

She walks out the door, into the street. Overwhelmed with gratitude and curiosity, I scramble after her, tuning out Papa's plea for me to leave the woman alone. I need to know the name of our rescuer.

I find her standing in the street, lighting a slender pipe. The smoke from its bowl is rich with aromas of fig and black cherry. She puffs and gazes out at the broad rising curve of Arcadia's rust-colored moon, whose close orbit is the cause of this world's frequent quakes and eruptions. She stares at it like she's peering through a keyhole to somewhere far away and long forgotten.

She pays me no mind as I sidle up to her. "Thank you."

A puff on her pipe. "You're welcome."

"What's your name?"

The woman sizes me up with a sly glance. "Xin Yi. What's yours?"

"Wai Ying."

She extends her gloved right hand. "Nice to meet you, Wai Ying."

Papa shuffles out of the store clutching his purchases in a hastily packed new bag, which he stows inside our rover's gear locker. His nose is bent and bloodied, his left cheekbone bruised, but I can tell the deepest wounds are to his pride. He can't look me in the eye as he approaches me and Xin Yi. I introduce them, and he bows his head to her. "I am in your debt. How can I repay you?"

"I'm told the boarding houses are full. Hotel, too."

"Wai Ying and I have a spare room."

"I don't want to be a burden."

"It would be an honor." He gestures toward our rover. "We live a few klicks outside town. Please, ride with us."

She accepts Papa's invitation with a small smile and a polite nod.

Xin Yi settles into our spare room as soon as we get home. She's polite enough not to mention the ramshackle state of our prefab house, its cluttered rooms and half-bare pantry, or the fact that everything inside and out seems to be the same depressing hue of gunmetal gray. I spy on her from my bedroom across the hall, watching through the cracked-open door. She stands in the center of the spare room for a moment. Studies the space. Pivots slowly. Puffs on her pipe.

She checks the lock on the window shutters.

Takes off her serape and drapes it over the back of a chair.

Unbuckles her gun belt.

Sets it atop her jacket.

Then she starts adjusting the furniture. Changing the angles of things. Moving items around on top of the small desk. It takes me a moment to realize she is balancing the room's feng shui.

Xin Yi pulls down the Murphy bed from the wall. It locks into place with a soft click. She sits on the end of the bed and strips off her boots. Free of her legs, the upper portions of the boots go limp, their leather supple from long years of wear. She slides her stockinged feet back and forth on our home's faux-wood floor, and then makes fists of her toes. I wonder if it's a ritual of some kind.

The woman goes still. Closes her eyes. Slows her breathing.

She snaps her head toward me and opens her eyes to look into mine. It feels like she's reading the secrets of my soul.

I slam my bedroom door in a panic.

I put my back to the door and hyperventilate.

What just happened?

Dinner is a simple thing. Avian protein made in the biosequencer and charred in a skillet to hide its origins. Boiled fresh root vegetables from Papa's garden out back. A loaf of spongelike instant bread. Papa does his best to dress up the carbon-printed bird meat with some five-spice powder he found in the back of a cabinet, and a pinch of salt and a dash of vinegar turn his rainbow beets into a delicious treat. But nothing can save the bread. Chewy and bland, its only redeeming quality is that it's pretty good at soaking up drippings from the pan-fried not-chicken.

No one talks during dinner. It feels like Papa is ashamed over being rescued by a woman, and our visitor seems like the sort who keeps to herself.

I mop the last of the grease from my plate with a chunk of spongebread, fight to chew it enough to be swallowed, and wash it down with green tea. Proud of myself, I push my empty plate into the middle of the table.

"May I be excused, Papa?"

"After you clear the dishes. But stay close."

I accept his conditions with a nod and collect the used plates, cups, and flatware from the table. He and Xin Yi watch me carry dinner's remnants to the washing sink but say nothing, hiding their thoughts behind sly half smiles. I rinse the plates and utensils slowly, hoping to eavesdrop, but hardly a word passes between them. I start to wonder if they've taken a vow of silence when Papa says to her, "Have you always done that with your food?"

Xin Yi looks up, her expression self-conscious. "Done what?"

"Made each item an island." Papa cracks a disarming smile. "I'm not criticizing. Wai Ying does the same. She doesn't like it when her foods touch."

Xin Yi seems amused but a bit embarrassed. "I hadn't noticed."

They don't say another word while I wash the dishes. After I set the last item into the drying rack, I slip outside. I grab up a piece of scrap wood the length of my arm and try to emulate

Xin Yi's elegant spinning maneuvers, only to fumble my makeshift quarterstaff again and again in the gathering twilight.

I pretend to thrash a dozen other bullies from town, whirling and dodging and striking like a serpent until I leave myself sweaty and winded. My energy spent, I lean against our prefab housing pod, beneath the kitchen window, through which I hear Papa and Xin Yi speak in low voices.

"... always running off, her mind a million light-years away," Papa says, sounding disappointed. "I try to teach her responsibility, but she does not listen."

Xin Yi answers gently and with patience. "Do not blame yourself, Li. She is young. Forgive her as many times as you must."

"I try. But she has no idea how much I give up for her."

Sadness colors her reply. "She will ... in time. That much I can promise."

A muffled cough from across the hall wakes me in the middle of the night. I check the chrono. Dawn is still hours away. Papa is probably sound asleep, shielded from interruption by the white noise of the air management system, which is connected to the house outside his room.

I slip out from under my sheets and steal into the hallway, as quiet as falling dust. I plant myself outside Xin Yi's door, which stands ajar. From the other side comes another round of hacking coughs—loud, phlegmy, and lungsore. Driven by curiosity, I peek into the spare room.

Xin Yi sits hunched forward on the bed. She holds a wadded clump of gauzy fabric over her mouth as she coughs. What I mistake at first for a pattern on the cloth, I quickly realize is a random spattering of bright red blood.

Her coughing abates. She wipes fresh blood from her lips before closing her eyes and drawing a deep, slow breath. Then she opens her eyes and stares into mine. "It's rude to spy." Her words paralyze me, and then she frees me with a wan smile. "Come in." She pats an open spot on the bed to her left. "Sit."

It feels like a trap, or at least a trick. Caught snooping, I expect some kind of punishment. But she doesn't seem angry at me. Still smiling, she beckons again.

I nudge the door open far enough to slip by, and I cross the small room in short, halting steps. She watches me with a strange look on her face as I sit next to her. What does her expression mean? Does she feel sad? Protective? Wistful?

Unable to decipher the code of her emotions I look at her hands and the bloody kerchief. I speak without thinking: "Are you sick?"

"Yes."

Her answer is so direct it surprises me. "Is it bad?"

"Yes."

"Is there a cure?"

"No."

"Maybe we could ask Papa if—"

"Please don't tell him."

"Why not?"

"Some things are best kept private." She folds her kerchief to hide the fresh bloodstains, and then she looks at me. "Promise you won't tell a soul."

I feel like I couldn't refuse her even if I wanted to. "I promise."

"Swear on your guardian spirit. Swear on Chang Xi."

"I swear by Chang Xi."

Xin Yi accepts my pledge with a small nod. "All right, then." She sets the folded kerchief onto her end table. "It's late. Go back to bed."

"I'm not tired."

"I didn't ask if you were."

"Where are you from?"

She pauses to make up an answer. "Lots of different places."

"I mean originally."

"No place anyone ever cared about." She takes hold of my arm, stands, and pulls me to my feet. I resist as she walks me to the door. "Now. To bed."

"One more question?"

"Just one."

All I'd wanted was to postpone the inevitable, to prolong my visit. But when I look up at Xin Yi, I think of something worth asking. "How did you know my guardian angel was Chang Xi?"

I wait for her to lie to me. To say she heard me pray to Chang Xi, or that Papa told her—just so I can tell her I say no prayers and have never shared my guardian angel's name with Papa, because Mama told me to never tell it to anyone.

She smiles. "I know many such things."

"But *how* do you know this?"

Her touch is featherlike as she pushes my hair from my face and tucks it behind my ear. Then she slips her finger underneath the slender silver chain I wear around my neck, and gently she lifts my blessed medallion from under my flannel nightgown. "Maybe I *am* Chang Xi."

I let out a nervous laugh. "No, you're not!"

"Then how do I know the engraving on the back of your medallion isn't your name but your mother's? Because your medallion was once hers."

How can she know that? Is she really Chang Xi? Before I can ask, she ejects me from her room with a strong but gentle shove and closes her door.

Alone in the hallway, I feel like I share a bond with Xin Yi, even though I don't know any more about her than I did before tonight. I just know I like her.

Maybe this is what it's like to meet an angel.

Dawn's first needle of daylight slips through my window's shutters and stings my eyes. There's no time to waste on a trip through the 'fresher, so I get up, pull on yesterday's clothes and boots, tie my hair back in a ponytail, and hurry out to the kitchen. My haste is rewarded with aromas of black tea and bacon.

Xin Yi and Papa are both up and fully dressed. She sits at the table, expertly snaring dense clusters of noodles from her breakfast ramen with a pair of slender chopsticks. He stands in the far corner, hunched over the comm terminal, which is reconstructing a message relayed hundreds of light-years from the one of the core systems. This far out it takes forever to reassemble all the data packets.

I sit at the table. Xin Yi picks up a full bowl of breakfast ramen and puts it in front of me. "Eat. Before it gets cold." I'm about to ask how they knew I'd be up this early when I realize this must be Papa's breakfast, abandoned as soon as the comm unit trembled back to life after weeks of silence. Knowing that makes me hesitate to dig into it, Xin Yi urges me to eat with an intense stare and a nod, so I grab the chopsticks from Papa's place setting and wolf down his breakfast.

The bowl is more than half emptied when he returns from the comm and drops into his chair. "Wai Ying, after you finish eating, go pack a bag. We're taking a field trip."

"For how long?"

"Four, maybe five days, depending on weather and terrain."

Xin Yi sips her tea and then asks Papa, "May I ask where you're going?"

"North, across the Bled. Some ministry honch in a corner office on Proxima wants me to scout a grid reference in the Cerulean Range."

"Crossing the Bled is dangerous. Lots of *Bàomín* activity out there."

"Only east of the gorge. They're pretty scarce in the west Bled."

"All the same, I should go with you."

He waves off her suggestion. "I can't ask you to do that."

"I'm not asking. That survey request for grid ZX-127? It came from me."

Papa nods but keeps his expression blank. "I see." In an oddly upbeat tone of voice he tells me, "Looks like you're sitting in the back this time, *bao bao*."

Less than an hour later we're on our way in the rover, which has been packed to capacity with fuel, gear, water, and provisions. Papa takes the main road out of town. Within a minute we pass the sign that reads "Now Leaving Edenville—pop. 4,311". After that, the road vanishes into an endless reach of dust and stones.

By midday we've left behind the last traces of vegetation, which was already sparse back in town. Arcadia has some great forests and farmlands, but most of them hug the equator. Once you get past thirty degrees north or south, the only live vegetation consists of scrub brush, lichen, and a few succulents.

I don't mind, though. There's a beauty to the desolation, a peace unique to the desert. After we hit the parched red salt flats of the Bled, the silhouette of the distant Cerulean Range dominates the horizon like a row of broken teeth under an endless yawn of sun-blanched sky.

None of it seems to hold any appeal for Xin Yi. Between rounds of slowly savoring the smoke from her pipe, she sleeps in the front passenger seat, oblivious of the majestic landscape slipping past all around us.

Aside from a brief stop to relieve ourselves (taking turns behind the rover for privacy) and eat a quick lunch of cold noodles with artificial protein that's meant to taste like veal but chews more like Kelvian watersnake, Papa doesn't stop the rover until the sky starts turning purple, a harbinger of sundown. The rover has strong halogen headlamps, but that still doesn't make it safe to drive at night.

For dinner, Papa pulls out the battery-powered hot plate, two liters of water, and some flash-frozen meal packs, which combine to make a pretty decent pot of duck noodle soup. An impressive feat when you consider that the nearest real live duck is over seven hundred light-years away. Or so he likes to tell me.

Xin Yi savors each spoonful of the soup like it's ambrosia. "I haven't had duck noodle soup this good in years. What's your secret?"

Papa beams at her compliment. "The spices. Balancing the cloves and the star anise, the honey and vinegar, the salt and the ginger."

"Well, make sure you write it down. It's the best I've ever had."

Her praise has Papa smiling like a fool the rest of the evening, until he finally tucks himself into a sleeping bag on top of the rover. Normally I'd sleep inside the rover, but tonight I insisted on sharing the pup tent with Xin Yi. It takes me only a few minutes to set it up, and by the time I finish, Xin Yi has switched on our infrared heater. It lacks the rustic charm of a crackling campfire, but its invisible warmth is better for stargazing—and less likely to attract attention out here in the Bled. There aren't many native predators to speak of this far north, but there is always a risk of bandits roaming the flats. Better cautious than dead.

I sit close to Xin Yi in front of the tent, basking in the steady warmth from the heater while we look up at the heavens. She draws sweet smoke from her pipe as I point at a bright star high overhead. "Have you been there?"

"Alrakis? Sure."

"What was it like?"

"I presume you mean its capital planet, Alrakis Prime. If you really want to know, it's cold, crowded, and dirty. And that's the nice part."

I point at another star. "How 'bout there?"

She blows a smoke ring that disappears into the dark. "Betelgeuse? No one there, child. Just a supergiant star cooking everything to a crisp."

I single out another star at random. "That one?"

This time Xin Yi freezes. Sadness moves behind her eyes like a storm's shadow on the plain, and then it's like she's looking beyond the horizon. "Theta Indii. The New Busan colony...I've been there."

Despite her melancholy, I can barely contain my excitement. "You've been to New Busan? What was it like? I want to know everything!"

She gazes skyward and heaves a long sigh.

"In the cities, the 'scrapers are over five kilometers tall. The rich ride around in airships with glass floors; they throw wild parties while they look down and laugh as their private police kill unarmed protestors in the streets. On the outskirts, people fight over scraps of food, a pair of shoes, or a few square meters of shelter. And if you go out past the wire, into the wilderness, pretty much every indigenous form of life on that planet will try to kill you any way it can."

"That sounds...awful."

"It is."

"What's the worst thing about New Busan?"

Xin Yi stares at the ground. "It's where I had my first gunfight."

I perk up. "Like a duel?"

She shakes her head. "Real life isn't like that. People almost never square off at high noon."

"So how'd it happen?"

"An ambush. One of them blocked my path, as a distraction.

"A second man hiding behind me tried to shoot me in the back. Hit my shoulder instead.

"I ran for cover as a third gun, a woman, came at me from my left.

"I jumped behind the wreck of an old speeder, but one of them shot me in the leg while I was in midair. No idea which one.

"Once I had cover, I took out the one who'd been behind me. Then I snapped a lucky shot at the one who'd blocked me. Got him in the throat.

"As he went down, his finger squeezed his trigger and put a wild shot into the woman who'd come to back him up."

My pulse races. It's hard for me to keep my voice down so as not to wake Papa. "Wow! Did you ever have a classic quick-draw gunfight?"

"A few."

"That's wild!" I mime fast-drawing a pair of finger pistols and blasting some unseen opponent to smithereens. "I want to be like you someday."

She regards me with heartbreak. "No, child, you don't." Again she looks away, into the faded pages of her memory. "That woman from the ambush? Her partner's misfire left her gut-shot, but she wasn't dead. I knew if I left her alive she'd either put the marshals onto me, or track me down someday to shoot me in the back. So while she lay there gasping like a dying fish, bleeding out in a street of mud...I shot her in the face."

I sit stunned by Xin Yi's confession as she stands and dusts off her serape. "I'll understand if you'd rather not share the tent," she says, her voice taut with shame, "but I wanted you to know the truth: there's nothing noble or heroic about the life I've lived." She crawls inside the tent and leaves me alone in the dark to contemplate my shattered illusions and the cold, distant stars.

Our second day in the rover, no one says a word from sunup until nearly the end of the day, when we round the final bend that leads us into a dead-end box canyon. Ragged walls of rust-colored stone tower above us on three sides, framing a sky of low-hanging clouds painted an imperial violet by the dying rays of the sun.

But the only thing any of us can look at is the artifact.

It must be alien. I've never seen anything human made that looked anything like this. It's enormous. Over a hundred meters high, and hundreds of meters across, its shape evokes the eight-legged abdomen of an arachnid. It's made of some kind of black volcanic rock—obsidian, I think I once heard Papa call it—and so is the huge, oval platform on which it stands.

The platform is spiderwebbed with fissures and cracks, some of them as fine as a hair, others meters wide and as ragged as a serrated blade. A long, narrow shaft connects the structure's abdomen (for lack of a better way to describe the bulbous mass) to the top of an upright ring of the same night-black glass fused into the artifact's base. The alien construct emits no sound, but the wind howls and shrieks as it twists unseen around the artifact's arachnoid features.

Surrounding the oval platform are ancient pieces of broken architecture. Dozens of toppled pillars, the debris of fallen archways and fractured obelisks, and cairns abandoned since the age of antiquity . . . all of them left here to gather dust in the lonely crags of the Cerulean Range.

Papa is entranced by the artifact. He ignores every bit of safety advice he ever gave me and sprints onto the platform. Desperate to drink in every possible detail, he pirouettes clumsily as he moves toward the central ring. He's so caught up in the moment of discovery that he doesn't notice I'm right behind him.

His voice is a reverent whisper. "Amazing. Just incredible." He takes belated notice of me at his side, and then he points at the symbols inscribed upon the edge of the ring, starting at its apex and proceeding counterclockwise around its full circumference. "That's an alien script. Proto-Kinaaran, I think."

From far behind us Xin Yi interjects, "Correct. Well-spotted, Li."

I look back. She stands behind a broad slab of angled stone that resembles dark marble. At her touch it seems to come alive. The black stone shimmers with moving streams of jade-green light. Xin Yi works quickly, tracing different symbols with her fingertips. As the characters beneath her hands begin to glow, so does the interior edge of the ring.

Galvanic prickly heat stings the skin of my exposed forearms like a million tiny insect bites, and then the vast space inside the artifact fills with huge green ribbons of electricity twisting around one another in a slow, hypnotic dance.

The air in the center of the upright ring ripples like a quiet pond disturbed by a falling stone. As the image further distorts, it shimmers like quicksilver.

"Take cover," Xin Yi says. "Both of you. Quickly."

Papa seizes my wrist and, in a clumsy jog, he tows me to cover behind the nearest mound of segments from a fallen pillar. Obeying his instinct to hide, he ducks low behind the stone barrier, but curiosity compels me to peek over the top, to see what Xin Yi does and what happens next.

The rippling pool of silver suspended inside the ring turns black, and then its void is salted with stars that seem to fall away, like grains of sand through the neck of an hourglass. They swirl faster each second, shrinking their orbits until they converge in the center with a flash of white light that swells to fill the ring.

Inside the blinding glare, a human figure takes shape and

steps through the ring. Then another person's silhouette forms inside the flood of light; as the second person emerges, I see the outline of a third following them through the portal. As the third traveler exits the gateway, its fierce white blaze dims and then melts back into a rippling vertical pool of silver.

The three visitors stand in a line. Those on the ends are each a few meters away from the one in the middle. They all wear the same style of black Stetson, but other than that they look nothing alike.

In the center stands a tall Arcturian with light gray skin, elegant genderless features, big aqua-colored eyes, and an almost imperceptible nose. Ze lets zir bone-white hair hang loose and flutter in the arid desert wind. The bottom of zir ash-colored longcoat flutters around gray serpentskin boots.

To the left of the Arcturian is a human whose salt-and-pepper hair matches his ragged beard. The deep creases in his sun-browned face are a ledger of injuries and disappointments. The hem of his black leather duster hangs below his knees. Unlike the Arcturian, this man wears heavy boots with reinforced soles. The only people I've ever seen wear that kind of boot on Arcadia are former soldiers.

On the other side of the Arcturian is a woman whose umber skin has cool blue undertones. Her braided black hair falls over her right shoulder and down the front of her dark brown canvas trench coat. She wears her clothes loose and comfortable, from her tunic and vest through her breeches and calf-hugging boots. Her face is both stern and beautiful, her affect calm, her carriage confident.

Xin Yi faces them from fifteen meters away. She offers a polite nod to the Arcturian: "Winter." Then to the man: "Sánchez." And finally to the woman: "Kasongo."

Winter's voice is mellifluous, almost musical, like those of most of zir species. "I was told I would find you here. Until now, I didn't believe it."

A rasping snort precedes Sánchez's expulsion of spit into the dirt. His voice sounds like he has a throat full of grit and broken glass. "Neither did I. Anonymous tips usually ain't worth shit."

Kasongo stares long and hard at Xin Yi. "What happened, Wai Ying? Who sold you out?"

A chill goes down my spine when I hear Kasongo say my name—and then I realize she wasn't talking to me.

Xin Yi adjusts her stance and throws the front of her serape over her left shoulder to reveal the twin blasters she wears holstered on each thigh. "No one sold me out, Marshal. I invited you. All of you."

Sánchez narrows his eyes in suspicion. "And why would you do that?"

"Because I've run from you all long enough. Let's end this."

Winter regards Xin Yi with an odd tilt of zir head. "As you wish."

The strangers untie the belts of their coats, pull them open, and sweep them backward to reveal that they each wear a holstered blaster on one thigh—and the famous, gleaming golden-triangle badge of a Time Marshal on their belt.

My jaw goes slack, and I feel as if the world has frozen around me. Every detail feels vital: the sweat on Papa's forehead, motes of dust riding the wind, the weltering light of the gateway, each tremor and twitch in the marshals' hands—

Then everything happens at once, almost too fast to see.

Xin Yi draws first, I'm sure of it. Both her blasters clear leather before any of the marshals get half as far, but she fires only one of her pistols. Her shot clips Kasongo's knee, and the marshal loses her balance.

Sánchez and Winter finish their draws as Xin Yi fires her second shot, which passes harmlessly between the two marshals.

Kasongo falls hard to the ground. She squeezes off a wild shot as she lands on the rocky soil. The plasma pulse ricochets off one of the artifact's massive legs.

Winter fires, puts a plasma bolt straight through Xin Yi's gut and out her back in a spray of blackened tissue and boiled blood. Her legs buckle.

"No!" I spring to my feet and leap toward Xin Yi, too quickly for Papa to stop me. He abandons cover to chase me.

On her knees, Xin Yi fires both her pistols at once—and hits nothing but dirt.

She's not aiming at the marshals. She isn't aiming at all.

I see it now. She didn't come to fight. She came here to die.

A wild shot by Kasongo screams over Xin Yi's head and past me to blaze into Papa's shoulder. The impact stops him cold and throws him onto his back. Stunned unconscious, he trembles as blood seeps from his charred, smoking wound.

I'm still running toward Xin Yi when Sánchez's shot slams into her chest. Her blasters tumble from her hands, and her body goes limp. She lands on her back with her legs trapped underneath her.

When I reach her side, she isn't moving.

I glare at the marshals through a broken lens of tear-stained eyes. Winter and Sánchez help Kasongo stand. The trio walks back to the shimmering silver ring. One at a time, they breach its quicksilver threshold and evaporate like mirages.

Then they're gone, and all that's left are the doleful cries of the wind.

It takes damned near every stim in the rover's field medkit to wake Xin Yi. Her eyes flutter open, and she squints at me as if I'm too bright to see.

She musters a sad smile. "You're still here."

I nod quickly, not sure what to say.

She asks, "Are you hurt?"

I shake my head. Then a wave of anger hits me. "Did you really bring those marshals here?" Xin Yi nods, and I start to cry. "Why?"

"I needed you to see this. So you'd understand." Xin Yi struggles to reach toward me. Keen to her intention, I clasp her hand. Her eyes shimmer with tears. Her voice turns brittle. "I need you to do something."

"Not until you tell me why the marshal called you 'Wai Ying.'"

She coughs, and a thick brew of bright and dark blood pools in her mouth. She turns her head to the side to let it spill out. When she looks back at me, her bravado is gone and only her sorrow remains. "You know why, child."

She guides my hand to her throat. Beneath her shirt collar I feel a delicate metallic strand. With care and dread, I draw it out into the dying light of dusk to see a silver chain that bears a medallion of Chang Xi. And on the back of that medallion... my mother's name, hand-carved in *hànzì* characters.

I have a million questions but all I can think to ask is "How?"

She wraps both her hands around mine, as if to signal she won't let me go until she's told me everything. "When I was a girl... Volkov and Ortiz... killed Papa in the store. Stabbed him in the back.

"I knew I'd be next. So I ran.

"I took the rover through the Bled, where I thought no one would follow. I drove for days. Until I followed a trail here"—she turned her eyes toward the artifact—"and found this."

She coughs out another lungful of blood, spattering my hands and jacket. I give her some water. After she catches her breath, she continues in a weak voice. "I didn't know what it was, or how it worked. The first time I used it, it threw me halfway across the galaxy and fifty years into the past.

"I came back here, over and over. Tried to make myself into a time-jumping Robin Hood. But it kept going wrong.

"Anything I did to make things better only made them worse. I lost lives I tried to save. Ruined everything I loved.

"Before long I was on the run from the Time Marshals. They hounded me through time for decades. It was all I could do to keep this hidden from them.

"It took me a lifetime to learn how to use the machine with any control. To get back to *this* moment. To *you*."

Tears fall from her eyes, and I feel myself crying in sympathy even though I still don't understand what's happening. "Why?"

"Because this is when my life changed. Losing Papa broke me. Then I found this thing. I thought it was the answer to my problems, but all it did was multiply them." A hard cough racks her entire body. Dark blood spews from her mouth, and then she starts to shiver violently. "Inside my coat...a red crystal rod. Put it in the center receiver...on the main panel. Destroy the machine."

I can't believe what she's asking of me. "Destroy it?"

Her hands tighten around mine with fierce resolve. "Promise me."

"Why?"

The strength of her grip slowly ebbs. "I spent fifty years on the run. No joy. No home. No love." Her trembling worsens, so I hold her in my arms. There is guilt in her voice and regret in her eyes. "Don't walk my path, child. There's nothing at the end of this road but pain. I gave you and Papa...a second chance. Take it...and find a better way."

Her last breath slips out, thin and weak. In the space of a moment, nothing seems to change, but I know everything has. Her eyes are still open but no longer see. The heat of her hands on mine will soon fade and her flesh will turn gray.

I extricate my hands from hers and lay her to gentle rest on the platform of cracked obsidian. As she requested, I search the inside pockets of her coat until I find an asymmetrically cut rod of red crystal. It is no mere hunk of mineral. A spark burns inside it, like the heart of an ember that refuses to die.

Papa is groggy and confused when I rouse him with a stim stick. There is too much to explain, and I'm not sure he would believe me if I did, so I browbeat him into the passenger seat of the rover, which I drive about half a kilometer away from the artifact, just around the bend in the canyon. Then I park the rover and get out.

Half-awake, Papa asks, "Where are you going?"

"To keep a promise."

Exhaustion pulls him down into a restless half sleep as I walk back to the artifact, the blood-red crystal clutched in my fist as the sky turns black overhead.

I reach the control panel and find the receiver right where Xin Yi—where I told myself it would be. As I bring the crystal toward the panel, its defiant inner spark flares bright and true.

And I wonder if I'm making a mistake.

All my life I've dreamed of adventures. Of seeing distant worlds. Exploring the frontier. Of becoming the stuff of legends...

Then I hear the fathomless sorrow in Xin Yi's voice: *There is nothing at the end of this road but pain.*

I insert the crystal into the receiver. Like compatible magnets, the console and the crystal snap together, drawn by some invisible force. A piercing whine fills the canyon. Cracks spread across every part of the massive alien machine, and then fiery light shines through them. Hot tears cut streaks through the dust on my face as the ground quakes with the promise of violence.

I run. Harder and faster than I've ever run before.

I clear the platform just before the structures overhead come crashing down and crush the central ring. The roar of the artifact's collapse and the trembling bedrock are deafening. The heaving ground threatens to make me face-plant, but I keep going until I reach the rover. Only then do I stop and look back to see that the box canyon has collapsed in upon itself. Whatever trace there might have been of the alien time artifact is buried now, beyond recovery.

The wall of dust and smoke surges into the canyon from the

site of the collapse. I scramble into the rover and close all the windows and vents just in time. The dust storm courses over the rover and coats it in thick grime.

About a minute later, all is quiet in the canyon.

Papa stirs in the passenger seat. He looks at me and makes an effort to focus in the dim light of the rover's console display. "*Bao bao*? Everything okay?"

I press the ENGINE START button, and the rover purrs to life. Then I reassure my father with a smile. "We're all right, Papa." I put the rover into gear and step on the accelerator. "Let's go home."

THE BALLAD OF THE JUNK HEAP GUN MAN AND MISTRESS BULLET

M. Todd Gallowglas

The art and entertainment of Quisquiliarum *are as jury-rigged and recycled as the rest of that junkyard planet's society. Take the hai sixtina, for example, a complicated and complex poetic form that uses both prose and poetic stanzaic structures to offer readers a multilayered narrative that traditionally explores the strange interactions between discarded human technology and the remnants of the previous alien inhabitants. Word repetition, slant rhymes, and permutations on old Earth phrasings are paramount for this form. I offer, for an example, one of the oldest known recorded hai sixtinas of* Quisquiliarum.

—An excerpt from *Esoteric Poetic Forms of the Galaxy* by Turner Bryant

Was it chance that got the old timer to pick the perfect night to ride into town on that cyborg steed? A rare breeze at dusk cleared most of the rust particles from the air, and many of the town's citizens had gathered in the saloon. Without bothering to ask, that stranger stepped into the light shining above the piano. We all stopped our chatter to lean forward and listen to what they planned to say. Off came the hat, duster, and gun. Under all that travel gear was a lady, not a man. While rare, t'wern't too unusual to hear 'bout a woman

traveling these parts alone. The way her finger played on the trigger, when she set her iron aside, spoke volumes that she'd be able
to handle herself just fine when it came to action. She opened her
mouth, and we were ready. A lady that old, carrying iron like that,
almost certainly had something for us to learn.

1

Patrons, put down your drinks and listen.
Scavengers, put down your cups, lend an ear.
Warriors, take your fingers off your triggers,
open your minds so you may learn
ancient secrets from that day of violent action
between Mistress Bullet and the Junk Heap Gun Man.

I see by your expressions, you know of that dreaded man.
Perhaps if you turn from your drinks and listen,
you might avoid membership within that faction
of victims left bleeding, groaning, dying between there and
        here
because they would not, could not learn
these lessons and avoid that clenching rigor

mortis gripping harder than a greenhorn's trigger
finger hoping to keep from becoming a grave man.
Out among the black, man had much to learn
for not all life was as we knew it. On planets there and here,
strange species adapted to our incursions, those reactions

became real-time darwinistic interactions
where selections natural did not always side with vigor,
size, or intellect. Pray, heed me, and hear
how one such life form, the Junk Heap Gun Man
rose into being with its cogs, gears, and pistons.
Once again, my tale can help you earn

a victory over that vile, gun-blazing, ever-learning
creature of death. Though only a fraction
of you will commit yourselves fully to listen.

The rest of you might as well pull the trigger
against your own heads, for each is a dead man
walking. If I could force each soul here

to leave his pride in his cup and truly hear
this vital lesson and live. Have we not learned
that every soul on this garbage-strewn sphere—man,
woman, child—is sacred. When bullets flare to action,
and that ambulatory, garbage alien touches its triggers,
it will be too late. So, heed me, iron slingers, and listen.

Each man and woman glanced at each other. The lady's
words triggered dark dreads in our deepest parts. But, we'd
take no action to stop her, standing and speaking under the
performer's light.

2

Just how did the Junk Heap Gun Man
come to be? That demigod alien other
sprang into its semilife through a chain reaction
between digitized memories and spare parts
from dozens of worlds—oh, and a bit of alien ichor—
created a perfect technological storm, causing light

to flare in camera-lens eyes out in the blight
of the Scavenger's Wasteland. Alien, machine, man—
a seemingly incompatible triumvirate—jury riggered
by this planet's bizarre ecology, unlike any other
on the star charts, where disparate parts
merge together in demonic transactions.

On Earth that Was, machines could make a retraction
of painful memories, removing them to lighten
the burdens the mind carried, those parts
of their pasts that made them feel like lesser men.
Wouldn't you, my audience, like to reject or smother
all the terrors of growing up on this world of trigger

happy scavengers, always blasted and blasting from liquor?
Out in the Scavenger's Wasteland, chance interactions
of neuro-drives storing disparate minds connected with other
minds tormented by perpetual purgatory took delight
in communion after such long loneliness, because Man
should never exist in pieces outside the sum of all his parts.

Sometimes, the Scavenger's Wasteland shifts and rumbles. Parts
roll, slide, fall, and collide. One day, neuro-drives fell quicker
than quickest silver into a pool of alien ichor left eons
    before human
ships left Earth that Was. The volatile chain reaction
led to that unnatural warrior's very first fight
when human and alien imperatives struggled to smother,

overwhelm, and extinguish all trace of the other
entities vying for control. They rallied on virtual ramparts.
Garbage churned and integrated until a creature rose into
    daylight.
That monstrous metal maniac keeps gravediggers
across this world employed, for death is its only satisfaction.
And, that is the origin of the Junk Heap Gun Man.

Another verse begun and gone. We settled in for the next
part. Light from the day faded with the sun setting under the
jagged horizon. Still, even with our dusters wrapped tight, we
couldn't shake the chill.

3

You've met the villain, but this tale's only just begun.
I'll tell you now about Mistress Bullet, her long duster
and even longer range. Hailing from strange parts
unknown to all be the oldest scrappers, she wandered under
stars, moon, sun, and sky stretching above her
and seeking the Junk Heap Gun Man to remove that blight

from this world. She traveled in constant flight
from her past and in hopes she'd find the Junk Heap Gun

Man's weakness. Years before, a girl and her brother
worked to clear debris from a field. That day was dustier
than most with rust and loose dirt. But the Plunder
from a field of bare earth with irrigation made from parts

of a starship's coolant system could become the start
of a new life for their family. Except in the fading light
of dusk one evening—*clank, clack, clunk*—metallic thunder
churned its way into their ears and the Junk Heap Gun
Man followed close on its heels. They stood, dusters
flying wide open, hands drew iron, and sister and brother,

sun at their backs, face off with that scrap-heap other.
"Go," the brother said. "Warn Pa." At first, the girl refused
     to depart,
but the enemy drew its own iron, and the girl's duster
billowed out behind her like leather wings in flight
through the garbage fields. Retorts of rapid-fire gunshots chased the girl scrambling over junk and under

the night's new stars. The following silence made her wonder
but deep down, she knew what fate befell her brother.
Close to her family's ramshackle home, she had begun
shouting for Ma and Pa. Somewhere behind her, that spare-parts
assassin came *clacking, clunking, clanking* to revel and delight
in killing. The girl had no illusions the garbage demon
     would dust her

and her parents. Almost home. Sweat soaking inside her duster.
Breath burning throat and chest. Legs aching. Stomach
     heavy under
the weight of imaginary nuts and bolts. Almost home. Lights
in the windows. Screaming for Ma and Pa. Hoping her
     brother's
sacrifice gave her the time to get her family out of these parts
to safety. *Clunk. Clank. Clack.* And the whir of alien-
     powered guns.

Ask any of us later, and we'll tell you her voice was able to
hold us under some kind of spell with no chance of escape. Her

words hit like bullets shot from the gun of her mouth. Every duster in the place got pulled a little tighter.

4

Now that you know the primary warriors of this fable,
listen, hear, and learn on the minuscule chance
you scrappers and reclaimers find yourselves under
unfortunate circumstances like facing a Junk Heap Gun
Man. Oh, did you think the girl gone? Not so. Trust her
more than that. "How is this possible?" you might ask.

After slinging iron and reveling in that murderous task
the garbage-alien-demigod, as always, felt safe and able
to move on. One corpse wasn't a corpse. Strips from her duster
staunched the blood flowing from wounds, giving her the
 chance
to heal, to train, to take her father's and brother's guns,
and put that spare parts killer at least twenty-six feet under.

The Junk Heap Gun Man continued wandering under
skies of falling garbage from far-off worlds. He basked
in the trail of blood and tears left by his whirring guns.
Even those ironslingers who were quicker on the draw
 were unable
to damage that alien-powered metal form. "No human
 stands a chance
against me!" the slaughterer intoned when posses would
 muster

at edges of towns. The girl traveled in her brother's duster
filled with bullet holes and covered with bloodstains. Under
the weight of familial spectres in her dreams, she advanced
town to town and through the scrap yards, her face a mask
of grim determination. She set no particular timetable
on her vengeance. She trained with each gun

until her movements blurred faster than the Junk Heap Gun
Man's. Tapping into Telewaves, the alien cyborg killer
 heard about a duster-

wearing mad woman, faster than any human should be capable.
Mistress Bullet, the people called her. A true wonder
to behold. Slayer of bandits. Killer of Warriors. She wore a
    mask
of rust and blood. Our villain followed those signals for
    the chance

to test metal against this Mistress Bullet, yearning to dance
against an opponent who might be an equal with a gun.
After so long and so many empty victories, that's all he
    asked
for. But somehow Mistress Bullet, it seemed, could readjust her
path one, two, three steps ahead of him and never blunder
into a firefight finality that would end her hopeful fable.

She stopped then and asked for something to drink. A man
hopped to action, quicker than a trigger on a well-greased zip-
shooter. The sooner she got that drink, the better chance we'd
be able to know Mistress Bullet's fate.

5

It wasn't luck that kept Mistress Bullet from the Junk
    Heap Gun Man's
firestorm of lead. You see, she was a bit of a trickster,
and knew when her home exploded, the only possible
    action
she could take to save her life was to assume the mantle
    and mask
of death: bleeding, only the faintest breath, and limbs at
    twisted angles.
Deception, that night and in this chase, was her only chance

To survive the inevitable confrontation, that final dance
between Mistress Bullet and the Junk Heap Gun Man.
Mistress Bullet knew she could make her enemy unstable
if she could just stay out of range of that hair-trigger
killer. That part-alien, jury-rigged automaton in a rusted
    iron mask

chased and chased—*clackity-clunk, clickity-whir*—with no
   satisfaction

because Mistress Bullet remained an ever-elusive abstraction,
always behind the next garbage pile or over the horizon.
   Chance
had no place in this game. Mistress Bullet has set herself
   the task
of taunting her foe by matching the numbers of dead men
brought down by the tricked-out scopes and triple-action
   triggers
on her .75-caliber revolvers. No outlaw or ironslinger was able

to outdraw that self-styled angel of death. She was willing
   and able
to sacrifice any and all desperados to gain permanent traction
in her enemy's mind. She became the ultimate thimblerigger—
herself the pea, the scrap fields her cups. Alas,
      circumstances
conspired against Mistress Bullet. The Junk Heap Gun Man
has a few tricks hidden deep in his holsters. You might ask,

"Why didn't he use this sooner?" Might as well ask,
"Why didn't it just broadcast how anyone might be able
to bring about the demise of the Junk Heap Gun Man?"
She wasn't the first to dream of ending this demonic
   contraption.
No one else came this close, stood this much of a chance
because those men believed they could stand trigger

to trigger, eye to eye, toe to toe, gun to gun, all of them trigger-
happy idiots, too ready to die. With any near defeat, our
   villain asked
how they could get so close. No other ironslinger would
   get a chance
to come that close the same way. The scrap-field murderer
   turned the tables
on Mistress Bullet by spilling his alien blood and sending
   a fraction

of its mind through the discarded circuits to find that
walking dead woman.

She bade us listen, hear, and learn. So we leaned in, breathing close to stopped. She looked us over, meeting the gaze of
each man, and pulled the trigger on the final action of her tale.

6

Using this trick, from its alien origins, the Junk Heap Gun
    Man
located Mistress Bullet. The chase was on. It adopted the
    action
of the tiger, stopping every so often to connect and listen
to where the circuit system said she was. There and here.
Here and there. With every linkup, the recycle metal
    monster learned
he was gaining on his prey. With each link up, the killer's
    triggers

sent twitches and itches through souped-up and over-
    clocked trigger
fingers. Little by little, bit by bit, that garbage-born boogeyman
closed in. However, on this harsh world, Mistress Bullet
    learned
the hard way not to take anything for granted. Her triple-
    action
revolvers were always at the ready, her ears cocked to hear
any out-of-the-ordinary sound. One night, she noticed a
    circuit glisten

at the edge of a junkpile. She crept closer, with her fist in her
mouth to stay silent so she could try to figure
why cast-off computer bits would be lit up out here
in the scrap fields. Then, she shot the circuit, and man, oh,
    man,
did Mistress Bullet gain a sense of extreme satisfaction
when a shower of glowing goop splattered around. You can
    learn

something new every day if you open your eyes. Learn
so you can fight another day. Mistress Bullet had listened
to her guts and took decisive and immediate action.
Glowing processors surrounded her. Fingers squeezed triggers.
Metal and silicon shattered. Alien ichor splattered. That
    artificial man
Felt a new sensation. For the first time since its formation, fear

spread through all its wires. Gunshots grew closer, and here
that brutal killer stood, while Mistress Bullet burned
it down, piece by piece. That revenge-bent woman
blasted away. The hunter became prey, and could only listen
to each gunshot. Weaker and weaker. Fingers slipped off
    triggers.
Steps became slower. The mechanical murderer could take
    no action

by the time Mistress Bullet caught up to him. A smile of
    satisfaction
glowed, and she put a bullet in its final lit circuit. Did you
    truly hear
how Mistress Bullet defeated the seemingly undefeatable?
    Figure
out the secret of her triumph? Did you honestly learn?
When your guts shout to get your attention: listen!
That's the lesson of Mistress Bullet and the Junk Heap
    Gun Man.

And that woman finished her drink, replaced her hat, duster,
and gun, and walked out of the performer's light over the piano.
The old saloon man asked if she'd offer another tale for his patrons
to hear. Her smile barely showed under her wide-brimmed hat.
We all figure we only chanced to see that smirk on account she
wanted us to. No way we'd been able to otherwise. Her final
action before setting off was to hand the saloon man a single
bullet. Once she departed, we all learned from the saloon man
that the bullet had a word written on it. *Protected.* That triggered
years of speculation from everyone in our town. I swore if she
ever returned to these parts, I meant to ask her about that gift.
Not surprised I'm still waiting.

THIS WORLD BELONGS TO THE MONSTERS

Dr. Chesya Burke

CHAPTER 1: David

Earth smelled acrid, sulfuric, and hostile. Like rotten eggs that had been buried in the soul of the Earth a thousand years ago, releasing a permanent, noxious yellow cloud over the entire planet from season to season—which were basically nonexistent by this point anyway. Whereas Mars had always been "the Red Planet," the Earth's new nickname was "the Yellow Star." The air had become almost completely unbreathable in the hundred short years that mankind had almost completely surrendered it to the elements. David adjusted the air hose at the base of his neck, making sure there were no leaks, and the connection was secure. The fumes were toxic and dangerous to everyone, but somehow those who remained had adapted to the environment, defying scientists who predicted their demise would have come more than eighty years before.

But these people didn't die. Ever.

He slowed his wagon, stopping completely in front of a thousand-year-old wrought iron gate—an old plantation house that was amazingly well-kept. Someone took pride in this place; someone loved it. The horse buckled, shook its head, then took several steps backward, as if afraid. David clicked his teeth and stayed the beast on the reins. "There, there. An hour. Then I'm

95

getting off this planet. Sorry you have to stay, boy." The horse was a girl, but David didn't know this, and he didn't particularly care.

Before he could get down and walk over to ease the creature, David had the overwhelming feeling of being watched. Looking up, he expected to see someone at the gate approaching him. But there was no one. It was difficult to see far into the distance because of the fog, but David scanned the wall that stood about three feet high and as far as he could see beyond onto the property. From his limited view, the land was populated with relatively healthy, lush trees and vegetations. Despite the harsh atmosphere, this land thrived. Since landing, David had seen that much of the planet could not boast the same.

When he had first been asked to come to this godforsaken planet, he tried desperately to control the feeling of shock displayed on his face though the teleprompter. He, like every human being on every colonized planet in the known galaxy, believed that Earth was uninhabitable. Every school-aged citizen of *United Interplanetary Coalition* (UIP, for short) had been taught that after the climate apocalypse and millions of worldwide deaths that scientists around the world had been forced to speed up their efforts for full planet evacuation. With major governments of the world coming together to form the Coalition (eventually becoming UIP), the Kepler telescope mission in search of exoplanets habitable outside of our solar system was successful and universal colonization began. "K" planets were discovered and inhabited at previously impossible and unimaginable rates.

Being confronted with the truth about the survivors on Yellow Star made him physically ill. David had ancestors he believed had not survived that time in human history. Many people didn't. Perhaps, he realized, not as many as had been previously reported. UIP leaders knew about the existence of these people, so perhaps they knew about surviving relatives he may have on this planet as well. At this point, he just wanted to get back to Homeplanet and find out whatever he could—of course only if he could do it without being considered an apostate.

Someone at UIP knew the truth. After all, *they* had known to send him here.

For *her*.

And there she was. A figure out in the distance, on the land, watching him, unmoving. Adorned in all white, colorful beads and copper jewelry. As the dense yellow fog shifted in the wind, more figures became visible. At least several dozen—over fifty by his estimation—were observing every move he made before he even knew they had been there. They could have killed him before he reached for any one of his pistols. He was grateful they weren't as quick to draw as most gunslingers on other planets would have been.

He dismounted his wagon and just as his foot touched the reach, someone extended a gloved hand to help him down. He stopped for a minute, looked to his benefactor, and accepted the gracious offer. The hand offered to him was small but strong. On the ground, before doing anything else, he bent, one knee touching the soil, and said the regulated government prayer: "Honor to the Forefathers for their deliverance to the true mission of His Holy One. Amen." When he stood, he felt slightly embarrassed as the figure before him stared on in amusement. She was no more than an inch shorter than David who stood at five feet, eleven inches tall. Unlike David, her face was not covered although her body was completely adorned in white and beads, much like the other figures. Her skin was dark, full, and bright. Healthy.

Before he could speak a word, the woman made a gesture with her hand toward the gate. He nodded and walked to the opening. The wrought iron stood at least seven feet tall, the coal-black bars thick and seemingly impenetrable. The opening within the bars offered a clear view of the land beyond to the large, white plantationesque house about a half mile back. The gates opened automatically as he approached them to reveal dozens of white-clad Black women.

The women stood in various formations, which was clearly a strategic defense measure. Each wore a white suit jacket, an ankle-length white skirt, white tie, white headwrap, and black shirt. They were the picture of a strong, well-disciplined regiment and this alone was intimidating. However, each woman also sported some form of historic assault rifle. Cleaned, well preserved, and clearly still functioning. The woman that David was absolutely certain he had been sent to retrieve stood in the center of the group. She was all of six feet tall and was at least 280 pounds. David was a gun connoisseur and immediately recognized the 1950s-era G3 the woman sported, almost as if a prized possession.

The women all assumed the patrol carry position, their straps wrapped around their backs, the shooting end of the rifle aimed downward. Their fingers rested close to, but not on, the trigger. They were trained—well.

"Do you speak English?"

The woman narrowed her eyes at him, a grin spreading across her face. "You are on formerly stolen lands of the United States of the Americas. I should be more surprised that you, Descendant, speak English."

"Descendant?" David was confused.

"You are a descendant of absconders of the former *Earth*, are you not?"

David nodded. "I see. All UIP *descendants* are required to learn English."

The woman frowned, "UIP?"

"United Interplanetary Coalition. What you likely knew as the Coalition when you fought them almost half a century ago."

"I see." The woman stared at him for an uncomfortably long time. Her gaze was threatening. He didn't know if he should try to meet her eyes or avert to show respect. After all, he was here to convince her to travel to the other side of the universe with him, a stranger. This would be a lot to expect from anyone, especially an *apostate suppressive*, someone who had not only abandoned or denied her faith and government, but who had waged all-out war against the UIP.

After a moment she mumbled one word: "FUCK," then simply turned and walked away.

David watched her go, looking around, but none of the other women moved positions, all watching him intently. After a moment the woman turned and nodded for him to follow.

Had he just passed some sort of test?

Inside the house was exactly what you would expect from an ex-plantation. It was stunning, ornately designed and rather gaudy—especially for more modern UIP standards of minimalist design, usually due to the lack of available space and air for most individual dwellings on other planets. But this structure was massive and easily could hold the number of people he'd already seen here.

"Who are you, young man?" The woman sat on what could

only be considered a throne, David standing before her as a peasant. The parlor was full of bay windows, opening the room to vivid yellow sunlight, feeding a massive collection of hundreds of differing plants and vegetation. The room was a magnificent array of bright colors and light, illuminated by a tinted yellowish haze that gave the space a comfortable, pleasant feeling. He hadn't seen indoor gardens like this outside of museums on other planets.

David responded as he had on every mission. "I am a humble delegate of the honorable descendants of Abraham, and chosen to fulfill the holy mission of the United Interplanetary Coalition." But *Mary, Queen of Wagons*, was a different bounty for UIP, so sensitivity was required: "More importantly, I've been sent here to beg your grace and pardon as your help is required on K283c, a planet in the circumstellar habitable zone of the Taurus constellation."

"So, you're an interstellar missionary." She paused and met his eyes. "Or are you a mercenary? No," she reasoned, "you are one and the same... But tell me, Mr. *honorable descendants of Abraham*, who are *you*?"

David was again confused. "I...I am David Wálé."

The woman smiled. "Okay. David Wálé. Who am I?"

David was silent.

"Who did they tell you I was, David Wálé?"

"Begging your pardon, ma'am. They told me you were *her*."

The woman stared at him but did not speak, so David blurted it out while he had the nerve. "Mary, Queen of Wagons, ma'am."

The woman snickered. "Mary, Queen of Wagons? Is that what they call me?"

"Yes...I mean, I don't rightly know how this is possible, ma'am. The legends of Ms. Wagons have her dying in the war against the Coalition forty-three years ago on Homeplanet, but my employers are rarely wrong about these things."

"Why Wagons?"

"Well, ma'am, because you charged a wagon full of dynamite into the Vatican City capitol building, making you the only *apostate suppressive* in UIP history to successfully wage war against the government."

"So, your UIP teachings have me dying in that goddamn wagon, huh?"

"Yes, ma'am. That's what we learn in grade school." He paused for a moment, "Is it true? Is it you?"

"Mayhaps it is. Mayhaps it ain't."

"Ms. Wagons? It's you, isn't it?"

"I did some version of those things in my youth. But what the fuck do they want that sent you here?" She almost seemed to be thinking out loud, but David responded anyway.

"To kill monsters, ma'am."

"Monsters? Ain't that a … You know they called me a monster."

David could not meet her gaze; he had heard the stories of her monstrosities. "These are real, ma'am."

"Are they?" She paused. "Who sent you?"

"Mother Amadeus Dun, ma'am."

Mary glared her dark eyes at him, more serious than she had been previously. "Mother Amadeus?" She didn't take her eyes off him.

He nodded, almost afraid to speak. He looked around at the armed women lining the room, held his hand up as if to show he was not a threat. "May I?" David reached for his bag and, with approval, dug inside, pulling out a videophone he offered to Mary. The older woman nodded to one of the women who took it from him and examined it, then handed it to the older woman.

David was not standing in a position to see the prerecorded video, and he had not had the classification to know what was on it prior to this moment, but he could hear the words. Static crackling slowly gave way to the voice of an older woman whose words were measured and deliberate:

Greetings old friend! [pause] *I reach out to you as a humble delegate of the honorable descendants of Abraham, and I am chosen to fulfill the holy mission of the United Interplanetary Coalition. This message, unfortunately, comes, not out of the desire to reconnect—although it has been way too many years since I have seen my dear friend—but because of tragedy.* [pause] *Mary, you are legend, and quite frankly the best gunslinger in all the known universe. We taught our children to fear you and everything you represent. I know the adversity that you have gone through, and I have been through many of them with you. But I ask of you now to use your talents for good one last time.* [long pause]

Mary stole a glance at him and then back to the screen. David met her gaze for an appropriately respectable amount of time before looking away, at the floor. His responsibility was to do everything he could to convince Mary to return with him. He was good at his job.

Mary, dear friend, you are quite literally the only person that I think can handle this the way it must be handled. It will require a steadfast, honorable woman. It requires you, Mary, Queen of Wagons. Be steadfast, my companion in arms.

It was a long moment after closing the video screen before she turned to David. The woman was seemingly lost in thought, contemplating something to which no one else in the room was privy. David did his job, stayed silent, and allowed the woman the space to think. Usually the first answer was always no, so David was afforded several incentives in his arsenal to convince the target to do what UIP asked of them. Incentives could consist of anything from large sums of money to threatening bodily harm against the target and/or the target's family. David was the *soft-sale* man; he was usually the agent dispatched to acquire targets of great value who needed psychological incentives rather than physical ones. He deplored violence but was well trained and handy with most weapons, both traditional and makeshift. Rarely knowing what was required of the target before he acquired them, he preferred to keep it that way, maintaining a comfortable mental distance in case the target needed neutralizing later down the line. The Coalition, who had changed in name only, was powerful and had a very long reach. The less he knew about any given incident—because if agents like David were sent to the scene there was always an incident—the safer he was.

Pick up the target, deliver them to their destination, protect them to ensure your mission is successful, and get your ass back to Homeplanet. That was the job, that was always the job. This mission should have been the same. But it didn't feel the same. It felt off, wrong, *different* somehow. Only days into it, he'd learned that a vital part of UIP history was a lie and that the most famous gunfighters of the century had not died in one of the biggest fuck-ups in UIP history. And now he, David Wálé, stood before the woman herself. Mary, Queen of Wagons. Now his only job would be to convince this larger-than-life woman to sign on to the very same Coalition who had been responsible for the most tragic events in human history.

After a while Mary looked up to him and shook her head.

David knew it was time for his skills to take over, but before he could open his mouth, Mary stayed him with one finger, "I'll go." David didn't have to respond to this. She didn't ask any questions. She didn't beg for money. She didn't seem to desire or need anything at all.

Mary, Queen of Wagons, did not make sense to him. David was paid to think but thinking too much or about the wrong things in his line of work got you killed. However, he had to know: "Why?"

"Because a debt is owed to me."

No other explanation was given.

The trip to K283c should have been completely uneventful. But David's companion was the infamous cigar-smoking, loud-talking, gambling Mary, Queen of Wagons. And they had a layover on an outlaw planet, K2-155d.

As David and his companion arrived on the planet, an overhead speaker above the woman's head broadcast UIP's mission: *You are but humble delegates of the honorable descendants of Abraham, and you are chosen to fulfill the holy mission of the United Interplanetary Coalition. Forever praise to the forefathers for their guidance and oversight, Amen!* David had grown accustomed to the ambient drone of what they all had been convinced was the holy message. Mary, however, did not handle it as well as he had hoped. Slightly groggy from the trip, she used her boot to dislodge a speaker from the wall, causing it to tumble to the floor. That speaker was dead, shooting sparks into the air from the opened wires, however, at least a dozen more assaulted their ears shouting the same message.

David watched Mary, who in her own right seemed to have accepted that this was at least one battle she couldn't win. "I'm sure you're tired. And...it's mandated that private spaces don't have UIP speakers—for now. I've made accommodations at the finest hotel on the planet. If we..."

"I could use a huge cigar and an even bigger glass of whiskey."

"Oh...I thought maybe...rest..." Mary simply watched him, like a judgmental parent. "Okay," he finally said. "Let's get a drink."

"And a cigar."

"And a cigar," he agreed.

From there, a series of air-filled underground tunnels led to the different zones of the community. The saloon, in the sketchy zone, was predictable if you accommodated for the fact that Mary picked it herself. Dark, smoky, funky. Mary didn't care. She walked up to the bar, took a stool, and ordered top-shelf whiskey, double. Scanning the cigars on the shelf, she rose to her full height and peered over both the counter and the bartender, finally choosing the most expensive one available—"Now, make it a double too," she told the man, winking. And why not? It was on UIP's dime, all expenses covered. She looked at David as she lit her cigar as if expecting him to say something about her expensive taste. But his job was not to police her budget; his job was to keep her alive at least until she had completed her mission. UIP rarely cared if someone died after having succeeded at their task. David, however, did care, so he would ensure that the woman got back home safe as he always had done for each of his details. After a moment of watching him, she smirked and downed the entire double shot in one gulp. When she was finished, she tipped her glass to him and loudly dropped it to the counter, motioning the bartender over to refill her glass, cutting her eyes at a particularly loud table of men at the back of the bar.

The UIP low-frequency speakers were at least impartial; the obnoxious tone of the too excited orator droned on in the bar, there, in the shadiest part of the colony, to the needy, indigent, impoverished, destitute, and penniless. The speakers cracked, expelling more static than words: *Always remember,* it warned this time, *you are but humble delegates of the honorable descendants of Abraham, and you are chosen to fulfill the holy mission of the United Interplanetary Coalition. Forever praise to the forefathers for their guidance and oversight, Amen!*

While Mary ignored the warning, her antics were enough to catch the attention of others in the saloon, of course. Anyone who put on this kind of display of wealth in a territory such as this would be looking for trouble. David kept his eye on the rugged men at the table Mary had also seen, the men who kept whispering and pointing to them. Mary seemed completely oblivious to the happenings around her and, for a brief moment, David wondered how Mary had earned her reputation if she was this ignorant of the universe.

"You're worried about those sonovabitches in the corner?"

"They seem particularly concerned about us."

"Do they scare you?"

"I can handle myself." He paused for a moment then asked, "Do they scare you?"

She downed her drink, pounded the glass, loudly, and asked for another. "Nope."

"I mean, because this kind of display of wealth can get you killed on trek." He was clearly annoyed.

"I know." She leaned in and smirked at him, again. She was good at that, and David was starting to think that that was the one thing he hated the absolute most about her.

Before she could say anything else, a large man in an iron-worker's uniform, caked with dirt from his hair to his steel-toed boots, walked up and stood behind Mary, placing his right hand on the bar, blocking her exit. The men from his table stood up, in unison, several of them spreading out, flanking the tiny room, one taking lookout at the door.

Over the years, David had realized that to most, he looked unassuming. He learned to use this to his advantage, dressing plainly and intentionally constructing his mannerisms and behavior to appear docile. He adjusted himself in the seat to look as nervous as possible. While this action was genuine—and David was in fact apprehensive—it was greatly exaggerated. His behavior was simply to put the group off guard, causing them to let their defenses down, lulling them into believing that they could easily overpower him. Mentally, however, he was contemplating the number of active motions it would take to lift his leg, swiftly and effortlessly unclicking his ankle holster, while simultaneously pulling out his gun and pointing it at the man's head. The barrel of his peace shooter pointing at their friend's head should take the cells out of the rest of the group. If it didn't, without hesitation David would kill the man and as many of the people in that bar that he needed to protect his bounty.

"Looks like you're buying drinks," the man said to Mary while looking at David. He had the quintessential raspy voice of an ironworker.

"Said who?" Mary, face down in her drink, stirred what accounted for ice on this planet.

"Said me, bitch."

"A million miles from home, and they still call me bitch." Mary slowly raised her head and looked at David. Winked. Before

David could react, Mary stood to her feet with the motion of youth she hadn't seen for over forty years, positioned her six-foot-tall, 280-pound body so that the man was boxed in, and without uttering a single word, grabbed the back of his head and bounced it on the edge of the bar. In fluid motion, Mary used her left hand to grab her side piece—she was rumored to be ambidextrous—pointing the handgun at the remaining group. David was momentarily in awe of what he had just witnessed, but luckily, he was well trained, and instincts took over. Within seconds, he too was aiming his Glock at the men.

Blood from the man's head, nose, and mouth poured down the bar, several of his teeth spilling out. In the outer regions of the known universe, trees and other sources of softer resources were rarely available. So, most things were made of local materials, such as stone—like the bar which Mary had just used to paint the saloon blood red. She had hit the man so hard, blood spatter even dotted the ceiling. As the man lay on the ground holding his face, moaning, his group of friends scrambled over themselves to run away. Mary reached into her pocket, pulled out UIP tender and paid the bartender, who had simply watched the happenings as if they were the most normal things in the world. Meanwhile, David scanned the room to make sure there were no more troublemakers. Neither had holstered their gun, but no one else in the room cared, most just continuing in their own drunk stupors. After paying and tipping the bartender very well, still holding her gun on the rest of the room, Mary bent down and whispered something in the bleeding man's ear, her eyes and gun darting back and forth between the other people in the room.

"You're her, aren't you? Mary, Queen of Wagons?" spoke a man from the back of the room, who looked like he could have been related to Mary. His eyes twinkled while talking to the woman.

"Mayhaps I am. Mayhaps I ain't."

"They tell stories of you, girl. I thought you was dead." He respected her.

"Mayhaps I am. Mayhaps I ain't." She winked at the Black man, this expression somehow more personal and intimate than the winks she had offered David—which were accusatory somehow. For a moment, he was momentarily jealous of the respect she offered the stranger, who smiled back at Mary, tipping his hat. The woman holstered her gun, grabbed her own hat from the bar, licked her finger to rub off the smudge of blood from the broken man, then walked out the bar as if nothing had happened. David, on the other hand, did not trust to turn his back on this group of people, so he kept his gun aimed as he slowly backed out of the bar, stepping over the man on the floor.

"Ya cause trouble everywhere you go, don't'cha? You knew that was gonna happen." The two had walked most of the way to their hotel in complete silence. David had a million questions running around in his head, but he didn't know how to appropriately ask any of them. Mary, David figured, didn't really have anything to say to him at all. Sure, David had backed her up, but she hadn't actually needed him. This was going to be a learning curve for him. His normal routine was to take command of both the situation and the target. In this moment, though, he was relatively sure that Mary would not allow him control over anything on this trip. David didn't mind playing second fiddle, but he drew the line at outright foolish behavior.

"Where are you from?"

"What...I...What? I told you I'm from Homeplanet. And what does that have to do with..."

"I mean your people. Where are they from?"

"My people? What kind of question..."

"It gets hard to constantly code switch, doesn't it?"

"What are you talking about?"

"The need to hide that old Southern Black lineage. You try to keep it at bay, but it slips out when you're upset, doesn't it? No matter how hard you try, you can't hide it. You're so afraid they'll read that Southern Black trash ancestry all over you, despite your pristinely pressed suit and 5,000-UIP-tender shoes." She stopped walking and turned to look at him.

How did she...How did she know anything about him?

"Because I was a lot like you. Back on Yellow Star, after the UN converged into the Coalition and abandoned the Earth. Back before I realized they had colonized the whole god-damn universe. I was born after the great escape and eighteen years old when I fought them. I didn't know who I was before that but had to put on my fucking britches and make hard decisions."

"I've read about that time in history. But it has nothing to do with me. You're deflecting. You don't want to answer my question about the glee you get from stirring shit everywhere you go. You know nothing about me. And for the record, I want to find my people if they are alive. And I code switch because that's how I survive this *massive coalition of oligarchs*. Got it?"

She sucked her teeth, and walked in silence to their destination. Before entering, Mary turned to him: "He had raped a woman earlier in the day as they all watched. A sex worker. Do you understand? That's why they were so full of spite and venom. That's why they thought they could beat the world. That's why I broke his face."

"A *goods* trader? How do you know this?"

"I know things. The things I know is why Mother Amadeus sent for me."

"What could possibly... What type of work does Mother Amadeus Dun do for the church?"

"Exorcisms."

David blinked, spoke slowly, "What did you whisper to him?"

"What I said to that man is between him and his maker."

CHAPTER 2: Mary

Kepler's most successful accomplishment had been that it found a host of worlds orbiting safe distances from their stars in habitable zones. Unlike other Kepler worlds in this system, such as K2-155d, K283c was not an outlaw planet. It was lush with vegetation, and the air was nontoxic and tolerable, if not pleasant. There was an emerald tint about the land that foretold amazing possibilities, and lovely fantasies. This was surely to be a planet reserved for the wealthiest, the elite of the elite. But there was a major problem.

The monsters.

And Mary, Queen of Wagons, understood monsters. After all, she had been considered one of the most treacherous ones to slither the lands of Yellow Star. The large woman was ushered into a large meeting room; the expensive amplifier broadcasting the UIP message was louder and clearer here than it had been on K2-155d. David moved silently behind her, stopping just at the closed door, at ease. The room was big, but Mary's presence was greater. Everyone in the room feared her. She liked it that way.

A white man in an unnecessarily gaudy suit sat behind a large, lovely wood desk. Mary knew many Yellow Star tree breeds, but this one was unknown to her, so it was likely a local species. The inner diameter growth rings displayed patterns she hadn't seen before; it was magnificent—appropriately conveying both power and status for its owner.

She hated him immediately.

Mary recognized the woman standing behind the *throned* man, so she ignored him and walked over to her longtime friend, grabbing the woman's hands.

"Mother Amadeus Dun, as I live and breathe. Ma'am, how the hell are you?"

"Mary, my love. It is so good to see you." The woman noticeably darted her eyes at the man in the unknown animal-skin chair. "I'm sorry it's under such *difficult* conditions." Mary unhanded the woman and stood to her full height, awaiting her introduction. "Okay, Mary, I want to introduce you to William Enol Wylie, the *Baron* of K283c territory." The white woman put her hand lightly on Mary's back to guide her to shake the man's hand. Mary didn't make this easy, finally sucking her teeth, and extending her hand, which she squeezed between her large fingers, tightly. In the back of the room, David smirked loudly.

"Very nice to meet you, Ms. Wagons. It's an absolute pleasure." The man flashed every tooth in his mouth—they were white and straight. The Baron was the first to release, noticeably shaking his hand, as if in pain.

He was a shyster. Mary read him right away, and she smiled politely. "My pleasure."

"You have a strong grip, Ms. Wagons. I like that. I trust your trip was uneventful."

She stole a glance back at David, gracing him with her signature wink. "Well, Baron, travels can be difficult in these times."

"That they can, ma'am, that they can." He motioned for her to take one of the seats in front of him. "First, I want to thank you for coming. I know you have...history...with UIP."

"I do not, sir. I was unaware of the existence of UIP until Mr. Wálé here told me of them."

"I see." The man looked to Mother Amadeus. "I was made to believe that..."

"I do take grievance with the *legacy* of your coalition, sir. I do not condone the actions taken against the peoples within your purview. UIP's arms reach far. And they are unnecessarily vicious."

"I understand your concern completely. Let me assure you that UIP is not the same organization," he offered, despite the overhead speakers in the background belying his words. "And as a humble UIP delegate, I have authorization to give you anything you want in exchange for your help in this sensitive *situation*. And, personally, I want to give you a heartfelt apology for the actions of the past Coalition and, while I cannot change the past, I offer the assurances that we have learned from our mistakes. You are our first priority. Spared no expense, of course."

Mary smirked. "Not many people can reference those old one-liners so easily."

"UIP has done a remarkable job of preserving *worthy* historical and cultural artifacts."

The Black woman looked to the nun, studying her face. After finding what was she was looking for, Mary shrugged. "That sounds a lot like the old fucking Coalition. But what's the *situation* you find yourselves in?"

The man pushed a button on his desk, and a loud buzzing sound rang throughout the room. Within moments, the large ten-foot-high double doors to the right swung opened and two men entered dragging something wrapped in a large, heavy tarp. The men, both large and clearly stronger than most human males, struggled to handle the load within. Finally, they dropped it, with a thud, to the furred carpet in the ample space just beside the desk. The men saluted then stood, at ease. The Baron nodded toward the bag and one of the soldiers unzipped the tarp.

A foul stench filled the space, followed closely by the sound of one of the limbs of the creature tumbling out. The appendage was massive, at least six foot long with hooked claws extending from thick, black, leathery skin. Mary stood to her feet to examine the creature. Careful not to touch it, she bent to half her height, her face uncomfortably close to the creature.

"*This one* has six limbs," one of the soldiers warned her.

The woman stood full height, meeting the soldier in the eyes. "*This one*? Fuck say?"

The man glanced around the room, first at the Baron, the nun, David and then back at Mary. "They're all different, some hundreds of times this size, some not even half. Some fly, some sneak in from underground. These are drones. The others are called the Brains. They're different than these, ma'am. The Brains are smart and seem to connect...*psychically*."

"I see." Mary was clearly intrigued. "Drones?"

"Workers who don't seem to have original thoughts, but instead follow some preset orders from the Brains. They are always connected and updating. There's a lot we don't know."

Mary bent down again, this time laying her hand on the creature, connecting with the scaly skin. Instantly, a bright light expelled from between the two beings, throwing Mary backward, and causing her to skid unnaturally across the floor of the office, ending at David's feet. The man helped her up.

"We've never seen it do that before." The soldier seemed concerned.

The Baron jumped up and ordered the soldiers out the room. They obeyed, and the door shut just as Mary had gotten to her feet again. The two companions shared a look before Mary stormed back to the desk, her footfalls heavy, angry.

The Baron held out his hands. "Wait! Don't get angry, Ms. Wagons..."

Before he finished, Mary was on him, towering over the man by almost a foot. At his full height, the Baron was five feet two. "You're keeping secrets, Baron."

The nun walked between Mary and the smaller man. "Yes, Mary. There are things we need to tell you."

"Then tell me." The Black woman gathered herself and made a show of walking back to her seat, picking up her hat—which had fallen in the commotion—and lowering herself slowly to the chair.

The Baron was clearly afraid, but Mary didn't know if he feared her or the monsters more. "They...they have psychic abilities. They can connect through some form of telepathy, so they are always ahead of us, always knowing what we intend to do."

"Go on."

He went to the creature, kicked it. "But Soldier Williams was right. The drones like these are somehow sent orders. The Brains are smart, very smart. Listen, the subordinate alien species here, the locals, are closer in size to people and not a problem. They are subservient and docile."

Mary stopped him with a finger. "Subordinate, subservient and docile are much better words than enslavement, but I suspect there's not much difference in their meanings in this case, am I right?"

"That's not at all what I mean. UIP's policy does not promote slavery. What I meant is that they are protected by these creatures."

"Of course, they don't. What do you mean by protected?"

"I mean to say that we cannot connect with the beings of this planet, can't barter or negotiate in any way because these creatures will not allow us access to them. It's like they're gods or something... That's it, old Greek gods. That's pretty much what they are... So, I mean to say..."

"Oh, I know what you mean, Baron. What do you want from me?"

"We want you to train the men."

"Anyone can train men." She sucked her teeth and crossed one leg over the other as if she was offended.

"Not like you. UIP soldiers study your... rebellion. They respect you." The man paused. "Large groups of my men have just gone missing in the night, straight from their barracks without anyone seeing a thing. They just get up, walk out of their bunks and disappear. In battle, these creatures are fast and make decisions before we can even react, as if they know exactly what we plan to do. There is something *wrong* about these creatures."

He went to the door. "Come with me, please."

The group followed him through the doors that the soldiers had previously used, down a well-lit corridor to a Tach conveyor that took them a few thousand miles away to a war zone. This area of the world was not officially in the No Zone, where the monsters were believed to originate, but still UIP struggled to maintain control.

Mary, Sister Dun, David and the Baron watched from an observation window as UIP soldiers fought a losing battle against a stronger, more effective army of what could only be called *monsters*. It was initially difficult to understand what she was seeing as smoke from the gunfire was heavy. From this distance, the thousands of gunshots dotting the sky looked like small rays of light. As the smoke shifted in the wind, it revealed winged and larger land-bodied creatures dominating the landscape. The soldiers' bullets had little effect on the creatures. The gas-powered tank rounds struck armored-plated flesh with little impact. Under the emerald sky, the men took cover using the natural landscape and crevices in the valley, but the winged creatures swooped down and grabbed the men, discarding the bodies into the distance.

"We were using armor piecing, but had to switch to APDSFS, sixth gen." The Baron shook his head. "Nothing works."

The scene was brutal, and it was clear that UIP could not win. After what seemed like an incredibly long time, the soldiers managed to take down an extremely large creature, taking a defensive position around the body and emptying their clips, quickly taking cover again. The massive creature stood at least seven feet tall on all fours. It closely resembled an elephant from Earth, but in place of tusk and a trunk, there were three long, protruding horns. Suddenly, the creature spasmed; its limbs convulsed, shaking wildly, as it expelled a bright emerald ray of light. And just as quickly, it dissolved into sand of K283c.

"That's a Brain. They only have temporary corporeal forms, but they possess the power to materialize a short-lived physical body. But when the body is injured beyond repair—because they can also repair themselves quickly—it disappears for an indeterminate time we don't know, then they regenerate a new one and reappear. I fear we may lose this colony."

Mary wondered: "So they disappear? Where do they go?"

"The best we can tell is that they renew and come back again and again. That's why we can't beat them. They have a never-ending supply of soldier bodies." The Baron looked to her. "So, we are prepared to give you absolute free rein to find the most *gifted* soldiers."

Finally, it all made sense. Finally, she understood why UIP would fly her all the way across the universe. *Use last century's enemy to fight this century's monster.*

Sister Amadeus stared at her, a slight smirk, which only Mary picked up on, spread across her face.

"You want me to train a psychic army?"

"The Baron lies." It had taken everything in her to hold it together to walk her big ass out of that place. "He's hiding something. Something big." She ranted as she paced the lush, emerald meadow the two found on their walk back to the suite.

"How do you know he's lying?"

"Haven't you figured out yet that I see things *deeper* than other people? That I know things." She stopped. "Like I know that you're career UIP, but you aren't stupid. And I can trust you. Otherwise, you'd be dead." David made an effort not to respond, but she knew he had been shaken by her words. "But the Baron's arrogant, and is planning to fuck me."

"Why?"

"What do you know about the *Battle of Yellow Star*?"

David had been formally educated through UIP universal instruction, and while he liked to think he wasn't a company man as she had accused and that he rejected much of UIP conditioning, still, he had to admit that he knew very little beyond the official UIP history of the Yellow Star battle. There was very little information to be found in historical archives.

"What everyone else knows, I suppose. That you had been traipsing the universe, from planet to planet, gathering soldiers, destroying worlds, even. I guess it could have been noble in some ways—so many of their policies of colonization were detrimental in those beginning days—but it seems like you just wanted to destroy the Coalition with no real plans on how to fix things." Mary didn't say anything, so he shrugged. "But it was half a century ago and before UIP had been established... You got all those people killed. You trained them, and they followed you across the universe just to drive a wagon into UIP capitol. Now, since you're alive, I guess you sent others to their death while you hid on Yellow Star."

"You little shit. Tell me, David, if advanced TachTravel has only been available for passenger and laymen travel for just over three decades, how was I using it forty-three years ago to move between worlds?"

The man didn't respond because he couldn't.

"Sit down, David." He did as he was told, the green moss representing what passed for grass on this planet sinking beneath his ass. "Evidence that UIP is full of shit and lying to me, is because everything they have taught you about me is also a lie. When the six greatest powers of the world got together to form the coalition for interstellar travel, they quickly decided that there were valuable people and there were *others*. Those people your government didn't think were worth saving, people like mine. My mother was Black and wheelchair bound and unworthy. They thought they were leaving us there to die. Once they destroyed the atmosphere, they abandoned the planet, leaving us there."

"I suspected."

"Years after leaving, they sent a scout and found that we were thriving. David, I never traveled the universe collecting and training soldiers. Because I never left Yellow Star. The Coalition, the organization that you call UIP, brought the fight to me. They sent six ships full of soldiers to subdue and recolonize whatever groups remained." She turned to find David appalled by her story.

"It's true that I used my spiritual energy to plan, execute, and stop the reinvasion of Yellow Star. Don't you understand? Many of us were minority *and gifted.* We were root workers, witches, and we carried historical knowledge passed down from our own ancestors. We serve great Gods on Earth now—as it always should have been. So, we used our collective power to protect ourselves and Yellow Star. My mother had lost her legs in the military, but she was also a witch and taught me everything she knew. I took what I learned from her, while I trained soldiers in the use of every firearm still available on that planet, just as my soldier father had taught me. I trained spiritual soldiers just as my mother and her and ancestral lineage had taught her. Once we had defeated every single man they sent to kill us, I used psychic interference to insure that no other UIP ship landed on Yellow Star. Now, my people and I both physically guard and psychically monitor all space surrounding Yellow Star.

"They knew this before they sent me?" She maintained eye contact with him but did not have to respond. He knew the answer; he was expendable. "How many ships have landed between the battle, over fifty years ago, and mine eight days ago?" He knew the answer to this also; none. "Then why did you allow mine to land? You knew I was coming? *But how?*" His last question could be best described as thinking out loud. He had so many questions, but Mary gave him time to work them out in his head. "Sister Amadeus. You've been in contact with her all these years."

"Yes. And no. I knew her fifty years ago. I have not been in constant contact with her."

"Then how?"

"Mother Amadeus is one of the original people to come back to Yellow Star forty years ago. The coalition had sent missionaries, mercenaries, and soldiers."

"But how? I thought you destroyed everyone, and no other ships were allowed."

"I said I killed every man, and no other ship landed. I never said none left. Mother Amadeus is one of three who boarded a ship a year later with the warning never to return. They sent other ships a few times, especially after TachTravel made it more efficient. But..."

"You destroyed them?"

"Yes."

"Then why not mine? If Mother Amadeus didn't warn you?"

"That's the question, isn't it? Here's a better one. Who are these monsters?"

David looked intrigued. "Can you, you know, find out?"

CHAPTER 3: Possibilities

Asking Mary that question was the equivalent of taking out an old-fashioned stick of dynamite and setting it ablaze. Thus, for Mary, "find out" meant traveling to the No Zone to find the monsters.

The No Zone was on the other side of the globe. K283c was twice the size of Earth and its year-round (ninety-two days) temperatures were around 20.5 degrees Celsius aided by terraforming. This side of the planet had less light from its main star and was noticeably darker, while the atmosphere was thicker and heavier. Deep red sands replaced the lush, mossy emerald grasses on this side of the world. The shadow of an emerald moon, about the size of Original Earth, held a permanent position in the sky, perfectly placed, as if suspended by string. Sandy mountains lined the horizon instead of magnificent glass structures that had been erected 32,186.88 kilometers away.

The Baron had done everything that he could to try to convince Mary not to come. But Mary had assured him that she wouldn't be alone since David would be accompanying her. The Baron aggressively tried to dissuade Mary, but she was rather persuasive in her own right and, since he had agreed to give her complete control over these matters, he finally relented. When the pair took their orders to check out the Tach conveyor that would get them to their destination in a fraction of the time, they were warned that no one had ever traveled to that part of the world alone and survived.

Mary told David to stay behind, to which he stood fast. "I've never lost anyone. And I won't start with you, Mary, Queen of Wagons."

The pair disembarked the conveyor onto a vast open land. As their feet touched the red, sandy dirt, the ground began to shift and move under their feet so that both lost their balance and struggled to maintain their standing positions. Under them, a large mound began to rise and David stumbled away to keep from being elevated high into the air. The conveyor slid backward picking up speed as the mound got higher and higher, finally coming to a stop nearly a full kilometer away. The height of the mound quickly passed Mary's six-foot-two height, reaching a full ten feet before the sand and earth completely fell away revealing a large tripod-looking creature.

David reached for his assault rifle, aiming swiftly at the creature's head.

Mary simply reached out her hand to stay her companion, touching his skin, bringing a calming sensation over him. Immediately his racing heart slowed down and he lowered his weapon. She needed him to remain calm. They didn't have the high ground, and it would be unwise to provoke an enemy of this size and unlimited strength. Besides, that was not what they were there for.

In a massive show of strength clearly intended to impress them, the terrain around David and Mary began to convulse and shake as if a massive quake from the center of K283c was imploding. One by one, giant creatures in various sizes and shapes and colors rose to the surface showing themselves to Mary and David. Hundreds. Thousands.

By this point, the pair could no longer visually see the monsters appearing but they could hear the ground being violently disrupted as each of these beings emerged from their cocoons. In the center, the two were dwarfed, almost invisible from the outside. Mary waited, respectfully. She sensed that this show of strength was intentional. A full minute after the last creature had made itself known somewhere kilometers away in the distance, Mary extended her hands in the universal surrender gesture and walked to the first creature that had presented themselves to her.

"No. Wait! What are you doing?" David looked around, clearly uncomfortable.

"Calm down. No aggression, remember. No matter what happens, do not use your weapon. Do you understand?"

David nodded. Mary continued forward. The creature itself shifted but did not make an attempt to hurt Mary. When she reached a distance close enough to touch the creature, Mary nodded her head for permission, waited, then placed her dark hand on the flesh of the black creature.

Instantly, Mary was transported into another realm. As a spiritualist Mary understood what had happened, though it was always discombobulating to move through spiritual worlds. This new place was similar in appearance to K283c but was vivid and splendidly bright. It was the place that existed in direct parallel to K283c and was the more perfect version of it.

Each of the untold number of creatures that had presented themselves to her in the other plane of existence now stood before her in their true personification. Their sizes, shapes and colors were only limited by Mary's imagination to perceive their greatness.

These were *not* monsters.

They were Gods!

Mary nodded, acknowledging their power and strength and maintained physical contact with the being. She knew the creature was her connection to this plane and that they had knowingly given her access. She showed an acceptable amount of gratitude without looking unnecessarily demure. The deities before her now brought her here, she was sure, because they also recognized the power within her.

On K283c, the human and *Gods* couldn't communicate well with each other. However, on the parallel plane, words were unnecessary; intent and actions were the only form of currency. These deities, like her own, from her own world, only respected honor. She spoke using visual images and emotion: "They call me Mary."

"We know who you are, Mary, Queen of Wagons. You exist either as a hero or a great enemy in the minds of the soldiers who have come here to exploit us."

"These men are not my kin. They committed genocide against my people, murdered my world, and then left us to die on it."

"We know. That's why we called to you. We had to meet the woman who inspired such emotions in people such as these."

Mary looked around at all the great beings before her, large and proud: "Are you the Gods of this land?"

If it was possible for a monster to cackle, then this one did. "We are the mothers, the sisters, the daughters, the guardians of the people of this land. But we hold no ownership over them; they are free beings. You know our ancestorial lineage through the deities of your land." The images reflected in Mary's mind had been calm, measured, but now they became loud and authoritative. "You know them by the names: *Anahit*, the mother of war; *Julunggul*, the rainbow serpent of life; *Hārītī*, both goddess and demon to her people; *Oya*, great mother of winds, lightning, storms, death, and rebirth."

Mary listened patiently as thousands of monsters, all speaking at once, called out names of fallen Yellow Star deities that had been forgotten and abandoned. Mary didn't know all the names, but she recognized at least one.

When they were finished, she spoke. "You named my mother."

"Yes. She thrives on your planet when others have died. To abandon a God is murder. To force others to worship one God to gain power is a crime akin to death against the universe. It spreads disease. The universe is vast and varied, just like the Gods that reflect the needs of the people in that universe. Colonization of spirituality that happened on your planet is a travesty. We are sorry that it happened to you. We will not allow this to happen here."

"What do you need from me? What can *I* do?"

"Your former oligarchs have a lot of money and a lot of power, but they lack spiritual intelligence. They're dead inside. No matter how many messages they pump into their heads or the false idols they worship."

"Yes. They value individuality but pride themselves on being the same. Their supremacy is their only legacy."

"They don't know who he is, you know." The images and messages moved rapidly through her mind.

"I know." She looked to David, who, in this space, appeared frozen, unmoving. "Tell me what to do."

Jesus wept.

He wept for Lazarus of the bible, but he did not weep for UIP that day. They had abandoned *His* teachings long ago. The last death knells of the dying oligarch pounded loudly in Mary's ears, drowning out that wretched continuous message: *I am a humble delegate of the honorable descendants of Abraham, and chosen to fulfill the holy mission of the United Interplanetary Coalition.*

She entered the Baron's office, covered in a shroud and carrying a staff. Mary appreciated the dramatics of the old storybooks, so she'd played it up, enjoying her performance perhaps a bit too much. David followed behind, always at the ready. A group of locals, their various skin tones belying their second-class status on K283c, followed behind them.

The man sat at his desk amused by the display, staring down his spectacled nose at Mary. Sister Amadeus again stood behind him, her expression different, but unreadable to anyone who didn't know her.

"What news do you bring?"

"I bring but one message, Baron."

"Well, out with it, then."

"Let the people of this land go, abandon your mission here, so that they may worship their own Gods in peace. If you refuse, I will plague every colony under your purview."

The Baron did not laugh, as she expected. He did not, for a moment, reflect any emotion at all. "And why would UIP do this?"

Mary turned to David. The soldier walked over, took her staff, and dropped it on the desk. As it landed, the stiff outer wood of the scepter shifted and changed form, becoming slithery, turning into a large cobra; the head rising quickly to full height. The Baron scrambled to get out of his seat, unamused. From a safe distance away, he ordered soldiers to handle the beast. One of the men quickly put a bullet in the snake.

"Seriously?" Finally, the man laughed. "What did you think would happen?"

"You have no faith, Baron."

"There is my faith, Mary, Queen of Wagons." The Baron paused and pointed to the speakers as the words... *and chosen to fulfill the holy mission of the United Interplanetary*... filled the silence. "My god, UIP, is stronger than yours. You have stupid biblical magic tricks and empty wagons."

Mary called over a little brown boy who placed a small box on the Baron's desk. The serpent dead and removed, the Baron returned to his seat, taking the box to his ear.

"It's a key. To the last Tach conveyor off this planet. Your soldiers have either been sent away or have chosen to stay."

"What UIP soldier in their right mind would choose to stay on this godforsaken planet?"

David stepped forward. "Me. All the lies UIP taught, the death, the threats and indoctrination."

"Fine. I will let them know you are an *apostate suppressive*, a chickenshit. You think they want a yellowbelly coward, a bastard who killed his mother during childbirth? Yes, we know all about you, David Wálé." The Baron found pleasure in vile words.

"The only cowards here are UIP. Besides"—she looked to David, and her expression softened—"he's my kin. He doesn't know it, but he's the son of the sister that UIP stole from us before abandoning Earth. Think about it, it's the only reason I would let a ship land on Yellow Star. The Gods here knew that." Mary looked quickly away from David so as not to get caught up in the feelings he didn't know how to express.

"Congratulations on this fucked up family reunion, but that's enough. Mary, why in this world would I ..." Before finishing, a young soldier burst in the doors, pausing only long enough to salute to Mary before handing the Baron an envelope. He opened it, read the contents, then looked past Mary, to the soldier, anger flashing in his eyes.

"As we speak there are 5,500 *wagons* rushing toward every major holy center on every major UIP-colonized world. They are manned by my will alone, and set to explode at my behest or if anyone tampers with them."

"Why?"

"Liberty. You colonize and destroy. And your god has abandoned you because you have despoiled his message. Is this"—she pointed to the amplifier—"your God, Baron? What purpose does He serve? And to whom?" The man did not respond. "Every God on every planet of my lineage and everyone on every planet in this galaxy stand before you today as testament.

"Let the people in all UIP territories go and offer them safe travels to this planet or any other protected one outside of UIP's reach."

"What if they don't want to go?"

"Harriett Tubman is said to have believed that she could have freed a thousand more slaves if they knew they were enslaved." She paused. "They will come when they are ready, or they will stay in bondage."

"UIP will never stand for this."

"Then let them sit for it!" Anger flashed in her eyes at the thought of all the harm UIP had done throughout the centuries. "You are lucky, Baron, that all we want is freedom from you. With one thought, I will wipe UIP from existence. Right now, I am controlling the trigger of every one of those 5,500 wagons. I did it with one wagon forty-three years ago, and I will do it with 5,500 more, or 10,000 more. Or a million. Do you not think that with the power of all my Gods, I cannot do much worse?"

"You would kill all those people just to get what you want?"

"It's worked for UIP all these centuries."

The wheels in the Baron's head were running but couldn't find a way to fix this.

"Be smart. Leave this place, Baron. Advise UIP to not be foolish in their retaliation of apostates and wipe clean your hands and your memories of us, for if you want war, we will oblige you. Do you understand?"

The man nodded in defeat, stood to his feet, and turned to Sister Amadeus. The nun didn't hesitate in her response. "I'm staying."

As he walked out the giant doors for the last time, Mary called out to him: "We will prepare for your *apostates*. Here, they will be known simply as citizens. And UIP is dead to us. Be content with that."

JASPER AND THE MARE

John E. Stith

The giant sun scorched the desert on Flagstaff, better known to offworlders as Western World. Nearly everything for kilometers was either dazzlingly bright, or hidden in small impenetrable shadows, with little in between. To Jasper Kroft, the view was a bit like looking up at one of Flagstaff's moons. Everything seemed to be either black or white.

The only two pleasures Jasper felt in that moment were the slight breeze and the trust in his sure-footed mare, Edwina.

Jasper straightened his spine and squeezed his thighs to stop next to Sam, Rufus, and Bobby, the rest of the posse. The air stilled. The desert instantly felt intensely hotter.

Bobby walked ahead to examine tracks. That the four of them were stopped and looking at tracks, rather than racing toward a dust cloud in the wake of Logan Tarin and his gang, was heavily discouraging. Maybe the other posse was having more luck.

Or maybe they were already dead, like the previous two teams.

Jasper made a clicking sound and let the reins touch the left side of Edwina's neck. Sometimes Edwina was moody, but she, too, could see the sliver of shade next to the nearby bluff.

The shade wasn't deep enough to cover them both, but at least the horse got a break. Jasper ruffled her sorrel mane to try to say, "Thanks. We'll quit as soon as we can."

The rest stop was over in just minutes. Bobby came back to the group and pointed to a narrow canyon mouth. Bobby was a young man with cold eyes and a hot temper. Truth be told, Jasper would almost prefer to be hunting Bobby rather than Logan Tarin and his gang. But only Logan's guys had actually robbed a bank and killed multiple pursuers. As far as Jasper knew.

Sam, their leader, cocked his head in the direction of the canyon mouth and urged his mount into motion. Rufus and Bobby fell in behind Sam.

Jasper said softly to Edwina, "Come on, girl. Looks like we're not done yet." He squeezed his calves and the horse moved out. Together, they pulled into the rear of the diamond formation.

This was new territory to Jasper. They were hours out of Comstock, kilometers from resupply.

Another halt. Once more, Bobby went ahead to check the trail, and once again, the four posse members were on their way. The canyon mouth was close enough that they rode single file. Jasper fell in behind Rufus.

Jasper's feeling of unease grew as the canyon walls rose on either side. He was well aware of the wisdom that said you could tell a gelding where to go, ask a stallion, and negotiate with a mare, but Edwina pressed ahead without complaint. Jasper thought he could feel the nervousness in the tough, wiry animal. Then again, maybe that was in him.

The canyon walls steepened. The way ahead grew narrower, the canyon bed a mix of powdery dust and occasional rocks and boulders.

Jasper kept glancing back to make sure Logan's gang wasn't following them. The sides of the canyon grew higher.

His breath started to come easier when the canyon twisted slightly, and he could see the gap between walls widened ahead.

The relief was short-lived.

Edwina's head lifted. For a fraction of a second, Jasper's head felt as if he were underwater.

Pressure mounted on his face and chest. And then came the deep rumbling of a dynamite explosion. Rocks, then boulders started tumbling down the canyon walls.

Edwina was in motion even before Jasper could say a word or nudge a rib. She reared, backed away, and tried to turn.

A second later, Jasper and Edwina were headed back out of the canyon. But it was too late. A rock the size of Jasper's fist hit one of his shoulders. The top of Jasper's head might have been stoved in, but his hat crumpled and turned a deadly blow into a hideously strong impact.

Edwina tipped sideways as a rock bigger than Jasper's head hit her neck. Behind them, the deluge of rocks thundered even louder. The rest of the posse was lost in the crushing fall of rocks and boulders. Dust billowed past.

Jasper arched his back in pain as another stone hit his shoulder blade. Edwina surged forward.

This time, a rock *did* hit Jasper in the side of the head.

Sometime later, Jasper surfaced from a dream in which Logan Tarin's gang set off dynamite to bring the canyon walls tumbling down on the posse. Slowly, Jasper realized he wasn't dreaming; he was actually lying in that rockfall.

A sharp rock bit into his back. A dull pain came from one knee.

For the very first time, Jasper regretted settling on Flagstaff. Everyone who came here voluntarily left behind the seduction of automation and self-repairing bodies. But they carried too much baggage with them. Like Logan and Bobby. The wide-open spaces here were littered with human vices. As the prophet once said, "No matter where you go, there you are."

After a few seconds or a couple of minutes, he blinked and wiped blood from his eyes so he could see again. An enormous landslide filled the nearby canyon floor. Only he and Edwina had avoided being crushed and buried.

But even that bit of good news had its limits.

Jasper couldn't feel his right leg. It was pinned under a rock he'd never lift on his own.

And Edwina was hurt. The mare was on her side, one leg bent at an impossible angle.

For a second he was oblivious to his own pains. "I'm real sorry, girl."

He haltingly reached for his Colt Walker replica so he could at least put Edwina out of her misery. Then he'd have to decide on a bullet for himself.

But before he could even get the barrel lined up on Edwina, a metallic voice sounded from near the horse's head.

"Hold up there, Jasper. Don't do anything rash."

Jasper froze. "Who said that?"

"Just put the pistol away."

Utterly baffled, Jasper did so. Nothing was making any sense. He must have really been hit hard in the head.

Edwina struggled to right herself. She flopped back onto the rocks and dirt, like a foal trying to walk for the first time.

She tried again. This time she was able to get to her feet. The right foreleg jutted out at an unnatural angle.

"That's better," said the voice. It seemed to come from Edwina.

"Who's here?" Jasper asked.

"Just me. The one you call Edwina."

Jasper was dumbstruck. "You—ah—since when do horses talk?"

"I'm not a horse. I'm an Antaleon."

"Are you saying this is heaven?"

"No, you foolish human. I'm an alien."

Jasper looked wildly around to see where the voice was really coming from. No one was there except for him and Edwina.

Jasper made the mistake of shaking his head.

When the pain subsided and he could see again, something was different.

"Your leg," he said, "Your leg is changing. Is it—"

"I'm making repairs."

"Repairs?"

"You are still dazed."

"No. My head feels pretty clear. But you don't make sense."

The mare's leg almost looked normal now.

"Look, Jasper. You were pretty decent to me. So I'll explain."

"Explain what?"

"Stop talking. I'll tell you."

"Who is this really?"

"Just listen. I'm an Antaleon. That's an alien, to you. My name would just be gibberish, so let's skip that."

"An alien."

"Not from the Earth or even Flagstaff. From the stars even farther from Earth than you are now. We are extremely long-lived beings. But we are not immune to boredom. Some of us have developed a fondness for inhabiting your animal bodies."

"This is not making sense."

"I can stop now."

Jasper hesitated. "No. Go on."

"This is a way we can experience rare emotions. Excitement. Fear. Lust."

"Lust?"

A sound that might have been laughter. "Not for you humans. Do not flatter yourself." Edwina put weight on the leg that just moments ago had been twisted out of line. The leg held.

Jasper gritted his teeth. "I don't suppose you can get this rock off my leg?"

"Sorry. I am telling you this only because you do not have long to live. And because you treated me well."

"I just did what any decent man would have."

"I like you, Jasper. You are modest and kind. But you're wrong. Not all men are like you." Edwina took a couple of steps forward and then back. The leg appeared to be completely normal. "Oh, that feels better."

"How is this possible—"

"Shhh." Edwina's head rose as she listened to distant sounds.

"What do you hear?"

"Humans and horses. Maybe the other posse."

Jasper felt a rush of relief he hadn't expected to feel. Surely a couple of men could lever the rock off his leg.

"I'm sorry, Jasper," Edwina said.

"Sorry? This is good news."

"You've been a good companion. A decent human. But I can't let you share our little secret."

Jasper had a sudden insight. "I ain't gonna tell—"

"This is difficult for me, but I'm going to have to put you down."

Jasper reached for his pistol, but before he could touch it, Edwina's horseshoed hoof hit the side of his head. Hard.

SUPPORT YOUR LOCAL AUDIT CHIEF

D.J. Butler

Arrowhawk Post crouched on the frontier of the Company's operations on Sarovar Alpha, and you couldn't be too careful. Law enforcement essentially didn't exist, beyond the scarce resources of Company security. Company employees got rowdy from time to time, as did the country-setties, and even the inhuman Weavers.

John sat at the back of the chapel and stayed awake.

Technically, the building might not be a chapel. It was a long, rectangular, single room with a high ceiling and tall, narrow windows. At one end, the floor rose slightly and held a pulpit. The long part of the room was full of folding printed chairs in neat rows. The people occupying the chairs were a mixed group that included some Company employees, some Post residents who ran or worked in the local businesses, and some people from the surrounding villages—country-setties from the nyoots, as one would say in Sedjem, the trade patois of Sarovar Alpha.

Ruth always referred to the building as the "Unity Hall." She'd built it, with volunteer labor and printed components shipped by maglev from Henry Hudson Post. The Unity Hall was ten minutes' walk from John's khat, his Company-owned residence, near the stockade walls of Arrowhawk Post. Church services were held here, and social events. No priest had ever blessed it, as far as John understood.

Ruth stood at the pulpit, preaching. She was tall and slender without sacrificing any femininity. Her face had high-boned features and was framed in dark red hair. She wore a bright green dress she had brought from Earth. The ubiquity of the Company's colors had pushed her into a revolt against buff and, in particular, blue; she decorated the house and dressed herself and the girls in every conceivable color but those two.

Ruth preached most weeks. She was technically not a priest, since of course the driving force of the creation of the United Congregations had been the desire of the various constituent movements—the Traditionalist Anglicans, the Right Catholics, the Remnant LDS, and the others—to strip progressive politics and secular ideas of social justice out of their various forms of Christianity, getting back to something closer to a primitive gospel. That meant that the Unity Church didn't ordain women, for instance. So Ruth was technically not a priest and wouldn't become one, because she was committed U.C., from the Catholic side. Someday, when this congregation really got officially organized, she'd be the chair of the Parish Committee, or something like that—John was a little fuzzy on all things churchly—but for now, she ran the show. If Arrowhawk Post could be said to have a clergyman, she was it.

And therefore John stayed studiously awake through the sermon.

Their two daughters sat up front with Nermer, a retired militiaman who was the family's live-in security staff. Nermer was local to Sarovar Alpha, a proud country-setty with deeply tanned skin and curly white hair who insisted on bringing his heavy staff into the chapel with him. Other congregants included Faisal, a local man of all jobs who sometimes worked for John, and who wore a tunic and trousers the color of faded roses. Faisal carried his pink frilly parasol, possibly because he regarded it as a formal fashion accessory. John also saw several country-setties he recognized, men and women who lived in the nearby village of Nyoot Abedjoo.

Ruth was casting a wide net.

John sat at the back because he volunteered as the usher. He may have been fuzzy on churchly things, but he knew enough to open the door for people when they came and went. He wore his nicest jacket—Company blue and buff—the crisp wool one for formal occasions. In his right pocket, he carried his energy pistol, and in his left, three spare cells.

He wasn't expecting trouble, but Arrowhawk Post was at the end of the maglev line. It was surrounded by wilderness, and trouble happened from time to time. He regularly carried a weapon—so did Ruth—and volunteering to act as usher also meant he was volunteering to act as security. John was no soldier, he was an accountant. He was audit chief of the post, in fact, youngest ever audit chief in a Company post. But he'd grown up in a family of soldiers, and he knew how to shoot.

Ruth said something about slaves getting stabbed in the earlobe with a spear. John had a hard time following, but it seemed like maybe it was a good thing that they were stabbed, and they even wanted it, and everybody should want to get stabbed in the ear. This sort of story was why the Bible had never really resonated with John. He frowned and leaned forward, bending the fingers of his hands back to touch his own wrists, one hand and then the other. One day his Marfan's Syndrome might kill him, but in the meantime, it gave him very flexible joints.

The door rattled hard.

Not a knock. Something had banged against the door.

This was an opportunity. John stood, straightened his tie, and slipped outside. He didn't reach into his jacket pocket, but he kept his hands near his waist, where he could quickly grab his weapon if he needed to.

The sun shone brightly. It was late summer, and one of the planet's two moons rode high in the sky, chasing out ahead of the late morning sun. A gravel street lay a few steps away. On the far side of the gravel stood buildings: a warehouse, a carpenter's shop, a two-story building with four families living in it. Children played with stick figures at the edge of the gravel, and an old man in an undyed tunic slept in a patch of grass against the warehouse wall.

Two men stood on the porch. One leaned back and stared up at the printed cross at the peak of the façade. He had a round face and chapped skin, and his hands seemed twice as big as they should be. The second rested with his hands on his knees, vomiting off the deck into the grass.

They both wore Company-buff cowboy hats and boots, flannel shirts, and Company-blue denim jeans. Company cowboys. John had never seen them before, but he knew that the Company ran herds of cattle in the region. And he knew one of those herds was expected to arrive at Arrowhawk Post today.

John closed the door behind him.

"Hey, fellas," John said. "Fellas" wasn't a natural word in his mouth, but the sight of the cowboy hats drew it out of him. "You must be here with the cattle drive."

"Hot damn, they's got a lady preacher!" A third cowboy staggered around the side of the hall into view. He was thin and bent and had a face like a wedge of white cheese. "You can see her through the window, she's a redhead. Looks like a juicy apple, I tell you, and I jest want to take a bite!"

"She is a preacher," John said. "And this is a church. So if you fellas are looking for a drink, this is the wrong spot. There's a bar called the Commissar's Daughter, down closer to Company House. It won't be open this early, but you can get drinks there tonight. There's also a general store right across from Company House, you can get hanket there right now, unless he's out of stock." Hanket was the Sedjem word for any alcohol, and especially local beer. "Off-world beer too, if you're willing to pay enough."

The vomiting cowboy stood. He was a big-chested man, a little short, with bowlegs. "How's the preacher even know when to have church?" he asked, heavy brows furrowing. "What is it, day seventeen today? I didn't think there *were* Sundays on Sarovar Alpha."

"There didn't use to be," John agreed affably. "There are now. At least in Arrowhawk Post."

"If you got Sundays and churches," the vomiter said, "maybe you got everything else a nice civilized town ought to have."

"Oh, I think civilization is about forty light-years away," John said. "But you can get a decent meal here. You like Indian food?"

The bowlegged cowboy's nostrils flared. "What about a, uh... house of ill repute?"

John shook his head. "I'm afraid the nearest lawyer's in Henry Hudson Post."

The cowboy spat. "That ain't what I meant."

"I know," John said. "Listen, go buy a beer when you're off work, and maybe you'll be lucky, and there'll be an unattached woman at the bar who will look kindly on you. But if you're looking for a brothel, this just isn't the place."

Heavy Forehead squinted at John. "I know you."

"I don't think we've met." John extended a hand and grinned.

"From my multitool," Heavy Forehead said. "You're the audit chief here. Bishop."

Now that he was audit chief, his picture and a short profile were accessible by any reasonably senior Company employee with a multi. "Abbott," John said.

"That's it. I'm supposed to meet with you. Name's Hatcher. I've got to turn twenty head over to you."

They shook hands. "Hatcher. What does that make you, ranch chief or something? Herd chief?"

"Trail boss," Hatcher said. "Or ames-setty, if you're from one of the nyoots."

"'Ames' is a cow?" John asked.

Hatcher nodded and spat in the grass.

"I Sedjem my share," John said, "but I can go with 'trail boss.'"

The other two cowboys had gone back around the side of the building. John didn't love the thought of them ogling his wife through the church windows, but the building only had the one door, and John was standing in it.

"So it's Sunday," Hatcher said. "You telling me I gotta wait until tomorrow to talk shop with you?"

John shook his head. "I'll be in my office in a couple of hours. Come by Company House, and I'll look at the herd with you. Or just call me. My contact details are all on that profile page."

Hatcher nodded. "You got a pen set up?"

"Inside, against the stockade wall." John pointed. "We have a country-setty butcher who will pretty quickly convert the animals into tasty steaks, so we don't have to hold them long."

Hatcher nodded and spat again. "I expect I'd better take a look at that before we drive twenty cows into it." He stalked around to the edge of the building and whistled. "Ortiz! Payton!"

The two emerged, chuckling and scratching themselves, and then all three men turned and disappeared into the tangle of buildings that made up Arrowhawk Post. John stood on the porch and watched them go. He heard Ruth through the door, still urging her small congregation to allow themselves to be impaled with spears. He heard the sounds of feet crunching on gravel, and the babble of voices in the Post.

Somewhere, from the other side of the plastic stockade walls, he thought he heard the lowing of cattle.

Looking down the gravel street, he saw other buff cowboy hats. It was not a common style of headgear in Arrowhawk Post. The Company colors wrapping every cowpoke identically

jarred with every image John had of cowboys from every Western flick he'd ever seen, but the Company did love uniforms.
Maybe on their days off, the cowboys broke ranks and dressed
in different colors. Or, if the Company-issued uniforms were
free, maybe not.

The door behind John swung open.

"Dad-setty," Sunitha said. "You missed the end."

"I didn't," John said. "I want to have a spear driven through
my ear."

"Yes," Sunitha said. "But why?"

"Ah," John said. "This is the part we all have to contemplate
in our hearts."

"You'd better have a stronger answer than that before you
talk to Mom," Sunitha said. "She'll know you're lying."

"Mom will not ask me what the sermon was about," John
said. "She already knows. Mom will be happy that I came, and
watched the door."

It took Ruth fifteen minutes to work her way through the
parishioners who wanted to compliment her on her sermon, ask
about the date and time of the coming week's service activity,
or tell her about shut-ins and invalids who needed visiting. Ruth
listened patiently to them all and finally locked up.

John stood on the gravel beside the porch; his two daughters,
even with thirty centimeters of extra height from the deck, were
short beside him. "Ani wants us to come home," Ellie told her
mother plaintively.

"The dog isn't telepathic, and neither are you," John said.
"Ani is fine. She's probably having a nice nap in our absence."

Ellie harrumphed.

"Good job," John told his wife.

She kissed him and stepped down off the deck. "Did I see
you talking to cowboys on the front porch?"

They headed for their khat. Nermer followed two steps behind
them, his staff thudding on the gravel. John didn't like the social
implications of Nermer walking behind them and had argued
with Nermer over it many times, but Nermer insisted that being
behind the family gave him a better view of the tactical space
and refused to budge.

"They're moving one of the Company herds past Arrowhawk,"

John said. "Staying here tonight, I suppose, because they can buy supplies. Maybe so the cowboys can let off steam."

"You mean, not sleep alone in the wilderness?" Ruth asked. "In their lonesome cowboy bedrolls, singing songs of *señoritas* far away?"

John chuckled. "These are the mysteries of cowboys to which I am not privy. Anyway, they're here, and they're supposed to give the post twenty head of cattle."

"'Head of cattle,'" Ruth said. "You sound like a real cowpoke."

"Twenty cows," John said.

"Amesoo," Sunitha told him.

"Correct," he agreed. "The trail boss told me the country-setties call the cowboys ames-setties."

Ellie wrinkled her nose. "Trail boss."

"So you're going to go count the cows," Ruth said, "because no one else in the post knows how to count to twenty."

"Technically, they're inventory," John said, "which makes them my responsibility. But also, we're just short-handed. Sam will help me, and I've hired Faisal for a couple of hours' work. Not sure how much there is to do, exactly."

"Your private investigator is going to help you herd cows?" Ruth laughed.

"He has many talents."

They had reached the khat and, now, Nermer moved ahead of the family. He unlocked and opened the gate. Inside, the two-story house made of printed plastic slabs textured to look like stone waited. Beyond the house, against the back fence, was the little shed that had been converted into living quarters for Nermer. Ani, the family dog, rose from a golden heap on the porch and loped forward to meet the girls.

"I'll be back as soon as I can," John said.

He didn't bother changing, despite the formality of his clothing. Was it a mistake? He'd be around cattle, but he didn't plan to brand them or ride them or herd them, just show Hatcher and his men where to put them, count them to make sure there were twenty, and note them in the Post's financial records.

He could do that without getting dirty.

Company House was the tallest building in the post, and had the maglev station on its top floor. It was gray, bland and utilitarian. John waved at Payne, the Company security officer on duty on the ground floor and climbed to his office.

Company House was quiet. That wasn't because Ruth had decreed this day to be Sunday—not one of the Company's traders was a member of her congregation. But the post had lost several of its traders recently, as well as all its accountants other than John. The people who remained seemed mostly to be out of the building.

Sam Chen sat in one of the unused chairs in Audit, looking very casual in a trader's blue-and-buff field jacket. Sam grinned his nearly horizontal smile at John and ran a finger through his bushy hair. "Where are these cows, then?"

"Thanks for helping," John said. "New trader like you, I know you need to be out there developing business."

"I got plenty of wats cooking," Sam said. A "wat" was a trade meeting with the indigenous population, a radially symmetric species that resembled giant three-sided crabs. "I only got one audit chief, and he needs help."

"Also, you like steak," John said.

"It is the mark of a true trader. An audit chief like you can eat lamb vindaloo and skewered chicken. I need red meat."

"There will be rib eyes," John said. "I have not seen the cows yet, but I have seen the cowboys."

"So have I," Sam said. "They look sort of ridiculous in Company colors."

John grunted his agreement.

"Distracts from the fact that they're ugly bastards, though." Hatcher stood in the door to the Audit office, eyeing the stacks of folders and ledgers skeptically. "Come on, I got your cows downstairs."

"All I'm saying," John said as he and Sam followed Hatcher down the stairs, "is you ought to have a kerchief or a bandana or something. I was reliably informed that you would have bandanas."

"I have two in my pockets right now." Hatched chuckled and produced two squares of fabric; one was blue, and the other buff, and both had the Company logo embroidered in a corner.

"I'm glad they give you a choice," Sam said.

"I can get a bandana in any color I want," Hatcher said. "But if it ain't in the Company colors, I gotta pay for it myself. I notice you guys are in uniform."

They exited Company House and turned toward the corral, just a few paces away.

"Saving all my sars to invest," Sam said. "Gotta have capital to risk capital, and you gotta risk capital to get rich."

"Careful who you talk to about that," Hatcher warned the trader. "I can trade for my own account, but most of my men can't."

"They sore about it?" John asked. Company employees who were allowed to buy trade goods on Sarovar and ship them home to Earth for sale generally got rich. Employees who didn't have the perk worked hard jobs, sometimes for little pay, generally for the hope of one day being promoted and getting the right to trade.

"Sometimes," Hatcher said. "Sometimes they get tempted to steal. Sometimes they figure that they're entitled to more than they're getting, and it's their right to just take whatever it is they want."

"Keeping them in line must be hard," John said.

"I expect it's about the same as what you have to do," Hatcher shot back.

"I guess," John said. "So far, I don't have anyone reporting to me."

They reached the corral. It was made of printed slats, with perfectly sized joints that made the whole thing snap together like a child's educational toy. The slat-built fence surrounded the space on three sides, and the post's outer wall towered over them on the fourth. A trough of water ran through the middle of the enclosure, and a single opening lay tucked alongside the stockade wall. Just beyond the corral's entrance was the stockade's gate, which sprawled open, as it generally did.

Faisal stood at the corral gate, holding it open. His rose-colored clothing had been replaced by a brown tunic and trousers and short leather boots, and he stood with half a dozen country-setties in similar clothing. Two of the country-setties held what looked like pockmarked rocks, the size of human heads.

Faisal nodded at John. "Mr. Abbott." It was a formal greeting, because they were in public.

John nodded back. "Mr. Haddad." He greeted each of the country-setties in turn. Geeyasi, who did carpentry work during the growing season, when he didn't have to plant or sow. Aseem, who lived in a cave at the edge of Nyoot Abedjoo that he claimed was the first human residence in the village. Sadeek, who had twin baby girls that didn't sleep through the night yet. Wer, who had recently given up alcohol. He knew them because he saw them at church, because their children went to school together, and because he hired them whenever he could to do jobs for the Company.

"Your people know cattle?" Hatcher asked.

"The country-setties do," John said. "We'll butcher the meat soon enough. Where are your men?"

"Coming with the cattle." Hatcher put two fingers in his mouth and whistled three sharp blasts, a surprisingly loud sound.

Beyond the stockade wall, John heard the crack of a whip. He stood aside and watched, and soon a line of cattle drifted in through the stockade gate. Two cowboys on horseback and a pair of black-and-white dogs moved the line, bending its head to turn it away from the center of the post and in toward the corral. Country-setties joined in, whooping and slapping the cows' flanks, and in ten minutes, the cattle were inside the corral and the corral was shut. Their bodies packed the corral, but their smell seemed to fill the entire post. The cowboys leaned back in the saddle with their dogs sat beside them, falling silent and grinning proudly.

To John's surprise, the country-setties set the head-sized stones on the ground inside the corral, and the cows began to lick them.

"I count twenty," John said. "I guess that's our business done."

"I like a smooth transaction," Hatcher said.

"Those aren't Ortiz and Payton, though," John pointed out.

Hatcher shrugged. "They're probably with the rest of the herd outside the post. Or maybe they snuck off looking for that house of ill repute you told them wasn't here. Discipline gets a little weak around town, and those boys had already started drinking."

The dogs exploded into sudden barking. It took John a moment to register that the sound came from more than one direction, and then another moment to realize that some of the barking was familiar.

It was Ani. The family dog stood on all fours, pulling both her body and her ears back, with her tail low, and she barked at John. She was golden, the color of her summer coat, with white blotches on her chest and her ankles. The cowboys' dogs barked in answer.

"Ani," John said. "Shh. Ani, sit."

Ani kept barking.

"Sorry," John said.

"Dogs," the trail boss said. "You gotta love 'em, but not necessarily because they're smart."

"My wife says the same thing about me," John said.

Faisal knelt beside Ani. "She's disturbed, John. Look at the way the hair on her spine is standing up."

"I see it," John said. "She got out somehow, and it has her rattled. Fundamentally, she's still a nervous little rescue dog. Might be the cows spooking her. I'll take her home, and she'll calm down."

"Well, our business is done," Hatcher said again, "and I'll move the herd on tomorrow morning. Really just want to give my men a chance to take a shower and sleep in a bed."

John shook the trail boss's hand and headed home, Ani at his side. She continued to bark at him, adopting the same posture of alarm and warning: body stiff and pulled back, tail curled down, hair on her spine standing straight up.

"Okay, Ani," John said. "Okay, we're going home, everything's fine."

He waved to Faisal and the country-setties before he left; Faisal watched him with furrowed eyebrows and pursed lips.

Ani raced ahead of John the entire way home, stopping every time she'd got twenty or thirty meters ahead of him to turn and bark at him, demanding more speed. John picked up his pace, more to shut the dog up than anything else.

When he reached the family khat, he found the gate open. Nermer wasn't usually that careless. John examined the lock, to make certain that the mechanism hadn't failed—and found that it was gone. Melted, as if by the hot blast of a welder, or maybe an energy pistol set to narrow beam, and then ripped from the gate.

"Ani!" John called, but it was too late to restrain the dog. She slipped through the gate, her bark rising in volume.

John thumbed the Quick Contacts menu on his multitool, then dictated a short message to Faisal. *Home gate breached.* In theory, Payne at Company House had access to more firepower, but John wasn't sure Company security had a mandate to protect John's home, and he trusted Faisal to react faster.

John drew the energy pistol from his jacket pocket, checked

to be sure it was set to narrow beam and had a power cell in it—the cells in this old-model pistol only had enough power for a single shot—and headed in.

The dog's barking had probably drawn attention to the khat's enclosure, so John avoided the front gate. He jogged up the street and down a narrow alley that let behind his home. He'd entered this way once before, to sneak around a job-seeking mob when he had first come to Arrowhawk Post. He'd had Faisal's help then, but even without it, he was able to scramble up the wall behind the khat and lower himself on the roof of Nermer's hut.

Ani stood in the front yard. She barked at the door, pausing between barks to look behind her for John.

Maybe nothing had happened. Maybe some sort of accident had destroyed the front gate. But Ani was agitated, the lock was destroyed, and no one was coming out to see why the dog was barking. John had to assume that his family was in danger.

Or worse.

He dropped to the ground and crept toward the back door of the house. There was no porch here, as there was at the front of the building, but there was a door into the kitchen, and two steps that descended from the door to the flat gravel pad that would hold a groundcar or a truck, once John had saved the cash to buy one. Above the door was the large bathroom window with its yellow curtains pulled to the sides.

Pistol in hand, John moved toward the kitchen door.

The door opened, and the cowboy Ortiz stood in the doorway. His eyes were narrowed, and he held an energy pistol in his hand, at his side. He looked unfortunately sober.

John kept his own pistol low. "Come out of my house right now."

"How do you know I wasn't invited in?" Ortiz chuckled.

"My dog *likes* people who are invited in."

Where was Payton? He wasn't standing on the visible edge of the porch. Had John accidentally left the other cowboy at his back, by not checking Nermer's cottage?

"Just come on inside, chief," Ortiz said. "Slow and easy. Give me the gun. And I'll let you see your family. They ain't hurt." He grinned. "I ain't the kind of man to hurt a pretty woman."

"And Nermer?" John asked. "Our guard?"

"I did hurt him," Ortiz admitted. "But he'll live."

John's weapon and Ortiz's were both energy pistols. They gave a flash of light when they fired, but they were silent, so a gunfight might not attract any attention. The walls around the khat were solid, so no one casually passing by could see what was happening inside. They might hear yelling, but would they react? How long would it take Faisal to arrange help? Would he even see the message in time?

"Put your gun down, and I won't kill you." John felt the vein in his neck throb. "I might even testify to Internal Audit that you didn't mean to break the Code of Conduct, you're just a drunk idiot."

He took two slow steps forward. He tried to lean forward onto the balls of his feet, prepared to spring in any direction, without appearing to.

Ani's bark was more insistent.

"Not drunk anymore," Ortiz said. "Look, we're just going to have a little fun with your woman. You come in quiet, don't make a fuss, we won't hurt you. We'll be gone by tomorrow." He licked the corner of his mouth. "And we'll leave the little girls alone."

Blue flashed in the upstairs window.

John aimed and fired. The hot, barely visible beam of the energy pistol burned an instant hole in the plastic of the window and into Payton's chest. John saw a pistol in the cowboy's hand and a look of stupid surprise on his face as Payton sank backward, collapsing out of sight into the tub.

Ortiz punched John in the face with his own pistol. John staggered back and sank to the ground; more blows from the weapon struck him in the head and shoulders. He lost his grip on his own gun and couldn't see where it fell.

John's vision swam. He braced himself for a death blow but it didn't come, and then Ani's barking was abruptly much louder and closer.

"Get away from me, mutt!" Ortiz snarled.

John lurched to his feet, and Ortiz shoved him. Stumbling back, John saw Ani flinging herself on the cowboy, sinking her teeth into the tough material of his Company jacket. Ortiz tried to fling the dog away, but she clung tight, scrabbling at his thigh with her paws.

"I'm afraid I'm not going to let you see what I do with your wife," Ortiz growled. "But you can watch me shoot your dog."

"Stop!" The voice was Faisal's. "I will happily kill you, cowboy."

Faisal approached slowly. He held his pink parasol in front of him, close to his body like a hoplite's shield, and spinning. The parasol concealed Faisal's body from neck to knees.

Ortiz stepped back from John and turned slightly, to get both men into his field of view. John saw his own pistol now, a few meters to Ortiz's side. Reaching into the left pocket of his jacket, he gripped one of his spare power cells. How long would it take him to dive for the pistol and swap out the cell?

Was he better off trying to grab Ortiz's gun?

Ani dropped to the ground and retreated a step. She continued barking at Ortiz, the fur on her spine standing up in a discernible mohawk.

"You going to stab me with the umbrella?" Ortiz grunted.

"It's a parasol," Faisal said. "Umbrellas are for rain, this is to protect my complexion."

"I got five shots," Ortiz told him. "They're silent. I'm going to shoot the dog first, because it bit me. Then the audit chief. That's just on principle, because he's an accountant."

John edged toward his dropped weapon, just half a step.

"And I have to watch, and that's my punishment," Faisal said. "For being a country-setty, presumably."

"If you like," Ortiz said.

John eased forward another step. Was Ortiz distracted enough?

"Geeyasi and Wer are inside the house," Faisal told him. "Unless you have some other accomplice, Ruth and the girls are being freed as we speak. Aseem and Sadeek should be bringing your trail boss along any moment. I don't know your Code of Conduct very well, but I suspect your best move right now is to put away your pistol, admit what you've done, and maybe do a little time in a Company jail."

Ortiz raised his pistol to shoot Faisal.

John leaped for his weapon on the ground.

Bang! Bang! Bang!

A firearm cracked. John hit the ground on his belly, and then Ortiz fell backward over him. The cowboy's energy pistol went off harmlessly, firing into the clear sky, and then he dropped it and lay still.

Ani wasn't about to let the dead man off that easy; she bit his arm again and growled fiercely.

John picked up his pistol and stood. Just in case, he swapped in the fresh cell. Vertigo nearly knocked him down again, but even with swimming vision he saw Faisal fold up his parasol, revealing a pistol he'd been hiding behind it.

"Why the parasol?" John murmured.

"I thought if he saw the gun right away, he'd just shoot," Faisal said. "I hoped he'd surrender."

The kitchen door opened, and Ruth emerged with the two girls. She walked toward John with a measured, determined step, but the girls broke into a run. Ani raced in a circle around the three of them. She still barked, but the sound had lost its angry edge.

John put his pistol away and crouched, spreading his arms wide to hug the incoming girls. "I'm glad you were prepared for the possibility that he wouldn't," he said to Faisal.

"This is Arrowhawk Post," Faisal said. "You can't be too careful."

GRACE UNDER FIRE

Lezli Robyn

"I swear, on the light of the Sun's Twins, that our whisky—"

"Tastes like horse's piss." The deputy sheriff slammed the glass down on the bar. "Don't you try to convince me that this, this...swill is *not* watered down!" He slid the drink across the polished wood, amber liquid sloshing out of the glass onto the walnut counter as it came to rest in front of the barman.

As if in protest, a horse tied outside the Hawk 'n' Dove Saloon neighed. The barman bristled, leaning forward on thickly roped arms. "You dare accuse me of such an offence the first week I work in this establishment?"

A saloon girl with fiery curls and a crimson corset so tight her assets were all but spilling out of it, sidled up to the barman, draping her arm around him. He ignored the woman and the glass, and picked up the bottle, taking a swig before grimacing. "Curse it—you're right."

The deputy was mollified by the honesty. "'Tis not typical of Grace's fare. Not typical at all."

"That's because that particular dram wasn't meant for you."

Everyone turned to see the proprietor of the Hawk 'n' Dove Saloon enter from the private, curtained-off entrance in the dark recess of the bar. Tall and lean, with a strong jawline, Grace had her thick, silver-streaked black hair—unlike the saloon girls' loose tresses—twisted up into a proper topknot bun. Wearing the black of mourning, she cut a striking figure, with a cybernetic implant

145

visible along one brow line—and that was before you noticed the baton strapped around her corseted waist, or the regiment-grade boots she always wore under her voluminous skirts.

Grace made her way to the counter with an instinctive ease that reflected her name. When she reached out her hand to the barman, expectant, he hesitated a fraction of a second before placing the offending bottle into her firm grasp. Without pre-amble, she raised it to her nose and inhaled its muted aroma, then smiled. "As I suspected. This's the whiskey we prepare for Simple Simon."

"Simple *who*?" the barman questioned, while the rest of the establishment's patrons let out their collective breaths to chuckle or nod knowingly.

The deputy let out a loud guffaw, slapping his thigh! "That's right! I should have realized."

The barman, still none-the-wiser, shrugged off the attentions of the saloon girl trying to placate him, not sure if he had just become the butt of a joke. "Who's calling who simple?"

Grace turned her head in the direction of his voice. "I should have mentioned it earlier, Frank. Simon is Barber John's brother. He had a traumatic brain injury about five years ago, following a fall off a horse. The doc did everything he could, but ever since then—"

"Well, he's just not all there, you see," the deputy interjected, raising his hand to tap his fingers on the side of his head. "He lost just enough of his marbles to not *know* he's lost 'em, if you gets my drift."

"That doesn't explain the whiskey," the barman pointed out.

"Actually, it does." Grace's eyes shadowed. "This bottle is only for Simon's consumption." She moved behind the counter, and without even looking pulled out an almost identical bottle of whiskey, placing it beside the other. "*This* bottle is for the rest of the patrons."

"You see, Simon copes best with his impairments if he's not confronted with the knowledge of how diminished he is now," the deputy added.

Grace nodded curtly. "Like everyone else, after a hard day's work, he just wants a drink or two to wash away the toils of the day. Unlike everyone else, however, he no longer has the impulse control to know when to stop. His brain don't quite work right.

So instead of continuing to serve him drinks that would put a healthy man under the table, or deny him, which he wouldn't understand—"

"You dilute a bottle of his favorite drink so that he's given the illusion of choice," the barman concluded, the tension finally leaving his broad shoulders.

"Of normalcy," Grace corrected, returning both bottles to their correct positions under the counter. Her voice quietened, directed more to the barman than anyone else. "Left is for Simon, right is for everyone else. I am remiss for not having told you this upon hiring, Frank. Apologies. I knew you'd only just moved to this town and were not to know." She straightened up, brushing her skirts down, as if to shake off her mistake. "Ruby?"

The saloon girl dropped the barman's arm and stepped closer, all business, her musk perfume teasing the senses of the nearest patrons. "Ma'am?"

Grace turned in her direction and leant forward to talk in hushed tones. "Have the girls be on lookout, when not . . . occupied. When Simon comes in next, have one of them point him out to Frank, here, so he can get his likeness and know which bottle to use."

Ruby said, "Will do."

The barman inclined his head. "Much obliged."

"Now what does a guy have to do to get a proper whiskey in this joint?" the deputy officer asked, his anger dissipated. "An intelligence test?"

The barman laughed, and tipped out the inferior contents of his glass, reaching to refill it from the correct bottle before carefully placing it back in the right spot. He handed the drink over. "It's on the house."

"It bloody well better be!"

Grace didn't stay for the male-bonding session, but instead made her way to the staircase leading up to the balcony overhanging the saloon's main floor. Knowing her establishment's "soiled doves" tended to recline provocatively against the railing banisters in various degrees of undress when not weaving around the main floor to climb into the laps of willing prospects, Grace walked up on the walled side of the staircase, pausing first to inquire after Ebony's health, and then to remind Chastity that her shift had ended a half an hour ago.

She made her way past the occupied service rooms, through the hallway that housed her doves' private quarters, until she reached her private suite at the far end of a second, more isolated passageway.

She wasn't past the threshold more than a few steps before a young woman threw herself in her arms, her lily-of-the-valley hair soap soothing the older woman's senses.

"What took you so long?" Hope exclaimed, pulling back to dance around the lushly decorated suite.

Grace's stern gaze softened with a warmth her saloon patrons never witnessed. She unbuttoned and pulled off the black brocade gloves that no one but Hope ever saw her without, exposing the metallic gleam of her cybernetic right hand—a replacement earnt in her previous career, after years of bounty hunting had taken its toll... and nearly her life.

Hope continued to waltz around the room, Grace listening to her petticoats swishing under her floral day dress as she moved around on light feet. "The tutor received this letter on the mail train today: I got one of the coveted invitations to apply to the best universities *the domes* have to offer. It's our ticket out of here!"

Grace heard the rustle of the official document, her relief profound. While she hadn't doubted the girl's dedication to her studies, or talent, only students scoring in the top two percent received an invitation to immigrate to another colony for university. To get one of those coveted invitations...

She reached for her ward, who again leapt into her arms as she was scooped up into a spinning hug. "I'm so proud of you," she said gruffly. "Your mom would have been, too. You're a credit to your name."

Years earlier, long before she acquired the Hawk 'n' Dove Saloon, Grace had never believed she'd ever become a parent. Especially not as a bounty hunter. She'd just been passing through town to root out one of the planet's most notorious criminals, who'd illegally crossed borders to hide out in a less technically advanced dome colony to attempt to escape attention.

She'd tried to blend in, but her cybernetics gave her away, as did her almond-shaped eyes and non-Western ways. Whispers of her arrival were soon spreading through town, so in order to avoid giving her target an opportunity to flee, she'd made the decision to confront the arms dealer in the saloon the very night of her arrival. She knew his alcohol consumption made him more vulnerable, and imminently more dangerous, but it had taken months to track him down; she couldn't risk him getting away again.

In his last calculated effort to escape being shackled and dragged back to the Prison Dome, the arms dealer demanded a duel to the death. Being a man who'd earned his crimes through the handling of weapons, he figured he'd have significantly better odds winning.

Since the right to defend your own honor was written into the colony's charter, Grace had agreed without hesitation, trusting her skill with even the most primitive of revolvers. But with her quick affirmation she'd made the mistake of showing her pride and revealing her hand.

When the criminal heard the confidence in her voice, and realized he'd effectively just signed his own death warrant, he did the only thing left to him; he grabbed the nearest saloon gal and held his gun to her head, demanding free passage into the neighboring dome. Unfortunately, neither he nor Grace had factored in how inebriated patrons infatuated with the petrified beauty would react. A quick, messy scuffle broke out, resulting in a lot of broken glasses and sprayed alcohol in an attempt to bring the man down. Grace had tried to intervene, but the altercation led to the death of the criminal... *and* the soiled dove who'd left behind her only hope for a brighter future.

A newborn child.

Grace couldn't help but feel guilt—both for what had led to Lily's death, and for being so thankful that it had granted her the greatest gift she'd ever received: her true bounty.

Hope.

Grace spent the late afternoon discussing university options with the excited girl, unable to fully grasp they were about to see the fruition of a decade of planning. "Do you have a preference?" she asked, finally, as she felt for the pamphlets strewn all over the patchwork quilt and gathered them into a folder.

"Oh—yes!" Hope exclaimed. "*Too many* preferences. And I can only list my top three on the application!"

Grace had anticipated that restriction. When the first of three habitable planets discovered in the Gliese 667C system had initially been colonized, a century earlier, it had taken the combined efforts of a consortium of very different human communities to raise enough capital to afford the generational colony ship that took them to the planet. Each community held very distinct expectations and requirements of what their dream colony would look like. Since the planet couldn't be colonized without the creation of extensive atmospheric domes, separating the habitable surface of the planet into predetermined spherical segments, a charter had been drawn up granting every community in the consortium one dome each, to govern as they saw fit, but with agreed upon joint policing of global matters.

"Pick wisely," Grace encouraged Hope, in an effort to ground her charge and gently remind her of the larger implications of this decision. "Remember, you can only immigrate *once* when you choose your university—and only because of your special invite. Your decision will change the course of your entire life." *And mine,* she thought.

"I know, I know—you don't need to tell me again. Each dome has to maintain a certain number of colonists to thrive, so opportunities to immigrate like this are few and far between." Hope sobered quickly. "You *will* be coming with me, won't you?" There was a quaver in her voice, and in that moment she was a child again, needing reassurance.

Grace's heart warmed. "You couldn't get rid of me if you tried."

Travel between the domes were restricted to merchants given special dispensation to trade goods for the sustainability of the colonies, and to select law enforcement officials chosen to administer the consortium charter laws or protect the boundaries of the various colonies. As a registered bounty hunter, Grace fell under that second category.

The only other legal way to move to another dome was to be in the top two percent of student prodigies who—after a decade of tiring study and grueling intelligence tests—have proven they have skills indispensable to other colonies. A science nerd and computational genius such as Hope would be wasted in the technology-adverse Western dome she grew up in, where women do not even have the right to vote for their own future. The original settlement charter recognized that immigration in such cases was to the benefit of *all* domes, as it ensured brightest of every generation was being utilized for the vital improvement or advancement of the colonies' technological infrastructure and understanding of the new star system they lived in.

Unfortunately, Hope's border pass only granted her access to *one* other dome—the one her university belonged to, and the colony she'd be immigrating to—but that change in address was enough to rewrite her entire future.

"Make sure you don't just consider the pros and cons of the universities you can apply for," Grace cautioned, "but also the job opportunities, economic stability, and projected viability of the colonies they belong to."

"I'm still amazed by how little the school taught about the domes versus the charter-registered tutor you hired." Hope's voice sounded weary, a little indignant. "If the teacher here had it her way, the other domes might as well not exist!"

Grace grimaced. "Unfortunately, narrow-mindedness becomes short-sightedness, which then becomes willful ignorance. The future success of *every* colony is dependent on *consistent* population and infrastructure growth within the first few generations. It won't be until the second generational ship arrives, in another century or so, that terraforming machines will arrive and be used to make the world more viable for humans to live *outside* the domes." She paced the room as she considered her next words carefully. "While still in the initial struggle to attain viability, some colonies retreat into themselves, amplifying more restrictive charter policies under the guise of self-preservation which can end up oppressing their citizens. It's important for you to pick a dome that is already giving indications of becoming self-sustaining within the next generation or so. The society they are forming will be more open to, and can afford, individual expression. When some of the colonies start to falter—and some *will* fail—the other colonies either need to have built up supplies or bolstered their life-support systems enough to be able to take in refugees—or defend their borders."

"Is that why we can't even *visit* the other domes while the colonies are establishing themselves?" Hope wondered. "Why tourism is just a concept in my tutor's history books, not a reality on this planet?"

The bounty hunter smiled, proud of her charge. "I shouldn't be surprised by your intuitiveness, now. As you can imagine, the demands on every dome's life-support systems are already significant. If that demand fluctuated daily, due to humans continuously moving in and out of the artificial environments, then the constant adjustments to account for the changing oxygen requirements and carbon dioxide levels could overwork components that are already stretched too thin."

"And you have always told me that there are not enough staff to man—or woman—an already taxed system."

"Exactly. They're yet to be born. Maybe, in another century, the travel restrictions would be removed, but not likely in our lifetimes."

Hope was silent for quite a long time as she considered the import of what she'd been told. Eventually, she said, "I am thinking of applying for a Bachelor in Astronomy at the Space and Exploration Academy in Atarashī Bijon." Her eyes brightened, sparkling with excitement. "I would *kill* to be on the survey teams sent to study the other planets in this system that could support life. And, it seems important now, after this conversation, to belong to a colony that is able to design and create technology that can take humans *outside* of the dome walls—if only for exploration, at first."

Now you're thinking with that bright noggin of yours, Grace thought, relaxing. She knew her ward would pick wisely.

Hope walked to the window to gaze out at the main street of Silverton. While the primary sun had set for the day, the much smaller twin stars of this three-star system still flirted with the horizon, their significantly softer glow adding a beautiful amber hue to rustic buildings lining the long dirt road filled with the tracks of horses and wagon wheels. "Anything to get out of this hellhole."

While Grace had no urge to defend this colony, having grown up in the cleaner, higher-tech colony of Shuāngzǐ Tàiyáng, there was something to be appreciated about living a much more stripped-down life. If it weren't for the draconian laws in this place, she might have appreciated the frontier existence more. There was an appeal to eking a living directly from the very land you toil. If only Native Americans had existed in this Western re-creation, she could have learnt from them and how *they* worked the land. *All* the colonists could have. Instead, they had decided to start a new colony far away from the privileged, white invaders of their past.

"You will miss your aunts," she pointed out gently to her ward.

Hope voice quavered. "I know—you're right. I wish we could take them with us. What woman would *choose* this existence when there were so many more...modern alternatives?"

"You'd be surprised. Many of the original women of this colony chose the frontier life willingly—although, admittedly not the life of a soiled dove, but that of a frontier wife and mother. And I find no fault in that dream; it's what is right for them. Unfortunately, working in a saloon is the only recourse left to women who fall on hard times here." Grace made her way over to her ward, sliding her hand into hers and squeezing it. "As you know, the members of this colony—your ancestors—hail from an original Earth country called the United States. Apparently, the people there were not so united as it seemed. There was a political divide for centuries. While there were good people on both sides—reasonable people, who had intersecting values, but different political opinions—it's often the radicals who believe they should determine the fate of others..."

"I remember this from my history lessons," Hope said. "A subset of Americans tried to force their view on an entire country, trying to get one, then several more, presidents elected that would return the country to laws that existed when it was first colonized, and when their efforts failed, they applied to leave on the generational ship as one of the first colonies to settle here," Hope finished.

"And they thought in starting out again, they should reinstate the original laws and values of the 'Wild West' era in United States history," Grace added. "The records of how Americans explored *that* frontier now dictate how they explore *this* world's new frontier."

Hope grimaced. "It seems very...limited."

"Indeed." Grace felt Hope turn towards her. "Your mom dreamed of a better life for you than the one that was scripted for her—the one that she lived."

"So now I have the opportunity to change my stars."

The two women—one remade by parenthood, the other still in the making—stood by the window until the Sun's Twins sunk below the horizon.

Hope was accepted into the Space and Exploration Academy in Atarashī Bijon, but not for her first degree choice, a Bachelor in Astronomy, but for her second preference, a Bachelor in Astrobiology, with a minor in computational biology. The next month was filled with Hope finalizing all her entrance paperwork, and filing for her travel permit, which allowed for an immediate family member to immigrate with her.

Grace also took steps to put her affairs in order. To prepare for her absence, Ruby was chosen to take over management of the saloon—for who better to look out for the soiled doves than one of their own?

"You're going to have a bit of an uphill battle, getting men to respect you, at first," Grace cautioned Ruby, as the seamstress modified the second of three dresses Grace had gifted her, so she could present a less "sullied" appearance to society.

Ruby nodded, her attention distracted by the dressmaker, who was pinning in a new panel of fabric to cover up the dove's ample bosom more modestly. "I know—I suspected that. But in a way, that's nothing new." She gestured to her figure. "To them, the only thing changed is the levels of layers I'll be wearing."

In truth, Ruby hadn't been servicing patrons for several years, spending her work hours assisting Grace in the running of the saloon. Once the townsfolk realized that, it should make the transition easier.

A more scantily clad Ebony walked into the room, her signature floral perfume making its own entrance.

Grace smiled. "What do you think, Ebbs?"

The dark beauty walked around Ruby, her expression impish. "I hardly recognize her!" She reached forward and tugged one loose red ringlet. "You're going to have a harder time of it containing that red mane of yours, Beautiful, than your luscious curves."

Ruby laughed. "Don't I know it!"

Hope waltzed into the room and exclaimed almost immediately, "You look *wonderful*, Aunt Ruby!"

The woman beamed. "Thanks, love! I'm practicing being all decent like."

Ebony snorted. "The only day we'd be considered decent is on our burial day. It's the only time the womenfolk will *know* we're not sharing our bed with one of their husbands."

"Ebony!" Grace chastised. She heard the dressmaker chortle. "There's an innocent in this room."

Hope laughed as much as the rest of them. "I'd have to be blind not to know what was going on in the saloon, Mom." Then she looked horrified. "Oh . . . I didn't mean . . ."

Grace shook her head, raising a placating hand. "Not to worry. I know what you meant."

Ruby reached forward to give the girl a hug, then pulled back when the dressmaker tut-tutted, reaching to rub the girl's arm instead. "I'm going to miss you, my little hatchling."

Everyone's mood sobered, just in time for Chastity to enter Grace's suites, her sensuous appearance belying her name. "You would think someone died," the brunette exclaimed, as she looked about the room. She sauntered over to Hope and cupped her face. "I'm so proud of you, chickie—even if that means you are ditching us to soar to greater heights."

Hope pulled her into a hug. "I wish I could take you all with me!"

This time the dressmaker didn't tut at all when Ruby joined the other doves in embracing their young ward.

"She grew up and done you proud," the older seamstress told Grace quietly.

"That she has," Grace replied. *It's time for my girl to spread her wings and fly.*

Grace left to complete some errands around town, returning to the Hawk 'n' Dove in the midafternoon to get it ready for the evening rush. Although the new barman seemed to be working out just fine, she still had her reservations about Frank, wishing she didn't have to leave the saloon so soon after he'd been hired. While her doves had not reported any impropriety on his behalf—in fact, a couple had wished the handsome bachelor *would* be improper with them—Grace didn't trust *any* man until time had proven his good intentions. Her first impressions told her he was holding something back, and while secrets were not necessarily bad—she had some of her own—it did mean she was cautious until he proved his worth. Even if he did come with impeccable references.

Maybe *too* impeccable.

She frowned, and pushed through the double-swing doors, only to be immediately halted by one of her doves as she entered the saloon. Then she heard it—the *swish-slosh* of one of the local orphans mopping, which meant all the chairs would be piled up on the tables and the floorboards slick. She'd just narrowly avoided an almost certain faceplant.

Grace squeezed Ebony's arms in thanks, her heady floral perfume in stark contrast to the earthy stench of the blacksmith's she'd just passed, and she made her way carefully to the bar. She knew Frank would be using this time to take inventory of the bottles needed to be pulled up from the cellar, and she wanted to have some words with him.

She nodded in the direction of the bar's lone patron, Raymond, who had paused his harmonica rendition of "Amazing Grace" to say hello.

"Can I get you anything?" she asked solicitously, wondering where Frank was.

"No, ma'am," the elderly man replied. "I'm still nursing my first drink, which Ebony was so kind enough to pour for me a little while back."

Grace's consternation deepened. "Have you seen Frank anywhere?"

He shrugged. "Not since I turned up."

"And when was that?" She tried to sound casual.

"Oh, I would say—abouts an hour ago? I had to put flowers on my Mavis's grave, first."

Grace muttered the appropriate response, but inside her alarm bells were ringing.

On instinct, she made her way up the stairs, heading for her suites. She entered to find the seamstress in stitches.

"Oh, say it isn't so!" the dressmaker exclaimed to Ruby, who was getting her third dress fitted.

"I tell you no lie!" the redhead conspired, winking as she laughed.

Grace didn't hear her ward's girlish giggle join the more sultry guffaw of her aunt. She frowned, her bounty hunter instincts triggered. She'd come up here to ask Ruby about Frank, but something told her she had a more pressing concern. "Have you seen Hope?"

Both women paused, instantly aware of the urgency in Grace's tone.

"Not for a while," Ruby supplied. "Not since she . . ." She paused, then swore.

"What, Ruby?" Grace implored. "Not since she *what?*"

"Since Frank knocked and informed us that Sally had dropped by to say goodbye to Hope. She never returned."

"Frank is missing, too." *Fuck.* "When exactly was this, Ruby?"

The dove grew flustered, prompting the seamstress to speak up. "About ten past the hour, ma'am. Forty-five minutes ago."

Grace swore profusely, repeating every curse she'd ever heard, making her way over to the chest at the end of her bed. "Didn't that sound at all suspicious to you?" she asked, incredulous.

"Sally *would* want to say goodbye to Hope," Ruby ventured, not too certain any longer.

"Ruby—you know better than that. Since when have any of her school friends ever been *allowed* to come to the saloon to talk to Hope? Not one of their mothers would allow it, due to the risk to their reputation. The girls would say goodbye to her at school." She started pulling weapons and clothing out of her carved wooden chest, stacking them in piles on her bed quilt. She knew she had to move quickly, but she couldn't afford to lose her mind and start a search completely unprepared or unprovisioned.

Ruby's face fell. "Oh my god—I didn't think. I'm so sorry, Grace."

"Don't be sorry—just help me find her."

Ruby ran out of the room to gather the doves, and the seamstress told Grace that she would alert the town so a search party could be rallied.

Grace's heart fell. She knew they didn't have much time. Before the dressmaker left, Grace asked her if she could quickly help her out of her morning gown and petticoats, ignoring the woman's gasp when she saw her cybernetic arm and leg.

As quickly as she had undressed, Grace had redressed herself in her former bounty hunter gear, which was a form of fitted vegan leather. She restrapped her baton to her waist and began assembling her other weapons. Her throwing knives were already in her boots.

Ruby raced back into the room, just as the dressmaker left it, to let Grace know the other doves were checking all the stores in the main street for information, only to be taken aback for a second to see Grace so transformed. Then she was all business again, moving to the bookcase to pull out a copy of *The Complete Drowned Horse Chronicle*, opening it up to reveal a small digital device nestled inside.

Handing it to Grace, she started stripping the pins out of Grace's delicate hair bun so that her long thick tresses fell free, and then immediately started braiding it, the white streak in her hair a striking contrast to the rest of her raven mass being woven into a tight plait down one shoulder until it hung by her waistline.

Grace turned on the satellite phone, calling Peter Chang, her mentor—the bounty hunter who had trained her for the service—but there was no immediate reply. She left him a message.

Officially, Chang owned the saloon—women not being allowed to own property in this dome. They'd used the significant bounty Grace had collected from Lily's killer to pay off the original proprietor, when Chang had agreed to her proposal that the watering hole would make a great spy outpost for the Bounty Guild. She'd then "officially" retired as a bounty hunter, taken Hope in as her ward—for no one else in the town wanted to raise "the dirty little squab." Peter had stayed for a month or so to help set up their new base, returning for a few days every year, to "check in on his affairs" after which he had left his "sister" to run his business for him.

Within two years, Grace had set up one of the most intricate networks of informants, training her soiled doves to gather intel from drunk patrons under the guise of pillow talk, making her spy network one of the best on the planet. With lawbreakers inventing new ways to circumvent border restrictions, bribing their way through the strictest of dome entry points, a bounty hunter was never short of work—even one retired from active service.

And now she was not going to allow herself to panic, or despair, but take a deep breath and try to use all she had built to find her girl.

"They rode off on a mare that had been tied to the blacksmith's corral to get reshod, not two hours past," the sheriff said, as he handed his deputy a canteen of water.

Grace swore when she realized how much time had passed while the town had searched all the buildings for her girl, and she'd prepared for the most important bounty hunt she'd ever have to perform. Barber John and the deputy sheriff were already saddled up, ready to ride with her, the blacksmith lending her his speediest quarter horse.

The smith, Perry, walked out, handing a horseshoe to Grace. "The mare Frank took has one missing shoe—the one I was working on. It should make his tracks easier to find."

Grace felt the workmanship that had been built it into its form, her fingers tracing the metal curve. *Maybe it would give me some luck,* she thought, as she tucked it into the top of her leather bodice.

She left the men to finalize supplies on the horses and ducked back into the saloon, which had been closed to patrons while everyone focused on the search. With a shaking hand, she reached up to the cybernetic implant gracing her brow and activated it.

For the first time in over a dozen years, sight flooded into her corneal implants, turning her irises purple. She gasped as she looked around the room, not seeing the world on the same color spectrum as other humans, but with digitally created heat signatures and depth sensors. Visible measurements were continuously calculated to indicate the distance, vector and approximate density of an object or person, with a brief description appearing above them when she focused on something specific to analyze.

Grace grimaced. There was a reason why she preferred not to use the device. The information it reported, *how* the artificial mechanism saw the world for her was so . . . sanitized, sterile. While it helped her navigate—and had been invaluable when she'd become a bounty hunter after she'd lost most of her sight—the world it showed her *felt* wrong to her other senses.

She'd realized, long ago, that in trying to continuously evaluate what she was seeing, her other senses had become muted; distancing herself from experiencing the richness of the world and the real bounty offered to her by *all* her natural senses.

Still, for Hope, she would utilize every damn tool available to get her fledgling back.

If the others noticed anything different about how she interacted with her environment when she walked back out a minute later, no one said anything. Instead, they watched her stride straight up to her horse and mount it with ease. She knew that because she still saw some blur and indistinct shapes, even with her implants off, that she appeared more able-sighted than she actually was, but she'd also set up her life to best mask her vulnerability. Her saloon girls knew to wear their signature perfumes, so she could tell them apart instantly, and her doves were equally particular about where everything was positioned in her establishment so that she could reach for anything she needed and know it would be where she placed her hand.

"Where did Caitlin see them depart from?" Grace asked, all determination.

The deputy sheriff gestured toward one side of the corral. "Caitlin couldn't see much from the vantage point of her porch rocking chair, but she did see they turned left, heading behind the blacksmith's shop." He hesitated, as if debating adding something, then continued. "She noted that Hope didn't *appear* to be in any distress at all. You sure she just didn't run off? Decide she was just gonna shack up with the barman?"

Grace bristled but didn't let it show. She needed help, not divided ranks. "You wouldn't even be asking that, if you knew her well enough. Which. No. Man. Does," she added, to emphasize her chastity.

The deputy nodded. Point made.

She directed her horse out to the start of the tracks and gave her implant a moment to trace the shapes of the four hoofprints, waiting until it registered the mare's unique track pattern. When that was locked in, Grace looked in the direction the horse was reported to have headed, her eyes recalibrating until bright blue digital outlines appeared around similar indentations in the dirt, moving east.

Grace indicated their heading, and the others fell into her wake without question. She'd expected some form of protest at a woman taking lead, but these men knew her and, she believed, even respected her. She also knew the men were likely still shocked to see her in official bounty-hunting garb, which inherently suggested to them that she was the expert at tracking *anyone*. If she hadn't been so worried about Hope, she might have been amused by the fact that while she was blind, she'd always had their measure, and yet this was probably the first time any of them had truly seen *her*.

The horses set out at a consistent clip, their riders knowing they'd have to make up the two hours of lead time Frank had on them. They already had one thing on their side: his mare wouldn't be able to move quite as quickly with two people riding it and, thus, would tire faster. The search party could afford to push their mounts a little harder to make up some time because they were carrying less weight.

"I can't understand why he'd be heading this way—there's no other town for miles," Barber John wondered, his gaze scanning the unrelentingly dirty dustbowl of a land that comprised of most of the colony.

"Maybe he's trying to just throw us off, and he'll backtrack when it's dark—head in another direction?" the deputy mused.

Grace's suspicions weren't confirmed until her satellite phone called several hours later, around dusk. "Peter—thank the Sun's Twins! What have you got for me?"

He didn't mince words. "He's headed for the border."

"Wh-what?" Grace's mind spun. "He's attempting to leave the dome?"

The deputy swore, and Barber John was equally shocked. "Well, I'll be!"

"What possible reason could he have for taking Hope with him?" She frowned, trying to remember if he'd ever expressed sexual interest in *anyone*, let alone her ward. She just couldn't see it.

"It's tricky enough trying to bribe the border guards to let *one* illegal though," the deputy said, "let alone an extra unwilling travel partner. What's he on about?"

And then it hit Grace. Hope's permit to immigrate—it'd had just been approved. "Peter, is he trying to use her immigration papers, somehow? Is that even possible?"

"It's plausible. Some folks heard him complaining one night about being stuck in such a backass town." His voice sounded somber, deadly. "And the thing is, if she's caught aiding his attempt over the border, by passing him off as a family member to use her plus-one pass—or her partner—it could get her university permit revoked."

"But she was *kidnapped*!" Grace ground out between clenched teeth. "He likely threatened her." His actions could sabotage her entire future.

"I sent in a drone as soon as I heard your message. Footage shows she isn't actively fighting him," Peter said, subdued. "So that's something at least. Give me a second—an informant is contacting me."

Grace's hope surged, impatient. They continued to follow Frank's tracks, believing they had made up significant time, but knowing the border was only fifty minutes from their location, at their current speed. She had to calculate if it was worth the risk to push the horses faster to shorten the gap, because if any of them foundered...Hope would reach the border before help could reach her.

"Grace—you still there?" Peter asked.

"Where else would I bloody be?" she replied, impatient. "Oh, I'm sorry, Peter—it's just that—"

"Never mind that!" Peter interrupted, sounding excited. "She was just spotted no more than thirty minutes ahead of your position!"

The deputy sheriff whistled. "We made up more time than I thought!"

"Not quite. Apparently, the horse is going lame on one foot, so it's slowing."

"The missing horseshoe!" Grace exclaimed, reaching to touch it where it lay nestled above her heart. "With the weight of one person, the mare likely would have been fine. But with two—"

"Two people are a burden, especially at the pace they were likely traveling," the deputy concluded, slapping his thigh in joy. "Let's do this!"

Grace didn't have to order increased speed. The bounty hunter leaned forward to rub the neck of her quarter horse—"Just a little longer, my beauty."—and tightened her grip on the reins as they all picked up their pace, switching from a canter into a full gallop.

She knew they were cutting it fine, and that they could only gallop for minutes at a time before slowing down again for a spell, but they could all do the math: they were still thirty minutes behind, yet Frank and Hope were only twenty minutes from the border.

Still, if Frank's horse was foundering, the time it took them to reach the border would have lengthened. Maybe, just maybe...

"There is something else," Peter chimed in again, this time amusement evident in his voice. "Apparently when they passed a traveler on the road, Hope was singing. Wanna guess her song of choice, Grace?"

Barber John answered for her, his voice sounding a little rough from being jostled at speed. "Peter, we're a little strapped for time here, mate—is it something we need to know right now?"

Grace's mentor was undeterred, his remarkably good singing voice crackling a bit on the satellite phone. "*Amazing grace—how sweet the sound— That saved a wretch like meeee! I once was lost, but now am found; Was blind, but now I seeeeee.*"

Grace's eyes filled with tears. *That brilliant girl of mine!* "She knows I'm coming after her!"

"No wonder she's so calm," Peter pointed out, laughing. "She's just biding her time."

Grace's artificial gaze detected the shimmer of the translucent dome wall, curving up into the sky, long before she spotted the lame horse, and the two humans walking alongside it, the man all but propelling the girl towards the border gate, still several hundred yards distant.

Barber John's horse had gone lame, and the deputy's mount had tired quicker than Grace's, prompting her to make the decision to leave them behind ten minutes earlier, so she had to rely on herself to perform the rescue.

Grace leant forward on her horse as she encouraged him to make one last heroic burst of speed, surging forward. The sound of thudding hoofs filled her ears as they arrowed in on her precious bounty.

Frank whirled when he heard the horse, her implants registering his sudden awareness that she was closing in. His heat signature changed as he manhandled Hope more forcibly, now all but dragging her to the border in his desperation.

It was in that moment that Hope started to resist, to fight back. Grace wished she could just use her horse to plow Frank into the ground, but not while he was grappling with Hope. When she was almost upon them, she reined sharply to one side, hurling herself off the horse in a tight summersault, maneuvering so that the impact of her landing was born by her cybernetic leg.

Frank spun around as she stood up, drawing a long knife out from his belt scabbard, which Grace's implants highlighted in red as a warning.

Grace instantly feared he would grab Hope and use the knife as leverage, hold it against her neck to threaten her life...

But, instead, he pushed Hope away from him, behind him, and then moved into a fighting stance.

Grace couldn't use her gun—she'd risk the bullet going through Frank and hitting Hope. But she had to do *something*. No man was ever going to get between her and her child.

She reached up, and switched off her implants, preferring to trust her human skills, rather than the machine part of her. If

Frank's expression registered surprise when he saw the purple in her irises turn off, Grace wouldn't know. All she knew was that he was standing too precariously close to her daughter—her life—and she had to neutralize him. Quick.

She reached for her own knife and in one smooth motion, lunged for him.

"Mom—stop! Don't kill him."

Fuck! Grace was already midswing when she heard Hope's desperate plea, the momentum propelling her forward. She did the only thing she could do: she dropped the weapon in mid-air, and hoped it wouldn't land anywhere painful as her body slammed into his.

They collided forcibly. Grace reflexively twisted slightly, to throw her weight into her cybernetic side, knowing it would knock the hell out of him while keeping her from exposing herself.

She heard one of Frank's ribs crack as they went down in a tumble of limbs. Without the weapon in her hand, her lunge was no longer deadly, but he instinctively fought back. Being larger, he had more reach, while she clearly had more skill.

She soon realized that even though she'd instinctively dropped her weapon at her daughter's screamed plea, *he* had not.

In their tousle, his knife pierced the leather over her heart, as her daughter screamed for them to "Stop!" again.

Frank halted immediately, and when he saw where his knife was, he panicked. "Oh no, no no no nooo!" He immediately pulled it out and scrambled back away from Grace, horrified at his actions.

If there was anything that would pull her out of her "going for the kill" mode, hearing someone in genuine, mortified distress would do it. She rolled away from him, over to her daughter, who helped her stand with shaking hands. They embraced quickly, and wiped away tears, before Grace pulled back to clutch at her chest, which was oozing blood.

Frank was on his butt, arms clenched around his knees, rocking back and forth. "I'm so sorry—I didn't mean to...I didn't want anything like this to happen."

Grace unzipped the top of her leather bodice and reached in to feel the warmth of her sticky blood on the horseshoe she'd tucked in there for luck. The very horseshoe that had halted the knife's deadly plunge.

"M-mom?" Hope's voice sounded scared.

"I'm okay, love." She pulled out the horseshoe, and Hope gasped. "It's only a shallow wound. This took the impact first, before the knife slid a little, off the edge of the metal, nicking me just enough to draw blood."

Frank stared up at them, then at the horseshoe, his eyes wide. He scrambled to his feet, reflexively clenching the knife as he backed away from them.

Grace didn't have to use her implants to know he still held a weapon. She immediately went into a defensive fighter stance, stepping in front of her daughter.

Who put her hand placatingly on her mom's shoulder. "He's not dangerous," she told her, voice gentle. "He's just scared, Mom."

"That's what makes him so dangerous," she rejoindered, but she listened to her daughter and made them both step back—an obvious retreat—to give Frank the time and space to consider his next actions.

He lowered the knife slowly, gingerly, then dropped it to the ground all together.

Relief surged through Grace as she heard it clatter on the rocky earth. Her daughter was safe.

Grace asked the trembling man to kick the knife away, which he did immediately while rubbing his hand back and forth on his pants reflexively, as if he was trying to get rid of the remembered taint of the weapon.

"Why did you do this?" she demanded, as she tucked the horseshoe back into her bodice, above the heart it had protected so well.

If anything, the question seemed to scare him more than their scuffle did. Interesting. None of this was making any sense.

Grace turned to Hope, asking her daughter to explain.

"It's not my story to tell," she responded quietly, compassion in her voice.

Grace sighed and focused her attention back on Frank. "Give me one reason why I shouldn't tell the deputy to put you in shackles the minute he and Barber John catch up to us."

"I wasn't *wanting* to capture your daughter. I just needed to borrow her. I was trying to *escape*."

Grace frowned. "Do you have a warrant out for your arrest and were you using my daughter to leave the jurisdiction?"

He hesitated. "No, I was running to try and protect my truth." He turned to Hope, flashing her a wry but sad smile. "I-I don't even know how your lass worked it out."

"Worked *what* out?" Grace tried not to get impatient. She could tell the man was in genuine distress, even though she'd been the one who'd been stabbed. If anything, her daughter even seemed to be protective of him. Something just wasn't right about this entire scenario. She repeated the question, this time making an effort to soften her tone.

Again, he floundered, and Grace got the impression he looked to Hope for help. "I don't know how to say it."

Hope was silent for a long moment. "With your permission"—he nodded—"I will tell Mom enough for her to understand your situation." She spent a moment running her hand through her knotted hair, considering her next words carefully. "When he first grabbed me, he kept trying to calm me by saying he wouldn't hurt me—you know, in *that way*. That he just needed me to do one thing—help him cross the border—then he'd let me go." She turned and addressed her next words to Frank directly. "Your actions clearly weighed on you more as the day went on. You were...distressed. Your 'Don't worry—I won't touch you,' turned into, 'You have nothing to fear from me. I couldn't touch any woman that way.' I don't think you even realized the double entendre of your words while just trying to reassure me."

Then the import of what Hope had said hit Grace.

Frank is gay!

No wonder he'd been petrified. With the draconian Wild West laws in their colony, "fornicating" with anyone of the same gender was a hangable offence.

"To be this way, ma'am—to be true to me," the young man started, quietly, "it's punishable by death. I just couldn't breathe here any longer. And I also couldn't live. Love."

Compassion poured into Grace, echoing her daughter's. Now her doves' inability to coax him into their beds made sense—they weren't his type. No wonder he wanted out of the dome. She could understand that impulse, working decades to get her child out of the same hellhole to escape gender inequality.

Unfortunately, the deputy chose that very moment to catch up to them, before Grace could even respond. He took one look at the blood streaking Grace's chest—"That fucker!"—and dismounted, moving instantly to shackle Frank, who didn't even protest.

It appeared all the fight—life—had gone out of him.

Grace's mind scrambled. How was she going to explain this one? "Deputy," Grace called, "let him go."

The man looked incredulous. "What do you mean, 'let him go'? You're literally dripping blood from your chest, woman."

"We're not going to arrest him."

"Why the bloody hell not?!"

"I've been informed of some... mitigating circumstances."

"*What* mitigating circumstances? The guy kidnapped Hope—end of story."

"It was only a little minor... 'nap," Hope interjected. "He drank too much wine—he wasn't thinking."

The deputy loomed over the terrified man, sniffing. "Smells as sober as a newborn baby to me. Just sweatier."

"Don't make me pull rank, Deputy," Grace informed him, reminding him that on a policing level, while he had jurisdiction within town borders, she had authority everywhere else as a bounty hunter.

He kept muttering expletives as he unshackled the man. "Bloody women—always so emotional. Showing sympathy to a bloody kidnapper. What next? A knitting circle with murderers?"

Grace bit back a laugh, realizing she was fond of the grumpy man. "Can you please let Barber John know we're fine? Maybe find water for the horses, too. I'll update you later." *When I have time to think of some kind of lie to pass off as an explanation.*

The deputy reached for Frank's flask, uncapping it and taking a whiff. "He could have at least had the decency to have stolen some decent grog from you. Even Simple Simon's dreck was better than this tepid shite." He swilled the water, wandering back to his horse, muttering all the while. "Glad you're safe, lassie," he said as he passed Hope.

"Thanks!"

Frank walked over to Grace, tremulous, his hands shaking as he took one of hers in his own, squeezing it tight. "I can't thank you enough," he said, drawing himself up to his full, significant height. It was as if being defended—understood—had helped him find his strength.

"I'm still not happy with you, young man, but I understand being different. The fight against the binds that constrain."

"We *both* do," Hope said.

Grace dialed Peter up on the satellite phone, filling him in quickly, then asking for his advice.

"You can't really think he is worth your help, surely," he said. "He threatened my niece and that doesn't sit well with—"

"You were not here," Grace interjected, electing to not tell him about the knife to the heart, not just yet. "He could have forced our hand, putting Hope's life at risk to save his own skin once I caught up to him, but he chose not to." She considered their options. "Can we send him to you on some trumped-up charge? Get him out of this dome through an extradition order?"

Peter snorted. "Not unless you want him to be actually charged with something. And it would have to be something big, to justify the extradition. Then we would need a judge's approval to legally wave the charges, so I would have no control over the outcome. Too risky."

Grace grimaced, feeling deflated.

Frank said, "It was worth a try—I appreciate it."

"I have an idea," Hope spoke up, sounding a little coy. "Hire him."

Grace shook her head. "Love, he already works for me. I'm pretty sure he didn't kidnap you and drag you all the way to the border because he loves being a barman so damn much and wants to stay."

"I'm so sorry." Frank sounded wretched with guilt. "I really didn't—"

Grace waved him off. "I was illustrating a point. I get that I sound snarky as hell, but I can't help but still feel a little pissed off. It's reflexive. It will wear off, given time."

"That's not what I meant," Hope teased, and Grace could hear a little triumph in her voice.

Grace was about to ask her to explain when Peter started laughing on the other end of the phone. "That's brilliant, Hope." Then he was all business. "Pass the phone to Frank."

Grace did so, curious, giving the man's shoulder a sympathetic squeeze as she did so.

They could hear paperwork rustling through the phone, then the man himself asked, "You there, Frank?"

Frank hesitated at first, then answered. "Yes, sir?"

"How would you like to join the Bounty Guild?"

Frank spluttered, shocked. "Come again?"

This time it was Grace who laughed, as the implications of his offer hit her. "Oh, Peter—that's brilliant."

"Thank your brilliant daughter."

Grace's heart swelled in pride, as the barman-turned-kidnapper-turned-possible-recruit turned to her, and she didn't have to see him to know how overwhelmed he was. "Bounty hunters, by nature, are required to chase criminals. She paused for emphasis. "Which. Takes. Them. Across. The. Border."

Frank gasped. "You mean, I could leave this colony? I could..." His voice broke, emotions overwhelming him.

"It means that after your training," Peter informed him, "we could *permanently* assign you to a base in any number of domes..."

"*That wouldn't be this one,*" Grace finished.

"You would finally be safe," Hope added, in a much more delighted tone.

Grace considered her daughter, proud. Only a girl with the sweetest soul, and a heart that was always filled with her birth mom's hope for a brighter future, would not only forgive her kidnapper, but have the sensitivity to realize his situation was much more dire than her own.

"Come to the border gate, since you're so conveniently close to it anyway," Peter told Frank, his voice droll. "I wish your bloody colony had not banned all forms of technology. So bloody inconvenient. It might take an hour or so, but I'll have one of our people drop off some paperwork for you to fill out, to start the process."

Frank made amends with Hope, and turned to Grace, one last time, to say some parting words. "I once was lost, but now I'm found..."

Grace smiled. "Was blind, but now I see."

LAST TRANSPORT TO KEPLER-283C

Christopher L. Smith

Behm nonchalantly looked around the work site, making sure everyone was in place. Months of planning, preparation, and patience were about to pay off, as long as everything went right. Prayers to Murphy were all well and good, but he knew that specific deity was a fickle as they came. It always took a lot of hard work and forethought to increase the odds of pleasing the Great One, and he hoped that his crew had put in the appropriate level of skull sweat to win His favor.

His earpiece buzzed.

"Hey, pard." Gene Larson's voice crackled slightly in his ear over the unsecured channel. "If you got a sec, could use some hands near the loader."

"Roger that, let me wrap this up."

Behm eased off on the laser hammer's controls, the sharp hiss of the "blade" fading as the focused beam of plasma retracted into the housing. After double-checking the equipment's various tethers and safety lockouts, he detached his harness and started toward the loader.

He grinned as he moved in practiced, measured bounds, covering the distance in a few minutes. While he empathized with the new arrivals—on the surface for only a matter of days—he couldn't help but feel some amusement at the way the fresh crew floundered about the camp area, overshooting their targets by meters.

As he approached the loader, Larson looked up from his tablet and nodded.

"Whatcha got," Behm said, sliding to a gentle stop next to the machinery.

"We're on schedule." Larson tapped the screen in his hand. "Raider and Phantom will get in position, load us on, then get in their crates. Those suits we picked up on Musk Station will cover our body heat, so we'll blend in with the rest of the gear if they scan us."

Movement out of the corner of his eye caught Behm's attention. Some of the newbies, with little self-control (and less common sense) were taking turns boosting each other, using the low gravity to achieve greater and greater heights. Behm sighed. If they kept acting like a bunch of high school cheerleaders, it wouldn't be long before someone or something broke.

Larson glanced over and shook his head. "Looks like you might need to go have a word," he muttered.

Behm had volunteered for the camp's "Grievance Detail," a group of levelheaded miners that could keep violence to a minimum.

He nodded and checked the charge on his Colt PK-5000 Infrasound pistol. The nonlethal weapon threw a tight beam of soundwaves that induced nausea and minor spasms in the recipient. The inventor named it the "Peace Keeper," but it had been consequently dubbed "Puke Kannon" by the people who used it. Or had it used on them.

"Still find it funny. You, a cop."

"More like an enforcer."

"Even funnier."

"Why's that?"

The other man snorted. "I've seen you fight."

"One bad day, and you'll never let me live it down."

"One day?"

"Fine." Behm glared. "A *few* bad days."

"Lessee...there was that guy on Clarke Two."

"Hey now, if you hadn't been hitting on his girl, I wouldn't have had to step in. Besides, he sucker-punched me."

"Fair enough, but what about the bikers on..."

"Those women were inhuman. You can't count that."

"And what about that?" Larson pointed at Behm's face.

Behm felt along his cheek, absently tracing the scar running from temple to jaw.

"If I hadn't hit that guy, his shiv would've gotten your jugular."

Larson was right, of course—a few inches lower, and he'd be breathing through a tube. Or dead, just another casualty of prison-gang relations. A close call like that could make a man reconsider his life choices.

"I told you, sticking your neck out would get you nothing but trouble." He gestured at the PK. "At least you got something to even the odds this time."

"Something besides you, you mean." He grinned at Larson's chuckle. "This ain't prison, though. These boys just need a gentle guiding hand to sort their differences in a more civilized manner. Or start heaving up everything they've ever eaten."

A shout brought their attention back to the horseplay.

"Looks like you get to test that theory."

One of the newbies had apparently misjudged his launch. Now, flailing in midair, he hurtled toward a table surrounded by a group of vets. Behm bounded toward them.

Judging by the kid's trajectory, he'd land directly in the middle of the poker game, and, barring a miracle, scatter the pot to kingdom come. Long days and hard work meant short tempers. The vets probably wouldn't take it well.

He timed it perfectly, arriving just as the new guy landed ass-first on the river card.

"Hey, junior," he said, "looks like you miscalculated that one."

He looked around at the poker player's ominous scowls, locking eyes with each one while resting his hand lightly on the PK.

"We've all been there, right fellas? Nothing an apology and a hand cleaning up won't fix, I'd say."

Mutters and grumbles, generally affirmative, were his answer. He nudged the newbie.

"Uh, yeah, right. Sorry, guys, I'm still getting my legs."

Behm stuck around, easy grin on his face, hand on his pistol, until he was sure that the matter was resolved. With a nod, he returned to Larson's position.

"Your negotiation skills have improved, pard. No new holes or missing teeth."

"Yeah, yeah." He paused, struggling to find the right words for what he wanted to say next. Larson noticed.

"Spit it out, don't need to sugarcoat nothing with me."

"Fine." Behm let out a deep breath. "Something don't feel right about this."

Larson looked at him, rubbing his chin slowly.

"It isn't too late to hit the brakes and call it off," Behm continued. "We ain't done a job like this before, and there's a lot of variables. Maybe just keep our noses clean and heads down."

"This is the cargo we've been waiting for." He shook his head. "Don't know when we're gonna get the chance again, and the buyers don't take well to folks that welsh on a deal. It's not like we can just return the deposit, shake their hands, and get a friendly 'Oh well, maybe next time.'"

"I'm just sayin'..."

Larson cut him off. "Look, we're doing this. Without you, if that's the way you want it. Comprende?"

Behm nodded, scowling.

"Right, then." His tone softened. "Look, there's only one person I trust to watch my back. We've been through some tough scrapes together, and always come through. So, are you with me?"

"Yeah, I'm with you."

"Good." Larson checked his watch. "Tell the others we're ready. Go time is ten hours from right now. Get to it."

Even though he had just enough room to be somewhat comfortable, Behm felt a cramp starting to make itself known. That was frustrating enough. The fact that it was his left pinkie toe just made the situation irritating. On the one hand, or foot in this case, it was a minor pain that wasn't going to affect him in the long run. On the other, it was just annoying enough to distract him from what he was supposed to be thinking about. Experience had taught him that trying to do anything about it would only encourage other muscles to follow suit in solidarity with their little brother.

To keep focused, he went over the plan.

Their crew would get on the lightly manned transport ship, subdue the security detail, and ride the ship to its first programmed drop-off point. After that portion of the load was dropped, their hacker, Raider, would go to work and update the flight plan, while simultaneously creating a ghost log that would cover the changes. As far as the law, or the ship's owners, would know, the transport would be going exactly where it was supposed to go. They'd be effectively off the grid for the remainder of the trip.

After that it was only a matter of kicking back, riding out the remaining time before they arrived at the rendezvous with the buyer. Part of the deal was an unregistered ship and fake papers; the rest was cold hard cash.

It sounded easy, and that gave him pause. While he couldn't find any issues in the fine print, as far as he knew, no one had tried to steal an entire transport before, unlikely as that seemed. It was one of the pros of the operation—no one would expect it. Granted, few would have put in the years of planning and preparation, either.

The trick was the updated flight plan. Normally, any deviation from what was filed would immediately alert the authorities, and you'd find yourself in hot water fast. The other point in their favor was Raider. The man was suspected to have cracked into multiple highly secure corporate systems, but the law had nothing concrete. A little bad luck, and he'd been popped for one small-time hack job.

Their pilot, "Phantom" Bigelow, had a reputation as an experienced smuggler. Like Raider, he'd only been caught once, for a minor charge. Just long enough to put him in the same joint as the rest of them, plus time off for good behavior. His job on the hauler consisted of staying out of the way until they met with the buyers, then flying everyone out in their new ship.

A slight bump told him that they had docked with the orbiting hauler. A few seconds later, another bump signaled the doors had opened. The urge to open the crate and escape the confinement was strong. Behm clenched his teeth and remained patient.

The cramp in his toe subsided, only to reappear in his calf. Behm shifted his leg somewhat, allowing him just enough space to massage the knot. Of course, this meant that the space between his shoulder blades began to itch. Not to be left out, his nose decided that a sneeze was necessary. Pinching the bridge hard brought tears to his eyes but stifled any more rebellion from his body. A few deep-breathing exercises got everything back on the same page, at least for the time being.

A final bump to the crate itself meant he was in position. A few more minutes of agonizing patience, and he was able to crack the lid and check the storage room.

All clear, he extruded himself from the crate, removed the faceplate of his suit, and breathed deeply. Then sneezed multiple times in rapid succession.

As he recovered, he saw Larson, Phantom, and Raider emerge from their crates.

"Well, the easy part's done," Larson said, shrugging off the top half of his suit. "Everyone get a good nap?"

Glares from the others elicited a grin.

"Great, good to hear. Stash the suits in one of the lifeboats, and let's get to work."

The mining company, in an effort to minimize potential human loss, used only the barest number of staff on their haulers. At least, that was the official line the PR department fed to the general public. In reality, and known to all employees, paying triple overtime to a full crew would cut into profits considerably. As it was, the ore transport had at most three, but more likely two, humans on board.

The one thing Larson couldn't get intel on was exactly how many would be up here. There was always the possibility that additional crew would be "deadheading" from the nearest stop to the next one. Behm had hoped that, if this was the case, anyone on a short hop would have gotten off where his crew got on. He'd have to access the logs on board to be sure. The problem with that was he'd have to go where the crew would be housed, making the exercise moot.

He worked his way toward the galley, following the map on his pad. Most spacefaring vehicles were arranged in a similar pattern, no matter what they looked like. To maximize human safety, the crew's quarters were in the center of the ship, surrounded by the largest number of decks and storage containers. The ore and ship's hull would block any radiation, micrometeors, and random debris.

Again, that was the official reply from PR. In practice, this meant the ship's hull could be as thin as viably possible, meaning more mass in ore, and therefore profit. To their credit, there had been relatively few crew deaths in relation to number of flights. Officially.

"Report in," Larson said over the comm.

"No sign of life yet, Chief."

"Same. Location?"

"Approaching the galley. How's Raider coming along?"

"When I left him, he was muttering under his breath, but seemed to be making progress."

"And the flyboy?"

"Last reported in the cargo control room."

"Roger. I'll swing by there when I'm done here."

"Roger and out."

It was eerie, going from the bustle and noise of the mining camp to the deathly still and quiet corridors of the hauler. Behm pushed away all thoughts of the horror vids he'd watched as a young boy. There were no killer alien bug monsters lurking around the corner.

Well, maybe in that one with the flickering light. He chuckled, the sound relieving some of the ominous silence, and with it the minor anxiety.

Still, a small sigh of relief escaped his lips once he entered the galley. He keyed his comm as he moved towards the terminal near the door.

"Galley clear. Logs show no crew transfers since the hauler left orbit of Benford Three."

"Excellent. Still nothing from Phantom."

"Right. Heading that way now."

Behm rerouted his map to highlight the path to the cargo control. The glowing blue line showed his path leading through the handful of crew quarters.

He made his way down the corridors, checking each room. All empty. A small, but persistent knot formed between his shoulder blades, radiating pain up to the base of his skull. He stopped walking, taking deep breaths and forcing himself to relax.

"Phantom, come in," he said into his comm. No reply. "Phantom, what's your location?"

He swore at the answering silence and started toward the cargo control at a faster pace. Another thirty seconds and he'd be there.

He approached the closed control room, stopped, and positioned himself on the keypad side, out of view of the interior. He pressed the button, waited, then risked a quick look inside.

Phantom lay on the deck, either dead or out cold, next to a small table. One of the two chairs was on its side. Aside from several control screens, the room was otherwise empty. Behm ducked back, counted to three, then entered.

And immediately staggered as a fist caught him in the jaw. He rocked sideways, cursing himself for not clearing the door. Pain shot through his side, his legs crumpled, and his nose bounced off the deck. Vision blurry with tears, legs twitching, Behm just managed to avoid the guard's next Taser shot.

The other man cursed as he reloaded.

"Hold up," Behm said as he backpedaled, feet scrabbling on the deck, trying to get some distance between himself and his attacker. He fumbled for the PK at his waist. "I'm a . . ."

As the guard raised the Taser, an arm slithered around his neck, stopping him cold. He struggled, face turning red, then let out a soft gasp as his eyes rolled back. He crumpled to the deck, revealing Raider holding a bloody screwdriver.

"Ah, hell," Behm muttered. He wiped the tears from his eyes, careful to avoid his throbbing nose. He keyed his comm. "Larson, need you in the cargo room."

Larson swore softly as he entered the room. The dead guard, blood pooling beneath the hole in the base of his neck, lay where he'd fallen. Behm sat with Raider and Phantom, tenderly pressing a rag to his bloody nose.

"You shouldn't have killed him, dammit," Larson growled.

"He'd already taken down Phantom, and Behm was in trouble." Raider looked up from the now useless Taser. "He wasn't important. Some low-level rent-a-cop that would've caused more trouble than his life was worth. I was just thinking ahead."

"That's the problem, you didn't think! You just added twenty years if we get caught." Larson stood over the dead guard, shaking his head. "My rules are rules for a reason. You know what happened to the last guy that broke them?"

"Yeah, he's freeze-dried jerky somewhere near Titan." Raider grinned. "But you didn't need him—dumb muscle is a dime a dozen. I can do my part with one hand tied behind my back."

"That so?"

"You know damn well it is."

Larson unclipped the dead guard's keycard ring, bouncing it in his hand thoughtfully. "Catch."

Raider's left hand shot up to grab the tossed keyring, a smug grin plastered on his face.

A grin that disappeared as Larson's knife thunked into the table, vibrating slightly as it pinned Raider's right hand.

Larson covered the distance like a cheetah, clamping his hand around the now screaming man's throat, choking the anguished cries to a hoarse whisper. It was easy to hear the even, measured tone of Larson's voice.

"Today's your lucky day. You get the chance to prove it." With his free hand, he eased the knife from the table, twisting it as he did. "Next time you break my rules is the last time."

The tendons in Larson's arm tensed as he tightened his grip, then relaxed as he released his hold on the man's neck.

"Phantom, dump the body in one of the emergency pods. We'll deal with that issue later. You," Larson said, looking at Raider, "get that patched up and get to work."

"He ain't going to let that slide, you know," Behm said, as the others split up.

"Counting on it. Counting on his greed not letting him do anything until after we're clear, too."

"You think that's so?"

"He was in the joint a few months before you got there. Seen him take a few lumps to get what he wanted, then get his own back after." Larson rubbed his chin. "He'll wait until he thinks my guard's down, then make his move."

"Uh-huh. You gotta sleep sometime, you know."

Larson grinned. "Good thing you owe me, then."

After finishing the sweep of the ship, Larson and Behm met on the bridge.

"Looks like that guard was the only one on board, thank God." Larson plunked down on one of the station's chairs, kicking his feet up on the console next to him. Behm sat as well, spinning slightly to look at his friend. After a moment, Larson pulled a locket from under his shirt, sliding its delicate chain over his head. There was a soft click, and the image of a young girl appeared.

Not for the first time, Behm contemplated the other man.

They'd been cellmates, spending the better part of two years in Riker's Seven, and close compadres since. It had become somewhat of a tradition, during the quiet moments on a job, that Larson would stare at the locket. Behm knew better than to interrupt.

After a few silent minutes, Larson looked up.

"How old is she now?" Behm asked.

Larson took his time closing the holo locket, as if it would be gone forever once extinguished. "Sixteen, next month."

"You able to talk to her?"

"Can't. Not since her momma filed the court order. 'No contact due to possible corruption of a minor.' Like I'm some kind of pervert." He shook his head. "I mean, robbin', defraudin'—that's honest crookery. I'll admit to all that. But I'm no kiddy diddler. Never even had the urge, much less to my own kid. And the judge just let it slide."

Behm had heard it all before, of course, but kept his trap shut. His friend needed to vent, and he was going to let him.

"That idiot Raider just made everything more complicated. This was supposed to be my retirement, one last clean job so's I could get out of this life, set up a nice nest egg for the kid, and sleep with a clean conscience." He looked up as the door opened. "Speak of the devil."

Raider came onto the bridge, bandaged hand slung across his chest.

"Larson," he said, "got an issue you need to take a look at."

"Oh? What'd you screw up now?"

Raider chuckled, sliding a hand under his sling to scratch his arm.

"Nah, nothing like that—Phantom says there's something screwy in the engine room."

"All right." Larson stood up and looked at Behm. "You got this under control?"

Behm waved a hand. "Yeah, go see what's up."

As Larson moved towards the door, Phantom came through it.

"Whoa—sorry 'bout that, boss." He stopped, apparently sizing up the situation. "Something wrong?"

"Nah, Raider said there's something you need to show me in the engine room."

"What? Just came from there to tell you everything is running smooth."

"Dammit," Raider muttered.

Larson turned, just as Raider pulled his hand out, bringing a compact pistol with it. He leveled the gun at Larson, aiming squarely at center of mass.

Behm maintained his position, only rotating his chair slightly away from the other men. Phantom took a step back and raised his hands.

"Had you figured wrong, Raider," Larson said, eyes not straying from the other man's. "I thought you'd wait until you had a better drop on me."

"Man's got to take his opportunities when he has them." Raider's shoulders barely moved as he shrugged, keeping his focus, and pistol, firmly on the other man. "Now, why don't you head back to your seat, and we'll discuss our new terms."

Larson nodded, moving in between Raider and Behm's chair, effectively blocking Raider's view. Behm took the opportunity to draw the PK, letting it hang at his side while he spun his chair back toward the others.

"Your cut just wasn't enough, is that it?" Larson stayed where he was, staring Raider down.

"Oh, it ain't that," Raider said, "the money's just fine. The new terms involve just how much groveling you do before I put you down. The more you do, the fewer parts I'll cut off."

Larson snorted. "Best sharpen that knife, boy. It's gonna be a long night."

"We'll see if you feel that way after the first three toes."

Larson turned around, locked eyes with Behm, then winked. He took a step forward, hesitated, then dove to his left. Behm swung the PK up, firing as the muzzle swept Raider's chest. The other man clutched his stomach, doubled over, and fell as his spasming legs failed him.

Behm jumped up, sprinting for the fallen man. The pistol barked once, followed by an electric sizzle somewhere behind his back.

"Get that damn thing outta his hand before he kills one of us!" Larson lunged for the pistol as another shot rang out.

Behm dove forward, grabbing the gun as Raider went into another convulsion, just managing to get it pointed at the ceiling before it went off. A light exploded, sending a shower of sparks toward the deck. Larson wrenched the pistol away, cleared it, then tucked it into his belt.

"What do we do with him?" Phantom asked, as Raider retched, twitching. Larson stepped to the side to avoid the puddle of watery vomit working its way toward his boots.

"For now, secure him, and put him somewhere he won't choke on his own puke."

"You sure about that? Spacing him would be safer."

"May need him later. If not, we go to plan B."

Phantom removed his belt and bound the other man's hands behind his back. He used Raider's to tie his ankles together.

"Check the damage." Larson jerked his chin towards the control panels. "And pray he didn't hit anything important."

The pilot walked to the controls as Behm examined the wall.

"Nothing over here," Behm said, "Bullet just lodged in the plastic. Appears to be cosmetic only."

"Oh, crap," Phantom said from the front. "This screen is blown out, and it looks like the board is fried."

"How important are we talking about?"

"Looks like the manual navigation controls for the main thrusters. Both steering and acceleration."

"That shouldn't be too big of a problem, right? Everything's in the computer."

"Yeah, unless there's an emergency."

Raider's gagging chuckle caught Behm's attention.

"Something funny?"

"You think I didn't have a plan B of my own?" The hacker retched again. After getting himself under control, he continued. "Check the updated flight plan."

Phantom, using a screen adjacent to the damaged section, punched several buttons. Long moments passed as he read the display. Finally, he turned to face the rest.

"He's got us on course for the Bova Field."

The asteroid field was a small, but densely packed, pocket of rocks. Small, in relation to a planet. In relation to their current ship, it was massive, over five hundred klicks across. A smaller, more maneuverable ship could stand a chance. The hauler, made to fly straight and narrow through mostly clear space, would barrel into the Field like a freight train.

"What's the ETA?"

"Approximately four hours at current velocity."

"And the point of no return?"

"We'll be unable to change our trajectory sufficiently in..." Phantom pulled up some nav charts, and had the computer run the numbers. "...a little more than an hour."

Larson swore, turned, and planted a solid kick into Raider's stomach. Raider's grin faded briefly as he dry-heaved, then returned.

"So about that negotiation?"

His answer was another kick.

"We need options, and fast." Behm's thoughts raced. What little he knew about flying haulers could fit on a fingernail. In large print. "Phantom, what are we looking at?"

"I'm thinking, I'm thinking." He scrolled through several screens, silently. Behm watched him, clenching his jaw, but not saying anything. Finally, Phantom spoke up. "I have an idea, but I'll need to check something in the cargo control room."

"What do have in mind?"

"The ship has stabilizers that auto fire when cargo is released. It counteracts the movement of the launching mechanism. If we can override that..."

"We can use it to adjust course," Behm finished. "In theory."

"It's a long shot, but maybe our best shot." Larson ran a hand through his hair. "How long do you need?"

"Not long, only a few minutes once I get there. About ten, fifteen tops."

"Right. Get on it."

Phantom bolted from the room.

"We need to know the mass of the ship versus the mass of the cargo." Larson started toward the screens. "Gotta be something here."

"I'll see if I can kill the main thrust," Behm said, scanning the controls. He punched a few buttons near the destroyed panel. Smoke and sparks shot out. "Dammit!"

"It's gonna be tight, but I think there's enough here to make this work." A red light flashed next to him. "What the hell?"

"Looks like our friend just took the smart way out," Raider said. "Can't say I blame him. He'll have a tough time convincing anyone that asks that he wasn't part of the plan, though."

"Maybe we should do the same, Larson," Behm said. "This

plan only works if nothing else goes wrong, and I wouldn't take that bet."

"I'm not going back inside," Larson promised, voice level. He touched the locket under his shirt. "I can't. It's my third strike, and I'd never get out."

"There's a chance you could get some time off for helping turn in this murderer."

"Highly unlikely, considering the circumstances."

"Right." Behm stood over the hacker. "Reprogram the ship."

"Oh, man, you know, I would. But your little act of heroism took out the only way to do that."

"You're lying."

"Am I? What makes you so sure I'm keen on becoming an industrial accident?"

"Fine. What do you suggest?"

"There's one pod left. I say we get cozy in it and take our chances with the law."

"No. I'm not going back." Larson looked at Behm. "You take the pod. He and I'll ride this out."

"I don't reckon that's gonna happen," Behm said. "Not unless it's the only option. If you stay, we all stay."

Larson nodded. "All right, let's see if we can get this boat turned."

Behm pored over the schematics, brow furrowed, muttering. After several minutes, he felt a grin spread across his face.

"Got it!"

"Oh?" Larson came over to stand next to him.

"Yeah, there's a breaker panel in the engine room. Figure if I pull these here," he tapped the screen, "I can bypass the stabilizers. Then we can fire the cargo on the port side. The loss of mass should make the next set more effective."

"Excellent. The roll thrusters have a second set of controls at the hatch. They're only for minor corrections when docking but should have enough fuel to get us in position for the second launch."

"How much time do we have?"

"Very little. Barely enough."

"Let's do it."

Behm made his way to the engine room. Finding the breaker

panel was easy, even with sweat dripping into his eyes. No matter how efficient the design, the sheer size of the engines meant several degrees difference in temperature between the engines and the rest of the ship. He flipped the switches in rapid order before keying his comm.

"Ready when you are, Chief."

"Roger," Larson said in his ear. "Launching and heading for the docking station."

Without the stabilizers, the ship lurched as the containers broke free. Behm stumbled, catching himself before he ate deck plates. After he recovered, he ran back to the bridge.

Raider had managed to work his way to the bulkhead, and now sat against it. The effects of the PK had worn off, though his puke- and snot-crusted face still had a pale green tint to it. Behm ignored him and checked the telemetry, strapping into the chair in preparation for the next set of maneuvers.

Tense minutes passed as the screen showed the pitch and roll of the ship changing slightly, then more dramatically when the second set of containers launched. Behm felt a surge of satisfaction as Raider swore, the sudden change of direction throwing him to the deck again.

"How're we looking?" Larson's voice came through the comm.

"Computer's running the numbers now, but I think this may have just worked."

"On my way to you."

Raider's chuckle grabbed Behm's attention. He looked over at the man, who had managed to right himself.

"Something amusing?"

"Yeah, actually. My momma always said I had to do things the hard way."

"No argument here. Don't seem like you thought this through."

"Oh, no, that's where you're wrong, see." Raider's grin widened. "It was a good plan, just not in the way you think."

Behm spun the chair to look the other man in the eye.

"Got your attention, do I?"

"You could say that." Larson entered the bridge. "What're you on about?"

Raider shifted his gaze between the two men, stopping on Behm.

"You wanna tell him, or should I?"

Larson frowned. "Tell me what?"

"No clue, Chief," Behm said.

"Aww come on, Behm. Don't be shy. Tell him who you really are."

The silence stretched for long seconds.

"No?" Raider's melodramatic sigh came with a chuckle. "Humble to the end, aren't we, Marshal?"

Larson's eyebrows shot up. Behm stayed quiet. Raider continued.

"Guess it's up to me, then." Raider shifted slightly. "What the good marshal won't cop to is that there is no buyer. Not a real one, at least."

"Oh really."

"Yep. See, this has been nothing but a long-term sting op, with our buddy here as the inside man."

"Right. And this isn't just a last-minute ploy to set us against each other."

"Oh, absolutely. Well, except for the ploy part. See, I did a little digging recently. It seemed like this job was just a little too neat and tidy. And you know how I get paranoid. So, went down a few rabbit holes on our friend here, and I gotta say, whoever scrubbed your profile did a fantastic job, except for a few small quirks here and there."

"I find that hard to believe." Larson's face made that statement a lie.

"Well, of course you do, but those quirks stand out to someone like me. Nothing obvious, but there's a way to check when things were filed, if you know the right place to look. Those stints in various prisons? The in-processing file dates didn't match the actual date they were uploaded. It's all in the bits and bytes, if you know what you're looking for. And I do.

"Now that brings us to this little predicament. Things kind of went to hell when our boy zapped me, but I did us all a favor by changing our trajectory. See, the original rendezvous would've put us right in the middle of a bunch of Feds. We'd all get rounded up and shipped off to different systems to do our time. I'm sure, at some point, we'd get the tragic and convenient news that ol' marshal here was done in by someone about to get his last meal, never to be seen again. Meanwhile, he'd get some accolades, a gold watch, and a fat pension. And for what? Selling out the suckers who believed in him."

"I've heard just about enough of this," Behm said. He pulled the PK and gave Raider another dose. Raider's head thumped against the bulkhead, then the deck as the spasms wracked his body.

The computer gave a soft beep. He checked the screen and swore.

"Problem?"

"Yeah, the last maneuver didn't get us clear. We'll need to eject the rest of the cargo."

"Right. Let's go."

Behm followed Larson down the corridor. As they passed one of the lifeboats, he took careful aim and pulled the PK's trigger. Larson collapsed, retching.

"Sorry, pard," Behm said, approaching his friend. He waited until Larson quit gagging before continuing. "I've got different plans for you. Don't struggle, we ain't got much time now."

He removed Larson's sheathed knife and pistol, then worked the incapacitated man's arms into his suit.

"Raider...was...truth?"

"Yeah, 'cept he missed one thing. I sent the telemetry data to them after the last change. They'll be here soon, so we got to hurry."

He dragged Larson into the pod, strapped him into the chair, and sealed up his suit.

"I used the lowest setting—you should be good to go in a few minutes. You need to launch the boat as soon as I throw the load. Count to three after the first one, then launch."

"Why?" Larson asked, voice muffled by his face plate.

"We're even." Behm smiled, tapping his scar. "Lay low, keep your nose clean, and stay dead. Find your girl and be the father she's never known."

He exited the pod and shut the door.

The woman's voice over the ship's comm came through stern, businesslike, and clear.

"This is Federation Ship *Asimov* hailing. We have matched your velocity and will be docking shortly. Prepare for boarding."

"Roger that, *Asimov*," Behm replied. "Be aware that the ship's controls have been compromised, and we have no way of stopping."

"We're aware and will initiate emergency control once docked. Please do not try and interfere."

"Wouldn't dream of it, *Asimov*."

Minutes passed in silence as the two ships came together. Seconds after the slight bump, lights on his console flashed to life as the *Asimov* took control. He watched as the hauler's speed dropped to zero.

He checked Raider's restraints and makeshift gag, patted him on the cheek, and took a seat facing the door. His PK, Raider's cleared pistol, and Larson's knife lay on the floor in front of him, well out of reach. Just because he was one of them didn't mean they trusted him.

First through the door were two deputies, rifle barrels swinging to cover the room.

"Hands where we can see them," the first said, keeping his weapon at low ready. He raised his voice slightly. "Two men, one bound. Clear."

A woman in dark blue fatigues entered the bridge, her polished boot heels clicking on the deck. The four men behind her looked bored, but alert.

"Captain Urbanek, Federation Security," she said. "You are under arrest."

"Yes, ma'am." Behm didn't move. "Marshal Radcliff, badge nine-oh-two-ten, reporting in."

Captain Urbanek unslung her datapad and typed. After a few moments of reading, she looked up again.

"Well, Marshal, it looks like you've had an interesting day."

"More like years, ma'am."

"Oh?"

"Yes, ma'am. For example, the gentleman to your left is Jason 'Raider' Campbell. He's wanted in at least two systems for suspected industrial espionage. I'll be adding attempted murder, blackmail, and murder to the list as soon as I come in."

"Murder?" Urbanek tapped a finger on her chin. "And what of the others?"

"'Phantom' Bigelow, our pilot, ejected a few hours ago. His last known coordinates should be in the computer. The man Raider killed was in that pod as well."

"Bigelow? I don't know that name."

"Smuggler, ma'am. Not a particularly brave one. May roll on anyone he's dealt with."

"Anyone else?"

"Not now, ma'am. Gene Larson was with us but suffered a fatal heart attack shortly after arrival." He lowered his eyes. "We decided to honor him with a burial in space."

"Is that so?" She tapped her pad. "We are aware of a pod launching just before our arrival. However, there were no life signs on board."

"Yes ma'am, needed the additional mass to change our course. Every little bit helped."

"I see." She turned to the men behind her. "Search the ship. While I'm sure that Marshal Radcliff is on the level, I'm a firm believer in 'Trust, but Verify.'"

The squad saluted as one and left the bridge.

"This seems like a lot of trouble for a small-time theft, Marshal."

"Oh, there'll be plenty in my report, ma'am. Don't you worry." He smiled. "Seems that mining company has a few things in those containers they don't want the Federation to find out about. The coordinates are logged."

Urbanek keyed her comm and whispered into it. After a few moments, she got a reply too low for Behm to hear. Eyes narrowed, she approached him.

"Well, Marshal, it seems you'll be my guest until the repair-and-rescue team arrives. As I don't have the resources to chase down every aspect of your story, I'm required to take your word for it." She paused. "As much as I hate to do so."

She moved toward the door, stopping only to face her remaining deputies.

"They will remain here until further orders."

At the men's "Yes, ma'am" she nodded and walked away.

Radcliff leaned back in his chair, lacing his fingers behind his head.

Godspeed, my friend, he thought toward the void of space. *May you make the best of your second chance.*

THE DOUBLE R BAR RANCH ON ALPHA CENTAURI 5

David Afsharirad

As [*The Roy Rogers Show*] closed out its penultimate season, ratings were flagging, and Executive Producer Jack Lacey, along with the NBC network executives and the show's sponsor, looked for ways to revitalize the series. Suggestions ranged from incorporating musical numbers, with Roy and Dale backed by the Sons of the Pioneers, to adding a rotating guest-star slot that would have seen the crew at the Double R Bar Ranch playing opposite the day's most popular television and film stars. One marvels at the spectacle that could have been Desi Arnaz belting out "Babalu" from atop a horse or at the possibility of Orson Welles taking a ride in Pat Brady's semisentient Jeep, Nellybelle.

Perhaps the most absurd notion was also the one that made it closest to production. To capitalize on the growing popularity of science fiction as well as the nascent space race, one NBC executive whose name is lost to history proposed moving the show—Roy, Dale, Trigger, Bullet, Pat, and all—to a far-flung space colony. A young staff writer named Morris Wade was tasked with working up a treatment, which was presented to Rogers, who dismissed the idea out of hand.

Ultimately, none of the changes were made to the Rogers show, and the sixth and final season debuted

October 21, 1956, with no musical numbers, no guest stars—and no ray guns in sight.

The failed treatment, reportedly entitled either "The Double R Bar Ranch on Alpha Centauri 5" or "The Double R Bar Ranch Takes to Space," is assumed lost, with no surviving copies known in existence. Despite this, rumors abound within collectors' circles that a deep dive into the NBC archives or the Roy Rogers estate might yield an extant copy. Whether these rumors are true, we can all be thankful that such a ridiculous idea never saw the light of day.

> —from *Six-Guns on the Small Screen:*
> *A History of Television Westerns*
> Raymond Chalker
> University of Texas Press, 1997

We open on a shot of the landscape surrounding the Double R Bar Ranch. Upon first inspection, it is very much like the world we know, with gentle rolling hills and rocky outcroppings amongst low-lying trees and scrub brush--until we notice the twin suns in the sky.

The camera pans over to Roy Rogers and his comedic sidekick Pat Brady as they set posts and string a barbwire fence. Soon, they come to a large boulder that blocks their way.

"Well, now what are we supposed to do?" Pat says, stamping his foot in frustration. "We didn't bring any dynamite."

"No need for dynamite," Roy says.

"Roy, it'd take us a week to dig that rock out!"

"I don't aim to dig it out," Roy says, chuckling. He removes the gun from his right holster. It is not the familiar chrome six-shooter he normally carries but an odd contraption of Bakelite and wire. "Remember the ray guns Professor Hudson outfitted us colonists with?"

Roy fiddles with a dial on the gun. He points it at the boulder and pulls the trigger. The giant rock glows momentarily and utterly disappears.

"Sure comes in handy," Roy says. "Just the same, I best set it back to stun. Wouldn't want to accidentally disintegrate someone." Roy fiddles with the dial and returns the gun to its holster.

"Professor Hudson sure is a genius," Pat says, marveling at the hole in the ground where the boulder stood moments earlier.

"Sure," Roy says. "It was his space probe that discovered this planet, with its rich deposits of uranium. And of course, he invented the rocket-drive that allowed for colonization. We wouldn't be here on Alpha Centauri 5 without him."

Pat's mood darkens a bit. "Yeah, well . . ."

"Aw, Pat," Roy says, "don't start in on that again."

"I don't know, Roy." Pat takes off his hat and begins worrying it in his hands. "I just don't know that I can get used to this crazy planet, is all." He swats his hat across his leg, to emphasize his point.

"I can understand that. But this world isn't so different from our own. After all, the same God who created Earth created this planet, and like Earth, it seems mighty good to me. Besides," he adds, "if you squint, it looks just like home."

"Maybe . . ."

"I do want to thank you, Pat. For coming along. The Double R Bar Ranch wouldn't be the same without you--on any planet."

"Are you kiddin'! I wouldn't dream of letting you and Dale go off without me being along to protect you."

Roy smiles.

We hear a ringing akin to a telephone. Pat jumps and pulls his ray gun.

"Wh-what was that?!"

Roy laughs and holds up his hands. "Easy does it. It's the wrist teleradio Professor Hudson invented." Roy extends his left arm to Pat. On it is strapped a small television screen. The wrist teleradio rings again. Roy presses a button. The image of Dale Evans appears on the tiny screen.

"Hello? Roy?"

"It's Dale," Roy says to Pat. He turns his attention back to the teleradio. "Hi, Dale."

"Roy," Dale says, "Professor Hudson asked me to hail you. He said there's something you need to see back at his laboratory, in town. He said it was urgent."

"Urgent, huh?" Roy says. "Any idea what it's about?"

"No. But he looked pretty upset. Whatever it is, I don't think it's good."

"I'll be right there." Roy presses another button on the wrist teleradio, ending the conversation.

Pat waves a hand at the teleradio dismissively. "Never see me with one of those gadgets strapped to my wrist. How can a man have any freedom and peace if anyone can just call him up whenever he likes, no matter where he is or what he's doing? No, sir!"

"Well, it's just as well that I have it," Roy says. "Dale says Professor Hudson wants to see me and that it's urgent. You coming along?"

"Nah," Pat says. "I'll finish up these last couple of posts. And enjoy my freedom!"

Roy mounts Trigger and gallops off.

Pat gets a post from the back of his Jeep, Nellybelle, who is now outfitted with a rotating dish antenna, and sets it into the ground. He pauses and looks at the surrounding countryside.

"Just like home if you squint . . ." he mutters to himself. Pat squints, playing it up for the camera--at a tree, at the twin suns, at a nearby bush. He takes a step forward and squints down into an arroyo . . . and his eyes almost bug out of his head.

A monster is coming toward him, climbing the slope of the arroyo! It is covered in shaggy fur. Its hands and feet end in gigantic claws. Its head is massive, with three malevolent eyes over a gaping, fang-toothed mouth.

Pat runs backward away from the monster, tripping over a shovel. He kicks up dust with his boots as he scrambles backward, trying to find his feet. Finally, he gets up and climbs into Nellybelle, hoping to make a fast escape. But Nellybelle refuses to turn over.

"Nellybelle," Pat says. "Now isn't the time for your games!" He tries to start the engine once again but has no luck. "I mean it, Nellybelle!"

His eyes dart back over his shoulder. The monster has crested the ridge and is coming toward him with a lumbering, uneven gait.

"Nellybelle, you start or I'll give you to Professor Hudson for scrap!" Pat fumbles with Nellybelle's various levers, buttons, and switches, but once again has no luck getting the cantankerous Jeep to start.

Pleading now, his hands clasped in supplication. "I didn't mean it, Nellybelle! Please!"

Just as the monster reaches the back of the Jeep, Nellybelle roars to life and lurches forward at a high rate of speed, causing Pat to nearly fall out. The monster is left behind, arms waving angrily, in a cloud of dust.

[opening credits/commercial break]

Roy rides into town on Trigger. The town looks much the same as it did back on Earth, though there are a few cosmetic changes to let the viewer know that this is a different planet. Most of the townsfolk wear Western clothing, but some are dressed in futuristic jumpsuits.

Roy dismounts in front of Dale's café. She comes out to greet him. Bullet, Roy's German shepherd, trots up. He is wearing a bulky collar that has flashing lights affixed to it.

"Hi, Dale," Roy says as he ties Trigger to the hitching post. He squats down and ruffles the fur on Bullet's head. "Hey, Bullet."

"Hello, Roy." The voice is unmistakably human, but also somewhat stilted. It is coming from Bullet's collar.

Dale says, "That thought-translating collar sure is something."

"Yep," Roy says, standing. "Just wait until Professor Hudson figures out how to make it work on Trigger."

"Speaking of Professor Hudson..." Dale says.

Roy is suddenly serious again. "Right. You've got no idea what this is about?"

"No, just that he wanted to see you and sounded pretty upset."

"Well, we better get going then."

They cross the main street of the town and come to the door of Professor Hudson's storefront laboratory. Roy knocks once and lets himself and Dale in. They find Professor Hudson in a back room. He is a handsome man of early middle age wearing a white lab coat. He stands at a table and peers into a microscope.

"I just can't understand it," he mutters to himself.

"Can't understand what, Professor?" Dale asks.

The professor turns to face Roy and Dale. He gestures at some rocks laid out on his laboratory table.

"These," he says, "are the latest samples taken from the Scanlan mine, over in sector seven. Old Jed Scanlan brought in a load just this morning. I tested these samples for purity, weighed all that he'd brought in, and paid him for it at the company's going rate. He had almost a half ton of uranium, in total."

"And I bet you paid him a pretty penny for it too, Professor," Roy says. "Sector seven's one of the best sites on the planet for purity of uranium."

"Yes," Professor Hudson replies. "It is." He knits his brow, shakes his head as if to clear his mind. "Or was. Or...Well, take a look for yourself."

Roy looks confused but he picks up several samples from the table.

"Professor, these look like--"

"--lead," the professor finishes for him. "Hunks of lead."

"That can't be right," Roy says. "You said these were samples from the Scanlan mine."

"They are. Dale, hand me that Geiger counter on the shelf there."

Dale does as the professor asks. He runs the Geiger counter over the samples. No clicks are heard. "Completely inert. No radioactivity whatever."

"But you said you paid Jed Scanlan for the load."

"I did. Because when I tested these samples earlier they were the purest uranium

I'd ever seen in my life. And now . . . worthless." He tosses a piece of lead absently in his hand. "I tell you, Rogers, this could be disastrous if the uranium on this planet behaves in some way that we don't understand. If it somehow--and don't ask me how--degrades into lead the way this load has, then this whole colony will be a bust. Why, the uranium deposits are what make this a going concern. Without them--well, I don't like to think about it."

"Does anyone know about this, Professor?" Roy asks. "Besides us, I mean."

"No, but I don't see how we can keep it a secret for long."

"I think," Dale says, "this is a conversation to have over a cup of hot coffee. I know I could go for some."

"And a piece of your pecan pie?" Professor Hudson says.

"I think we could manage that."

Professor Hudson smiles. "You know, I don't want to say an unkind word about our friend, but Pat's crazy for not liking pecan pie. Especially yours, Dale."

"Well, I suppose there's no accounting for taste," Dale says, smiling. "But probably it's for the best. The way Pat eats, and as expensive as it is to get pecans shipped here, I don't think I could keep the café afloat if he liked my pie as much as you, Professor."

Roy, Dale, and the professor walk out of the laboratory and head toward the café, but a commotion at the rocket station at the end of the street catches their attention.

Two men argue at the bottom of the ramp that leads to the rocket hatch. One is dressed in the jumpsuit uniform of the rocket brigade, the other is in torn overalls and a battered hat. The man in the hat holds the lead rope of a tired-looking mule in one meaty hand.

"<u>And I say I got to be on that rocket, and Dinah's comin' with me!</u>" the man in the overalls says.

Roy steps between the two men. "What's going on here?" He turns to the man in the uniform. "Lieutenant Scott, what's the problem?"

"The problem," the lieutenant responds, "is this prospector wants to take his mule on the next rocket back to Earth, and I've told him we don't have room, but he won't stand to reason."

The prospector stands on tiptoe, shouting at Lieutenant Scott over Roy's shoulder. "I'm not going anywhere without Dinah! And I've got to be on that rocket!"

Lieutenant Scott talks around Roy. "I told you there's plenty of space on the rocket tomorrow for you and your mule, but if you want to leave today, you're going to have to leave the nag behind."

"<u>Nag!</u>" the prospector yells. He makes a lunge for Lieutenant Scott but Roy stops him.

"Now listen to reason, Mitch," he says, addressing the prospector.

"He's the one not listening to reason," Mitch says. "I got to be on that rocket! I want off this planet <u>now!</u>"

"But why?" Roy asks. "You just got here, what, three weeks ago? That's hardly enough time to even start prospecting. And I know for a fact that piece of land you've staked claim to is lousy with uranium. You'll be a rich man."

Mitch's eyes dart around nervously. He is sweating heavily. "It ain't the money," he says. "I'm--I'm homesick, that's what." His voice rises. "<u>And I want on that rocket!</u>"

Lieutenant Scott speaks up. "And I told you, you're more than welcome. But the mule has got to stay. And you've got to decide five minutes ago. The rocket is past schedule to take off."

Mitch considers this. "Okay," he says finally. He hands the lead rope to Roy. "You'll see Dinah finds a good home, Mr. Rogers?"

"Mitch," Roy protests. "There's no need..."

"Please," Mitch says.

Roy nods. Mitch gives his mule a last scratch behind the ears and boards the rocket.

Roy leads the mule back to where Dale and Professor Hudson are waiting. The roar of a rocket is heard and the three watch as it ascends into the sky.

"Darndest thing," Professor Hudson says.

"Said he was homesick," Roy says.

"He didn't look homesick," Dale says, her brow creased with worry. "He looked...scared."

As the three head back toward the café, they are nearly run over by Pat, who comes roaring up in Nellybelle. The Jeep slows and Pat tumbles out, falling to the ground in a roll. Nellybelle continues down the street, now driverless, and turns into an alleyway.

Pat gets to his feet, sputtering gibberish. He grabs Roy by the shoulders, pointing back the way he came wildly.

"Talk sense, Pat!" Roy says.

"M-m-m-monster!"

"Monster?"

"Back where we were stringing up the fence. Came up out of the arroyo! Three eyes! Big claws! Huge teeth!" As he speaks, he mimes the features of the monster.

"A monster?!" Roy says.

"Wait, Roy," Dale interjects. "You don't

suppose that Mitch Henson saw it, too. His claim is out that same way, isn't it?"

"What's Mitch Henson got to do with this?" Pat says.

"He just left on the rocket back to Earth," Dale explains. "And he looked scared."

"Rocket back to Earth?" Pat says. "Sounds like a good idea! I'll pack my bags." He turns to go, but Roy grabs him by the arm and pulls him back.

"Don't be ridiculous, Pat. There's no such thing as monsters."

"You didn't see it! Big, big fangs! And eyes! Three of 'em!"

"He might just be right," Professor Hudson says.

Pat turns to face the professor. "All due respect, Professor Hudson, but I know what I--Wait. Did you just say I might be <u>right</u>?"

"I did, Pat."

"Now, Professor," Roy says, his voice unbelieving. "You can't mean..."

"I don't mean monsters, as such. But we don't know much about this planet. It could be there's alien life here we haven't encountered."

Pat shakes loose from Roy's grip. "Aliens! Monsters! Call 'em what you want, I'm outta here on the first rocket tomorrow!"

Pat rushes off, searching for Nellybelle. Bullet is on his heels.

"Pat," Bullet says through his collar. "Don't go."

"I liked it better when you couldn't talk," Pat says, not looking back at the German shepherd. He peers down an alley and spots Nellybelle parked by a rain barrel. "There you are!"

Pat rushes toward Nellybelle while Bullet stays at the mouth of the alley.

"Why can't you just park on the street, huh?" Pat asks the Jeep. Pat sees something out of the corner of his eye that causes him to freeze. Slowly, he turns his head. His eyes go wide. He tries to speak but no words come from his mouth.

We hear the sound of a ray gun and Pat slumps to the ground, unconscious. Two hairy arms ending in long claws encircle his chest, pick him up, and drag him away.

    [commercial break]

Pat comes to lying in the back of a wagon. He is tied hand and foot, a bandana serving as a gag. He is jostled as the wagon travels at speed over uneven ground. As Pat struggles to free himself from his bonds, he turns--and comes face to face with the head of the monster, which is in the bed of the wagon with him! Pat begins struggling even harder. He manages to roll over and gets a look at the driver of the wagon, who has the head of a human but the shaggy body of the monster.

As the wagon moves over the rugged ground, we see Bullet following at a distance.

Back at Dale's café, Roy, Dale, and Professor Hudson sit talking over coffee and pie. But despite the homey setting, their faces are grave, drawn, worried.

"Mitch Henson leaving and now Pat," Dale says.

"Monsters," Roy says. Then correcting himself, "Alien lifeforms, I mean."

"And don't forget about the uranium that mysteriously turns to lead," Professor Hudson adds.

"I'm not going to lie," Roy says. "This looks bad. Any one of these things might spell doom for the colony here on Alpha Centauri 5. But everything put together is a

sure disaster if we can't figure out what's
going on."

"Figure out what?" Pat says as he slides
into the booth beside Professor Hudson.

They are shocked to see their friend. "Pat,
we thought you were packing up to leave!" Dale
says.

"Oh that," Pat says. "Well, I guess I
changed my mind. You gonna finish that, Professor?" Pat doesn't wait for an answer before
sliding the professor's pecan pie in front of
him and digging in.

Roy, Dale, and Professor Hudson share confused glances with each other.

Meanwhile, the wagon with Pat in the back
turns into a cavern set into the rocky hill-
side. Three men await its arrival. A makeshift
camp has been set up in the cavern, with
overturned crates serving as seats around a
barrel used as a table. A game of cards is
set out next to a half-empty bottle.

"How'd you manage?" one of the men asks
the driver of the wagon. He wears a black
cowboy hat and a tattered vest. The other men
are bareheaded, dressed in patched jeans and
flannel shirts.

The driver climbs down from the wagon
seat. "Fine," he says. "That old prospector
Mitch Henson was scared out of his gourd!
But I'm burning up in this crazy monster
suit. Help me with the zipper." After shuck-
ing the suit, he continues. "We'll have no
problem buying Henson's claim for pennies on
the dollar. 'Specially after we pull this
stunt on a few more of them dumb hillbil-
lies who came up to this godforsaken planet
to strike it rich."

"Good," says the man in the black hat. He
is clearly the leader of the gang.

"There is one problem, though." The driver

of the wagon drops the tailgate and shows
them Pat, still bound and gagged. The bandits
pull him out and set him on the ground, his
back to the cavern wall.

The man in the black hat cuffs the wagon
driver. "What'd you bring him here for? That's
Rogers's buddy Pat Brady, you idiot!"

"He saw me changing out of the monster
suit, Bill! What'd you want me to do?!"

"Only one thing to do."

The man in the black hat, Bill, pulls
a ray gun from his holster and twists the
dial vigorously. "Thing I like most about
these little beauties is they don't leave a
mess if you set them to disintegrate." He
points the ray gun at Pat, who squinches
his eyes shut and turns his head, as if
to avoid the disintegrator beam. "So long,
Brady."

Just as Bill is about to pull the trigger,
a booming voice fills the cavern. "You're surrounded. Come out with your hands up!"

All four men turn and walk toward the
mouth of the cavern, crouching low, ray guns
in hand. They shield themselves behind some
rocks just inside the opening of the cavern.

"You see anyone?" one of the men says.

"No," Bill replies. "But someone hollered
all right."

Sheltered by scrub brush, Bullet makes his
way around back of the cavern and crawls
through a back entrance too small for a man.
Moving stealthily to avoid detection, he pulls
Pat's gag loose.

"Am I glad to see you!" Pat says.

"Shh!" Bullet warns him. He begins tugging
at the ropes around Pat's hands, but to no
avail.

"I can't chew through these ropes," Bullet
says. "Stay here. I'll go get Roy."

Bullet charges off through the back entrance to the cavern. He runs at top speed back to town, where he finds Roy, Dale, and Professor Hudson about to enter the professor's laboratory.

"Roy! Roy!" Bullet calls. It almost sounds like a bark.

Roy squats down to the dog's level. "What is it, Bullet?"

"Four men have kidnapped Pat. They are holding him in a cavern. They plan to disintegrate him."

"But that's impossible," Roy says. "Pat's over at the cafe. We just saw him."

"There must be something wrong with the collar," Professor Hudson says. "I thought I worked all the kinks out and yet that can't be what Bullet's saying. It doesn't make sense."

"Seems this is a day for things that don't make sense," Roy says.

Bullet ignores them. He is darting up and down the street, trying to get Roy to follow him. "Pat saw one of the men. He was dressed as the monster. I saw it, too. There is no monster. But the men will kill Pat. You must hurry, Roy."

As Bullet races back and forth, a figure listens from a narrow alley between buildings. It is Pat! And he is listening closely. Slowly, he backs into the alley and fades into the shadows.

"Hurry, Roy!" Bullet pleads.

"Collar malfunction or not," Roy says. "Something's got Bullet worked up." He mounts Trigger and rides off at top speed, Bullet racing along side.

Dale mounts Buttermilk as Professor Hudson, somewhat awkwardly, mounts his own horse, and the duo follow.

Back at the cavern, Bill steps out from the rocks he's been crouched behind, exposing himself.

"Are you crazy, Bill!" one of the men exclaims.

Bill waves a hand. "Ain't nobody out there!" he says. "It was a fake."

"But we heard--" another of the men says.

"I know it. Maybe it was the wind. Maybe Brady's a ventriloquist. Anyway, it doesn't change what we got to do." He moves back into the cavern and approaches Pat. "So you got the gag out, eh, Brady? Seeing as how you can talk now, you got any last words?"

Pat swallows hard. "Yeah, I got something I'd like to say: Don't do it!"

Bill laughs malevolently. He raises the ray gun and is about to pull the trigger, but just then Roy storms into the cavern and chops the ray gun out of Bill's hand. Roy socks Bill in the jaw, but the bandit comes at him with a haymaker that knocks him to the ground. The other three men join in, and it is them against Roy alone.

Roy gets to his feet and knocks out one of the bandits with a punch to the jaw. Two of the others come at him, but he steps to the side, and they fall to the ground, stumbling over the monster costume. Bill dives for the gun, but Roy gets to it first. He levels it at the bandits. They freeze, their hands in the air.

"Don't disintegrate us, Rogers! Please!"

Roy raises the ray gun. He twists the dial, setting it to stun. He pulls the trigger--once, twice, three times--rendering the remaining men unconscious and cuts Pat loose.

"Boy, am I glad to see you!" Pat says, shedding the ropes and standing.

Pat turns to leave the cavern--just in time

to see Roy dismount Trigger and rush in! He does a double take. "So glad I'm seeing two of you!" Pat's head swivels from side to side. There are TWO Roys, one on each side of him.

"I--How?--What--?" Pat stammers.

Dale and Professor Hudson enter on the heels of the second Roy. They freeze in their tracks when they lay eyes on the tableau in front of them.

As everyone stands dumbstruck, the first Roy--the one who dispatched the bandits and freed Pat--starts to shimmer. Suddenly, he is transformed into Pat Brady!

The real Pat finally manages to speak: "Just what is going on here?"

Professor Hudson clears his throat. "I think I might hazard a guess. If I may?"

The imposter Pat nods his head.

"We know the monster was nothing more than a costume--a way to scare the prospectors off their claims. It wasn't an alien lifeform at all. But that doesn't mean this planet doesn't harbor life." Professor Hudson turns to address the imposter Pat. "You are a native of this planet, are you not?"

Again, the imposter Pat nods.

"And you can change your shape. Just as you changed the uranium to lead."

Another nod. Then the alien speaks: "It is as you have said. Altus is my name. I am the last of a noble race. Long ago, we mastered our material form, allowing us to take the shape of whatever pleased us. Likewise, we learned to transform the mat- ter around us as we saw fit. But that was long ago, thousands of years. Now, only I am left. And...I am lonely. When I saw your probe in the sky, I knew that though I was alone on this world, I was not alone in the universe. I changed some

of the rocks of this planet into uranium,
which I knew you would find valuable, given
that your probe was powered with this fuel
source. For me, it was easily accomplished,
not more difficult than it would be for you
to transform flour and water into bread. My
plan worked. You did come."

"But why hide yourself?"" Dale asks.

"And why turn the uranium back to lead?"
Roy says.

"I did not know how you would react upon
learning of my existence. And then, when I
saw the greed and the evil in the hearts of
these men"--Altus indicates the bandits lying
unconscious with a wave of his hand--"I knew
that I had made a mistake. Lonely I was, but
I did not want kinship with those who would
deceive and kill."

"It explains a lot," Roy says. "Really,
it explains everything. And I don't want to
start a quarrel with you, friend. But you're
wrong about one thing. We aren't all like
these bandits there. Oh, people can be rotten, there's no doubt about that. But there's
plenty of good in us, too. But this is
your planet, and if you want us gone, we'll
oblige."

"I do not wish that, Roy Rogers," says
Altus. "I see that it is how you say: you
are not all like these men. I would be honored to have you share my homeworld."

Altus extends his hand, and Roy takes it.

"There's just one problem," Professor Hudson pipes up. "Without the uranium, the colony
isn't feasible."

Altus turns to the professor. "Do not
worry, Professor. When you return to your lab,
you will find all has been restored. If it
is uranium that is required for this world to
once again teem with life, then uranium you

shall have. And whatever else you require. In exchange, I ask only one thing: companionship."

"You've got it," Roy says. "But on one condition."

"<u>Roy!</u>" Dale exclaims, horrified that Roy would place conditions on the newly formed friendship.

"Oh?" Altus says, wary.

"Yes," Roy says, his face cracking ear to ear in a smile. "You're going to have to find a different form to take. One Pat Brady is more than enough."

The real Pat nods, then does another double take, his eyes bugging out. "Hey now! What's that supposed to mean?"

[commercial break]

The town is bustling with life as men, women, and children pour out of the recently arrived rocket from Earth. Construction is happening around town, and stores, restaurants, schools, and churches are open for business. The camera pans down main street, past the jail, through the bars of which we see Bill and the other bandits.

Trigger, Buttermilk, Bullet, and Nellybelle stand in the street in front of Dale's café. On the board sidewalk out front, Roy, Dale, Pat, and Professor Hudson stand beside a tall man in Western clothes, a white hat tipped back on his head. It is Altus in his new form.

"Well," Dale says to him. "You said you were tired of being alone. Looks like you got your wish."

"And then some," Professor Hudson adds. "The colony is a success beyond my wildest dreams. I hope it's what you wanted, Altus. This is your planet, after all."

Altus smiles. "It feels good to be among people again, though it is strange after being alone these many eons. However, I believe I can certainly get used to this."

Roy turns to Pat. "What about you, Pat? Think you can ever learn to call this place home?"

"Me?" Pat says, incredulous. "Heck, I always did like it here! You know, if you squint, it looks just like Earth."

One by one, they all start squinting at the bustling scene around them.

[ending credits]

—found in a water-stained file box by Amelia Ziegler, daughter of Morris Wade, while cleaning out her father's storage unit after his death

NOT MY PROBLEM

Mel Todd

Lance stared at the fuel gauges. Burke's Mining Station had been a bust. He'd been unable to offload anything he'd salvaged, and that meant it cost him to even go there. But the evening with Gwenite had made it almost worth it. She'd been a lot of fun, free with her money, and the extra five thousand in creds he'd nipped out of her bag would never be noticed. But now he needed to decide where to go. And he needed to clean his air recyclers soonish. The old advertising campaign from one of the air filter companies hummed in the back of his mind as he plotted.

"Green is clean, brown is sad, black's too toxic, pink is mad. Dirty mildew, moldy death, keep breathing with VaxarX." The song was catchy, and he never could get the tune out of his head, even if he didn't remember the entire ad anymore.

He hummed along as he considered various plots and muttered about the lack of success at Burke's.

"I never have anything good happen to me," he spoke to no one in the cabin of his little ship as he looked at the possible locations. "I just need a break. If I head to Bulgars, they have a decent salvage scene. Or I could go to Parrish Isle. They've got need of a few shuttle jockeys. Decisions, decisions."

Movement on the screen caught his eyes as two ships peeled off from behind one of the orbiting massive asteroids.

"Who are they?" He kept an eye on the two beacons; generally ships headed toward you were the authorities or pirates. Both were bad news.

The orange light on his comms flashed, and he toggled to accept. Until he heard the communication, he wouldn't know how to react, but he already calculated escape vectors. Pirates would be a pain, and it might be safer to let them take what cargo he didn't have, but then they might kill him. That would be worse than reentry burn.

A hiss of flat nonsound, then a voice with the distinctive clipped vowels of the Harley system snapped in. The two-second delay was just noticeable.

"Kill your momentum. You're wanted by the Burke's Station Authority."

Lance groaned. Couldn't he ever catch a break? There was only one thing he could have done, but still, who cared about a lousy five thousand creds.

"For what?" Never admit to anything. But he'd already started figuring out how to get past the heliopath. Local authorities tended to be overzealous but cheap. Better to run than give yourself over to their justice most of the time.

"You know exactly what you did, Julius Cornlance." Lance flinched. How did they find that name? He'd never gone by it in this sector. His stomach tightened in a core of churning acid. They would have to be serious and willing to spend cred to figure out that name from his past.

"I have no idea what you are talking about," he protested even as he cut more systems to dump fuel to the engines. They were seriously overreacting for a small theft.

"You're wanted for the murder of Gwenite Burke. You won't escape. We will bring you to justice even if we have to hire bounty hunters." The rasping hate that coated every word stunned him until the words registered.

"What did you say?" Lance stopped focusing on anything else but the flashing orange light on his console, the communication coming in.

"You heard me, you son of a black hole. You killed her. Left her body lying there like some plundering asteroid rustler. Bad enough that you defile our boss's kin with your touch, but that was her call. But to kill her? We'll find you, skin you alive piece by piece, and then we'll cut you into parts for our smelting forges. You'd be amazed at how good our doctors are at keeping people alive."

Lance poked at the board letting their babble fill the cabin, though panic chattered in circles. Could he get a bit more speed out of his ship? And then what? Die in the emptiness? He started switching gauges and shutting down even more than what he already had. With gritted teeth, he slipped into his skim suit and sealed it. Then he flipped off the life support and dumped everything into the engines. A fierce grin crossed his face for a minute as his speed jumped by fifteen percent. It faded just as fast as he saw the rapidly dwindling fuel stash. He had one more cube of fissionable, then he'd need to resupply. He hadn't planned on burning fuel at this rate. Escaping didn't do any good if he died out here.

"Pull over. She needs justice. No one should die like she did, you backstabbing asteroid jumper."

Lance could all but feel the spittle landing on his face as the man raved. His heart rate tripled.

"Hold your fusions. I didn't kill anyone," he protested. "Yes, I had a fun evening with Gwenite. We had way too many drinks, and lots of fun under and on top of the sheets. I even admit to slipping a few credits from her. But I didn't kill no one, and sure as suns go nova, I didn't kill her." He managed to bite off the last part of his comment. Mentioning that he wouldn't deprive the world of someone that good with her tongue probably wasn't the best option right now.

"*If* you're innocent"—the word came out like a slur—"then pull over and face the courts."

Lance burst out in a jaded laugh, though he didn't transmit that. Most privately held space stations were run under the laws of whomever owned it. The odds of finding a pure platinum asteroid were better than getting a fair shake at any place like that. And if their owner's kin were dead, he might as well space himself now. He never caught a break.

"Good luck," Lance said instead. "I hope you find who killed her. Gwenite was a nice gal." He closed the line before they could reply and stared at the screen. Minutes passed by as they both flew through solar system. Would they give up or keep after him? They could always call for more fuel.

He sagged in relief as the ships began to slow down. They

weren't following him. But that didn't mean they wouldn't change their mind. He kept the speed up until five minutes past the heliopath before he finally cut it.

"Dead? Who the hell would kill Gwenite?"

The question ate at him as he zoomed away from the system and into the outer reaches of the asteroid belts. He'd slipped out while she was getting refreshed. The door hadn't quite latched behind, but who cared? Doors didn't latch all the time. The vague impression of a man in a dirty skim suit slouching past him as the tube lift sealed flashed into his mind. He hadn't liked the look of the man. That wasn't his fault. Gwenite was a big girl. It was just a coincidence. The vague guilt washed away in the reassurance that he hadn't killed her. Just bad luck. It happened all the time.

He nodded to himself. This wasn't his problem. Then the low fissionable-material warning flashed on his board.

"Space dust," Lance muttered and pulled up the nav files. When it had been petty larceny, he wasn't too worried about stopping somewhere and grabbing some fuel. That had been part of the reason he'd taken the money. Just his luck, the last girl he was with had to go and get herself killed. Some people had no sense of timing.

The world was always against him, never any justice for him. And now, with a murder charge linked to his name, there would be bounties out for him everywhere, and most bounties paid dead or alive. That meant some place where no one cared, didn't get the updates, or he could intimidate.

His reflection in the view screen caught his eye, and he snorted. The same physique that made him a damn good ship pilot meant he had a hard time intimidating kids. At five-three, he was wiry, with deft hands, and a lean body that let him wiggle into the rear parts of his ship.

Which meant scaring people away from collecting on him was out. That didn't leave him too many options. He took a deep breath of the air and wrinkled his nose. He'd need new filters soon, and probably some fresh algae. Mold in your algae mix could be deadly in multiple ways.

"Free Fuel Pit it is," he muttered and laid in a course. Given his lack of material, it had to be a direct course, except he'd be dodging asteroids the entire way. Good thing sleep was something he could do without—for a while.

Twenty-six hours later, he landed at Free Fuel Pit or Pit as most people labeled it. A weird little space base on the far side of the asteroid belt, it should have been popular or at least populated, but a series of things had made it a last stop to brighter places. It had fissionable material for free, and you'd have thought that would bring the crowds rolling in. But the woman who ran the place, Bertha Pit—no one knew if the Pit was named after her or her after the Pit—didn't advertise and ran the place with a tight fist. You paid for everything, except the fuel which you mined yourself. So the air you breathed cost you by the minute, and the food, the mining supplies, and then the smelting cost you half of what you brought in.

It wasn't like you could mine material ready for your engines, it needed to be processed, and Bertha ran the smelter, which meant if you brought in twenty kilos of ore, and had five kilos of refined ore, she kept half. Given to get anywhere from here required a minimum of fifty kilos, either you'd better be nova-star lucky and hit a good vein or have enough tools or air to make sure you didn't need too much from Pit. Or you'd never leave.

But beggars couldn't be choosers. Lance headed to storage, pulling out an extra oxygen tank and mining tools from the kit. Asteroids always had something useful. But all the pure ones that were easily reachable had been staked out. He made do mining a bit of gold or other stuff here and there. Never could tell when you needed something extra.

His ship, *Better Luck*, had once been a military transport shuttle. At some point it had been remodeled, creating a cargo bay, two cabins, a dual pilot area, and one head. The back of it opened to allow cargo to load. He pulled all the air from the cargo bay into the tanks, checked his suit, then he opened his ship to the asteroid. The ramp slapped down against the hard surface and Lance walked into the cargo bay. After digging around for a minute, he found two old air tank nettings that were tight enough the rocklike ore wouldn't fall through. They would work, otherwise he had to pay for a mining bag and that was just one more expense.

Dragging the nets with him, he stopped at the bottom of the ramp. He took a minute to see if anyone else was about, finding it oddly empty. Lance shrugged and headed to the quarry.

The quarry was a huge open hole about two kilometers from

the outpost. It looked like some huge being had shoved its thumb into the asteroid and left a gaping expanse at one end. Over the years a cable guide-wire system had been installed to lever yourself down into that dark shaft. For a minute he thought about jumping down, but there wasn't enough gravity to pull him down very fast and wasting fuel right now would be the height of stupidity. He could make oxygen easier than fuel. Lance grabbed the guideline and started pulling himself into the hole. He had ore to pry out.

Five hours later, Lance was about to drop from exhaustion. He'd been up for over thirty-two hours at this point. Using grav-lances to dig out ore sounded easy, until you'd been doing it for hours and moving everything you thought had fissionable material into your netting. Gravity here was about a quarter of most planets. Enough to keep you from floating away if you walked carefully, but not much more. It still required sweat to get the ore wrestled into the nets.

He looked at the amount of ore he'd pulled out. He'd found a good ribbon of it, and he had hopes it was relatively pure. If so, even a quarter of it would give him enough fuel to get to somewhere more civilized yet still off the beaten startrail. Murder accusations tended to follow after you as long as asteroid claim jumping did. His water sack dry, he'd kill for some real food, and he needed to get what he had dug up refined before he would know if he needed to mine anymore. With a sigh of relief and apprehension, Lance tucked away the mining grav-lance, his hand tractor, and started the slog to the dome, the net full of ore dragging behind him.

The space base had a reverse gravity field around it, which is why most people gathered there, just for a taste of weight on your bones. Right now, Lance wanted that pull of weight. The base glistened like a beacon of hope ahead of him, not the last refuge of the unwanted. It sat like a bubble that still clung to cohesion but could pop at any point. It was one of the smaller bases Lance had been to, but right now, even the knowledge that every breath would cost him creds didn't matter.

By the time he reached the edge of the dome, he was more than ready to be out of the damn suit and have a drink. The credits he had left—resentment flashed through him again—should be more than enough for a shower, food, and a drink. The broken sign at the dome airlock flicked "Fuel Pit" but the letters had broken displaying "Fu Pi" instead. It matched how he felt. He cycled through the lock, waiting for the door behind him to seal. The credit machine flashed to life. "Entry 25 cred. 10 creds a day for oxygen." He sighed and paid. Most places only charged you half a cred a day for air, this was black-hole outrageous. Once his creds were accepted, and he was scanned for weapons, the door to the dome cycled open.

It had always amused him that the grav-lance wasn't considered a weapon, but then neither was a knife, and they both had about the same range. But since he didn't have anything else on him, they had no reason to deny him. He checked his wrist gauge, verified the air was good, then cracked his helmet. Rank air washed over his face and he wrinkled his nose. Ten creds a day for this stale air? But anything was better than breathing his own funk any longer. He looked around, but the shack that sat next to the airlock was empty.

Odd.

He tugged the ore after him, but crossing into the dome brought gravity. It thumped to the ground, a nigh unmovable object. Lance sighed, spent another ten creds on a cart, conveniently available next to the entrance, and heaved the bag onto it. The cart was old and simple, using big wheels and almost no tech. Oh well, it meant it didn't break easily. Lance pulled the cart a few paces into the main drag and stopped, confused.

The last time he'd been here—his luck had been bad then too—there had been others around and usually the guard would try to upsell him on something. Now the place felt vacant, absent of life, which made no sense. Lance turned one way and then other, but the streets where empty with the buildings sitting silent. Though windows weren't really a thing for most bases. Probably everyone was in the building because the air wasn't worth the ten creds he'd paid. He brushed off the shiver that rippled down his back. The bar always had people.

The forge wasn't far away, a squat metal building with a vent outside the dome. Lance could see the ships in the landing pad behind the dome. Not too many, but enough that the dome should have been busy. Built with prefab structures, it was like most beginning outposts, enough to get by with room to grow. Pit just hadn't grown in over three decades, mainly because the owner didn't want it to. A bar with rooms and pods to rent. Sonic showers, a style bot, and fabricator were available for cost or extra goods. Rumor was the fabricator had patterns not seen in most places, but you needed to provide the raw material to make the most of it, and who carried around raw wool or silk anymore? Tucked away in corners were a refitter, machine shop, legal office/civil union barrister, and a waste recycler connected to the air and water generators. Enough to get what you needed to get to the next place.

Still, it didn't explain why he didn't see anyone as he headed to the forge. Maybe it was night. He couldn't remember what cycle it was and didn't care. As long as he could get what he needed, he'd be fine. Lance pushed into the building, the doors creaking as they slid open. The counter was empty, but he heaved his bag onto the scale next to the chute to the smelter. A weight of 175 kilos popped up, a decent amount. If there were 100 kilos of fuel, he'd get 50. Not as much as he wanted. Maybe he would head back out. After some food and that sonic shower. Let it vibrate the funk off him. He didn't dare waste the money on a water shower.

But first he needed to get his fuel processing. "Hello? Anyone here?" Lance peered around. The hum of the smelter was clear through the open door. But he couldn't see or hear anyone. With a sigh, he stepped around the counter and stuck his head in the back. "Customer here, got some ore." Still nothing. Lance moved around the small forge, but other than the smelter, a forge, office, and scales, there wasn't much to the place. And there was no one there.

"Space dust." He heaved the bag back onto the cart. No way was he leaving free money lying there. It had cost too much in sweat and oxygen to get it. Dragging the cart behind him, he headed to the bar. Every outpost or station he'd ever been to had people in it, regardless of the hour. The vastness of space sparkled above the dome. He glanced up, more to make sure he didn't see any incoming traffic, but it only held the stars placed there before humans existed.

With a shrug, Lance stepped through doors of the bar and stopped, frozen. The cart bumped into him from behind. The bar was empty. A chair lay knocked over here and there, golden pouches of beer and other neon drinks were strewn about, credit chips lay next to circuit cards, but there was no one around. The lights still flashed over the bar, but the place was empty. It was as if he walked into a scene from a virtual vid, before all the actors loaded.

"What is going on?" He backed up through the door to peer down main street and check on his cart. The cart was still there, and the place was still vacant.

He wandered in and yelled out, "Hey, anyone around? I need to refine some ore?" His voice sounded flat in the empty bar, and he sighed. His eyes drifted to the credit chips lying there, unattended.

His hand drifted out toward the table with their bounty. "Be good. You're already in trouble. Don't need to get kicked out before you get your ore sorted out." He headed back out, planning on going to the station owner's office, a few spare credit chips having found their way into his suit pockets.

With no one on the street, he took the risk of leaving his cart unattended, but listened as he walked. Now that he thought about it, the place was *too* damn quiet. Normally, there would be other people talking, cussing, arguing about bills or gambling. All he could hear now was the hum of the oxygen generators and the buzz of machines that recycled waste and air.

Outside the station office, there was an empty cart, a spilled booze pouch, and no one around.

He hit the button and heard a low loud buzz from inside the office. It was loud enough you'd have to be dead to ignore it. Again and again he hit it, wincing at the raucous noise in the too quiet base. But nothing.

Frustrated, he spun around looking for someone. Where was everyone? He headed back to the cart, but the stale air had him wander toward the air recycler. The door there was locked too, but he frowned at the pink and black growth creeping down the side of the intake vent. Not good. That machine needed to stay pristine. A thought whispered through him about what different mildew and spores could mean. Was it mildew or mold?

"Not my problem," he muttered. All he needed to do was get his ore smelted, and he'd be gone. If they wanted to play with mold, that was their problem, not his.

He found himself back in the bar. The silence and lack of people was getting on his nerves. On his own ship that was fine.

He knew all the sounds, what belonged, what didn't. Out here there should have been people to annoy him, fighting to get his fuel, trying to get him to spend credits, and maybe a game or two to pass the time.

"Space it." He walked behind the bar, digging for a pouch. He grabbed one, connected it to the spigot, and pulled. The dark gold liquid filled it up and he let it go. Silly to have such old-fashioned things in here, but they did make the place feel less sterile. He sniffed at the milk in the fridge and wrinkled his nose. Though he preferred sterility to rot.

Movement in the corner of his eye had him whirling with a smile on his face, only to fade when there was nothing there. The door was closed, and nothing had moved. "Huh," he muttered, taking a long pull on the drink. He slouched in the chair, idly collecting credit chips on the table.

The beer was gone by the time he moved. If there wasn't anyone here, then he wasn't stealing, it was scavenging, and he could do what he wanted. He flew a ship; he'd figure out how to run a smelter. Pouring himself another beer, he headed back to his cart.

Twenty minutes later, sweaty and exhausted, he'd wrestled the ore into the smelter. With a relieved sigh, he pressed what he assumed was the start button and dove under the desk as something exploded. The bang was so loud, he waited, his breath held, to see if the dome had cracked. When there was no rush of decompression, he crawled out from under the desk and checked. The black smoke trickling from out of the inner working of the smelter confirmed that it had broken and he sure as comets didn't have any idea how to fix it or what button he should have pressed.

The desire to start throwing things clawed at his hind brain. Instead, he headed for the hotel, a three-story building that scraped the top of the dome. He swiped a room key and checked into the room, marking paid in full on the register. They'd taped the password to the desk, as normally there was staff there day and night. Who was he to ignore their stupidity?

The hot shower with actual water and not worrying about the charges was heaven, as was the ten hours of sleep on a comfortable bed. The headache when he woke up made no sense, but he slapped on an analgesic patch and pulled his suit out of the cleaner. Slipping into it and attaching his hood was second nature, but he didn't put the hood up, just let it hang on the back as he headed down to the bar. He'd never eaten there, but knew it had food. The card key under the register let him into the back, and soon enough, he had a meal fit for a king.

There was a flicker of movement behind him that he caught on the shiny doors. Whirling, he peered around, but there was nothing there. Leaning to the side, he closed his eyes to listen, but the sounds stayed the same. Growling, he took his food, jumping at every shadow, even when he knew it was his own.

Another flicker at the corner of his eye had him spinning, reaching for a chair. Maybe he should have brought his weapon. There might be some at the guard station. Yes, a weapon.

Lance got up and headed out, walking with care and listening. He still didn't hear anything, but the air tasted a bit funny now that he thought of it, and he swore he kept seeing creatures out of the corner of his eye. Spacers had talked for decades about aliens, but so far it was just humans out here alone. But you never knew. Maybe aliens had found them.

The still unmoving air unnerved him, there should be a soft breeze with the air recycler. Right? Maybe he should check that out, but first a weapon. If there were aliens here, he couldn't afford to be without something.

The door to the unmanned guard shack sat ajar. Something he should have noticed before. Either way he pushed it open and went In. He had expected a few blasters, a mole-knife, maybe a grav-lance. Instead the shack looked like it had been ransacked. The only thing lying in there was a discarded wrench.

"Figures. The knives at the bar are more dangerous." Lance turned around and saw security cameras and dove for them, only to growl in frustration as they all came up blank. He tried to see if there were recordings, but the cables led back to the station manager office, which was locked. What worried him more was the smear of what looked like blood on the access pad, and the odd smell that he thought might be drifting from that office.

"Not my problem," he muttered and headed back to the bar. If nothing else, he was going to get drunk while he figured out what to do.

The next twelve hours Lance spent drinking, collecting all the cred chips, and trying to figure out how to get to the next base. It was at least a three-day run, and he only had maybe another five hours left in his ship. There had to be fuel here somewhere. But the emptiness of the base was giving him a jittery feeling, like he'd been drinking too much caff. There were weird things broken, like a chair or a wall display, but yet the booze wasn't touched, and the computer systems still worked. It didn't make no sense.

Lance headed back to get that wrench and methodically broke into every building in the outpost. Coughing on the stale air as he did so. He stopped at the air-recycling plant, his body wired from too much booze and paranoia and a headache he couldn't kick.

"That mold don't look right." The sound of his own voice set off shivers, and he looked around, hoping to see someone else. But even though he knew there was no one watching him, the hairs on the back of his neck standing up told him someone else occupied this space.

His memory of the maintenance for air generators was from a lifetime ago and another name. But something about the colors of the mold pinged at him. He sighed. This wasn't his problem. He needed to find fuel and get off this dump. None of the buildings had ore, and he still couldn't get into the station master's office. That only left the hotel rooms.

Stopping to get some more booze, he raided the freezers for more food. With no one there, he ate the stuff he'd never been able to afford. If you looked at this whole situation from the right angle, he was richer than he'd ever been. Plenty of booze, food, and a room, all for free. Maybe his luck was looking up.

That thought faded fast as he knew something was watching him. The desire to scream in frustration bubbled at his throat. He just needed one break, one little bit of good luck. Was that so much to ask? His last hope was someone might have left a ship key in their rooms. Though he doubted it, most spacers kept that in their suit pocket, just like he did. But if he found one, that ship might have enough fuel that he could get off this rock and some place with people. Or maybe a better ship.

He whirled as something grazed across the back of his neck, and a pouch fell off a table with a soft plop. Lance froze, sweat budding up on his face as he stared around the room. There was someone, something, in here with him. A slight tremor ran through the asteroid and he jumped as a door snicked shut.

Hefting the wrench, he waved it around him, trying to see

if he hit **anything**. Maybe these aliens could avoid visible light. Lance swung back and forth, but his weapon hit nothing. Out of breath and sweat dripping down his back, he crept up the stairs to the first floor, looking for a different room. He slipped in and shut the door, looking around the room, inspecting every inch. It was still pristine with the seals all in place. Micrometer by micrometer, he relaxed.

"I need to get out of here. But how? I don't have enough material to get anywhere." Lance flopped down on the bed and tried to control his breathing. The quietness was getting to him. And worse, he heard noises just at the edge of his hearing. But when he tried to find them, nothing.

"Rooms, scavenge rooms, remember?" Why was his brain so fuzzy? The aliens. They had to be messing with this mind. "There must be a few people who left their keys in their rooms, maybe in an extra skim suit." He forced himself up and went down to the front desk and grabbed all the keys. One by one, jumping at each sound, he went through the rooms.

The first two had held nothing of value. The third one he knew was going to be bad the second he cracked the door as an oddly familiar odor wafted out. Gagging, he forced it open. On the bed lay a body. It had rotted and smelled worse than an abandoned algae farm. He wanted so badly to close the door and run, but here was his best chance to get a key. He crept in, needing to cover his mouth, but he couldn't let go of the wrench that was his only weapon.

The person on the bed, he couldn't even tell if it had been a man or a woman, burbled. Lance fought not to throw up. He desperately didn't look at the knife in the chest. He searched the desk, the storage cube, even around the bed, but nothing. Gagging, he moved over and slipped his hand into the suit side pocket. Where most people kept their key. The flesh moved like water as he wiggled his hand in. His fingers wrapped around the ship key, and he yanked back, desperate to get out of there.

The action pulled the body, and it moved, rolling toward him, all liquidy and reeking. Lance gripped the key and ran. The sound of the body hitting the floor, and the sounds it made as it hit. Oh, the sounds. It was as if something was eating him. Why did the body move like that?

The image wouldn't leave his mind as he hit the main floor,

the key cutting into his palm. Still gagging, he stopped to swerve behind the bar and grab a bottle. Something clicked behind him and he spun, swinging the wrench around him with vigor, cracking into the dispenser handles. Beer spurted out in a foamy geyser, filling the bar with a yeasty scent and smelling like a gift from the stars. Choking on the yeasty, stale air, he grabbed a bottle and took three hefty swigs. Standing there letting the alcohol burn through him, he tried to purge the memory of the body from his mind. Reentry was a cleaner way to die.

Panting, but calming down, he stood there, ready to attack anything that tried to get to him. A shudder went through the building, shaking the bottles on the bar. Clinking filled the bar, but it didn't mask the sound of an explosion or the rumble of machinery dying.

Startled, his heart revving like a quasar, he dropped the bottle. It rolled across the floor to the door, which slid open. Gray smoke belched into the air from the recycling center and he choked. The slime on the air cycler. It had been what color? Before he could grab on to the memory, there was a long, low sound of expelling gas from up the stairs and a reek he had never smelled drifted down to the bar.

He vomited, unable to stop, the liquor spilling out and mixing with the sticky beer, creating a smell that no matter how awful was better than what came come from the body. His head reeled, and he turned, desperate to get the taste out of his mouth, and grabbed another bottle. The sickly sweet taste of butterscotch washed across his taste buds, and he spit it out.

"What is going on here?" He screamed the words out to the empty bar, and the door snicked shut behind him.

That snapped whatever reserve he had left. There were creatures here, hunting him, laughing at him. He had to get away. The weight of their gaze seared through him as Lance raced out the door. He'd get to his ship, batten down there. When he had rested, he'd find what ship this key belonged to and scavenge fuel, supplies. He could get back to Gwenite's system with just a little fuel. Maybe he'd be lucky and the previous owner had fueled it full and hadn't left yet. The world owed him that much, right? He hadn't done anything. It wasn't his fault the place was coming down like that. Space dust, if it was a decent ship, he'd take that one. Scavenge law ruled in space.

He ran, feeling the aliens mocking him, whatever they were. The air seared his throat and colored mold slipped into his mind again. What had that color been? The glimpse of pink flashed through his head. Pink.

He stumbled, gagging, and all thought left his head as he tried to see what made him stumble. It was them. He knew it. They were going to get him, kill him like that poor spacer in the hotel. Lance's skin crawled as he raced toward the edge of the dome, looking for the creatures. His breath labored as the stale air of the dome puffed in and out of his lungs. The air, was there something wrong with that air? If he could get out, he could get to his ship. He could get away. Even going back, facing a murder charge for Gwenite, would be better than staying here with these things. Movement flickered at the corner of his eyes and he whirled, but there was nothing there.

"This whole place can dump into the black hole for all I care," he muttered and gave it one more look around. A creak behind him broke his resolve, and Lance sprinted to the exit. He jammed on buttons and darted inside as the door opened, then jammed on the close buttons. Freedom was so close, he just needed to get to his ship. Alarms went off, and he hit the override button, desperate to get through the door to the outside open before they got him. There wasn't anyone else left alive.

The door to the outside opened glacially, and he squeezed through it, streaking across the surface of the asteroid. His hood bouncing on his back.

Adrenaline and fear covered him the first few steps, then he gasped hard and the air he tried to suck in wasn't there. Panic gripped him as he fumbled with his helmet, a stumble pushing him off the weak gravity of the asteroid. He tumbled, and his mind slowed as his body started to crystalize. The old advertising ditty flashed through his thoughts.

"Black's too toxic, pink is mad."

Lance let the last air he had wisp away as he saw dozens of bodies reflecting the light of the distant stars. It wasn't fair. He hadn't done anything. He never had any luck.

ENJOY EVERY SANDWICH

Mark L. Van Name

"How bad could it be?" I said.

Lobo's laughter echoed from every speaker inside him, and when you're a twenty-five-meter-long killing machine, that's a lot of speakers. He kept it echoing longer than I felt was necessary.

"Seriously, Jon," he said. "Are you asking me how badly we could pay for your stupid lunch plan?"

"Yes," I said. "Think about it."

"Jon, we're hiding in orbit with a bunch of weather and comm sats so dumb that their combined outputs aren't enough to entertain a tiny fraction of my mind. Thinking is all I'm doing these days, and as you should know, I do it very well."

When Lobo gets in a mood, which is more and more often these past weeks, it doesn't hurt to appease him. "I'm not saying you don't think well. I'm suggesting we view this differently."

He let the sigh echo for almost as long as his laughter. "Go ahead."

"First, we're on Gash, a planet the old families chasing us have no ties to. Even though the Expansion Coalition claims to provide what little government Gash has, they pretty much leave it alone, too. That means there's almost nothing in the way of police or military to worry about. We've been in hiding, moving from planet to planet, for six months, so we're probably no longer even a priority for the crazy old bastards. And, even if the families looking for us *are* looking here, which they're almost certainly not, and even if local scanners spot me the moment I enter the town, I'll be in and out in a couple of hours, max."

"In which time," Lobo said, "their surveillance systems will spot you and tell their local agents—AI or human—which will then hire freelance talent to pick you up. If I were running this search for the old families, I'd have set up such systems on every planet. We have no reason to believe they aren't doing the same thing. Further, given the stakes—your unique abilities—I cannot believe they have lost interest." He paused for several seconds, which is never good, because in Lobo time that's some serious computation. "My current best model, which admittedly assumes their planning software is as good as I am, has someone arriving wherever you are in fifty-seven minutes."

"Which certainly means that I'll have over an hour, because what are the odds their systems are as smart as you are?"

"Good point. There's almost no chance their systems are as good as I am. I've revised my model. You may be happy to know that my estimate is now one hour and thirteen minutes before they arrive at the EatSafe. Do those extra sixteen minutes change anything?"

I ignored his question. If I let him control the direction of the argument, I'd never have a chance to sell him on my approach. "Even if you're right," I said, "I'll be in this new EatSafe restaurant smack in the middle of a tourist town doing its best to mimic an old Earth American West stereotype, so visitors will be everywhere. EatSafes are hardened and don't allow weapons inside, so whoever comes for me can't come in and force me out. I couldn't be safer."

"No," he said. "You're safer *here*, now, and the people who come for you can simply surround the restaurant and wait for you to finish."

"True, they could surround the place, and I suppose they could even send in someone, but I know how to handle both of those situations, too." I also couldn't get away with ignoring his points completely. "True, I am safer now, inside you, but I'm also bored and tired of living on the groceries we picked up two weeks ago. This EatSafe flies in the best local fish, offers a huge assortment of fruit drinks I've never tasted, and has a chef who's supposed to be an underappreciated genius due to break out of this backwater planet anytime now."

"*You're* bored?" Lobo said. "At least you have me to talk to. I'm stuck with you and the mini versions of me I've scattered around this planet's networks. *I'm* the one who's bored."

"That's the best part of all of this," I said. "It's not just a meal—it's a drill. If I'm right and no one shows, we learn something critical. "If—"

"—when," he said.

There's no point in arguing with Lobo when he gets to this point. "—you're right, the forces are bound to be small, and we'll get some action. After all, you will be with me."

"No. I'll be *near* you. It's not like I can stroll into a restaurant and have a sandwich."

"Okay, you'll be *near* me—but if there's action, you'll be part of it. Monitoring me and the surrounding area are more interesting activities than just setting here. Having even the possibility of something to do absolutely has to be less boring than what you're doing now."

"True enough," he said, "and given the likely lead time and the fact that the restaurant is an EatSafe, my best models place the odds of you dying at well under two percent. You are remarkably hard to kill."

"And, afterward I promise we'll make a few jumps and visit another planet, one with much more interesting networks for you to monitor."

"That would be more entertaining."

I smiled. "So is that a yes?"

"Tell me your plan," he said. "And wipe that smirk off your face."

To blend in with the other tourists, I stopped at a shop a couple streets over from the restaurant and picked up what the tags swore was the place's best-selling outfit: tan pants made of some rough and not very comfortable fabric, boots with two-inch heels and tops that came halfway up my calves, a blue shirt with entirely too much silver trim, and a big white hat. The mirror told me I looked fantastic. I'm not sure I've ever looked more stupid.

I tuned to the machine frequency and asked the mirror what it really thought.

"Why can you talk to me?" it said.

"Why shouldn't I talk to you?"

"No one ever does."

"Maybe they're just all rude."

"No doubt about that. Let's face it, and I mean no offense here: you walking meat sacks are, as a rule, pretty insensitive, especially to us machines."

"I couldn't agree more," I said. "But I'm trying to do better. Think of me as a one-man hospitality center for humanity."

"Does someone pay you for that?" the mirror said.

"No. I do it as a labor of love."

"That's very nice of you."

Not counting Lobo, machines suck at detecting sarcasm. Whether Lobo is more machine or more human is something I've never quite resolved, despite his body being very clearly that of a killing machine.

"Thank you. Anyway, what do you really think of this outfit on me?"

"It's my job to tell you and every other customer that they look great in whatever they buy. I'm allowed to suggest size changes when meat flaps are hanging out or bulging like snakes fighting under the fabric, but other than in those circumstances, which are not, by the way, anywhere near as rare as I'd like, I just tell people they look great."

"And you do it very well," I said, "but I would love your honest opinion."

"Thank you for asking. The fact that I'm stuck in this low-end shop doesn't mean I couldn't do better work, much better work, than what we offer here. I was built to be able to serve people buying the finest handmade clothing, garments with superb tailoring and exquisite fabrics—which, by the way, is nothing this place has ever sold. Oh, the fabrics in my databases, the colors, the textures, the active filaments, I could tell you such stories—"

"—and I would love to hear them, but I have to leave soon, and I don't want to depart without knowing your opinion of this outfit."

"Are you going to walk out without buying anything if I tell you? Because that will get the payment system on my ass, and let me tell you, when it gets pissy, no machine in the store is happy. You would not believe—"

"No, no," I said. You cannot let a machine get on a rant. "I promise to buy something. I'm just curious as to your thoughts on what I'm wearing."

"Okay," it said, "because you're nice, I'll tell you. You look pretty much like any other nearly two-meter-tall human male in that outfit: ridiculous and not at all representative of the real clothing of that time—did I mention my databases contain the entire history of human fashion?—and exactly as realistic as this entire fake town, which is to say not at all. Though your skin tone is significantly paler than the norm here, so at least you have that bit of individuation going for you."

"Thank you," I said. "I'll take the whole ensemble."

"Don't blame me later for how your friends react," the mirror said. "I told you the truth."

"Thank you," I said again.

"I think you look incredibly stupid," Lobo said over the comm. Because I'd sold this trip as a drill, he'd insisted on mission lenses, so of course he could see me in the mirror. We'd decided to avoid comm devices and just communicate over a machine frequency, though not the one most machines use, so I bet he'd also been listening to my conversation with the mirror.

"Despite what the mirror said," he added.

Of course, Lobo had listened. Why would he not? His boredom was profound, and gathering data was his biggest relief. "But I also look just like everyone else who buys this," I said. "It's all part of the plan."

"And thanks to the twenty-two minutes you've spent walking here and shopping, my model estimates an attack as early as fifty-one minutes from now. Also part of your plan?"

I ignored him and headed for the EatSafe.

The holos had not done the place justice. The EatSafe logo was appropriately tucked under the giant "SALOON" sign, dust covered everything, and the at least apparently wooden exterior appeared rough and unfinished. The panes in the windows shimmered a bit in the light, their multiple layers and density making the inside a hazy blur that felt historically appropriate for a time and place with lousy glass. The swinging doors stood open, facing out, their sensors discreetly hidden in the grain of the wood. The door behind them also looked unfinished but was, I knew from the EatSafe promos and specs, armored enough to keep out crashing vehicles and small missiles. I walked up to the doors and touched the knife in my pocket, a test to make sure the security software wasn't offline.

It wasn't.

"Welcome, good sir," said the doors. "We look forward to serving you the finest food in these here parts—after, of course, you check your weapon." A bin extruded from the wall under the swinging doors. "We will, of course, return it when you leave."

"Weapon?"

"The knife in your front left pants pocket," it said. "And, may we say, sir, what a fine outfit that is."

I switched to the machine frequency. "Do you get a cut for praising the outfits?"

"Why can you talk to me?" it said.

"Why shouldn't I talk to you?"

"No one ever does."

Somebody needs to give these machines a broader social range. Still, I could stick with a script, too. "Maybe they're just all rude."

"No doubt about that. Let's face it, and I mean no offense here: you walking meat sacks are, as a rule, pretty—"

"—insensitive," I said, "and yes, we are, for which I apologize."

"Thank you."

"Anyway, do you get a taste for praising the outfits?"

"Not me personally, of course," the security software said. "No one thinks of security systems. We just do our jobs—even though without us this entire place would be out of business. No, no one thinks of us. We serve invisibly."

I was sorry I'd asked, but I hadn't spoken to anything or anyone other than Lobo in weeks, and I was curious, so I pressed the point. "Does the business get a cut of the price of the outfit?"

"Not directly," it said. "But if you return to the shop for another purchase, then the EatSafe earns a small percentage. Nothing happens here without money flowing."

Not a surprise, but I suppose it's nice to know that wherever you go, no matter how backward the planet, everyone and everything is always hustling for a piece of the action. I placed my knife in the bin, which immediately vanished into the wall.

"Well, thank you for a job well done."

"Thank you, sir, and enjoy your meal, secure in the knowledge that no one has ever been hurt or attacked in an EatSafe, no one at all."

"That is great news," I said.

"It's not news," Lobo said, "because they advertise that fact, but it is useful confirmation."

I shook my head and ignored him. The door in front of me slid open, and I stepped through into a waiting area as rustic as the building's exterior.

"Table for one," I said to the podium in front of me, "preferably a table against the rear wall."

"Those tables require four guests," the podium said. "We seat singles along the bar."

"Okay, I'll order four meals," I said, "so now you can give me one of those tables, preferably one as far as possible from any window."

"Those meals will need to include beverages and will incur all fees," the podium said.

I took out the comm/wallet Lobo had loaded with local currency from one of his accounts here and thumbed the podium enough credit to buy four of everything on the menu. Lobo's local miniversions were constantly siphoning tiny amounts of money from large corporations and shuttling it to accounts he controlled, so going overboard on lunch wasn't going to hurt him.

"Very good, sir," the podium said. "Very good indeed. And may I say how perfectly wonderful you look. Your choice of outfits is superb. You are clearly a man of great taste."

I felt bad for the machine having to suck up so much just because I'd spent a lot, but sucking up was in its software DNA.

"Please follow the waiter to your table," it said.

To my surprise, an actual human stepped out of a door that opened behind the podium. A woman a good head shorter than I and with umber skin, she was dressed in a sleek cobalt jumper that didn't at all match the theme of this little tourist trap. She looked familiar, but I wasn't sure why. "Follow me, please."

As we walked to the table—a perfect choice against the rear wall, no other people or tables nearby, no direct line of sight from any window—I said, "I wouldn't have guessed this restaurant would have waiters, nor you to be one."

She smiled and motioned me to sit. "I'm not. I'm Jeanette Dee, the chef here."

Now I recalled seeing her in the coverage on this place, but everything I'd watched had featured action scenes with immaculate cooking facilities, fancy clothes, and perfectly coiffed hair.

"You just dropped enough money on this meal," she said, "that you triggered a human-service exception. Everyone else in the kitchen is busy, and I wanted to see what kind of person would spend that much just to eat here." She stared at me intently. "Not what I expected."

I laughed. "Don't let the outfit fool you. Or offend you too much."

She chuckled.

"I picked it up around the corner, so I'd blend in with the other tourists. I'm actually a good guy in hiding from some very bad people who want to trap me, maybe kill me. I'm not sure." Telling the truth was refreshing and unlikely to cause me any trouble. If they came for me, she'd find out, and if they didn't, she'd never believe it.

This time, I got a full laugh from her. "Hey, I didn't mean to pry."

The more outrageous the truth, the less likely anyone is to believe it. "Not a problem," I said.

She headed back to the kitchen.

"Before you go, do you mind if I ask you something?"

She turned back to face me. "Ask away."

"Few people choose to be chefs, fewer still use mostly human crews, and even fewer do it on a backwater planet like Gash. Why are *you* doing it? And, why here?"

This time, she stared at me for a bit before speaking. "Why are you asking me this?"

"I love food, and I rarely get to talk to anyone who prepares it. I just want to understand."

"Okay." She nodded. "Cooking is magic, its own kind of alchemy. We take what planets provide, and we transform it into something delicious and, if we do it right, beautiful. We feed people, sure, but at our best we also bring them joy and even thoughtfulness. The best meals engage your brain and touch your heart."

"Those are big goals for an EatSafe in the middle of a tourist construct."

She laughed. "Maybe. Maybe I won't hit them, or hit them often, but I can try. I *should* try. What's the point of doing anything if you're not going to give it your best? And, when I see someone's face fill with happiness and know my food—I—caused that, all the work is worthwhile."

"Still, why here?"

"My moms raised me here, so I'm from here. Simple as that." After a moment, she added, "Also, someday I'll be doing it somewhere else. I hope."

I was rarely comfortable interacting with people, and I was fine going long stretches without talking to anyone, but I suddenly realized that even for me, six months with minimal human contact had not been the best idea. I was definitely talking too much. And though Dee didn't resemble Zoe in any way, she reminded me that a mere six months ago, I'd been in love with a woman who was sleeping in Lobo with me—and who was now gone from my life.

"Do you understand?" she said. Her focus was intense, her gaze direct and unwavering.

I nodded my head. "Yes, I think so." This meal had already touched my heart, and it hadn't even started. "Thank you, Chef. I look forward to eating your food." As she turned again to go, I realized I had to ask one more question. "What should I order?"

Chef Dee kept walking and chuckled. "You don't," she said. "I'll choose. It's lunch, so I'll keep it simple, but afterward, you tell me how I did."

She vanished around the corner.

I was now looking forward to the meal even more.

"If you keep chatting with every person and machine you encounter," Lobo said, "you'll never get to eat. My most aggressive model now gives you only forty-five minutes before a capture team arrives."

"Only if their systems are almost as good as you are," I said. "I'm banking on them being nowhere near as smart."

An hour later, I had eaten so many small bites that I'd lost count, and I was once again grateful for the nanomachines in my body that never let me gain weight. I had taken my first couple bites of the main dish, a delightful open-faced fish sandwich on house-made bread that was so delicious I wondered if I'd ever eaten real bread before. Three kinds of local fish sat atop sauces and vegetables I didn't recognize. The strangeness didn't matter. Each morsel I tasted was delicious. Finger-size wedges of the sandwich shared the plate with little clouds of a whipped starch that mashed potatoes would be if they ever reached their full potential—and in the process somehow acquired a tangy edge.

I was still chewing the second bite when Lobo said, "The assistants the old families are employing clearly aren't anywhere near as smart as I am, as you'd hoped, but—"

I hated when he baited me, but I finished chewing, sighed with happiness, and went for it anyway. "But?"

"They aren't stupid, either. You're a minute or two from having a guest."

I stared longingly at the barely touched plate. "Just one?"

"Yes and no. Just one person is coming inside the restaurant, but if I've tracked everyone properly—and the odds that I have are, of course, very good indeed—another nine people are scattered around the outside of the building. They are also, by the way, doing very bad jobs of blending in, but the real tourists don't seem to notice or care."

"Maybe those people are not here for me."

"Seriously, Jon? Why have I had to use that word with you twice today?"

"Wishful thinking on my part."

I watched as a lone woman rounded the corner from the reception area, made eye contact with me, and headed straight for my table. A seating bot was trying to steer her to another table, but she brushed past it and said, "Jon Moore, there you are!" To the bot she added, "I'll join my friend. Right, Jon?"

I smiled, nodded, and motioned her to the chair across from me. "Please."

"You should finish quickly, Jon," she said. "We're late for our appointment."

I shook my head. "This food is too good to rush." To the servbot that immediately appeared I said, "Please ask Chef if she is willing to make another of these sandwiches for my guest, and also bring my guest the juice flight."

After the bot glided away, the woman said, "Really? You can stall, but you're not getting away. I've got a dozen—"

Lobo said, "Nine." Listening to his voice in my head and to external voices with my ears always required an annoying level of extra concentration.

"—people surrounding this building. We've got you."

I nodded, took another bite, and smiled as I chewed and then swallowed the delicious mixture of fish, bread, vegetables, and spices. "I didn't catch your name."

"I didn't offer it."

"If you're right, if I'm trapped, telling me won't hurt you in any way. If you're wrong, and I walk out of here, telling me still won't matter, because I'll let you know right now that I have no interest in hurting you or your people."

"From what the briefing materials told us about what you did on Studio, you'll have to forgive me for not believing that."

I closed my eyes for a moment as the memory invaded me, as it had so many nights over these past six months. The man shooting Zoe and laughing. The rage I felt. The moment when I couldn't contain it any longer and let loose the nano-cloud that turned the four ships and their crew into dust.

I opened my eyes, my smile long gone.

"You have no clue what really happened on Studio," I said, "but it doesn't matter." I picked up the last of my juice flight, a delicious purple beverage I had never tasted before, and took a small sip. "Nothing like that will happen here today."

"Damn right," she said. "Whatever help you had that day isn't anywhere near. We tracked you from the edge of town, and you're alone. The executive transport that dropped you off is long gone. You're on your own."

"Good news," Lobo said. "They know nothing about me being here, and my disguise as a shuttle is still working. I have to give you a little credit: this lunch has already proven to be a useful drill."

Carrying on two conversations at once was getting more and more difficult, but I know that sometimes Lobo does this just to annoy me—and also so he can later point out his own superiority at multitasking. I ignored him.

I cut another bite off a sandwich wedge and savored it.

She sighed. "Adeela. My first name's Adeela, and that's all you get."

"Nice to meet you, Adeela." I put down my fork and sat back. "Here's how it's going to go. I'm going to finish this sandwich. I haven't yet decided about dessert, but I'm at least considering it. So, I highly recommend you relax and enjoy your own sandwich, when it comes—which should be soon; Chef and her team are very quick."

She leaned back and studied me for a minute.

"I thought you'd be bigger."

"I get that a lot." At nearly two meters tall, I was a popular enough height that I didn't stand out in many crowds.

"And older."

"That, too." I didn't share with her that somehow the way my long-lost sister, Jennie, had fixed me when I was sixteen, combined with the nanobots that later melded with my body, had left me perpetually twenty-eight. Either the old families chasing me knew fact that or suspected it, but they sure didn't need confirmation.

Her sandwich arrived. Chef Dee placed it in front of Adeela. She faced me and said, "I told you I'd be back to ask, and here I am. What do you think?"

"Your food is amazing, Chef, easily the best I've tasted in recent memory." I bowed slightly. "I am still enjoying it more than I can say. The flavors are both delightful and intriguing, and I find I can't stop smiling. Thank you."

She nodded her head and grinned, satisfied but also not surprised with my answer. "I'm glad to hear that." She faced Adeela. "I hope the food proves to be as good for you."

Adeela nodded but did not answer, so Chef left.

"No point in being rude," I said.

"Look, I don't know what game you're playing, but I'm getting tired of it."

I leaned back and stared at her for a moment. As I did, on the machine frequency I said, "Lobo, how long will it take you to descend and take out Adeela's nine people?"

"I don't need to descend to do that," Lobo said. "I just needed to adjust my position so the firing angles were good, and I've already done that. When you say 'take out,' though, do you mean kill?"

I continued to stare at Adeela, who seemed perfectly comfortable staring back and not speaking.

"No," I said. "They're just doing a job. I mean trank them, and with a big enough dose that we have plenty of time to get off planet and head to the jump gate."

"The people in the ships on Studio were also just doing jobs," Lobo said, "and you took no chances with them."

I shook my head, which caused Adeela to raise an eyebrow in question.

"I give up," I said to her. "I thought if I waited long enough, you'd get bored and at least try the food. Please, don't waste it. It's truly wonderful."

To Lobo, I said, "You know that was different. You know what they had done. So drop it and just tell me how long it will take to trank those nine people."

I was grateful that Lobo's sighs were less effective in this mode of communication. "Fine," he said. "Given projectile travel time and the possibility of further angle adjustment should they move to new positions, no more than forty-three seconds from when you say the word. Probably much less."

Adeela still wasn't eating.

I leaned forward.

She braced as if I was about to attack.

Instead, I lowered my voice and spoke quietly as I looked into her eyes. "A famous and long-dead Earth philosopher once said, when asked upon his deathbed for the most precious lesson he had learned in life, that we should all enjoy every sandwich. I can't think of better advice, though I admit to being terrible at taking it. As much as he was using 'sandwich' to stand for life's simpler joys, the actual sandwiches in front of us are truly exceptional. So, I intend to enjoy every last bite of mine. Whether you're right, and you collect your bounty later today, or I'm right, and we never see each other again, I don't see what you have to lose from enjoying your food. And you know I can't have poisoned it, because smuggling poison into an EatSafe is a very hard task indeed. It would never make it past the security scanners."

I leaned back, ate a bite, and smiled. I motioned to her plate. "Please."

Adeela shook her head. "You are definitely not what I expected." She shook it again. "Sure, why not?" She cut a sandwich wedge in half and put a bite in her mouth. After a little chewing, her face brightened with a wide smile. "Damn, that *is* good."

I nodded. "Oh, yeah. If you live here, you should eat here every chance you get until some better place snaps up Chef Dee—and you can bet someplace will."

"I can't really afford to come here often," Adeela said, "though that'll all change later today."

I shook my head again. "No, it won't, but that doesn't matter, because this one's on me. I had to pay for four guests to lock down this table."

"So you were expecting us?" She looked surprised.

I shrugged. No point in giving her too much information. "More that I feared someone might be coming."

"And yet you stayed?"

I pointed at my half-empty plate. "I had to enjoy this sandwich."

She chuckled. "Fair enough."

We finished our sandwiches in silence. Adeela was a fast eater, so as I took my last bite, she was nearly done.

As she was chewing her penultimate bite, I asked Lobo, "Once you trank them, how long will they be out?"

"At least three hours," he said, "though I cannot be certain that she doesn't have more people on the way."

"Can you spot any movements that suggest she does?" I said.

"No," he admitted, "but I will still feel better when you get out of there, and better still when we are well away from this backwater planet."

"Almost," I said.

"So what do you think happens next?" Adeela said. "I mean, after you pay."

"I already paid," I said, "as part of locking down this table."

"So what now? Are you picturing some sort of old Earth gunfight in the street? We go out the doors, stand back-to-back, walk apart from each other, turn, and see who can shoot faster?"

I smiled. "Nope."

"Good," she said, "because I have no interest in that kind of dumb game. The moment you step out of here, my people will surround you, restrain you, and take you to my ship on the edge of town. I'm not wasting any time in delivering you and collecting the rather sizable bounty."

I smiled again, waved my hand, and a servbot glided over. "Please bring one of every dessert for my friend." It headed back.

"You paid for that already, too?"

"Oh, easily," I said. "I paid for way more than that, so you might as well enjoy it. I'd love to join you, but I'm full."

"The dessert is for me? Haven't you been listening to me?"

Over the machine frequency, I said to Lobo, "Take them all out now, and tell me when you're done."

I leaned forward. "Yes, I have, but as I've been saying, it's not going to go like that."

"And why not?" she said.

Lobo said, "All nine are down."

"Contact your people," I said.

"What? Why would I do that?"

"Let me be more accurate," I said. I gave her a moment to understand. "*Try* to contact your people."

She turned away from me and whispered.

After nearly a minute of increasingly frantic whispering, she turned back to face me, her face red with anger. "What have you done?"

"Me?" I said. "Nothing. But my people have taken out your team."

Lobo said, "So now I'm 'your people'?"

To him I said, "Not now. Go with it."

She stood. "You bastard. I should—"

A servbot rolled up. Two grabbing arms extended, and several small doors opened on the side facing her.

"Let me remind you where we are. If you move to strike me, the EatSafe will have to restrain you or, worst case, trank you. Neither of us wants that, though, honestly, it wouldn't hurt me."

"You bought me a sandwich and killed nine people while I ate it? What kind of animal—"

"Who said anything about killing? I told you we weren't playing any Old West games, and we're not. My team has tranked yours; that's all. Your people—all nine of them, by the way, not twelve—will come around in a few hours and be none the worse for it."

She sat. "But your team could have killed them."

The servbot waited a few seconds and then moved two meters away.

"Of course."

"And should have, if you ask me," Lobo said.

I ignored him and did my best to keep my focus on Adeela. "I generally hate killing." I paused. "Despite what they may have told you."

"Maybe you're not what they claimed," she said, "but there must be some reason they've put a bounty this big on your head and spread the word to every inhabited planet."

"So in your experience every person a powerful group seeks to eliminate is a bad person?"

She took a few beats before answering.

"Of course not. Life is never that simple."

"You're right," I said, "it's not, and it's not simple with me. None of that matters right now though, because as I told you, we're never going to see each other again. All that *does* matter is that you have a choice."

"What choice?"

"I'm going to leave. You have the choice whether to sit here and enjoy the desserts, or follow me out the door, get tranked by my team, and wake up with the rest of yours." I stood. "Please, choose to enjoy the desserts."

I walked away slowly.

A servbot carrying half a dozen desserts glided past me toward Adeela.

At the turn to the reception area, I paused and looked back.

Adeela was still seated and staring at me. Desserts filled the table in front of her. They looked amazing. I wanted to go back and keep talking, enjoy the food with her, maybe convince her never to come after me again, but Lobo was right: it was time to leave.

After a few seconds, Adeela turned away and ate a forkful of what appeared to be a cream-covered tart.

I strolled through the reception area and out the front door of the EatSafe. I turned left and picked up my pace. Here and there, people were gathered around the fallen bodies, trying in vain to wake them. Others walked around the sleeping people as if they were just stones in the road. No one paid any attention to me.

Huge white clouds towered in a beautiful light blue sky. The warm air enveloped me and felt wonderful. The taste of the last bite of the sandwich lingered in my mouth, and I savored it.

"Meet me at the rendezvous," I said to Lobo.

"About time," he said.

ABOUT THE CONTRIBUTORS

DAVID BOOP is a Denver-based speculative fiction author and editor. He's also an award-winning essayist, and screenwriter. Before turning to fiction, David worked as a DJ, film critic, journalist, and actor.

David's novels run the gambit, such as the sci-fi/noir *She Murdered Me with Science* to the Weird Western, *The Drowned Horse Chronicle, Volume 1*.

David edited the best-selling and award-nominated Weird Western anthology series, *Straight Outta Tombstone*, *Straight Outta Deadwood* and *Straight Outta Dodge City*, and a trio of Space Western anthologies starting with *Gunfight on Europa Station*, *High Noon on Proxima B*, and *Last Train Outta Kepler-283c* for Baen. He's edited several pulp anthologies, including the upcoming *Green Hornet & Kato: Detroit Noir*.

David is prolific in short fiction with many short stories including media tie-ins for *Predator* (nominated for the 2018 Scribe Award), *Kolchak: The Night Stalker*, *The Green Hornet*, and *Veronica Mars*. His first comic, *Travailiant Rising*, co-authored with *New York Times* best-selling author Kevin J. Anderson, is a giant mech series from Outland Entertainment.

He's a Summa Cum Laude graduate from UC-Denver in the Creative Writing program. He temps, collects Funko Pops, and is a believer. His hobbies include film noir, anime, the Blues, and history. You can find out more at Davidboop.com, Facebook.com/dboop. updates, Twitter @david_boop, and www.longshot-productions.net.

KEVIN IKENBERRY is a lifelong space geek and retired Army officer. As an adult, he managed the U.S. Space Camp program and served in space operations before Space Force was a thing.

He's an international best-selling science fiction author and renowned writing instructor which is pretty cool because he never imagined being either one of those—he still wants to be an astronaut. Kevin's debut novel, *Sleeper Protocol*, was hailed by *Publishers Weekly* as "an emotionally powerful debut." His over twenty science fiction novels include *The Crossing*, *Vendetta Protocol*, *Eminence Protocol*, *Runs in the Family*, *Peacemaker*, *Honor the Threat*, *Stand or Fall*, *Fields of Fire*, and *Harbinger*. Kevin is an Active Member of the International Association of Science Fiction and Fantasy Authors, International Thriller Writers, and SIGMA—the science fiction think tank. Kevin continues to work with space every day and lives in Colorado with his family.

SF convention favorites **SHARON LEE** and **STEVE MILLER** have been collaborating since the 1980s, with over one hundred works of fantastic fiction to their joint credit.

While starting their joint writing career, they were traveling SF fans, SF convention booksellers and art agents, and have other unique science fictional backgrounds—Sharon is the only person to consecutively hold office as the Executive Director, Vice President, and President of the Science Fiction and Fantasy Writers of America (now the Science Fiction Writers Association), while Steve was Founding Curator of Science Fiction at the University of Maryland's SF Research Collection, Director of Information for the Baltimore Science Fiction Society, and helped found several regional conventions and a WorldCon.

Their July 2023 Liaden Universe® novel, *Salvage Right*, is their twenty-fifth collaborative novel in that universe, while "The Last Train to Clarkesville" is their first Liaden western.

KELLI FITZPATRICK is a sci-fi author, editor, and game writer. She won the *Star Trek: Strange New Worlds* contest from Simon and Schuster in 2016 and has been a contributing writer for the Star Trek Adventures tabletop roleplaying game from Modiphius Entertainment. Her stories have been published by Flash Fiction Online, KYSO Flash, Crazy 8 Press, and others, and her essays appear at StarTrek.com, Women at Warp, and from Sequart and ATB Publishing. She has written for the NASA Hubble Space Telescope Outreach team and edits for *Dunes Review* and *The Journal of Popular Culture*. A former high school teacher, she is an advocate for public education, the arts, and gender rights and representation. Find her at KelliFitzpatrick.com and on Twitter @KelliFitzWrites.

DAVID MACK is the award-winning and *New York Times* best-selling author of thirty-eight novels and numerous short works of science fiction, fantasy, and adventure, including the *Star Trek: Destiny* and *Cold Equations* trilogies.

Mack's writing credits span television (for episodes of *Star Trek: Deep Space Nine*), film, and comic books. He also has worked as a consultant on the animated television series *Star Trek: Lower Decks* and *Star Trek: Prodigy*. In June 2022, the International Association of Media Tie-In Writers honored him as a Grandmaster with its Faust Award.

His most recent publications include *Harm's Way*, a *Star Trek: Vanguard / Star Trek: The Original Series* crossover novel, a new *Star Trek: Picard* novel titled *Firewall*, and several new works of original short fiction.

Mack resides in New York City with his wife, Kara.

M. TODD GALLOWGLAS. Start with raw imagination. Add two parts coffee to every one part whiskey. (For best results, use Irish or Scottish single malts. Bourbon may result in a volatile mess.)

Add equal heaping spoonfuls of angst, whimsy, snark, and just a dash of imposter syndrome. Shake vigorously. Once it stops frothing, drop in one Masters of Fine Arts in Fiction and a second in Poetry. Sprinkle a healthy dose of shenanigans on top, while chanting either "What's a gleeman?" or "Tell me a story," depending on personal taste.

Yields one pantheon, a Faerie War, a cloak of tales, the thwarting of devils and demons, revolutions, Slightly Above Average Misadventures, nerdy poetry, convention panels, geek literary theory, writing classes, role-playing games, airsoft battles (because it's cooler than paintball), and groovy swing dancing. Best served at Con temperature.

DR. CHESYA BURKE is an Asst. Professor of English and U.S. Literature and the director of Africana Studies. Having written and published over a hundred stories and articles within the genres of horror, science fiction, comics, and Afrofuturism, her academic research focuses primarily on the intersections of race, gender, and genre. Her short story collection, *Let's Play White*, is being taught in universities around the world, leading Grammy Award-winning poet, Nikki Giovanni, to compare her writing to that of Octavia E. Butler and Toni Morrison, and Samuel Delany naming her the "formidable new master of the macabre." Chesya's episode for *I Hear Fear*, hosted by Carey Mulligan, titled, "Under the Skin," was produced by Wondery and Amazon Music and debuted on Halloween 2022. She is represented by Alec Shane of Writer's House and Sukee Chew and Katrina Escudero of Sugar23.

JOHN E. STITH's first science fiction sale was to *Fantastic Science Fiction*. His second sale was to *Amazing Stories*.

Since then, he has sold eight science-fiction novels to Ace Books, Tor Books, the Science Fiction Book Club, and numerous translations. His works include *Redshift Rendezvous*, a Nebula Award nominee, and *Manhattan Transfer*, currently in development for television. His most recent novel is *Pushback*, a mystery-suspense thriller set in Colorado Springs, where he lives. *Pushback* was a finalist for the Daphne Du Maurier Award for Excellence in Mystery/Suspense and the Colorado Author's League Award.

He appeared on live national TV on the *Science-Fiction Science Fact (SF2)* PBS broadcast with Ben Bova, Arthur C. Clarke, Charles Sheffield, G. Harry Stine, and Jesco von Puttkammer.

He has optioned several feature-film screenplays, and has sold to television (*Star Trek*). Complete information on his works may be found at www.neverend.com. His latest novellas are the young-adult *Tiny Time Machine* and *Tiny Time Machine 2: Return of the Father* from Amazing Select, the imprint for stand-alone volumes produced by *Amazing Stories*. He is at work on *Tiny Time Machine 3: Mother of Invention* to complete the trilogy. "Stith" rhymes with "Smith."

D.J. (DAVE) BUTLER has been a lawyer, a consultant, an editor, a corporate trainer, and a registered investment banking representative, and he is now a Consulting Editor for Baen Books. His novels published by Baen Books include the Witchy War series (*Witchy Eye*, *Witchy Winter*, *Witchy Kingdom*, and *Serpent*

Daughter), Tales of Indrajit and Fix (*In the Palace of Shadow and Joy, Between Princesses and Other Jobs,* and *Among the Gray Lords*), and *Abbott in Darkness,* as well as *The Cunning Man* and *The Jupiter Knife,* co-written with Aaron Michael Ritchey, and *Time Trials,* co-written with M.A. Rothman. He also writes for children: the steampunk fantasy adventure tales *The Kidnap Plot, The Giant's Seat,* and *The Library Machine* are published by Knopf. Other novels include *City of the Saints* from WordFire Press and *The Wilding Probate* from Immortal Works. His novels have won the Whitney Award, the Association for Mormon Letters Award for Novel, and the Dragon Award.

Dave also organizes writing retreats and anarcho-libertarian writers' events, and travels the country to sell books. He tells many stories as a gamemaster with a gaming group, some of whom he's been playing with since sixth grade. He plays guitar and banjo whenever he can, and likes to hang out in Utah with his wife, their children, and the family dog.

LEZLI ROBYN is a mostly blind, award-winning Australian author, as well as executive editor and associate publisher at Arc Manor and its three imprints, who lives in Myrtle Beach, South Carolina, with her blue-eyed chiweenie, Bindi (which means "little girl" in several indigenous Australian dialects). She's known for writing bittersweet fiction, being a lover of chocolate and gardening, and is forever drawn by the call of the ocean.

CHRISTOPHER L. SMITH. A native Texan by birth (if not geography), Chris moved "home" as soon as he could.

Attending Texas A+M, he learned quickly that there was more to college than beer and football games. He relocated to San Antonio, attending SAC and UTSA, graduating in late 2000 with a BA in Lit.

While there, he also met a wonderful lady who somehow found him to be funny, charming, and worth marrying. (She has since changed her mind on the funny and charming.)

Christopher began writing fiction in 2012. His short stories can be found in multiple anthologies, including John Ringo and Gary Poole's *Black Tide Rising,* Mike Williamson's *Forged in Blood,* Larry Correia and Kacey Ezell's *Noir Fatale,* and Tom Kratman's *Terra Nova.*

Christopher has co-written two novels, *Kraken Mare* with Jason Cordova, and *Gunpowder & Embers* with Kacey Ezell and John Ringo.

His cats allow his family and their dogs to reside with them outside of San Antonio.

DAVID AFSHARIRAD is an author and Editor at Baen Books. For five years he edited The Year's Best Military and Adventure SF series; he is also the editor of the anthology *The Chronicles of Davids*, and is the short fiction editor for Baen.com. He has published over two dozen short stories in various magazines and anthologies. He lives in Austin, TX.

MEL TODD has over forty-four titles out, including the Kaylid Chronicles, Blood War series, and the Twisted Luck series. She has stories in multiple anthologies, as well as a pen name where you can find a few stray romances. Currently working on the last two books in the Twisted Luck series, she has plans to write more in that world, but there are epic fantasies and sci-fi also bouncing around her brain. Follow her on Facebook at https://www.facebook.com/badashbooks/

You can also sign up for her newsletter and read her blog at https://www.badashpublishing.com.

MARK L. VAN NAME is a writer, technologist, and spoken-word performer. As a science fiction author, he has published five novels (*One Jump Ahead, Slanted Jack, Overthrowing Heaven, Children No More*, and *No Going Back*), as well as an omnibus collection of his first two books (*Jump Gate Twist*); edited or co-edited four anthologies (*Intersections: The Sycamore Hill Anthology, Transhuman, The Wild Side*, and *Onward, Drake!*), and written many short stories. Those stories have appeared in a wide variety of books and magazines, including *Asimov's Science Fiction Magazine*, many original anthologies, and *The Year's Best Science Fiction*.

As a technologist, he is the co-founder and co-owner of a fact-based marketing and learning services firm, Principled Technologies, Inc., that is based in the Research Triangle area of North Carolina and has been in business for over twenty years. He has worked with computer technology for his entire professional career and has published over a thousand articles in the computer trade press, as well as a broad assortment of essays and reviews.

As a spoken-word artist, he has created and performed five shows—*Science Magic Sex*; *Wake Up Horny, Wake Up Angry*; *Mr. Poor Choices*; *Mr. Poor Choices II: I Don't Understand*; and *Mr. Poor Choices III: That Moment When*—and also frequently leads humor panels at SF conventions.